Mary Roberts Rinehart

The Bat & The Circular Staircase

OK Publishing 2021

Mary Roberts Rinehart
The Bat & The Circular Staircase

Miss Cornelia Van Gorder Mystery Novels

Published by
MUSAICUM
Books

- Advanced Digital Solutions & High-Quality book Formatting -

musaicumbooks@okpublishing.info

2021 OK Publishing

ISBN 978-80-272-7825-1

Contents

The Circular Staircase	13
I Take a Country House	13
A Link Cuff-Button	16
Mr. John Bailey Appears	19
Where is Halsey?	21
Gertrude's Engagement	23
In the East Corridor	26
A Sprained Ankle	29
The Other Half of the Line	32
Just Like a Girl	36
The Traders' Bank	39
Halsey Makes a Capture	42
One Mystery for Another	44
Louise	47
An Egg-Nog and a Telegram	52
Liddy Gives the Alarm	54
In the Early Morning	56
A Hint of Scandal	58
A Hole in the Wall	62
Concerning Thomas	64
Doctor Walker's Warning	66
Fourteen Elm Street	69
A Ladder Out of Place	74
While the Stables Burned	75
Flinders	78
A Visit from Louise	81
Halsey's Disappearance	84
Who is Nina Carrington?	87
A Tramp and the Toothache	90
A Scrap of Paper	93
When Churchyards Yawn	96
Between Two Fireplaces	98
Anne Watson's Story	100
At the Foot of the Stairs	102
The Odds and Ends	106
The Bat	111

Chapter One. The Shadow of the Bat   111
Chapter Two. The Indomitable Miss Van Gorder   115
Chapter Three. Pistol Practice   121
Chapter Four. The Storm Gathers   126
Chapter Five. Alopecia and Rubeola   131
Chapter Six. Detective Anderson Takes Charge   137
Chapter Seven. Cross-Questions and Crooked Answers   142
Chapter Eight. The Gleaming Eye   147
Chapter Nine. A Shot in the Dark   152
Chapter Ten. The Phone Call from Nowhere   157
Chapter Eleven. Billy Practices Jiu-Jitsu   162
Chapter Twelve. "I Didn't Kill Him."   168
Chapter Thirteen. The Blackened Bag   173
Chapter Fourteen. Handcuffs   178
Chapter Fifteen. The Sign of the Bat   183
Chapter Sixteen. The Hidden Room   189
Chapter Seventeen. Anderson Makes an Arrest   192
Chapter Eighteen. The Bat Still Flies   196
Chapter Nineteen. Murder on Murder   200
Chapter Twenty. "He Is—The Bat!"   205
Chapter Twenty-One. Quite a Collection   207

The Circular Staircase

Mary Roberts Rinehart

I Take a Country House

This is the story of how a middle-aged spinster lost her mind, deserted her domestic gods in the city, took a furnished house for the summer out of town, and found herself involved in one of those mysterious crimes that keep our newspapers and detective agencies happy and prosperous. For twenty years I had been perfectly comfortable; for twenty years I had had the window-boxes filled in the spring, the carpets lifted, the awnings put up and the furniture covered with brown linen; for as many summers I had said good-by to my friends, and, after watching their perspiring hegira, had settled down to a delicious quiet in town, where the mail comes three times a day, and the water supply does not depend on a tank on the roof.

And then-the madness seized me. When I look back over the months I spent at Sunnyside, I wonder that I survived at all. As it is, I show the wear and tear of my harrowing experiences. I have turned very gray-Liddy reminded me of it, only yesterday, by saying that a little bluing in the rinse-water would make my hair silvery, instead of a yellowish white. I hate to be reminded of unpleasant things and I snapped her off.

"No," I said sharply, "I'm not going to use bluing at my time of life, or starch, either."

Liddy's nerves are gone, she says, since that awful summer, but she has enough left, goodness knows! And when she begins to go around with a lump in her throat, all I have to do is to threaten to return to Sunnyside, and she is frightened into a semblance of cheerfulness, —from which you may judge that the summer there was anything but a success.

The newspaper accounts have been so garbled and incomplete-one of them mentioned me but once, and then only as the tenant at the time the thing happened-that I feel it my due to tell what I know. Mr. Jamieson, the detective, said himself he could never have done without me, although he gave me little enough credit, in print.

I shall have to go back several years-thirteen, to be exact-to start my story. At that time my brother died, leaving me his two children. Halsey was eleven then, and Gertrude was seven. All the responsibilities of maternity were thrust upon me suddenly; to perfect the profession of motherhood requires precisely as many years as the child has lived, like the man who started to carry the calf and ended by walking along with the bull on his shoulders. However, I did the best I could. When Gertrude got past the hair-ribbon age, and Halsey asked for a scarf-pin and put on long trousers-and a wonderful help that was to the darning! —I sent them away to good schools. After that, my responsibility was chiefly postal, with three months every summer in which to replenish their wardrobes, look over their lists of acquaintances, and generally to take my foster-motherhood out of its nine months' retirement in camphor.

I missed the summers with them when, somewhat later, at boarding-school and college, the children spent much of their vacations with friends. Gradually I found that my name signed to a check was even more welcome than when signed to a letter, though I wrote them at stated intervals. But when Halsey had finished his electrical course and Gertrude her boarding-school, and both came home to stay, things were suddenly changed. The winter Gertrude came out was nothing but a succession of sitting up late at night to bring her home from things, taking her to the dressmakers between naps the next day, and discouraging ineligible youths with either more money than brains, or more brains than money. Also, I acquired a great many things: to say *lingerie* for under-garments, "frocks" and "gowns" instead of dresses, and that beardless

13

sophomores are not college boys, but college men. Halsey required less personal supervision, and as they both got their mother's fortune that winter, my responsibility became purely moral. Halsey bought a car, of course, and I learned how to tie over my bonnet a gray baize veil, and, after a time, never to stop to look at the dogs one has run down. People are apt to be so unpleasant about their dogs.

The additions to my education made me a properly equipped maiden aunt, and by spring I was quite tractable. So when Halsey suggested camping in the Adirondacks and Gertrude wanted Bar Harbor, we compromised on a good country house with links near, within motor distance of town and telephone distance of the doctor. That was how we went to Sunnyside.

We went out to inspect the property, and it seemed to deserve its name. Its cheerful appearance gave no indication whatever of anything out of the ordinary. Only one thing seemed unusual to me: the housekeeper, who had been left in charge, had moved from the house to the gardener's lodge, a few days before. As the lodge was far enough away from the house, it seemed to me that either fire or thieves could complete their work of destruction undisturbed. The property was an extensive one: the house on the top of a hill, which sloped away in great stretches of green lawn and clipped hedges, to the road; and across the valley, perhaps a couple of miles away, was the Greenwood Club House. Gertrude and Halsey were infatuated.

"Why, it's everything you want," Halsey said "View, air, good water and good roads. As for the house, it's big enough for a hospital, if it has a Queen Anne front and a Mary Anne back," which was ridiculous: it was pure Elizabethan.

Of course we took the place; it was not my idea of comfort, being much too large and sufficiently isolated to make the servant question serious. But I give myself credit for this: whatever has happened since, I never blamed Halsey and Gertrude for taking me there. And another thing: if the series of catastrophes there did nothing else, it taught me one thing-that somehow, somewhere, from perhaps a half-civilized ancestor who wore a sheepskin garment and trailed his food or his prey, I have in me the instinct of the chase. Were I a man I should be a trapper of criminals, trailing them as relentlessly as no doubt my sheepskin ancestor did his wild boar. But being an unmarried woman, with the handicap of my sex, my first acquaintance with crime will probably be my last. Indeed, it came near enough to being my last acquaintance with anything.

The property was owned by Paul Armstrong, the president of the Traders' Bank, who at the time we took the house was in the west with his wife and daughter, and a Doctor Walker, the Armstrong family physician. Halsey knew Louise Armstrong,—had been rather attentive to her the winter before, but as Halsey was always attentive to somebody, I had not thought of it seriously, although she was a charming girl. I knew of Mr. Armstrong only through his connection with the bank, where the children's money was largely invested, and through an ugly story about the son, Arnold Armstrong, who was reported to have forged his father's name, for a considerable amount, to some bank paper. However, the story had had no interest for me.

I cleared Halsey and Gertrude away to a house party, and moved out to Sunnyside the first of May. The roads were bad, but the trees were in leaf, and there were still tulips in the borders around the house. The arbutus was fragrant in the woods under the dead leaves, and on the way from the station, a short mile, while the car stuck in the mud, I found a bank showered with tiny forget-me-nots. The birds-don't ask me what kind; they all look alike to me, unless they have a hall mark of some bright color-the birds were chirping in the hedges, and everything breathed of peace. Liddy, who was born and bred on a brick pavement, got a little bit down-spirited when the crickets began to chirp, or scrape their legs together, or whatever it is they do, at twilight.

The first night passed quietly enough. I have always been grateful for that one night's peace; it shows what the country might be, under favorable circumstances. Never after that night did I put my head on my pillow with any assurance how long it would be there; or on my shoulders, for that matter.

On the following morning Liddy and Mrs. Ralston, my own housekeeper, had a difference of opinion, and Mrs. Ralston left on the eleven train. Just after luncheon, Burke, the butler, was taken unexpectedly with a pain in his right side, much worse when I was within hearing distance, and by afternoon he was started cityward. That night the cook's sister had a baby-the cook, seeing indecision in my face, made it twins on second thought-and, to be short, by noon the next day the household staff was down to Liddy and myself. And this in a house with twenty-two rooms and five baths!

Liddy wanted to go back to the city at once, but the milk-boy said that Thomas Johnson, the Armstrongs' colored butler, was working as a waiter at the Greenwood Club, and might come back. I have the usual scruples about coercing people's servants away, but few of us have any conscience regarding institutions or corporations-witness the way we beat railroads and street-car companies when we can-so I called up the club, and about eight o'clock Thomas Johnson came to see me. Poor Thomas!

Well, it ended by my engaging Thomas on the spot, at outrageous wages, and with permission to sleep in the gardener's lodge, empty since the house was rented. The old man-he was white-haired and a little stooped, but with an immense idea of his personal dignity-gave me his reasons hesitatingly.

"I ain't sayin' nothin', Mis' Innes," he said, with his hand on the door-knob, "but there's been goin's-on here this las' few months as ain't natchal. 'Taint one thing an' 'taint another-it's jest a door squealin' here, an' a winder closin' there, but when doors an' winders gets to cuttin' up capers and there's nobody nigh 'em, it's time Thomas Johnson sleeps somewhar's else."

Liddy, who seemed to be never more than ten feet away from me that night, and was afraid of her shadow in that great barn of a place, screamed a little, and turned a yellow-green. But I am not easily alarmed.

It was entirely in vain I represented to Thomas that we were alone, and that he would have to stay in the house that night. He was politely firm, but he would come over early the next morning, and if I gave him a key, he would come in time to get some sort of breakfast. I stood on the huge veranda and watched him shuffle along down the shadowy drive, with mingled feelings-irritation at his cowardice and thankfulness at getting him at all. I am not ashamed to say that I double-locked the hall door when I went in.

"You can lock up the rest of the house and go to bed, Liddy," I said severely. "You give me the creeps standing there. A woman of your age ought to have better sense." It usually braces Liddy to mention her age: she owns to forty-which is absurd. Her mother cooked for my grandfather, and Liddy must be at least as old as I. But that night she refused to brace.

"You're not going to ask me to lock up, Miss Rachel!" she quavered. "Why, there's a dozen French windows in the drawing-room and the billiard-room wing, and every one opens on a porch. And Mary Anne said that last night there was a man standing by the stable when she locked the kitchen door."

"Mary Anne was a fool," I said sternly. "If there had been a man there, she would have had him in the kitchen and been feeding him what was left from dinner, inside of an hour, from force of habit. Now don't be ridiculous. Lock up the house and go to bed. I am going to read."

But Liddy set her lips tight and stood still.

"I'm not going to bed," she said. "I am going to pack up, and to-morrow I am going to leave."

"You'll do nothing of the sort," I snapped. Liddy and I often desire to part company, but never at the same time. "If you are afraid, I will go with you, but for goodness' sake don't try to hide behind me."

The house was a typical summer residence on an extensive scale. Wherever possible, on the first floor, the architect had done away with partitions, using arches and columns instead. The effect was cool and spacious, but scarcely cozy. As Liddy and I went from one window to another, our voices echoed back at us uncomfortably. There was plenty of light-the electric plant down in the village supplied us-but there were long vistas of polished floor, and mirrors which reflected us from unexpected corners, until I felt some of Liddy's foolishness communicate itself to me.

The house was very long, a rectangle in general form, with the main entrance in the center of the long side. The brick-paved entry opened into a short hall to the right of which, separated only by a row of pillars, was a huge living-room. Beyond that was the drawing-room, and in the end, the billiard-room. Off the billiard-room, in the extreme right wing, was a den, or card-room, with a small hall opening on the east veranda, and from there went up a narrow circular staircase. Halsey had pointed it out with delight.

"Just look, Aunt Rachel," he said with a flourish. "The architect that put up this joint was wise to a few things. Arnold Armstrong and his friends could sit here and play cards all night and stumble up to bed in the early morning, without having the family send in a police call."

Liddy and I got as far as the card-room and turned on all the lights. I tried the small entry door there, which opened on the veranda, and examined the windows. Everything was secure, and Liddy, a little less nervous now, had just pointed out to me the disgracefully dusty condition of the hard-wood floor, when suddenly the lights went out. We waited a moment; I think Liddy was stunned with fright, or she would have screamed. And then I clutched her by the arm and pointed to one of the windows opening on the porch. The sudden change threw the window into relief, an oblong of grayish light, and showed us a figure standing close, peering in. As I looked it darted across the veranda and out of sight in the darkness.

A Link Cuff-Button

Liddy's knees seemed to give away under her. Without a sound she sank down, leaving me staring at the window in petrified amazement. Liddy began to moan under her breath, and in my excitement I reached down and shook her.

"Stop it," I whispered. "It's only a woman-maybe a maid of the Armstrongs'. Get up and help me find the door." She groaned again. "Very well," I said, "then I'll have to leave you here. I'm going."

She moved at that, and, holding to my sleeve, we felt our way, with numerous collisions, to the billiard-room, and from there to the drawing-room. The lights came on then, and, with the long French windows unshuttered, I had a creepy feeling that each one sheltered a peering face. In fact, in the light of what happened afterward, I am pretty certain we were under surveillance during the entire ghostly evening. We hurried over the rest of the locking-up and got upstairs as quickly as we could. I left the lights all on, and our footsteps echoed cavernously. Liddy had a stiff neck the next morning, from looking back over her shoulder, and she refused to go to bed.

"Let me stay in your dressing-room, Miss Rachel," she begged. "If you don't, I'll sit in the hall outside the door. I'm not going to be murdered with my eyes shut."

"If you're going to be murdered," I retorted, "it won't make any difference whether they are shut or open. But you may stay in the dressing-room, if you will lie on the couch: when you sleep in a chair you snore."

She was too far gone to be indignant, but after a while she came to the door and looked in to where I was composing myself for sleep with Drummond's *Spiritual Life*.

"That wasn't a woman, Miss Rachel," she said, with her shoes in her hand. "It was a man in a long coat."

"What woman was a man?" I discouraged her without looking up, and she went back to the couch.

It was eleven o'clock when I finally prepared for bed. In spite of my assumption of indifference, I locked the door into the hall, and finding the transom did not catch, I put a chair cautiously before the door-it was not necessary to rouse Liddy-and climbing up put on the ledge of the transom a small dressing-mirror, so that any movement of the frame would send it crashing down. Then, secure in my precautions, I went to bed.

I did not go to sleep at once. Liddy disturbed me just as I was growing drowsy, by coming in and peering under the bed. She was afraid to speak, however, because of her previous snubbing, and went back, stopping in the doorway to sigh dismally.

Somewhere down-stairs a clock with a chime sang away the hours-eleven-thirty, forty-five, twelve. And then the lights went out to stay. The Casanova Electric Company shuts up shop and goes home to bed at midnight: when one has a party, I believe it is customary to fee the company, which will drink hot coffee and keep awake a couple of hours longer. But the lights were gone for good that night. Liddy had gone to sleep, as I knew she would. She was a very unreliable person: always awake and ready to talk when she wasn't wanted and dozing off to sleep when she was. I called her once or twice, the only result being an explosive snore that threatened her very windpipe-then I got up and lighted a bedroom candle.

My bedroom and dressing room were above the big living-room on the first floor. On the second floor a long corridor ran the length of the house, with rooms opening from both sides. In the wings were small corridors crossing the main one-the plan was simplicity itself. And just as I got back into bed, I heard a sound from the east wing, apparently, that made me stop, frozen, with one bedroom slipper half off, and listen. It was a rattling metallic sound, and it reverberated along the empty halls like the crash of doom. It was for all the world as if something heavy, perhaps a piece of steel, had rolled clattering and jangling down the hard-wood stairs leading to the card-room.

In the silence that followed Liddy stirred and snored again. I was exasperated: first she kept me awake by silly alarms, then when she was needed she slept like Joe Jefferson, or Rip, —they are always the same to me. I went in and aroused her, and I give her credit for being wide awake the minute I spoke.

"Get up," I said, "if you don't want to be murdered in your bed."

"Where? How?" she yelled vociferously, and jumped up.

"There's somebody in the house," I said. "Get up. We'll have to get to the telephone."

"Not out in the hall!" she gasped; "Oh, Miss Rachel, not out in the hall!" trying to hold me back. But I am a large woman and Liddy is small. We got to the door, somehow, and Liddy held a brass andiron, which it was all she could do to lift, let alone brain anybody with. I listened, and, hearing nothing, opened the door a little and peered into the hall. It was a black void, full of terrible suggestion, and my candle only emphasized the gloom. Liddy squealed and drew me back again, and as the door slammed, the mirror I had put on the transom came down and hit her on the head. That completed our demoralization. It was some time before I could persuade her she had not been attacked from behind by a burglar, and when she found the mirror smashed on the floor she wasn't much better.

"There's going to be a death!" she wailed. "Oh, Miss Rachel, there's going to be a death!"

"There will be," I said grimly, "if you don't keep quiet, Liddy Allen."

And so we sat there until morning, wondering if the candle would last until dawn, and arranging what trains we could take back to town. If we had only stuck to that decision and gone back before it was too late!

The sun came finally, and from my window I watched the trees along the drive take shadowy form, gradually lose their ghostlike appearance, become gray and then green. The Greenwood Club showed itself a dab of white against the hill across the valley, and an early robin or two hopped around in the dew. Not until the milk-boy and the sun came, about the same time, did I dare to open the door into the hall and look around. Everything was as we had left it. Trunks were heaped here and there, ready for the trunk-room, and through an end window of stained glass came a streak of red and yellow daylight that was eminently cheerful. The milk-boy was pounding somewhere below, and the day had begun.

Thomas Johnson came ambling up the drive about half-past six, and we could hear him clattering around on the lower floor, opening shutters. I had to take Liddy to her room upstairs, however, —she was quite sure she would find something uncanny. In fact, when she did not, having now the courage of daylight, she was actually disappointed.

Well, we did not go back to town that day.

The discovery of a small picture fallen from the wall of the drawing-room was quite sufficient to satisfy Liddy that the alarm had been a false one, but I was anything but convinced. Allowing for my nerves and the fact that small noises magnify themselves at night, there was still no possibility that the picture had made the series of sounds I heard. To prove it, however, I

17

dropped it again. It fell with a single muffled crash of its wooden frame, and incidentally ruined itself beyond repair. I justified myself by reflecting that if the Armstrongs chose to leave pictures in unsafe positions, and to rent a house with a family ghost, the destruction of property was their responsibility, not mine.

I warned Liddy not to mention what had happened to anybody, and telephoned to town for servants. Then after a breakfast which did more credit to Thomas' heart than his head, I went on a short tour of investigation. The sounds had come from the east wing, and not without some qualms I began there. At first I found nothing. Since then I have developed my powers of observation, but at that time I was a novice. The small card-room seemed undisturbed. I looked for footprints, which is, I believe, the conventional thing to do, although my experience has been that as clues both footprints and thumb-marks are more useful in fiction than in fact. But the stairs in that wing offered something.

At the top of the flight had been placed a tall wicker hamper, packed, with linen that had come from town. It stood at the edge of the top step, almost barring passage, and on the step below it was a long fresh scratch. For three steps the scratch was repeated, gradually diminishing, as if some object had fallen, striking each one. Then for four steps nothing. On the fifth step below was a round dent in the hard wood. That was all, and it seemed little enough, except that I was positive the marks had not been there the day before.

It bore out my theory of the sound, which had been for all the world like the bumping of a metallic object down a flight of steps. The four steps had been skipped. I reasoned that an iron bar, for instance, would do something of the sort,—strike two or three steps, end down, then turn over, jumping a few stairs, and landing with a thud.

Iron bars, however, do not fall down-stairs in the middle of the night alone. Coupled with the figure on the veranda the agency by which it climbed might be assumed. But-and here was the thing that puzzled me most-the doors were all fastened that morning, the windows unmolested, and the particular door from the card-room to the veranda had a combination lock of which I held the key, and which had not been tampered with.

I fixed on an attempt at burglary, as the most natural explanation-an attempt frustrated by the falling of the object, whatever it was, that had roused me. Two things I could not understand: how the intruder had escaped with everything locked, and why he had left the small silver, which, in the absence of a butler, had remained down-stairs over night.

Under pretext of learning more about the place, Thomas Johnson led me through the house and the cellars, without result. Everything was in good order and repair; money had been spent lavishly on construction and plumbing. The house was full of conveniences, and I had no reason to repent my bargain, save the fact that, in the nature of things, night must come again. And other nights must follow-and we were a long way from a police-station.

In the afternoon a hack came up from Casanova, with a fresh relay of servants. The driver took them with a flourish to the servants' entrance, and drove around to the front of the house, where I was awaiting him.

"Two dollars," he said in reply to my question. "I don't charge full rates, because, bringin' 'em up all summer as I do, it pays to make a special price. When they got off the train, I sez, sez I, 'There's another bunch for Sunnyside, cook, parlor maid and all.' Yes'm —six summers, and a new lot never less than once a month. They won't stand for the country and the lonesomeness, I reckon."

But with the presence of the "bunch" of servants my courage revived, and late in the afternoon came a message from Gertrude that she and Halsey would arrive that night at about eleven o'clock, coming in the car from Richfield. Things were looking up; and when Beulah, my cat, a most intelligent animal, found some early catnip on a bank near the house and rolled in it in a feline ecstasy, I decided that getting back to nature was the thing to do.

While I was dressing for dinner, Liddy rapped at the door. She was hardly herself yet, but privately I think she was worrying about the broken mirror and its augury, more than anything else. When she came in she was holding something in her hand, and she laid it on the dressing-table carefully.

"I found it in the linen hamper," she said. "It must be Mr. Halsey's, but it seems queer how it got there."

It was the half of a link cuff-button of unique design, and I looked at it carefully.

"Where was it? In the bottom of the hamper?" I asked.

"On the very top," she replied. "It's a mercy it didn't fall out on the way."

When Liddy had gone I examined the fragment attentively. I had never seen it before, and I was certain it was not Halsey's. It was of Italian workmanship, and consisted of a mother-of-pearl foundation, encrusted with tiny seed-pearls, strung on horsehair to hold them. In the center was a small ruby. The trinket was odd enough, but not intrinsically of great value. Its interest for me lay in this: Liddy had found it lying in the top of the hamper which had blocked the east-wing stairs.

That afternoon the Armstrongs' housekeeper, a youngish good-looking woman, applied for Mrs. Ralston's place, and I was glad enough to take her. She looked as though she might be equal to a dozen of Liddy, with her snapping black eyes and heavy jaw. Her name was Anne Watson, and I dined that evening for the first time in three days.

Mr. John Bailey Appears

I had dinner served in the breakfast-room. Somehow the huge dining-room depressed me, and Thomas, cheerful enough all day, allowed his spirits to go down with the sun. He had a habit of watching the corners of the room, left shadowy by the candles on the table, and altogether it was not a festive meal.

Dinner over I went into the living-room. I had three hours before the children could possibly arrive, and I got out my knitting. I had brought along two dozen pairs of slipper soles in assorted sizes —I always send knitted slippers to the Old Ladies' Home at Christmas-and now I sorted over the wools with a grim determination not to think about the night before. But my mind was not on my work: at the end of a half-hour I found I had put a row of blue scallops on Eliza Klinefelter's lavender slippers, and I put them away.

I got out the cuff-link and went with it to the pantry. Thomas was wiping silver and the air was heavy with tobacco smoke. I sniffed and looked around, but there was no pipe to be seen.

"Thomas," I said, "you have been smoking."

"No, ma'm." He was injured innocence itself. "It's on my coat, ma'm. Over at the club the gentlemen —"

But Thomas did not finish. The pantry was suddenly filled with the odor of singeing cloth. Thomas gave a clutch at his coat, whirled to the sink, filled a tumbler with water and poured it into his right pocket with the celerity of practice.

"Thomas," I said, when he was sheepishly mopping the floor, "smoking is a filthy and injurious habit. If you must smoke, you must; but don't stick a lighted pipe in your pocket again. Your skin's your own: you can blister it if you like. But this house is not mine, and I don't want a conflagration. Did you ever see this cuff-link before?"

No, he never had, he said, but he looked at it oddly.

"I picked it up in the hall," I added indifferently. The old man's eyes were shrewd under his bushy eyebrows.

"There's strange goin's-on here, Mis' Innes," he said, shaking his head. "Somethin's goin' to happen, sure. You ain't took notice that the big clock in the hall is stopped, I reckon?"

"Nonsense," I said. "Clocks have to stop, don't they, if they're not wound?"

"It's wound up, all right, and it stopped at three o'clock last night," he answered solemnly. "More'n that, that there clock ain't stopped for fifteen years, not since Mr. Armstrong's first wife died. And that ain't all,—no *ma'm*. Last three nights I slep' in this place, after the electrics went out I had a token. My oil lamp was full of oil, but it kep' goin' out, do what I would. Minute I shet my eyes, out that lamp'd go. There ain't no surer token of death. The Bible sez, *Let yer light shine!* When a hand you can't see puts yer light out, it means death, sure."

The old man's voice was full of conviction. In spite of myself I had a chilly sensation in the small of my back, and I left him mumbling over his dishes. Later on I heard a crash from the pantry, and Liddy reported that Beulah, who is coal black, had darted in front of Thomas just as he picked up a tray of dishes; that the bad omen had been too much for him, and he had dropped the tray.

The chug of the automobile as it climbed the hill was the most welcome sound I had heard for a long time, and with Gertrude and Halsey actually before me, my troubles seemed over for good. Gertrude stood smiling in the hall, with her hat quite over one ear, and her hair in every direction under her pink veil. Gertrude is a very pretty girl, no matter how her hat is, and I was not surprised when Halsey presented a good-looking young man, who bowed at me and looked at Trude-that is the ridiculous nickname Gertrude brought from school.

"I have brought a guest, Aunt Ray," Halsey said. "I want you to adopt him into your affections and your Saturday-to-Monday list. Let me present John Bailey, only you must call him Jack. In twelve hours he'll be calling you 'Aunt': I know him."

We shook hands, and I got a chance to look at Mr. Bailey; he was a tall fellow, perhaps thirty, and he wore a small mustache. I remember wondering why: he seemed to have a good mouth and when he smiled his teeth were above the average. One never knows why certain men cling to a messy upper lip that must get into things, any more than one understands some women building up their hair on wire atrocities. Otherwise, he was very good to look at, stalwart and tanned, with the direct gaze that I like. I am particular about Mr. Bailey, because he was a prominent figure in what happened later.

Gertrude was tired with the trip and went up to bed very soon. I made up my mind to tell them nothing; until the next day, and then to make as light of our excitement as possible. After all, what had I to tell? An inquisitive face peering in at a window; a crash in the night; a scratch or two on the stairs, and half a cuff-button! As for Thomas and his forebodings, it was always my belief that a negro is one part thief, one part pigment, and the rest superstition.

It was Saturday night. The two men went to the billiard-room, and I could hear them talking as I went up-stairs. It seemed that Halsey had stopped at the Greenwood Club for gasolene and found Jack Bailey there, with the Sunday golf crowd. Mr. Bailey had not been hard to persuade-probably Gertrude knew why-and they had carried him off triumphantly. I roused Liddy to get them something to eat-Thomas was beyond reach in the lodge-and paid no attention to her evident terror of the kitchen regions. Then I went to bed. The men were still in the billiard-room when I finally dozed off, and the last thing I remember was the howl of a dog in front of the house. It wailed a crescendo of woe that trailed off hopefully, only to break out afresh from a new point of the compass.

At three o'clock in the morning I was roused by a revolver shot. The sound seemed to come from just outside my door. For a moment I could not move. Then —I heard Gertrude stirring in her room, and the next moment she had thrown open the connecting door.

"O Aunt Ray! Aunt Ray!" she cried hysterically. "Some one has been killed, killed!"

"Thieves," I said shortly. "Thank goodness, there are some men in the house to-night." I was getting into my slippers and a bath-robe, and Gertrude with shaking hands was lighting a lamp. Then we opened the door into the hall, where, crowded on the upper landing of the stairs, the maids, white-faced and trembling, were peering down, headed by Liddy. I was greeted by a series of low screams and questions, and I tried to quiet them. Gertrude had dropped on a chair and sat there limp and shivering.

I went at once across the hall to Halsey's room and knocked; then I pushed the door open. It was empty; the bed had not been occupied!

"He must be in Mr. Bailey's room," I said excitedly, and followed by Liddy, we went there. Like Halsey's, it had not been occupied! Gertrude was on her feet now, but she leaned against the door for support.

"They have been killed!" she gasped. Then she caught me by the arm and dragged me toward the stairs. "They may only be hurt, and we must find them," she said, her eyes dilated with excitement.

I don't remember how we got down the stairs: I do remember expecting every moment to be killed. The cook was at the telephone up-stairs, calling the Greenwood Club, and Liddy was behind me, afraid to come and not daring to stay behind. We found the living-room and the drawing-room undisturbed. Somehow I felt that whatever we found would be in the card-room or on the staircase, and nothing but the fear that Halsey was in danger drove me on; with every step my knees seemed to give way under me. Gertrude was ahead and in the card-room she stopped, holding her candle high. Then she pointed silently to the doorway into the hall beyond. Huddled there on the floor, face down, with his arms extended, was a man.

Gertrude ran forward with a gasping sob. "Jack," she cried, "oh, Jack!"

Liddy had run, screaming, and the two of us were there alone. It was Gertrude who turned him over, finally, until we could see his white face, and then she drew a deep breath and dropped limply to her knees. It was the body of a man, a gentleman, in a dinner coat and white waistcoat, stained now with blood-the body of a man I had never seen before.

Where is Halsey?

Gertrude gazed at the face in a kind of fascination. Then she put out her hands blindly, and I thought she was going to faint.

"He has killed him!" she muttered almost inarticulately; and at that, because my nerves were going, I gave her a good shake.

"What do you mean?" I said frantically. There was a depth of grief and conviction in her tone that was worse than anything she could have said. The shake braced her, anyhow, and she seemed to pull herself together. But not another word would she say: she stood gazing down at that gruesome figure on the floor, while Liddy, ashamed of her flight and afraid to come back alone, drove before her three terrified women-servants into the drawing-room, which was as near as any of them would venture.

Once in the drawing-room, Gertrude collapsed and went from one fainting spell into another. I had all I could do to keep Liddy from drowning her with cold water, and the maids huddled in a corner, as much use as so many sheep. In a short time, although it seemed hours, a car came rushing up, and Anne Watson, who had waited to dress, opened the door. Three men from the Greenwood Club, in all kinds of costumes, hurried in. I recognized a Mr. Jarvis, but the others were strangers.

"What's wrong?" the Jarvis man asked-and we made a strange picture, no doubt. "Nobody hurt, is there?" He was looking at Gertrude.

"Worse than that, Mr. Jarvis," I said. "I think it is murder."

At the word there was a commotion. The cook began to cry, and Mrs. Watson knocked over a chair. The men were visibly impressed.

"Not any member of the family?" Mr. Jarvis asked, when he had got his breath.

"No," I said; and motioning Liddy to look after Gertrude, I led the way with a lamp to the card-room door. One of the men gave an exclamation, and they all hurried across the room. Mr. Jarvis took the lamp from me —I remember that-and then, feeling myself getting dizzy and light-headed, I closed my eyes. When I opened them their brief examination was over, and Mr. Jarvis was trying to put me in a chair.

"You must get up-stairs," he said firmly, "you and Miss Gertrude, too. This has been a terrible shock. In his own home, too."

I stared at him without comprehension. "Who is it?" I asked with difficulty. There was a band drawn tight around my throat.

"It is Arnold Armstrong," he said, looking at me oddly, "and he has been murdered-in his father's house."

After a minute I gathered myself together and Mr. Jarvis helped me into the living-room. Liddy had got Gertrude up-stairs, and the two strange men from the club stayed with the body. The reaction from the shock and strain was tremendous: *I* was collapsed-and then Mr. Jarvis asked me a question that brought back my wandering faculties.

"Where is Halsey?" he asked.

"Halsey!" Suddenly Gertrude's stricken face rose before me the empty rooms up-stairs. Where was Halsey?

"He was here, wasn't he?" Mr. Jarvis persisted. "He stopped at the club on his way over."

"I—don't know where he is," I said feebly.

One of the men from the club came in, asked for the telephone, and I could hear him excitedly talking, saying something about coroners and detectives. Mr. Jarvis leaned over to me.

"Why don't you trust me, Miss Innes?" he said. "If I can do anything I will. But tell me the whole thing."

I did, finally, from the beginning, and when I told of Jack Bailey's being in the house that night, he gave a long whistle.

"I wish they were both here," he said when I finished. "Whatever mad prank took them away, it would look better if they were here. Especially—"

"Especially what?"

"Especially since Jack Bailey and Arnold Armstrong were notoriously bad friends. It was Bailey who got Arnold into trouble last spring-something about the bank. And then, too —"

"Go on," I said. "If there is anything more, I ought to know."

"There's nothing more," he said evasively. "There's just one thing we may bank on, Miss Innes. Any court in the country will acquit a man who kills an intruder in his house, at night. If Halsey—"

"Why, you don't think Halsey did it!" I exclaimed. There was a queer feeling of physical nausea coming over me.

"No, no, not at all," he said with forced cheerfulness. "Come, Miss Innes, you're a ghost of yourself and I am going to help you up-stairs and call your maid. This has been too much for you."

Liddy helped me back to bed, and under the impression that I was in danger of freezing to death, put a hot-water bottle over my heart and another at my feet. Then she left me. It was early dawn now, and from voices under my window I surmised that Mr. Jarvis and his companions were searching the grounds. As for me, I lay in bed, with every faculty awake. Where had Halsey gone? How had he gone, and when? Before the murder, no doubt, but who would believe that? If either he or Jack Bailey had heard an intruder in the house and shot him-as they might have been justified in doing-why had they run away? The whole thing was unheard of, outrageous, and-impossible to ignore.

About six o'clock Gertrude came in. She was fully dressed, and I sat up nervously.

"Poor Aunty!" she said. "What a shocking night you have had!" She came over and sat down on the bed, and I saw she looked very tired and worn.

"Is there anything new?" I asked anxiously.

"Nothing. The car is gone, but Warner"—he is the chauffeur—"Warner is at the lodge and knows nothing about it."

"Well," I said, "if I ever get my hands on Halsey Innes, I shall not let go until I have told him a few things. When we get this cleared up, I am going back to the city to be quiet. One more night like the last two will end me. The peace of the country-fiddlesticks!"

Whereupon I told Gertrude of the noises the night before, and the figure on the veranda in the east wing. As an afterthought I brought out the pearl cuff-link.

"I have no doubt now," I said, "that it was Arnold Armstrong the night before last, too. He had a key, no doubt, but why he should steal into his father's house I can not imagine. He could have come with my permission, easily enough. Anyhow, whoever it was that night, left this little souvenir."

Gertrude took one look at the cuff-link, and went as white as the pearls in it; she clutched at the foot of the bed, and stood staring. As for me, I was quite as astonished as she was.

"Where did-you-find it?" she asked finally, with a desperate effort at calm. And while I told her she stood looking out of the window with a look I could not fathom on her face. It was a relief when Mrs. Watson tapped at the door and brought me some tea and toast. The cook was in bed, completely demoralized, she reported, and Liddy, brave with the daylight, was looking for footprints around the house. Mrs. Watson herself was a wreck; she was blue-white around the lips, and she had one hand tied up. She said she had fallen down-stairs in her excitement. It was natural, of course, that the thing would shock her, having been the Armstrongs' housekeeper for several years, and knowing Mr. Arnold well.

Gertrude had slipped out during my talk with Mrs. Watson, and I dressed and went down-stairs. The billiard and card-rooms were locked until the coroner and the detectives got there, and the men from the club had gone back for more conventional clothing.

I could hear Thomas in the pantry, alternately wailing for Mr. Arnold, as he called him, and citing the tokens that had precursed the murder. The house seemed to choke me, and, slipping a shawl around me, I went out on the drive. At the corner by the east wing I met Liddy. Her skirts were draggled with dew to her knees, and her hair was still in crimps.

"Go right in and change your clothes," I said sharply. "You're a sight, and at your age!"

She had a golf-stick in her hand, and she said she had found it on the lawn. There was nothing unusual about it, but it occurred to me that a golf-stick with a metal end might have been the object that had scratched the stairs near the card-room. I took it from her, and sent her up for dry garments. Her daylight courage and self-importance, and her shuddering delight in the mystery, irritated me beyond words. After I left her I made a circuit of the building. Nothing seemed to be disturbed: the house looked as calm and peaceful in the morning sun as it had the day I had been coerced into taking it. There was nothing to show that inside had been mystery and violence and sudden death.

In one of the tulip beds back of the house an early blackbird was pecking viciously at something that glittered in the light. I picked my way gingerly over through the dew and stooped down: almost buried in the soft ground was a revolver! I scraped the earth off it with the tip of my shoe, and, picking it up, slipped it into my pocket. Not until I had got into my bedroom and double-locked the door did I venture to take it out and examine it. One look was all I needed. It was Halsey's revolver. I had unpacked it the day before and put it on his shaving-stand, and there could be no mistake. His name was on a small silver plate on the handle.

I seemed to see a network closing around my boy, innocent as I knew he was. The revolver—I am afraid of them, but anxiety gave me courage to look through the barrel-the revolver had still two bullets in it. I could only breathe a prayer of thankfulness that I had found the revolver before any sharp-eyed detective had come around.

I decided to keep what clues I had, the cuff-link, the golf-stick and the revolver, in a secure place until I could see some reason for displaying them. The cuff-link had been dropped into a little filigree box on my toilet table. I opened the box and felt around for it. The box was empty-the cuff-link had disappeared!

Gertrude's Engagement

At ten o'clock the Casanova hack brought up three men. They introduced themselves as the coroner of the county and two detectives from the city. The coroner led the way at once to the locked wing, and with the aid of one of the detectives examined the rooms and the body. The other detective, after a short scrutiny of the dead man, busied himself with the outside of the house. It was only after they had got a fair idea of things as they were that they sent for me.

I received them in the living-room, and I had made up my mind exactly what to tell. I had taken the house for the summer, I said, while the Armstrongs were in California. In spite of a rumor among the servants about strange noises—I cited Thomas-nothing had occurred the first two nights. On the third night I believed that some one had been in the house: I had heard a crashing sound, but being alone with one maid had not investigated. The house had been locked in the morning and apparently undisturbed.

Then, as clearly as I could, I related how, the night before, a shot had roused us; that my niece and I had investigated and found a body; that I did not know who the murdered man was until Mr. Jarvis from the club informed me, and that I knew of no reason why Mr. Arnold Armstrong should steal into his father's house at night. I should have been glad to allow him entrée there at any time.

"Have you reason to believe, Miss Innes," the coroner asked, "that any member of your household, imagining Mr. Armstrong was a burglar, shot him in self-defense?"

"I have no reason for thinking so," I said quietly.

"Your theory is that Mr. Armstrong was followed here by some enemy, and shot as he entered the house?"

"I don't think I have a theory," I said. "The thing that has puzzled me is why Mr. Armstrong should enter his father's house two nights in succession, stealing in like a thief, when he needed only to ask entrance to be admitted."

The coroner was a very silent man: he took some notes after this, but he seemed anxious to make the next train back to town. He set the inquest for the following Saturday, gave Mr. Jamieson, the younger of the two detectives, and the more intelligent looking, a few instructions, and, after gravely shaking hands with me and regretting the unfortunate affair, took his departure, accompanied by the other detective.

I was just beginning to breathe freely when Mr. Jamieson, who had been standing by the window, came over to me.

"The family consists of yourself alone, Miss Innes?"

"My niece is here," I said.

"There is no one but yourself and your niece?"

"My nephew." I had to moisten my lips.

"Oh, a nephew. I should like to see him, if he is here."

"He is not here just now," I said as quietly as I could. "I expect him-at any time."

"He was here yesterday evening, I believe?"

"No-yes."

"Didn't he have a guest with him? Another man?"

"He brought a friend with him to stay over Sunday, Mr. Bailey."

"Mr. John Bailey, the cashier of the Traders' Bank I believe." And I knew that some one at the Greenwood Club had told. "When did they leave?"

"Very early—I don't know at just what time."

Mr. Jamieson turned suddenly and looked at me.

"Please try to be more explicit," he said. "You say your nephew and Mr. Bailey were in the house last night, and yet you and your niece, with some women-servants, found the body. Where was your nephew?"

I was entirely desperate by that time.

"I do not know," I cried, "but be sure of this: Halsey knows nothing of this thing, and no amount of circumstantial evidence can make an innocent man guilty."

"Sit down," he said, pushing forward a chair. "There are some things I have to tell you, and, in return, please tell me all you know. Believe me, things always come out. In the first place, Mr. Armstrong was shot from above. The bullet was fired at close range, entered below the shoulder and came out, after passing through the heart, well down the back. In other words,

I believe the murderer stood on the stairs and fired down. In the second place, I found on the edge of the billiard-table a charred cigar which had burned itself partly out, and a cigarette which had consumed itself to the cork tip. Neither one had been more than lighted, then put down and forgotten. Have you any idea what it was that made your nephew and Mr. Bailey leave their cigars and their game, take out the automobile without calling the chauffeur, and all this at-let me see-certainly before three o'clock in the morning?"

"I don't know," I said; "but depend on it, Mr. Jamieson, Halsey will be back himself to explain everything."

"I sincerely hope so," he said. "Miss Innes, has it occurred to you that Mr. Bailey might know something of this?"

Gertrude had come down-stairs and just as he spoke she came in. I saw her stop suddenly, as if she had been struck.

"He does not," she said in a tone that was not her own. "Mr. Bailey and my brother know nothing of this. The murder was committed at three. They left the house at a quarter before three."

"How do you know that?" Mr. Jamieson asked oddly. "Do you *know* at what time they left?"

"I do," Gertrude answered firmly. "At a quarter before three my brother and Mr. Bailey left the house, by the main entrance. I—was there."

"Gertrude," I said excitedly, "you are dreaming! Why, at a quarter to three—"

"Listen," she said. "At half-past two the down-stairs telephone rang. I had not gone to sleep, and I heard it. Then I heard Halsey answer it, and in a few minutes he came up-stairs and knocked at my door. We-we talked for a minute, then I put on my dressing-gown and slippers, and went down-stairs with him. Mr. Bailey was in the billiard-room. We-we all talked together for perhaps ten minutes. Then it was decided that-that they should both go away—"

"Can't you be more explicit?" Mr. Jamieson asked. "*Why* did they go away?"

"I am only telling you what happened, not why it happened," she said evenly. "Halsey went for the car, and instead of bringing it to the house and rousing people, he went by the lower road from the stable. Mr. Bailey was to meet him at the foot of the lawn. Mr. Bailey left—"

"Which way?" Mr. Jamieson asked sharply.

"By the main entrance. He left-it was a quarter to three. I know exactly."

"The clock in the hall is stopped, Miss Innes," said Jamieson. Nothing seemed to escape him.

"He looked at his watch," she replied, and I could see Mr. Jamieson's eyes snap, as if he had made a discovery. As for myself, during the whole recital I had been plunged into the deepest amazement.

"Will you pardon me for a personal question?" The detective was a youngish man, and I thought he was somewhat embarrassed. "What are your-your relations with Mr. Bailey?"

Gertrude hesitated. Then she came over and put her hand lovingly in mine.

"I am engaged to marry him," she said simply.

I had grown so accustomed to surprises that I could only gasp again, and as for Gertrude, the hand that lay in mine was burning with fever.

"And-after that," Mr. Jamieson went on, "you went directly to bed?"

Gertrude hesitated.

"No," she said finally. "I—I am not nervous, and after I had extinguished the light, I re-membered something I had left in the billiard-room, and I felt my way back there through the darkness."

"Will you tell me what it was you had forgotten?"

"I can not tell you," she said slowly. "I—I did not leave the billiard-room at once—"

"Why?" The detective's tone was imperative. "This is very important, Miss Innes."

"I was crying," Gertrude said in a low tone. "When the French clock in the drawing-room struck three, I got up, and then—I heard a step on the east porch, just outside the card-room. Some one with a key was working with the latch, and I thought, of course, of Halsey. When we took the house he called that his entrance, and he had carried a key for it ever since. The door

25

opened and I was about to ask what he had forgotten, when there was a flash and a report. Some heavy body dropped, and, half crazed with terror and shock, I ran through the drawing-room and got up-stairs—I scarcely remember how."

She dropped into a chair, and I thought Mr. Jamieson must have finished. But he was not through.

"You certainly clear your brother and Mr. Bailey admirably," he said. "The testimony is invaluable, especially in view of the fact that your brother and Mr. Armstrong had, I believe, quarreled rather seriously some time ago."

"Nonsense," I broke in. "Things are bad enough, Mr. Jamieson, without inventing bad feeling where it doesn't exist. Gertrude, I don't think Halsey knew the-the murdered man, did he?"

But Mr. Jamieson was sure of his ground.

"The quarrel, I believe," he persisted, "was about Mr. Armstrong's conduct to you, Miss Gertrude. He had been paying you unwelcome attentions."

And I had never seen the man!

When she nodded a "yes" I saw the tremendous possibilities involved. If this detective could prove that Gertrude feared and disliked the murdered man, and that Mr. Armstrong had been annoying and possibly pursuing her with hateful attentions, all that, added to Gertrude's confession of her presence in the billiard-room at the time of the crime, looked strange, to say the least. The prominence of the family assured a strenuous effort to find the murderer, and if we had nothing worse to look forward to, we were sure of a distasteful publicity.

Mr. Jamieson shut his note-book with a snap, and thanked us.

"I have an idea," he said, apropos of nothing at all, "that at any rate the ghost is laid here. Whatever the rappings have been-and the colored man says they began when the family went west three months ago-they are likely to stop now."

Which shows how much he knew about it. The ghost was not laid: with the murder of Arnold Armstrong he, or it, only seemed to take on fresh vigor.

Mr. Jamieson left then, and when Gertrude had gone up-stairs, as she did at once, I sat and thought over what I had just heard. Her engagement, once so engrossing a matter, paled now beside the significance of her story. If Halsey and Jack Bailey had left before the crime, how came Halsey's revolver in the tulip bed? What was the mysterious cause of their sudden flight? What had Gertrude left in the billiard-room? What was the significance of the cuff-link, and where was it?

In the East Corridor

When the detective left he enjoined absolute secrecy on everybody in the household. The Greenwood Club promised the same thing, and as there are no Sunday afternoon papers, the murder was not publicly known until Monday. The coroner himself notified the Armstrong family lawyer, and early in the afternoon he came out. I had not seen Mr. Jamieson since morning, but I knew he had been interrogating the servants. Gertrude was locked in her room with a headache, and I had luncheon alone.

Mr. Harton, the lawyer, was a little, thin man, and he looked as if he did not relish his business that day.

"This is very unfortunate, Miss Innes," he said, after we had shaken hands. "Most unfortunate-and mysterious. With the father and mother in the west, I find everything devolves on me; and, as you can understand, it is an unpleasant duty."

"No doubt," I said absently. "Mr. Harton, I am going to ask you some questions, and I hope you will answer them. I feel that I am entitled to some knowledge, because I and my family are just now in a most ambiguous position."

I don't know whether he understood me or not: he took of his glasses and wiped them.

"I shall be very happy," he said with old-fashioned courtesy.

"Thank you. Mr. Harton, did Mr. Arnold Armstrong know that Sunnyside had been rented?"

"I think-yes, he did. In fact, I myself told him about it."

"And he knew who the tenants were?"

"Yes."

"He had not been living with the family for some years, I believe?"

"No. Unfortunately, there had been trouble between Arnold and his father. For two years he had lived in town."

"Then it would be unlikely that he came here last night to get possession of anything belonging to him?"

"I should think it hardly possible," he admitted. "To be perfectly frank, Miss Innes, I can not think of any reason whatever for his coming here as he did. He had been staying at the club-house across the valley for the last week, Jarvis tells me, but that only explains how he came here, not why. It is a most unfortunate family."

He shook his head despondently, and I felt that this dried-up little man was the repository of much that he had not told me. I gave up trying to elicit any information from him, and we went together to view the body before it was taken to the city. It had been lifted on to the billiard-table and a sheet thrown over it; otherwise nothing had been touched. A soft hat lay beside it, and the collar of the dinner-coat was still turned up. The handsome, dissipated face of Arnold Armstrong, purged of its ugly lines, was now only pathetic. As we went in Mrs. Watson appeared at the card-room door.

"Come in, Mrs. Watson," the lawyer said. But she shook her head and withdrew: she was the only one in the house who seemed to regret the dead man, and even she seemed rather shocked than sorry.

I went to the door at the foot of the circular staircase and opened it. If I could only have seen Halsey coming at his usual hare-brained clip up the drive, if I could have heard the throb of the motor, I would have felt that my troubles were over. But there was nothing to be seen. The countryside lay sunny and quiet in its peaceful Sunday afternoon calm, and far down the drive Mr. Jamieson was walking slowly, stooping now and then, as if to examine the road. When I went back, Mr. Harton was furtively wiping his eyes.

"The prodigal has come home, Miss Innes," he said. "How often the sins of the fathers are visited on the children!" Which left me pondering.

Before Mr. Harton left, he told me something of the Armstrong family. Paul Armstrong, the father, had been married twice. Arnold was a son by the first marriage. The second Mrs. Armstrong had been a widow, with a child, a little girl. This child, now perhaps twenty, was Louise Armstrong, having taken her stepfather's name, and was at present in California with the family.

"They will probably return at once," he concluded "sad part of my errand here to-day is to see if you will relinquish your lease here in their favor."

"We would better wait and see if they wish to come," I said. "It seems unlikely, and my town house is being remodeled." At that he let the matter drop, but it came up unpleasantly enough, later.

At six o'clock the body was taken away, and at seven-thirty, after an early dinner, Mr. Harton went. Gertrude had not come down, and there was no news of Halsey. Mr. Jamieson had taken a lodging in the village, and I had not seen him since mid-afternoon. It was about nine o'clock, I think, when the bell rang and he was ushered into the living-room.

"Sit down," I said grimly. "Have you found a clue that will incriminate me, Mr. Jamieson?"

He had the grace to look uncomfortable. "No," he said. "If you had killed Mr. Armstrong, you would have left no clues. You would have had too much intelligence."

After that we got along better. He was fishing in his pocket, and after a minute he brought out two scraps of paper. "I have been to the club-house," he said, "and among Mr. Armstrong's effects, I found these. One is curious; the other is puzzling."

The first was a sheet of club note-paper, on which was written, over and over, the name "Halsey B. Innes." It was Halsey's flowing signature to a dot, but it lacked Halsey's ease. The ones toward the bottom of the sheet were much better than the top ones. Mr. Jamieson smiled at my face.

"His old tricks," he said. "That one is merely curious; this one, as I said before, is puzzling."

The second scrap, folded and refolded into a compass so tiny that the writing had been partly obliterated, was part of a letter-the lower half of a sheet, not typed, but written in a cramped hand.

> "——by altering the plans for——rooms, may be possible. The best way, in my opinion, would be to——the plan for——in one of the——rooms——chimney."

That was all.

"Well?" I said, looking up. "There is nothing in that, is there? A man ought to be able to change the plan of his house without becoming an object of suspicion."

"There is little in the paper itself," he admitted; "but why should Arnold Armstrong carry that around, unless it meant something? He never built a house, you may be sure of that. If it is this house, it may mean anything, from a secret room——"

"To an extra bath-room," I said scornfully. "Haven't you a thumb-print, too?"

"I have," he said with a smile, "and the print of a foot in a tulip bed, and a number of other things. The oddest part is, Miss Innes, that the thumb-mark is probably yours and the footprint certainly."

His audacity was the only thing that saved me: his amused smile put me on my mettle, and I ripped out a perfectly good scallop before I answered.

"Why did I step into the tulip bed?" I asked with interest.

"You picked up something," he said good-humoredly, "which you are going to tell me about later."

"Am I, indeed?" I was politely curious. "With this remarkable insight of yours, I wish you would tell me where I shall find my four-thousand-dollar motor car."

"I was just coming to that," he said. "You will find it about thirty miles away, at Andrews Station, in a blacksmith shop, where it is being repaired."

I laid down my knitting then and looked at him.

"And Halsey?" I managed to say.

"We are going to exchange information," he said "I am going to tell you that, when you tell me what you picked up in the tulip bed."

We looked steadily at each other: it was not an unfriendly stare; we were only measuring weapons. Then he smiled a little and got up.

"With your permission," he said, "I am going to examine the card-room and the staircase again. You might think over my offer in the meantime."

He went on through the drawing-room, and I listened to his footsteps growing gradually fainter. I dropped my pretense at knitting and, leaning back, I thought over the last forty-eight hours. Here was I, Rachel Innes, spinster, a granddaughter of old John Innes of Revolutionary days, a D. A. R., a Colonial Dame, mixed up with a vulgar and revolting crime, and even attempting to hoodwink the law! Certainly I had left the straight and narrow way.

I was roused by hearing Mr. Jamieson coming rapidly back through the drawing-room. He stopped at the door.

"Miss Innes," he said quickly, "will you come with me and light the east corridor? I have fastened somebody in the small room at the head of the card-room stairs."

I jumped up at once.

"You mean-the murderer?" I gasped.

"Possibly," he said quietly, as we hurried together up the stairs. "Some one was lurking on the staircase when I went back. I spoke; instead of an answer, whoever it was turned and ran up.

I followed-it was dark-but as I turned the corner at the top a figure darted through this door and closed it. The bolt was on my side, and I pushed it forward. It is a closet, I think." We were in the upper hall now. "If you will show me the electric switch, Miss Innes, you would better wait in your own room."

Trembling as I was, I was determined to see that door opened. I hardly knew what I feared, but so many terrible and inexplicable things had happened that suspense was worse than certainty.

"I am perfectly cool," I said, "and I am going to remain here."

The lights flashed up along that end of the corridor, throwing the doors into relief. At the intersection of the small hallway with the larger, the circular staircase wound its way up, as if it had been an afterthought of the architect. And just around the corner, in the small corridor, was the door Mr. Jamieson had indicated. I was still unfamiliar with the house, and I did not remember the door. My heart was thumping wildly in my ears, but I nodded to him to go ahead. I was perhaps eight or ten feet away-and then he threw the bolt back.

"Come out," he said quietly. There was no response. "Come-out," he repeated. Then—I think he had a revolver, but I am not sure-he stepped aside and threw the door open.

From where I stood I could not see beyond the door, but I saw Mr. Jamieson's face change and heard him mutter something, then he bolted down the stairs, three at a time. When my knees had stopped shaking, I moved forward, slowly, nervously, until I had a partial view of what was beyond the door. It seemed at first to be a closet, empty. Then I went close and examined it, to stop with a shudder. Where the floor should have been was black void and darkness, from which came the indescribable, damp smell of the cellars.

Mr. Jamieson had locked somebody in the clothes chute. As I leaned over I fancied I heard a groan-or was it the wind?

A Sprained Ankle

I was panic-stricken. As I ran along the corridor I was confident that the mysterious intruder and probable murderer had been found, and that he lay dead or dying at the foot of the chute. I got down the staircase somehow, and through the kitchen to the basement stairs. Mr. Jamieson had been before me, and the door stood open. Liddy was standing in the middle of the kitchen, holding a frying-pan by the handle as a weapon.

"Don't go down there," she yelled, when she saw me moving toward the basement stairs. "Don't you do it, Miss Rachel. That Jamieson's down there now. There's only trouble comes of hunting ghosts; they lead you into bottomless pits and things like that. Oh, Miss Rachel, don't—" as I tried to get past her.

She was interrupted by Mr. Jamieson's reappearance. He ran up the stairs two at a time, and his face was flushed and furious.

"The whole place is locked," he said angrily. "Where's the laundry key kept?"

"It's kept in the door," Liddy snapped. "That whole end of the cellar is kept locked, so nobody can get at the clothes, and then the key's left in the door? so that unless a thief was as blind as-as some detectives, he could walk right in."

"Liddy," I said sharply, "come down with us and turn on all the lights."

She offered her resignation, as usual, on the spot, but I took her by the arm, and she came along finally. She switched on all the lights and pointed to a door just ahead.

"That's the door," she said sulkily. "The key's in it."

But the key was not in it. Mr. Jamieson shook it, but it was a heavy door, well locked. And then he stooped and began punching around the keyhole with the end of a lead-pencil. When he stood up his face was exultant.

"It's locked on the inside," he said in a low tone. "There is somebody in there."

"Lord have mercy!" gasped Liddy, and turned to run.

"Liddy," I called, "go through the house at once and see who is missing, or if any one is. We'll have to clear this thing at once. Mr. Jamieson, if you will watch here I will go to the lodge and find Warner. Thomas would be of no use. Together you may be able to force the door."

"A good idea," he assented. "But-there are windows, of course, and there is nothing to prevent whoever is in there from getting out that way."

"Then lock the door at the top of the basement stairs," I suggested, "and patrol the house from the outside."

We agreed to this, and I had a feeling that the mystery of Sunnyside was about to be solved. I ran down the steps and along the drive. Just at the corner I ran full tilt into somebody who seemed to be as much alarmed as I was. It was not until I had recoiled a step or two that I recognized Gertrude, and she me.

"Good gracious, Aunt Ray," she exclaimed, "what is the matter?"

"There's somebody locked in the laundry," I panted. "That is-unless-you didn't see any one crossing the lawn or skulking around the house, did you?"

"I think we have mystery on the brain," Gertrude said wearily. "No, I haven't seen any one, except old Thomas, who looked for all the world as if he had been ransacking the pantry. What have you locked in the laundry?"

"I can't wait to explain," I replied. "I must get Warner from the lodge. If you came out for air, you'd better put on your overshoes." And then I noticed that Gertrude was limping-not much, but sufficiently to make her progress very slow, and seemingly painful.

"You have hurt yourself," I said sharply.

"I fell over the carriage block," she explained. "I thought perhaps I might see Halsey coming home. He-he ought to be here."

I hurried on down the drive. The lodge was some distance from the house, in a grove of trees where the drive met the county road. There were two white stone pillars to mark the entrance, but the iron gates, once closed and tended by the lodge-keeper, now stood permanently open. The day of the motor-car had come; no one had time for closed gates and lodge-keepers. The lodge at Sunnyside was merely a sort of supplementary servants' quarters: it was as convenient in its appointments as the big house and infinitely more cozy.

As I went down the drive, my thoughts were busy. Who would it be that Mr. Jamieson had trapped in the cellar? Would we find a body or some one badly injured? Scarcely either. Whoever had fallen had been able to lock the laundry door on the inside. If the fugitive had come from outside the house, how did he get in? If it was some member of the household, who could it have been? And then —a feeling of horror almost overwhelmed me. Gertrude! Gertrude and her injured ankle! Gertrude found limping slowly up the drive when I had thought she was in bed!

I tried to put the thought away, but it would not go. If Gertrude had been on the circular staircase that night, why had she fled from Mr. Jamieson? The idea, puzzling as it was, seemed borne out by this circumstance. Whoever had taken refuge at the head of the stairs could scarcely have been familiar with the house, or with the location of the chute. The mystery seemed to deepen constantly. What possible connection could there be between Halsey and Gertrude, and the murder of Arnold Armstrong? And yet, every way I turned I seemed to find something that pointed to such a connection.

At the foot of the drive the road described a long, sloping, horseshoe-shaped curve around the lodge. There were lights there, streaming cheerfully out on to the trees, and from an upper room came wavering shadows, as if some one with a lamp was moving around. I had come almost silently in my evening slippers, and I had my second collision of the evening on the road just above the house. I ran full into a man in a long coat, who was standing in the shadow beside the drive, with his back to me, watching the lighted windows.

"What the hell!" he ejaculated furiously, and turned around. When he saw me, however, he did not wait for any retort on my part. He faded away-this is not slang; he did-he absolutely disappeared in the dusk without my getting more than a glimpse of his face. I had a vague impression of unfamiliar features and of a sort of cap with a visor. Then he was gone.

I went to the lodge and rapped. It required two or three poundings to bring Thomas to the door, and he opened it only an inch or so.

"Where is Warner?" I asked.

"I—I think he's in bed, ma'm."

"Get him up," I said, "and for goodness' sake open the door, Thomas. I'll wait for Warner."

"It's kind o' close in here, ma'm," he said, obeying gingerly, and disclosing a cool and comfortable looking interior. "Perhaps you'd keer to set on the porch an' rest yo'self."

It was so evident that Thomas did not want me inside that I went in.

"Tell Warner he is needed in a hurry," I repeated, and turned into the little sitting-room. I could hear Thomas going up the stairs, could hear him rouse Warner, and the steps of the chauffeur as he hurriedly dressed. But my attention was busy with the room below.

On the center-table, open, was a sealskin traveling bag. It was filled with gold-topped bottles and brushes, and it breathed opulence, luxury, femininity from every inch of surface. How did it get there? I was still asking myself the question when Warner came running down the stairs and into the room. He was completely but somewhat incongruously dressed, and his open, boyish face looked abashed. He was a country boy, absolutely frank and reliable, of fair education and intelligence-one of the small army of American youths who turn a natural aptitude for mechanics into the special field of the automobile, and earn good salaries in a congenial occupation.

"What is it, Miss Innes?" he asked anxiously.

"There is some one locked in the laundry," I replied. "Mr. Jamieson wants you to help him break the lock. Warner, whose bag is this?"

He was in the doorway by this time, and he pretended not to hear.

"Warner," I called, "come back here. Whose bag is this?"

He stopped then, but he did not turn around.

"It's—it belongs to Thomas," he said, and fled up the drive.

To Thomas! A London bag with mirrors and cosmetic jars of which Thomas could not even have guessed the use! However, I put the bag in the back of my mind, which was fast becoming stored with anomalous and apparently irreconcilable facts, and followed Warner to the house.

Liddy had come back to the kitchen: the door to the basement stairs was double-barred, and had a table pushed against it; and beside her on the table was most of the kitchen paraphernalia.

"Did you see if there was any one missing in the house?" I asked, ignoring the array of sauce-pans rolling-pins, and the poker of the range.

"Rosie is missing," Liddy said with unction. She had objected to Rosie, the parlor maid, from the start. "Mrs. Watson went into her room, and found she had gone without her hat. People that trust themselves a dozen miles from the city, in strange houses, with servants they don't know, needn't be surprised if they wake up some morning and find their throats cut."

After which carefully veiled sarcasm Liddy relapsed into gloom. Warner came in then with a handful of small tools, and Mr. Jamieson went with him to the basement. Oddly enough, I was not alarmed. With all my heart I wished for Halsey, but I was not frightened. At the door he was to force, Warner put down his tools and looked at it. Then he turned the handle. Without the slightest difficulty the door opened, revealing the blackness of the drying-room beyond!

Mr. Jamieson gave an exclamation of disgust. "Gone!" he said. "Confound such careless work! I might have known."

It was true enough. We got the lights on finally and looked all through the three rooms that constituted this wing of the basement. Everything was quiet and empty. An explanation of how the fugitive had escaped injury was found in a heaped-up basket of clothes under the chute. The basket had been overturned, but that was all. Mr. Jamieson examined the windows: one was unlocked, and offered an easy escape. The window or the door? Which way had the fugitive escaped? The door seemed most probable, and I hoped it had been so. I could not have borne, just then, to think that it was my poor Gertrude we had been hounding through the darkness, and yet — I had met Gertrude not far from that very window.

I went up-stairs at last, tired and depressed. Mrs. Watson and Liddy were making tea in the kitchen. In certain walks of life the tea-pot is the refuge in times of stress, trouble or sickness: they give tea to the dying and they put it in the baby's nursing bottle. Mrs. Watson was fixing a tray to be sent in to me, and when I asked her about Rosie she confirmed her absence.

"She's not here," she said; "but I would not think much of that, Miss Innes. Rosie is a pretty young girl, and perhaps she has a sweetheart. It will be a good thing if she has. The maids stay much better when they have something like that to hold them here."

Gertrude had gone back to her room, and while I was drinking my cup of hot tea, Mr. Jamieson came in.

"We might take up the conversation where we left off an hour and a half ago," he said. "But before we go on, I want to say this: The person who escaped from the laundry was a woman with a foot of moderate size and well arched. She wore nothing but a stocking on her right foot, and, in spite of the unlocked door, she escaped by the window."

And again I thought of Gertrude's sprained ankle. Was it the right or the left?

The Other Half of the Line

"Miss Innes," the detective began, "what is your opinion of the figure you saw on the east veranda the night you and your maid were in the house alone?"

"It was a woman," I said positively.

"And yet your maid affirms with equal positiveness that it was a man."

"Nonsense," I broke in. "Liddy had her eyes shut-she always shuts them when she's frightened."

"And you never thought then that the intruder who came later that night might be a woman- the woman, in fact, whom you saw on the veranda?"

"I had reasons for thinking it was a man," I said remembering the pearl cuff-link.

"Now we are getting down to business. *What* were your reasons for thinking that?"

I hesitated.

"If you have any reason for believing that your midnight guest was Mr. Armstrong, other than his visit here the next night, you ought to tell me, Miss Innes. We can take nothing for granted. If, for instance, the intruder who dropped the bar and scratched the staircase-you see, I know about that-if this visitor was a woman, why should not the same woman have come back the following night, met Mr. Armstrong on the circular staircase, and in alarm shot him?"

"It was a man," I reiterated. And then, because I could think of no other reason for my statement, I told him about the pearl cuff-link. He was intensely interested.

"Will you give me the link," he said, when I finished, "or, at least, let me see it? I consider it a most important clue."

"Won't the description do?"

"Not as well as the original."

"Well, I'm very sorry," I said, as calmly as I could, "I — the thing is lost. It-it must have fallen out of a box on my dressing-table."

Whatever he thought of my explanation, and I knew he doubted it, he made no sign. He asked me to describe the link accurately, and I did so, while he glanced at a list he took from his pocket.

"One set monogram cuff-links," he read, "one set plain pearl links, one set cuff-links, woman's head set with diamonds and emeralds. There is no mention of such a link as you describe, and yet, if your theory is right, Mr. Armstrong must have taken back in his cuffs one complete cuff-link, and a half, perhaps, of the other."

The idea was new to me. If it had not been the murdered man who had entered the house that night, who had it been?

"There are a number of strange things connected with this case," the detective went on. "Miss Gertrude Innes testified that she heard some one fumbling with the lock, that the door opened, and that almost immediately the shot was fired. Now, Miss Innes, here is the strange part of that. Mr. Armstrong had no key with him. There was no key in the lock, or on the floor. In other words, the evidence points absolutely to this: Mr. Armstrong was admitted to the house from within."

"It is impossible," I broke in. "Mr. Jamieson, do you know what your words imply? Do you know that you are practically accusing Gertrude Innes of admitting that man?"

"Not quite that," he said, with his friendly smile. "In fact, Miss Innes, I am quite certain she did not. But as long as I learn only parts of the truth, from both you and her, what can I do? I know you picked up something in the flower bed: you refuse to tell me what it was. I know Miss Gertrude went back to the billiard-room to get something, she refuses to say what. You suspect what happened to the cuff-link, but you won't tell me. So far, all I am sure of is this: I do not believe Arnold Armstrong was the midnight visitor who so alarmed you by dropping-shall we say, a golf-stick? And I believe that when he did come he was admitted by some one in the house. Who knows-it may have been-Liddy!"

I stirred my tea angrily.

"I have always heard," I said dryly, "that undertakers' assistants are jovial young men. A man's sense of humor seems to be in inverse proportion to the gravity of his profession."

"A man's sense of humor is a barbarous and a cruel thing, Miss Innes," he admitted. "It is to the feminine as the hug of a bear is to the scratch of-well, anything with claws. Is that you, Thomas? Come in."

Thomas Johnson stood in the doorway. He looked alarmed and apprehensive, and suddenly I remembered the sealskin dressing-bag in the lodge. Thomas came just inside the door and stood with his head drooping, his eyes, under their shaggy gray brows, fixed on Mr. Jamieson.

"Thomas," said the detective, not unkindly, "I sent for you to tell us what you told Sam Bohannon at the club, the day before Mr. Arnold was found here, dead. Let me see. You came here Friday night to see Miss Innes, didn't you? And came to work here Saturday morning?"

For some unexplained reason Thomas looked relieved.

"Yas, sah," he said. "You see it were like this: When Mistah Armstrong and the fam'ly went away, Mis' Watson an' me, we was lef' in charge till the place was rented. Mis' Watson, she've bin here a good while, an' she warn' skeery. So she slep' in the house. I'd bin havin' tokens —I tol' Mis' Innes some of 'em-an' I slep' in the lodge. Then one day Mis' Watson, she came to me an' she sez, sez she, 'Thomas, you'll hev to sleep up in the big house. I'm too nervous to do it any more.' But I jes' reckon to myself that ef it's too skeery fer her, it's too skeery fer me. We had it, then, sho' nuff, and it ended up with Mis' Watson stayin' in the lodge nights an' me lookin' fer work at de club."

"Did Mrs. Watson say that anything had happened to alarm her?"

"No, sah. She was jes' natchally skeered. Well, that was all, far's I know, until the night I come over to see Mis' Innes. I come across the valley, along the path from the club-house, and I goes home that way. Down in the creek bottom I almost run into a man. He wuz standin' with his back to me, an' he was workin' with one of these yere electric light things that fit in yer pocket. He was havin' trouble-one minute it'd flash out, an' the nex' it'd be gone. I hed a view of 'is white dress shirt an' tie, as I passed. I didn't see his face. But I know it warn't Mr. Arnold. It was a taller man than Mr. Arnold. Beside that, Mr. Arnold was playin' cards when I got to the club-house, same's he'd been doin' all day."

"And the next morning you came back along the path," pursued Mr. Jamieson relentlessly.

"The nex' mornin' I come back along the path an' down where I dun see the man night befoh, I picked up this here." The old man held out a tiny object and Mr. Jamieson took it. Then he held it on his extended palm for me to see. It was the other half of the pearl cuff-link!

33

But Mr. Jamieson was not quite through questioning him.

"And so you showed it to Sam, at the club, and asked him if he knew any one who owned such a link, and Sam said-what?"

"Wal, Sam, he 'lowed he'd seen such a pair of cuff-buttons in a shirt belongin' to Mr. Bailey-Mr. Jack Bailey, sah."

"I'll keep this link, Thomas, for a while," the detective said. "That's all I wanted to know. Good night."

As Thomas shuffled out, Mr. Jamieson watched me sharply.

"You see, Miss Innes," he said, "Mr. Bailey insists on mixing himself with this thing. If Mr. Bailey came here that Friday night expecting to meet Arnold Armstrong, and missed him-if, as I say, he had done this, might he not, seeing him enter the following night, have struck him down, as he had intended before?"

"But the motive?" I gasped.

"There could be motive proved, I think. Arnold Armstrong and John Bailey have been enemies since the latter, as cashier of the Traders' Bank, brought Arnold almost into the clutches of the law. Also, you forget that both men have been paying attention to Miss Gertrude. Bailey's flight looks bad, too."

"And you think Halsey helped him to escape?"

"Undoubtedly. Why, what could it be but flight? Miss Innes, let me reconstruct that evening, as I see it. Bailey and Armstrong had quarreled at the club. I learned this to-day. Your nephew brought Bailey over. Prompted by jealous, insane fury, Armstrong followed, coming across by the path. He entered the billiard-room wing-perhaps rapping, and being admitted by your nephew. Just inside he was shot, by some one on the circular staircase. The shot fired, your nephew and Bailey left the house at once, going toward the automobile house. They left by the lower road, which prevented them being heard, and when you and Miss Gertrude got downstairs everything was quiet."

"But-Gertrude's story," I stammered.

"Miss Gertrude only brought forward her explanation the following morning. I do not believe it, Miss Innes. It is the story of a loving and ingenious woman."

"And-this thing to-night?"

"May upset my whole view of the case. We must give the benefit of every doubt, after all. We may, for instance, come back to the figure on the porch: if it was a woman you saw that night through the window, we might start with other premises. Or Mr. Innes' explanation may turn us in a new direction. It is possible that he shot Arnold Armstrong as a burglar and then fled, frightened at what he had done. In any case, however, I feel confident that the body was here when he left. Mr. Armstrong left the club ostensibly for a moonlight saunter, about half after eleven o'clock. It was three when the shot was fired."

I leaned back bewildered. It seemed to me that the evening had been full of significant happenings, had I only held the key. Had Gertrude been the fugitive in the clothes chute? Who was the man on the drive near the lodge, and whose gold-mounted dressing-bag had I seen in the lodge sitting-room?

It was late when Mr. Jamieson finally got up to go. I went with him to the door, and together we stood looking out over the valley. Below lay the village of Casanova, with its Old World houses, its blossoming trees and its peace. Above on the hill across the valley were the lights of the Greenwood Club. It was even possible to see the curving row of parallel lights that marked the carriage road. Rumors that I had heard about the club came back-of drinking, of high play, and once, a year ago, of a suicide under those very lights.

Mr. Jamieson left, taking a short cut to the village, and I still stood there. It must have been after eleven, and the monotonous tick of the big clock on the stairs behind me was the only sound. Then I was conscious that some one was running up the drive. In a minute a woman darted into the area of light made by the open door, and caught me by the arm. It was

Rosie-Rosie in a state of collapse from terror, and, not the least important, clutching one of my Coalport plates and a silver spoon.

She stood staring into the darkness behind, still holding the plate. I got her into the house and secured the plate; then I stood and looked down at her where she crouched tremblingly against the doorway.

"Well," I asked, "didn't your young man enjoy his meal?"

She couldn't speak. She looked at the spoon she still held—I wasn't so anxious about it: thank Heaven, it wouldn't chip-and then she stared at me.

"I appreciate your desire to have everything nice for him," I went on, "but the next time, you might take the Limoges china It's more easily duplicated and less expensive."

"I haven't a young man-not here." She had got her breath now, as I had guessed she would. "I—I have been chased by a thief, Miss Innes."

"Did he chase you out of the house and back again?" I asked.

Then Rosie began to cry-not silently, but noisily, hysterically.

I stopped her by giving her a good shake.

"What in the world is the matter with you?" I snapped. "Has the day of good common sense gone by! Sit up and tell me the whole thing."

Rosie sat up then, and sniffled.

"I was coming up the drive—" she began.

"You must start with when you went *down* the drive, with my dishes and my silver," I interrupted, but, seeing more signs of hysteria, I gave in. "Very well. You were coming up the drive—"

"I had a basket of-of silver and dishes on my arm and I was carrying the plate, because-because I was afraid I'd break it. Part-way up the road a man stepped out of the bushes, and held his arm like this, spread out, so I couldn't get past. He said-he said —'Not so fast, young lady; I want you to let me see what's in that basket.'"

She got up in her excitement and took hold of my arm.

"It was like this, Miss Innes," she said, "and say you was the man. When he said that, I screamed and ducked under his arm like this. He caught at the basket and I dropped it. I ran as fast as I could, and he came after as far as the trees. Then he stopped. Oh, Miss Innes, it must have been the man that killed that Mr. Armstrong!"

"Don't be foolish," I said. "Whoever killed Mr. Armstrong would put as much space between himself and this house as he could. Go up to bed now; and mind, if I hear of this story being repeated to the other maids, I shall deduct from your wages for every broken dish I find in the drive."

I listened to Rosie as she went up-stairs, running past the shadowy places and slamming her door. Then I sat down and looked at the Coalport plate and the silver spoon. I had brought my own china and silver, and, from all appearances, I would have little enough to take back. But though I might jeer at Rosie as much as I wished, the fact remained that some one had been on the drive that night who had no business there. Although neither had Rosie, for that matter.

I could fancy Liddy's face when she missed the extra pieces of china-she had opposed Rosie from the start. If Liddy once finds a prophecy fulfilled, especially an unpleasant one, she never allows me to forget it. It seemed to me that it was absurd to leave that china dotted along the road for her to spy the next morning; so with a sudden resolution, I opened the door again and stepped out into the darkness. As the door closed behind me I half regretted my impulse; then I shut my teeth and went on.

I have never been a nervous woman, as I said before. Moreover, a minute or two in the darkness enabled me to see things fairly well. Beulah gave me rather a start by rubbing unexpectedly against my feet; then we two, side by side, went down the drive.

There were no fragments of china, but where the grove began I picked up a silver spoon. So far Rosie's story was borne out: I began to wonder if it were not indiscreet, to say the least, this midnight prowling in a neighborhood with such a deservedly bad reputation. Then I saw something gleaming, which proved to be the handle of a cup, and a step or two farther on I found a V-shaped bit of a plate. But the most surprising thing of all was to find the basket sitting comfortably beside the road, with the rest of the broken crockery piled neatly within, and a handful of small silver, spoon, forks, and the like, on top! I could only stand and stare. Then Rosie's story was true. But where had Rosie carried her basket? And why had the thief, if he were a thief, picked up the broken china out of the road and left it, with his booty?

It was with my nearest approach to a nervous collapse that I heard the familiar throbbing of an automobile engine. As it came closer I recognized the outline of the Dragon Fly, and knew that Halsey had come back.

Strange enough it must have seemed to Halsey, too, to come across me in the middle of the night, with the skirt of my gray silk gown over my shoulders to keep off the dew, holding a red and green basket under one arm and a black cat under the other. What with relief and joy, I began to cry, right there, and very nearly wiped my eyes on Beulah in the excitement.

Just Like a Girl

"Aunt Ray!" Halsey said from the gloom behind the lamps. "What in the world are you doing here?"

"Taking a walk," I said, trying to be composed. I don't think the answer struck either of us as being ridiculous at the time. "Oh, Halsey, where have you been?"

"Let me take you up to the house." He was in the road, and had Beulah and the basket out of my arms in a moment. I could see the car plainly now, and Warner was at the wheel-Warner in an ulster and a pair of slippers, over Heaven knows what. Jack Bailey was not there. I got in, and we went slowly and painfully up to the house.

We did not talk. What we had to say was too important to commence there, and, besides, it took all kinds of coaxing from both men to get the Dragon Fly up the last grade. Only when we had closed the front door and stood facing each other in the hall, did Halsey say anything. He slipped his strong young arm around my shoulders and turned me so I faced the light.

"Poor Aunt Ray!" he said gently. And I nearly wept again. "I—I must see Gertrude, too; we will have a three-cornered talk."

And then Gertrude herself came down the stairs. She had not been to bed, evidently: she still wore the white negligee she had worn earlier in the evening, and she limped somewhat. During her slow progress down the stairs I had time to notice one thing: Mr. Jamieson had said the woman who escaped from the cellar had worn no shoe on her right foot. Gertrude's right ankle was the one she had sprained!

The meeting between brother and sister was tense, but without tears. Halsey kissed her tenderly, and I noticed evidences of strain and anxiety in both young faces.

"Is everything-right?" she asked.

"Right as can be," with forced cheerfulness.

I lighted the living-room and we went in there. Only a half-hour before I had sat with Mr. Jamieson in that very room, listening while he overtly accused both Gertrude and Halsey of at least a knowledge of the death of Arnold Armstrong. Now Halsey was here to speak for himself: I should learn everything that had puzzled me.

"I saw it in the paper to-night for the first time," he was saying. "It knocked me dumb. When I think of this houseful of women, and a thing like that occurring!"

Gertrude's face was still set and white. "That isn't all, Halsey," she said. "You and-and Jack left almost at the time it happened. The detective here thinks that you-that we-know something about it."

"The devil he does!" Halsey's eyes were fairly starting from his head. "I beg your pardon, Aunt Ray, but-the fellow's a lunatic."

"Tell me everything, won't you, Halsey?" I begged. "Tell me where you went that night, or rather morning, and why you went as you did. This has been a terrible forty-eight hours for all of us."

He stood staring at me, and I could see the horror of the situation dawning in his face.

"I can't tell you where I went, Aunt Ray," he said, after a moment. "As to why, you will learn that soon enough. But Gertrude knows that Jack and I left the house before this thing-this horrible murder-occurred."

"Mr. Jamieson does not believe me," Gertrude said drearily. "Halsey, if the worst comes, if they should arrest you, you must-tell."

"I shall tell nothing," he said with a new sternness in his voice. "Aunt Ray, it was necessary for Jack and me to leave that night. I can not tell you why-just yet. As to where we went, if I have to depend on that as an alibi, I shall not tell. The whole thing is an absurdity, a trumped-up charge that can not possibly be serious."

"Has Mr. Bailey gone back to the city," I demanded, "or to the club?"

"Neither," defiantly; "at the present moment I do not know where he is."

"Halsey," I asked gravely, leaning forward, "have you the slightest suspicion who killed Arnold Armstrong? The police think he was admitted from within, and that he was shot down from above, by someone on the circular staircase."

"I know nothing of it," he maintained; but I fancied I caught a sudden glance at Gertrude, a flash of something that died as it came.

As quietly, as calmly as I could, I went over the whole story, from the night Liddy and I had been alone up to the strange experience of Rosie and her pursuer. The basket still stood on the table, a mute witness to this last mystifying occurrence.

"There is something else," I said hesitatingly, at the last. "Halsey, I have never told this even to Gertrude, but the morning after the crime, I found, in a tulip bed, a revolver. It-it was yours, Halsey."

For an appreciable moment Halsey stared at me. Then he turned to Gertrude.

"My revolver, Trude!" he exclaimed. "Why, Jack took my revolver with him, didn't he?"

"Oh, for Heaven's sake don't say that," I implored. "The detective thinks possibly Jack Bailey came back, and-and the thing happened then."

"He didn't come back," Halsey said sternly. "Gertrude, when you brought down a revolver that night for Jack to take with him, what one did you bring? Mine?"

Gertrude was defiant now.

"No. Yours was loaded, and I was afraid of what Jack might do. I gave him one I have had for a year or two. It was empty."

Halsey threw up both hands despairingly.

"If that isn't like a girl!" he said. "Why didn't you do what I asked you to, Gertrude? You send Bailey off with an empty gun, and throw mine in a tulip bed, of all places on earth! Mine was a thirty-eight caliber. The inquest will show, of course, that the bullet that killed Armstrong was a thirty-eight. Then where shall I be?"

"You forget," I broke in, "that I have the revolver, and that no one knows about it."

But Gertrude had risen angrily.

"I can not stand it; it is always with me," she cried. "Halsey, I did not throw your revolver into the tulip bed. I—think-you-did it-yourself!"

They stared at each other across the big library table, with young eyes all at once hard, suspicious. And then Gertrude held out both hands to him appealingly.

"We must not," she said brokenly. "Just now, with so much at stake, it-is shameful. I know you are as ignorant as I am. Make me believe it, Halsey."

Halsey soothed her as best he could, and the breach seemed healed. But long after I went to bed he sat down-stairs in the living-room alone, and I knew he was going over the case as he had learned it. Some things were clear to him that were dark to me. He knew, and Gertrude, too, why Jack Bailey and he had gone away that night, as they did. He knew where they had been for the last forty-eight hours, and why Jack Bailey had not returned with him. It seemed to me that without fuller confidence from both the children—they are always children to me—I should never be able to learn anything.

As I was finally getting ready for bed, Halsey came up-stairs and knocked at my door. When I had got into a negligée—I used to say wrapper before Gertrude came back from school—I let him in. He stood in the doorway a moment, and then he went into agonies of silent mirth. I sat down on the side of the bed and waited in severe silence for him to stop, but he only seemed to grow worse. When he had recovered he took me by the elbow and pulled me in front of the mirror.

"'How to be beautiful,'" he quoted. "'Advice to maids and matrons,' by Beatrice Fairfax!" And then I saw myself. I had neglected to remove my wrinkle eradicators, and I presume my appearance was odd. I believe that it is a woman's duty to care for her looks, but it is much like telling a necessary falsehood-one must not be found out. By the time I got them off Halsey was serious again, and I listened to his story.

"Aunt Ray," he began, extinguishing his cigarette on the back of my ivory hair-brush, "I would give a lot to tell you the whole thing. But—I can't, for a day or so, anyhow. But one thing I might have told you a long time ago. If you had known it, you would not have suspected me for a moment of-of having anything to do with the attack on Arnold Armstrong. Goodness knows what I might do to a fellow like that, if there was enough provocation, and I had a gun in my hand-under ordinary circumstances. But—I care a great deal about Louise Armstrong, Aunt Ray. I hope to marry her some day. Is it likely I would kill her brother?"

"Her stepbrother," I corrected. "No, of course, it isn't likely, or possible. Why didn't you tell me, Halsey?"

"Well, there were two reasons," he said slowly. "One was that you had a girl already picked out for me—"

"Nonsense," I broke in, and felt myself growing red. I had, indeed, one of the-but no matter.

"And the second reason," he pursued, "was that the Armstrongs would have none of me."

I sat bolt upright at that and gasped.

"The Armstrongs!" I repeated. "With old Peter Armstrong driving a stage across the mountains while your grandfather was war governor—"

"Well, of course, the war governor's dead, and out of the matrimonial market," Halsey interrupted. "And the present Innes admits himself he isn't good enough for-for Louise."

"Exactly," I said despairingly, "and, of course, you are taken at your own valuation. The Inneses are not always so self-depreciatory."

"Not always, no," he said, looking at me with his boyish smile. "Fortunately, Louise doesn't agree with her family. She's willing to take me, war governor or no, provided her mother consents. She isn't overly-fond of her stepfather, but she adores her mother. And now, can't you see where this thing puts me? Down and out, with all of them."

"But the whole thing is absurd," I argued. "And besides, Gertrude's sworn statement that you left before Arnold Armstrong came would clear you at once."

Halsey got up and began to pace the room, and the air of cheerfulness dropped like a mask.

"She can't swear it," he said finally. "Gertrude's story was true as far as it went, but she didn't tell everything. Arnold Armstrong came here at two-thirty—came into the billiard-room and left in five minutes. He came to bring-something."

"Halsey," I cried, "you *must* tell me the whole truth. Every time I see a way for you to escape you block it yourself with this wall of mystery. What did he bring?"

"A telegram-for Bailey," he said. "It came by special messenger from town, and was-most important. Bailey had started for here, and the messenger had gone back to the city. The steward gave it to Arnold, who had been drinking all day and couldn't sleep, and was going for a stroll in the direction of Sunnyside."

"And he brought it?"

"Yes."

"What was in the telegram?"

"I can tell you-as soon as certain things are made public. It is only a matter of days now," gloomily.

"And Gertrude's story of a telephone message?"

"Poor Trude!" he half whispered. "Poor loyal little girl! Aunt Ray, there was no such message. No doubt your detective already knows that and discredits all Gertrude told him."

"And when she went back, it was to get-the telegram?"

"Probably," Halsey said slowly. "When you get to thinking about it, Aunt Ray, it looks bad for all three of us, doesn't it? And yet—I will take my oath none of us even inadvertently killed that poor devil."

I looked at the closed door into Gertrude's dressing-room, and lowered my voice.

"The same horrible thought keeps recurring to me," I whispered. "Halsey, Gertrude probably had your revolver: she must have examined it, anyhow, that night. After you-and Jack had gone, what if that ruffian came back, and she-and she—"

I couldn't finish. Halsey stood looking at me with shut lips.

"She might have heard him fumbling at the door he had no key, the police say-and thinking it was you, or Jack, she admitted him. When she saw her mistake she ran up the stairs, a step or two, and turning, like an animal at bay, she fired."

Halsey had his hand over my lips before I finished, and in that position we stared each at the other, our stricken glances crossing.

"The revolver-my revolver-thrown into the tulip bed!" he muttered to himself. "Thrown perhaps from an upper window: you say it was buried deep. Her prostration ever since, her-Aunt Ray, you don't think it was Gertrude who fell down the clothes chute?"

I could only nod my head in a hopeless affirmative.

The Traders' Bank

The morning after Halsey's return was Tuesday. Arnold Armstrong had been found dead at the foot of the circular staircase at three o'clock on Sunday morning. The funeral services were to be held on Tuesday, and the interment of the body was to be deferred until the Armstrongs arrived from California. No one, I think, was very sorry that Arnold Armstrong was dead, but the manner of his death aroused some sympathy and an enormous amount of curiosity. Mrs. Ogden Fitzhugh, a cousin, took charge of the arrangements, and everything, I believe, was as quiet as possible. I gave Thomas Johnson and Mrs. Watson permission to go into town to pay their last respects to the dead man, but for some reason they did not care to go.

Halsey spent part of the day with Mr. Jamieson, but he said nothing of what happened. He looked grave and anxious, and he had a long conversation with Gertrude late in the afternoon.

Tuesday evening found us quiet, with the quiet that precedes an explosion. Gertrude and Halsey were both gloomy and distraught, and as Liddy had already discovered that some of the china was broken-it is impossible to have any secrets from an old servant—I was not in a pleasant humor myself. Warner brought up the afternoon mail and the evening papers at seven—I was curious to know what the papers said of the murder. We had turned away at least a dozen reporters. But I read over the head-line that ran half-way across the top of the *Gazette* twice before I comprehended it. Halsey had opened the *Chronicle* and was staring at it fixedly.

"The Traders' Bank closes its doors!" was what I read, and then I put down the paper and looked across the table.

"Did you know of this?" I asked Halsey.

"I expected it. But not so soon," he replied.

"And you?" to Gertrude.

"Jack-told us-something," Gertrude said faintly. "Oh, Halsey, what can he do now?"

"Jack!" I said scornfully. "Your Jack's flight is easy enough to explain now. And you helped him, both of you, to get away! You get that from your mother; it isn't an Innes trait. Do you know that every dollar you have, both of you, is in that bank?"

Gertrude tried to speak, but Halsey stopped her.

"That isn't all, Gertrude," he said quietly; "Jack is—under arrest."

"Under arrest!" Gertrude screamed, and tore the paper out of his hand. She glanced at the heading, then she crumpled the newspaper into a ball and flung it to the floor. While Halsey, looking stricken and white, was trying to smooth it out and read it, Gertrude had dropped her head on the table and was sobbing stormily.

I have the clipping somewhere, but just now I can remember only the essentials.

On the afternoon before, Monday, while the Traders' Bank was in the rush of closing hour, between two and three, Mr. Jacob Trautman, President of the Pearl Brewing Company, came into the bank to lift a loan. As security for the loan he had deposited some three hundred International Steamship Company 5's, in total value three hundred thousand dollars. Mr. Trautman went to the loan clerk and, after certain formalities had been gone through, the loan clerk went to the vault. Mr. Trautman, who was a large and genial German, waited for a time, whistling under his breath. The loan clerk did not come back. After an interval, Mr. Trautman saw the loan clerk emerge from the vault and go to the assistant cashier: the two went hurriedly to the vault. A lapse of another ten minutes, and the assistant cashier came out and approached Mr. Trautman. He was noticeably white and trembling. Mr. Trautman was told that through an oversight the bonds had been misplaced, and was asked to return the following morning, when everything would be made all right.

Mr. Trautman, however, was a shrewd business man, and he did not like the appearance of things. He left the bank apparently satisfied, and within thirty minutes he had called up three different members of the Traders' Board of Directors. At three-thirty there was a hastily convened board meeting, with some stormy scenes, and late in the afternoon a national bank examiner was in possession of the books. The bank had not opened for business on Tuesday.

At twelve-thirty o'clock the Saturday before, as soon as the business of the day was closed, Mr. John Bailey, the cashier of the defunct bank, had taken his hat and departed. During the afternoon he had called up Mr. Aronson, a member of the board, and said he was ill, and might not be at the bank for a day or two. As Bailey was highly thought of, Mr. Aronson merely expressed a regret. From that time until Monday night, when Mr. Bailey had surrendered to the police, little was known of his movements. Some time after one on Saturday he had entered the Western Union office at Cherry and White Streets and had sent two telegrams. He was at the Greenwood Country Club on Saturday night, and appeared unlike himself. It was reported that he would be released under enormous bond, some time that day, Tuesday.

The article closed by saying that while the officers of the bank refused to talk until the examiner had finished his work, it was known that securities aggregating a million and a quarter were missing. Then there was a diatribe on the possibility of such an occurrence; on the folly of a one-man bank, and of a Board of Directors that met only to lunch together and to listen to a brief report from the cashier, and on the poor policy of a government that arranges a three or four-day examination twice a year. The mystery, it insinuated, had not been cleared by the arrest of the cashier. Before now minor officials had been used to cloak the misdeeds of men higher up. Inseparable as the words "speculation" and "peculation" have grown to be, John Bailey was not known to be in the stock market. His only words, after his surrender, had been "Send for Mr. Armstrong at once." The telegraph message which had finally reached the President of the Traders' Bank, in an interior town in California, had been responded to by a telegram from Doctor Walker, the young physician who was traveling with the Armstrong family, saying that Paul Armstrong was very ill and unable to travel.

That was how things stood that Tuesday evening. The Traders' Bank had suspended payment, and John Bailey was under arrest, charged with wrecking it; Paul Armstrong lay very ill in California, and his only son had been murdered two days before. I sat dazed and bewildered.

The children's money was gone: that was bad enough, though I had plenty, if they would let me share. But Gertrude's grief was beyond any power of mine to comfort; the man she had chosen stood accused of a colossal embezzlement-and even worse. For in the instant that I sat there I seemed to see the coils closing around John Bailey as the murderer of Arnold Armstrong.

Gertrude lifted her head at last and stared across the table at Halsey.

"Why did he do it?" she wailed. "Couldn't you stop him, Halsey? It was suicidal to go back!"

Halsey was looking steadily through the windows of the breakfast-room, but it was evident he saw nothing.

"It was the only thing he could do, Trude," he said at last. "Aunt Ray, when I found Jack at the Greenwood Club last Saturday night, he was frantic. I can not talk until Jack tells me I may, but-he is absolutely innocent of all this, believe me. I thought, Trude and I thought, we were helping him, but it was the wrong way. He came back. Isn't that the act of an innocent man?"

"Then why did he leave at all?" I asked, unconvinced. "What innocent man would run away from here at three o'clock in the morning? Doesn't it look rather as though he thought it impossible to escape?"

Gertrude rose angrily. "You are not even just!" she flamed. "You don't know anything about it, and you condemn him!"

"I know that we have all lost a great deal of money," I said. "I shall believe Mr. Bailey innocent the moment he is shown to be. You profess to know the truth, but you can not tell me! What am I to think?"

Halsey leaned over and patted my hand.

"You must take us on faith," he said. "Jack Bailey hasn't a penny that doesn't belong to him; the guilty man will be known in a day or so."

"I shall believe that when it is proved," I said grimly. "In the meantime, I take no one on faith. The Inneses never do."

Gertrude, who had been standing aloof at a window, turned suddenly. "But when the bonds are offered for sale, Halsey, won't the thief be detected at once?"

Halsey turned with a superior smile.

"It wouldn't be done that way," he said. "They would be taken out of the vault by some one who had access to it, and used as collateral for a loan in another bank. It would be possible to realize eighty per cent. of their face value."

"In cash?"

"In cash."

"But the man who did it-he would be known?"

"Yes. I tell you both, as sure as I stand here, I believe that Paul Armstrong looted his own bank. I believe he has a million at least, as the result, and that he will never come back. I'm worse than a pauper now. I can't ask Louise to share nothing a year with me and when I think of this disgrace for her, I'm crazy."

The most ordinary events of life seemed pregnant with possibilities that day, and when Halsey was called to the telephone, I ceased all pretense at eating. When he came back from the telephone his face showed that something had occurred. He waited, however, until Thomas left the dining-room: then he told us.

"Paul Armstrong is dead," he announced gravely. "He died this morning in California. Whatever he did, he is beyond the law now."

Gertrude turned pale.

"And the only man who could have cleared Jack can never do it!" she said despairingly.

"Also," I replied coldly, "Mr. Armstrong is for ever beyond the power of defending himself. When your Jack comes to me, with some two hundred thousand dollars in his hands, which is about what you have lost, I shall believe him innocent."

Halsey threw his cigarette away and turned on me.

"There you go!" he exclaimed. "If he was the thief, he could return the money, of course. If he is innocent, he probably hasn't a tenth of that amount in the world. In his hands! That's like a woman."

Gertrude, who had been pale and despairing during the early part of the conversation, had flushed an indignant red. She got up and drew herself to her slender height, looking down at me with the scorn of the young and positive.

"You are the only mother I ever had," she said tensely. "I have given you all I would have given my mother, had she lived-my love, my trust. And now, when I need you most, you fail me. I tell you, John Bailey is a good man, an honest man. If you say he is not, you-you—"

"Gertrude," Halsey broke in sharply. She dropped beside the table and, burying her face in her arms broke into a storm of tears.

"I love him-love him," she sobbed, in a surrender that was totally unlike her. "Oh, I never thought it would be like this. I can't bear it. I can't."

Halsey and I stood helpless before the storm. I would have tried to comfort her, but she had put me away, and there was something aloof in her grief, something new and strange. At last, when her sorrow had subsided to the dry shaking sobs of a tired child, without raising her head she put out one groping hand.

"Aunt Ray!" she whispered. In a moment I was on my knees beside her, her arm around my neck, her cheek against my hair.

"Where am I in this?" Halsey said suddenly and tried to put his arms around us both. It was a welcome distraction, and Gertrude was soon herself again. The little storm had cleared the air. Nevertheless, my opinion remained unchanged. There was much to be cleared up before I would consent to any renewal of my acquaintance with John Bailey. And Halsey and Gertrude knew it, knowing me.

Halsey Makes a Capture

It was about half-past eight when we left the dining-room and still engrossed with one subject, the failure of the bank and its attendant evils Halsey and I went out into the grounds for a stroll Gertrude followed us shortly. "The light was thickening," to appropriate Shakespeare's description of twilight, and once again the tree-toads and the crickets were making night throb with their tiny life. It was almost oppressively lonely, in spite of its beauty, and I felt a sickening pang of homesickness for my city at night-for the clatter of horses' feet on cemented paving, for the lights, the voices, the sound of children playing. The country after dark oppresses me. The stars, quite eclipsed in the city by the electric lights, here become insistent, assertive. Whether I want to or not, I find myself looking for the few I know by name, and feeling ridiculously new and small by contrast-always an unpleasant sensation.

After Gertrude joined us, we avoided any further mention of the murder. To Halsey, as to me, there was ever present, I am sure, the thought of our conversation of the night before. As we strolled back and forth along the drive, Mr. Jamieson emerged from the shadow of the trees.

"Good evening," he said, managing to include Gertrude in his bow. Gertrude had never been even ordinarily courteous to him, and she nodded coldly. Halsey, however, was more cordial, although we were all constrained enough. He and Gertrude went on together, leaving the detective to walk with me. As soon as they were out of earshot, he turned to me.

"Do you know, Miss Innes," he said, "the deeper I go into this thing, the more strange it seems to me. I am very sorry for Miss Gertrude. It looks as if Bailey, whom she has tried so hard to save, is worse than a rascal; and after her plucky fight for him, it seems hard."

I looked through the dusk to where Gertrude's light dinner dress gleamed among the trees. She *had* made a plucky fight, poor child. Whatever she might have been driven to do, I could find nothing but a deep sympathy for her. If she had only come to me with the whole truth then!

"Miss Innes," Mr. Jamieson was saying, "in the last three days, have you seen a —any suspicious figures around the grounds? Any—woman?"

"No," I replied. "I have a houseful of maids that will bear watching, one and all. But there has been no strange woman near the house or Liddy would have seen her, you may be sure. She has a telescopic eye."

Mr. Jamieson looked thoughtful.

"It may not amount to anything," he said slowly. "It is difficult to get any perspective on things around here, because every one down in the village is sure he saw the murderer, either before or since the crime. And half of them will stretch a point or two as to facts, to be obliging. But the man who drives the hack down there tells a story that may possibly prove to be important."

"I have heard it, I think. Was it the one the parlor maid brought up yesterday, about a ghost wringing its hands on the roof? Or perhaps it's the one the milk-boy heard: a tramp washing a dirty shirt, presumably bloody, in the creek below the bridge?"

I could see the gleam of Mr. Jamieson's teeth, as he smiled.

"Neither," he said. "But Matthew Geist, which is our friend's name, claims that on Saturday night, at nine-thirty, a veiled lady —"

"I knew it would be a veiled lady," I broke in.

"A veiled lady," he persisted, "who was apparently young and beautiful, engaged his hack and asked to be driven to Sunnyside. Near the gate, however, she made him stop, in spite of his remonstrances, saying she preferred to walk to the house. She paid him, and he left her there. Now, Miss Innes, you had no such visitor, I believe?"

"None," I said decidedly.

"Geist thought it might be a maid, as you had got a supply that day. But he said her getting out near the gate puzzled him. Anyhow, we have now one veiled lady, who, with the ghostly intruder of Friday night, makes two assets that I hardly know what to do with."

"It is mystifying," I admitted, "although I can think of one possible explanation. The path from the Greenwood Club to the village enters the road near the lodge gate. A woman who wished to reach the Country Club, unperceived, might choose such a method. There are plenty of women there."

I think this gave him something to ponder, for in a short time he said good night and left. But I myself was far from satisfied. I was determined, however, on one thing. If my suspicions- for I had suspicions-were true, I would make my own investigations, and Mr. Jamieson should learn only what was good for him to know.

We went back to the house, and Gertrude, who was more like herself since her talk with Halsey, sat down at the mahogany desk in the living-room to write a letter. Halsey prowled up and down the entire east wing, now in the card-room, now in the billiard-room, and now and then blowing his clouds of tobacco smoke among the pink and gold hangings of the drawing-room. After a little I joined him in the billiard-room, and together we went over the details of the discovery of the body.

The card-room was quite dark. Where we sat, in the billiard-room, only one of the side brackets was lighted, and we spoke in subdued tones, as the hour and the subject seemed to demand. When I spoke of the figure Liddy and I had seen on the porch through the card-room window Friday night, Halsey sauntered into the darkened room, and together we stood there, much as Liddy and I had done that other night.

The window was the same grayish rectangle in the blackness as before. A few feet away in the hall was the spot where the body of Arnold Armstrong had been found. I was a bit nervous, and I put my hand on Halsey's sleeve. Suddenly, from the top of the staircase above us came the sound of a cautious footstep. At first I was not sure, but Halsey's attitude told me he had heard and was listening. The step, slow, measured, infinitely cautious, was nearer now. Halsey tried to loosen my fingers, but I was in a paralysis of fright.

The swish of a body against the curving rail, as if for guidance, was plain enough, and now whoever it was had reached the foot of the staircase and had caught a glimpse of our rigid silhouettes against the billiard-room doorway. Halsey threw me off then and strode forward.

"Who is it?" he called imperiously, and took a half dozen rapid strides toward the foot of the staircase. Then I heard him mutter something; there was the crash of a falling body, the slam of the outer door, and, for an instant, quiet. I screamed, I think. Then I remember turning on the lights and finding Halsey, white with fury, trying to untangle himself from something warm and fleecy. He had cut his forehead a little on the lowest step of the stairs, and he was rather a ghastly sight. He flung the white object at me, and, jerking open the outer door, raced into the darkness.

Gertrude had come on hearing the noise, and now we stood, staring at each other over-of all things on earth—a white silk and wool blanket, exquisitely fine! It was the most unghostly thing in the world, with its lavender border and its faint scent. Gertrude was the first to speak.

"Somebody-had it?" she asked.

"Yes. Halsey tried to stop whoever it was and fell. Gertrude, that blanket is not mine. I have never seen before."

She held it up and looked at it: then she went to the door on to the veranda and threw it open. Perhaps a hundred feet from the house were two figures, that moved slowly toward us as we looked. When they came within range of the light, I recognized Halsey, and with him Mrs. Watson, the housekeeper.

One Mystery for Another

The most commonplace incident takes on a new appearance if the attendant circumstances are unusual. There was no reason on earth why Mrs. Watson should not have carried a blanket down the east wing staircase, if she so desired. But to take a blanket down at eleven o'clock at night, with every precaution as to noise, and, when discovered, to fling it at Halsey and bolt-Halsey's word, and a good one-into the grounds,—this made the incident more than significant.

They moved slowly across the lawn and up the steps. Halsey was talking quietly, and Mrs. Watson was looking down and listening. She was a woman of a certain amount of dignity, most efficient, so far as I could see, although Liddy would have found fault if she dared. But just now Mrs. Watson's face was an enigma. She was defiant, I think, under her mask of submission, and she still showed the effect of nervous shock.

"Mrs. Watson," I said severely, "will you be so good as to explain this rather unusual occurrence?"

"I don't think it so unusual, Miss Innes." Her voice was deep and very clear: just now it was somewhat tremulous. "I was taking a blanket down to Thomas, who is-not well to-night, and I used this staircase, as being nearer the path to the lodge. When-Mr. Innes called and then rushed at me, I—I was alarmed, and flung the blanket at him."

Halsey was examining the cut on his forehead in a small mirror on the wall. It was not much of an injury, but it had bled freely, and his appearance was rather terrifying.

"Thomas ill?" he said, over his shoulder. "Why, I thought I saw Thomas out there as you made that cyclonic break out of the door and over the porch."

I could see that under pretense of examining his injury he was watching her through the mirror.

"Is this one of the servants' blankets, Mrs. Watson?" I asked, holding up its luxurious folds to the light.

"Everything else is locked away," she replied. Which was true enough, no doubt. I had rented the house without bed furnishings.

"If Thomas is ill," Halsey said, "some member of the family ought to go down to see him. You needn't bother, Mrs. Watson. I will take the blanket."

She drew herself up quickly, as if in protest, but she found nothing to say. She stood smoothing the folds of her dead black dress, her face as white as chalk above it. Then she seemed to make up her mind.

"Very well, Mr. Innes," she said. "Perhaps you would better go. I have done all I could."

And then she turned and went up the circular staircase, moving slowly and with a certain dignity. Below, the three of us stared at one another across the intervening white blanket.

"Upon my word," Halsey broke out, "this place is a walking nightmare. I have the feeling that we three outsiders who have paid our money for the privilege of staying in this spook-factory, are living on the very top of things. We're on the lid, so to speak. Now and then we get a sight of the things inside, but we are not a part of them."

"Do you suppose," Gertrude asked doubtfully, "that she really meant that blanket for Thomas?"

"Thomas was standing beside that magnolia tree," Halsey replied, "when I ran after Mrs. Watson. It's down to this, Aunt Ray. Rosie's basket and Mrs. Watson's blanket can only mean one thing: there is somebody hiding or being hidden in the lodge. It wouldn't surprise me if we hold the key to the whole situation now. Anyhow, I'm going to the lodge to investigate."

Gertrude wanted to go, too, but she looked so shaken that I insisted she should not. I sent for Liddy to help her to bed, and then Halsey and I started for the lodge. The grass was heavy with dew, and, man-like, Halsey chose the shortest way across the lawn. Half-way, however, he stopped.

"We'd better go by the drive," he said. "This isn't a lawn; it's a field. Where's the gardener these days?"

"There isn't any," I said meekly. "We have been thankful enough, so far, to have our meals prepared and served and the beds aired. The gardener who belongs here is working at the club."

"Remind me to-morrow to send out a man from town," he said. "I know the very fellow."

I record this scrap of conversation, just as I have tried to put down anything and everything that had a bearing on what followed, because the gardener Halsey sent the next day played an important part in the events of the next few weeks-events that culminated, as you know, by stirring the country profoundly. At that time, however, I was busy trying to keep my skirts dry, and paid little or no attention to what seemed then a most trivial remark.

Along the drive I showed Halsey where I had found Rosie's basket with the bits of broken china piled inside. He was rather skeptical.

"Warner probably," he said when I had finished. "Began it as a joke on Rosie, and ended by picking up the broken china out of the road, knowing it would play hob with the tires of the car." Which shows how near one can come to the truth, and yet miss it altogether.

At the lodge everything was quiet. There was a light in the sitting-room down-stairs, and a faint gleam, as if from a shaded lamp, in one of the upper rooms. Halsey stopped and examined the lodge with calculating eyes.

"I don't know, Aunt Ray," he said dubiously; "this is hardly a woman's affair. If there's a scrap of any kind, you hike for the timber." Which was Halsey's solicitous care for me, put into vernacular.

"I shall stay right here," I said, and crossing the small veranda, now shaded and fragrant with honeysuckle, I hammered the knocker on the door.

Thomas opened the door himself-Thomas, fully dressed and in his customary health. I had the blanket over my arm.

"I brought the blanket, Thomas," I said; "I am sorry you are so ill."

The old man stood staring at me and then at the blanket. His confusion under other circumstances would have been ludicrous.

"What! Not ill?" Halsey said from the step. "Thomas, I'm afraid you've been malingering."

Thomas seemed to have been debating something with himself. Now he stepped out on the porch and closed the door gently behind him.

"I reckon you bettah come in, Mis' Innes," he said, speaking cautiously. "It's got so I dunno what to do, and it's boun' to come out some time er ruther."

He threw the door open then, and I stepped inside, Halsey close behind. In the sitting-room the old negro turned with quiet dignity to Halsey.

"You bettah sit down, sah," he said. "It's a place for a woman, sah."

Things were not turning out the way Halsey expected. He sat down on the center-table, with his hands thrust in his pockets, and watched me as I followed Thomas up the narrow stairs. At the top a woman was standing, and a second glance showed me it was Rosie. She shrank back a little, but I said nothing. And then Thomas motioned to a partly open door, and I went in.

The lodge boasted three bedrooms up-stairs, all comfortably furnished. In this one, the largest and airiest, a night lamp was burning, and by its light I could make out a plain white metal bed. A girl was asleep there-or in a half stupor, for she muttered something now and then. Rosie had taken her courage in her hands, and coming in had turned up the light. It was only then that I knew. Fever-flushed, ill as she was, I recognized Louise Armstrong.

I stood gazing down at her in a stupor of amazement. Louise here, hiding at the lodge, ill and alone! Rosie came up to the bed and smoothed the white counterpane.

"I am afraid she is worse to-night," she ventured at last. I put my hand on the sick girl's forehead. It was burning with fever, and I turned to where Thomas lingered in the hallway.

"Will you tell me what you mean, Thomas Johnson, by not telling me this before?" I demanded indignantly.

Thomas quailed.

"Mis' Louise wouldn' let me," he said earnestly. "I wanted to. She ought to 'a' had a doctor the night she came, but she wouldn' hear to it. Is she-is she very bad, Mis' Innes?"

"Bad enough," I said coldly. "Send Mr. Innes up."

Halsey came up the stairs slowly, looking rather interested and inclined to be amused. For a moment he could not see anything distinctly in the darkened room; he stopped, glanced at Rosie and at me, and then his eyes fell on the restless head on the pillow.

I think he felt who it was before he really saw her; he crossed the room in a couple of strides and bent over the bed.

"Louise!" he said softly; but she did not reply, and her eyes showed no recognition. Halsey was young, and illness was new to him. He straightened himself slowly, still watching her, and caught my arm.

"She's dying, Aunt Ray!" he said huskily. "Dying! Why, she doesn't know me!"

"Fudge!" I snapped, being apt to grow irritable when my sympathies are aroused. "She's doing nothing of the sort,—and don't pinch my arm. If you want something to do, go and choke Thomas."

But at that moment Louise roused from her stupor to cough, and at the end of the paroxysm, as Rosie laid her back, exhausted, she knew us. That was all Halsey wanted; to him consciousness was recovery. He dropped on his knees beside the bed, and tried to tell her she was all right, and we would bring her around in a hurry, and how beautiful she looked-only to break down utterly and have to stop. And at that I came to my senses, and put him out.

"This instant!" I ordered, as he hesitated. "And send Rosie here."

He did not go far. He sat on the top step of the stairs, only leaving to telephone for a doctor, and getting in everybody's way in his eagerness to fetch and carry. I got him away finally, by sending him to fix up the car as a sort of ambulance, in case the doctor would allow the sick girl to be moved. He sent Gertrude down to the lodge loaded with all manner of impossible things, including an armful of Turkish towels and a box of mustard plasters, and as the two girls had known each other somewhat before, Louise brightened perceptibly when she saw her.

When the doctor from Englewood-the Casanova doctor, Doctor Walker, being away-had started for Sunnyside, and I had got Thomas to stop trying to explain what he did not understand himself, I had a long talk with the old man, and this is what I learned.

On Saturday evening before, about ten o'clock, he had been reading in the sitting-room down-stairs, when some one rapped at the door. The old man was alone, Warner not having arrived, and at first he was uncertain about opening the door. He did so finally, and was amazed at being confronted by Louise Armstrong. Thomas was an old family servant, having been with the present Mrs. Armstrong since she was a child, and he was overwhelmed at seeing Louise. He saw that she was excited and tired, and he drew her into the sitting-room and made her sit down. After a while he went to the house and brought Mrs. Watson, and they talked until late. The old man said Louise was in trouble, and seemed frightened. Mrs. Watson made some tea and took it to the lodge, but Louise made them both promise to keep her presence a secret. She had not known that Sunnyside was rented, and whatever her trouble was, this complicated things. She seemed puzzled. Her stepfather and her mother were still in California-that was all she would say about them. Why she had run away no one could imagine. Mr. Arnold Armstrong was at the Greenwood Club, and at last Thomas, not knowing what else to do, went over there along the path. It was almost midnight. Part-way over he met Armstrong himself and brought him to the lodge. Mrs. Watson had gone to the house for some bed-linen, it having been arranged that under the circumstances Louise would be better at the lodge until morning. Arnold Armstrong and Louise had a long conference, during which he was heard to storm and become very violent. When he left it was after two. He had gone up to the house-Thomas did not know why-and at three o'clock he was shot at the foot of the circular staircase.

The following morning Louise had been ill. She had asked for Arnold, and was told he had left town. Thomas had not the moral courage to tell her of the crime. She refused a doctor, and shrank morbidly from having her presence known. Mrs. Watson and Thomas had had their hands full, and at last Rosie had been enlisted to help them. She carried necessary provisions-little enough-to the lodge, and helped to keep the secret.

Thomas told me quite frankly that he had been anxious to keep Louise's presence hidden for this reason: they had all seen Arnold Armstrong that night, and he, himself, for one, was known to have had no very friendly feeling for the dead man. As to the reason for Louise's flight from California, or why she had not gone to the Fitzhughs', or to some of her people in town, he had no more information than I had. With the death of her stepfather and the prospect of the immediate return of the family, things had become more and more impossible. I gathered that Thomas was as relieved as I at the turn events had taken. No, she did not know of either of the deaths in the family.

Taken all around, I had only substituted one mystery for another.

If I knew now why Rosie had taken the basket of dishes, I did not know who had spoken to her and followed her along the drive. If I knew that Louise was in the lodge, I did not know why she was there. If I knew that Arnold Armstrong had spent some time in the lodge the night before he was murdered, I was no nearer the solution of the crime. Who was the midnight intruder who had so alarmed Liddy and myself? Who had fallen down the clothes chute? Was Gertrude's lover a villain or a victim? Time was to answer all these things.

Louise

The doctor from Englewood came very soon, and I went up to see the sick girl with him. Halsey had gone to supervise the fitting of the car with blankets and pillows, and Gertrude was opening and airing Louise's own rooms at the house. Her private sitting-room, bedroom and dressing-room were as they had been when we came. They occupied the end of the east wing, beyond the circular staircase, and we had not even opened them.

The girl herself was too ill to notice what was being done. When, with the help of the doctor, who was a fatherly man with a family of girls at home, we got her to the house and up the stairs into bed, she dropped into a feverish sleep, which lasted until morning. Doctor Stewart-that was the Englewood doctor-stayed almost all night, giving the medicine himself, and watching her closely. Afterward he told me that she had had a narrow escape from pneumonia, and that the cerebral symptoms had been rather alarming. I said I was glad it wasn't an "itis" of some kind, anyhow, and he smiled solemnly.

He left after breakfast, saying that he thought the worst of the danger was over, and that she must be kept very quiet.

"The shock of two deaths, I suppose, has done this," he remarked, picking up his case. "It has been very deplorable."

I hastened to set him right.

"She does not know of either, Doctor," I said. "Please do not mention them to her."

He looked as surprised as a medical man ever does.

"I do not know the family," he said, preparing to get into his top buggy. "Young Walker, down in Casanova, has been attending them. I understand he is going to marry this young lady."

"You have been misinformed," I said stiffly. "Miss Armstrong is going to marry my nephew."

The doctor smiled as he picked up the reins.

"Young ladies are changeable these days," he said. "We thought the wedding was to occur soon. Well, I will stop in this afternoon to see how my patient is getting along."

He drove away then, and I stood looking after him. He was a doctor of the old school, of the class of family practitioner that is fast dying out; a loyal and honorable gentleman who was at once physician and confidential adviser to his patients. When I was a girl we called in the doctor alike when we had measles, or when mother's sister died in the far West. He cut out redundant tonsils and brought the babies with the same air of inspiring self-confidence. Nowadays it requires a different specialist for each of these occurrences. When the babies cried, old Doctor Wainwright gave them peppermint and dropped warm sweet oil in their ears with sublime faith that if it was not colic it was earache. When, at the end of a year, father met him driving in his high side-bar buggy with the white mare ambling along, and asked for a bill, the doctor used to go home, estimate what his services were worth for that period, divide it in half—I don't think he kept any books-and send father a statement, in a cramped hand, on a sheet of ruled white paper. He was an honored guest at all the weddings, christenings, and funerals-yes, funerals-for every one knew he had done his best, and there was no gainsaying the ways of Providence.

Ah, well, Doctor Wainwright is gone, and I am an elderly woman with an increasing tendency to live in the past. The contrast between my old doctor at home and the Casanova doctor, Frank Walker, always rouses me to wrath and digression.

Some time about noon of that day, Wednesday, Mrs. Ogden Fitzhugh telephoned me. I have the barest acquaintance with her-she managed to be put on the governing board of the Old Ladies' Home and ruins their digestions by sending them ice-cream and cake on every holiday. Beyond that, and her reputation at bridge, which is insufferably bad-she is the worst player at the bridge club —I know little of her. It was she who had taken charge of Arnold Armstrong's funeral, however, and I went at once to the telephone.

"Yes," I said, "this is Miss Innes."

"Miss Innes," she said volubly, "I have just received a very strange telegram from my cousin, Mrs. Armstrong. Her husband died yesterday, in California and-wait, I will read you the message."

I knew what was coming, and I made up my mind at once. If Louise Armstrong had a good and sufficient reason for leaving her people and coming home, a reason, moreover, that kept her from going at once to Mrs. Ogden Fitzhugh, and that brought her to the lodge at Sunnyside instead, it was not my intention to betray her. Louise herself must notify her people. I do not justify myself now, but remember, I was in a peculiar position toward the Armstrong family. I was connected most unpleasantly with a cold-blooded crime, and my niece and nephew were practically beggared, either directly or indirectly, through the head of the family.

Mrs. Fitzhugh had found the message.

"'Paul died yesterday. Heart disease,'" she read. "'Wire at once if Louise is with you.' You see, Miss Innes, Louise must have started east, and Fanny is alarmed about her."

"Yes," I said.

"Louise is not here," Mrs. Fitzhugh went on, "and none of her friends-the few who are still in town-has seen her. I called you because Sunnyside was not rented when she went away, and Louise might have, gone there."

"I am sorry, Mrs. Fitzhugh, but I can not help you," I said, and was immediately filled with compunction. Suppose Louise grew worse? Who was I to play Providence in this case? The anxious mother certainly had a right to know that her daughter was in good hands. So I broke in on Mrs. Fitzhugh's voluble excuses for disturbing me.

"Mrs. Fitzhugh," I said. "I was going to let you think I knew nothing about Louise Armstrong, but I have changed my mind. Louise is here, with me." There was a clatter of ejaculations at the other end of the wire. "She is ill, and not able to be moved. Moreover, she is unable to see any one. I wish you would wire her mother that she is with me, and tell her not to worry. No, I do not know why she came east."

"But my dear Miss Innes!" Mrs. Fitzhugh began. I cut in ruthlessly.

"I will send for you as soon as she can see you," I said. "No, she is not in a critical state now, but the doctor says she must have absolute quiet."

When I had hung up the receiver, I sat down to think. So Louise had fled from her people in California, and had come east alone! It was not a new idea, but why had she done it? It occurred to me that Doctor Walker might be concerned in it, might possibly have bothered her with unwelcome attentions; but it seemed to me that Louise was hardly a girl to take refuge in flight under such circumstances. She had always been high-spirited, with the well-poised head and buoyant step of the outdoors girl. It must have been much more in keeping with Louise's character, as I knew it, to resent vigorously any unwelcome attentions from Doctor Walker. It was the suitor whom I should have expected to see in headlong flight, not the lady in the case.

The puzzle was no clearer at the end of the half-hour. I picked up the morning papers, which were still full of the looting of the Traders' Bank, the interest at fever height again, on account of Paul Armstrong's death. The bank examiners were working on the books, and said nothing for publication: John Bailey had been released on bond. The body of Paul Armstrong would arrive Sunday and would be buried from the Armstrong town house. There were rumors that the dead man's estate had been a comparatively small one. The last paragraph was the important one.

Walter P. Broadhurst, of the Marine Bank, had produced two hundred American Traction bonds, which had been placed as security with the Marine Bank for a loan of one hundred and sixty thousand dollars, made to Paul Armstrong, just before his California trip. The bonds were a part of the missing traction bonds from the Traders' Bank! While this involved the late president of the wrecked bank, to my mind it by no means cleared its cashier.

The gardener mentioned by Halsey came out about two o'clock in the afternoon, and walked up from the station. I was favorably impressed by him. His references were good-he had been employed by the Brays until they went to Europe, and he looked young and vigorous. He asked for one assistant, and I was glad enough to get off so easily. He was a pleasant-faced young fellow, with black hair and blue eyes, and his name was Alexander Graham. I have been particular about Alex, because, as I said before, he played an important part later.

That afternoon I had a new insight into the character of the dead banker. I had my first conversation with Louise. She sent for me, and against my better judgment I went. There were so many things she could not be told, in her weakened condition, that I dreaded the interview. It was much easier than I expected, however, because she asked no questions.

Gertrude had gone to bed, having been up almost all night, and Halsey was absent on one of those mysterious absences of his that grew more and more frequent as time went on, until it culminated in the event of the night of June the tenth. Liddy was in attendance in the sick-room. There being little or nothing to do, she seemed to spend her time smoothing the wrinkles from the counterpane. Louise lay under a field of virgin white, folded back at an angle of geometrical exactness, and necessitating a readjustment every time the sick girl turned.

Liddy heard my approach and came out to meet me. She seemed to be in a perpetual state of goose-flesh, and she had got in the habit of looking past me when she talked, as if she saw things. It had the effect of making me look over my shoulder to see what she was staring at, and was intensely irritating.

"She's awake," Liddy said, looking uneasily down the circular staircase, which was beside me. "She was talkin' in her sleep something awful-about dead men and coffins."

"Liddy," I said sternly, "did you breathe a word about everything not being right here?"

Liddy's gaze had wandered to the door of the chute, now bolted securely.

"Not a word," she said, "beyond asking her a question or two, which there was no harm in. She says there never was a ghost known here."

I glared at her, speechless, and closing the door into Louise's boudoir, to Liddy's great disappointment, I went on to the bedroom beyond.

Whatever Paul Armstrong had been, he had been lavish with his stepdaughter. Gertrude's rooms at home were always beautiful apartments, but the three rooms in the east wing at Sunnyside, set apart for the daughter of the house, were much more splendid. From the walls to the rugs on the floor, from the furniture to the appointments of the bath, with its pool sunk in the floor instead of the customary unlovely tub, everything was luxurious. In the bedroom Louise was watching for me. It was easy to see that she was much improved; the flush was going, and the peculiar gasping breathing of the night before was now a comfortable and easy respiration.

She held out her hand and I took it between both of mine.

"What can I say to you, Miss Innes?" she said slowly. "To have come like this —"

I thought she was going to break down, but she did not.

"You are not to think of anything but of getting well," I said, patting her hand. "When you are better, I am going to scold you for not coming here at once. This is your home, my dear, and of all people in the world, Halsey's old aunt ought to make you welcome."

She smiled a little, sadly, I thought.

"I ought not to see Halsey," she said. "Miss Innes, there are a great many things you will never understand, I am afraid. I am an impostor on your sympathy, because I —I stay here and let you lavish care on me, and all the time I know you are going to despise me."

"Nonsense!" I said briskly. "Why, what would Halsey do to me if I even ventured such a thing? He is so big and masterful that if I dared to be anything but rapturous over you, he would throw me out of a window. Indeed, he would be quite capable of it."

She seemed scarcely to hear my facetious tone. She had eloquent brown eyes-the Inneses are fair, and are prone to a grayish-green optic that is better for use than appearance-and they seemed now to be clouded with trouble.

"Poor Halsey!" she said softly. "Miss Innes, I can not marry him, and I am afraid to tell him. I am a coward —a coward!"

I sat beside the bed and stared at her. She was too ill to argue with, and, besides, sick people take queer fancies.

"We will talk about that when you are stronger," I said gently.

"But there are some things I must tell you," she insisted. "You must wonder how I came here, and why I stayed hidden at the lodge. Dear old Thomas has been almost crazy, Miss Innes. I did not know that Sunnyside was rented. I knew my mother wished to rent it, without telling my-stepfather, but the news must have reached her after I left. When I started east, I had only one idea-to be alone with my thoughts for a time, to bury myself here. Then, I —must have taken a cold on the train."

"You came east in clothing suitable for California," I said, "and, like all young girls nowadays, I don't suppose you wear flannels." But she was not listening.

"Miss Innes," she said, "has my stepbrother Arnold gone away?"

"What do you mean?" I asked, startled. But Louise was literal.

"He didn't come back that night," she said, "and it was so important that I should see him."

"I believe he has gone away," I replied uncertainly. "Isn't it something that we could attend to instead?"

But she shook her head. "I must do it myself," she said dully. "My mother must have rented Sunnyside without telling my stepfather, and-Miss Innes, did you ever hear of any one being wretchedly poor in the midst of luxury?

"Did you ever long, and long, for money-money to use without question, money that no one would take you to task about? My mother and I have been surrounded for years with every indulgence everything that would make a display. But we have never had any money, Miss Innes; that must have been why mother rented this house. My stepfather pays out bills. It's the most maddening, humiliating existence in the world. I would love honest poverty better."

"Never mind," I said; "when you and Halsey are married you can be as honest as you like, and you will certainly be poor."

Halsey came to the door at that moment and I could hear him coaxing Liddy for admission to the sick room.

"Shall I bring him in?" I asked Louise, uncertain what to do. The girl seemed to shrink back among her pillows at the sound of his voice. I was vaguely irritated with her; there are few young fellows like Halsey-straightforward, honest, and willing to sacrifice everything for the one woman. I knew one once, more than thirty years ago, who was like that: he died a long time ago. And sometimes I take out his picture, with its cane and its queer silk hat, and look at it. But of late years it has grown too painful: he is always a boy-and I am an old woman. I would not bring him back if I could.

Perhaps it was some such memory that made me call out sharply.

"Come in, Halsey." And then I took my sewing and went into the boudoir beyond, to play propriety. I did not try to hear what they said, but every word came through the open door with curious distinctness. Halsey had evidently gone over to the bed and I suppose he kissed her. There was silence for a moment, as if words were superfluous things.

"I have been almost wild, sweetheart," —Halsey's voice. "Why didn't you trust me, and send for me before?"

"It was because I couldn't trust myself," she said in a low tone.

"I am too weak to struggle to-day; oh, Halsey, how I have wanted to see you!"

There was something I did not hear, then Halsey again.

"We could go away," he was saying. "What does it matter about any one in the world but just the two of us? To be always together, like this, hand in hand; Louise-don't tell me it isn't going to be. I won't believe you."

"You don't know; you don't know," Louise repeated dully. "Halsey, I care-you know that-but-not enough to marry you."

"That is not true, Louise," he said sternly. "You can not look at me with your honest eyes and say that."

"I can not marry you," she repeated miserably. "It's bad enough, isn't it? Don't make it worse. Some day, before long, you will be glad."

"Then it is because you have never loved me." There were depths of hurt pride in his voice. "You saw how much I loved you, and you let me think you cared-for a while. No-that isn't like you, Louise. There is something you haven't told me. Is it-because there is some one else?"

"Yes," almost inaudibly.

"Louise! Oh, I don't believe it."

"It is true," she said sadly. "Halsey, you must not try to see me again. As soon as I can, I am going away from here-where you are all so much kinder than I deserve. And whatever you hear about me, try to think as well of me as you can. I am going to marry-another man. How you must hate me-hate me!"

I could hear Halsey cross the room to the window. Then, after a pause, he went back to her again. I could hardly sit still; I wanted to go in and give her a good shaking.

"Then it's all over," he was saying with a long breath. "The plans we made together, the hopes, the-all of it-over! Well, I'll not be a baby, and I'll give you up the minute you say 'I don't love you and I do love-some one else'!"

"I can not say that," she breathed, "but, very soon, I shall marry-the other man."

I could hear Halsey's low triumphant laugh.

"I defy him," he said. "Sweetheart, as long as you care for me, I am not afraid."

The wind slammed the door between the two rooms just then, and I could hear nothing more, although I moved my chair quite close. After a discreet interval, I went into the other room, and found Louise alone. She was staring with sad eyes at the cherub painted on the ceiling over the bed, and because she looked tired I did not disturb her.

An Egg-Nog and a Telegram

We had discovered Louise at the lodge Tuesday night. It was Wednesday I had my interview with her. Thursday and Friday were uneventful, save as they marked improvement in our patient. Gertrude spent almost all the time with her, and the two had grown to be great friends. But certain things hung over me constantly; the coroner's inquest on the death of Arnold Armstrong, to be held Saturday, and the arrival of Mrs. Armstrong and young Doctor Walker, bringing the body of the dead president of the Traders' Bank. We had not told Louise of either death.

Then, too, I was anxious about the children. With their mother's inheritance swept away in the wreck of the bank, and with their love affairs in a disastrous condition, things could scarcely be worse. Added to that, the cook and Liddy had a flare-up over the proper way to make beef-tea for Louise, and, of course, the cook left.

Mrs. Watson had been glad enough, I think, to turn Louise over to our care, and Thomas went upstairs night and morning to greet his young mistress from the doorway. Poor Thomas! He had the faculty-found still in some old negroes, who cling to the traditions of slavery days-of making his employer's interest his. It was always "we" with Thomas; I miss him sorely; pipe-smoking, obsequious, not over reliable, kindly old man!

On Thursday Mr. Harton, the Armstrongs' legal adviser, called up from town. He had been advised, he said, that Mrs. Armstrong was coming east with her husband's body and would arrive Monday. He came with some hesitation, he went on, to the fact that he had been further instructed to ask me to relinquish my lease on Sunnyside, as it was Mrs. Armstrong's desire to come directly there.

I was aghast.

"Here!" I said. "Surely you are mistaken, Mr. Harton. I should think, after-what happened here only a few days ago, she would never wish to come back."

"Nevertheless," he replied, "she is most anxious to come. This is what she says. 'Use every possible means to have Sunnyside vacated. Must go there at once.'"

"Mr. Harton," I said testily, "I am not going to do anything of the kind. I and mine have suffered enough at the hands of this family. I rented the house at an exorbitant figure and I have moved out here for the summer. My city home is dismantled and in the hands of decorators. I have been here one week, during which I have had not a single night of uninterrupted sleep, and I intend to stay until I have recuperated. Moreover, if Mr. Armstrong died insolvent, as I believe was the case, his widow ought to be glad to be rid of so expensive a piece of property."

The lawyer cleared his throat.

"I am very sorry you have made this decision," he said. "Miss Innes, Mrs. Fitzhugh tells me Louise Armstrong is with you."

"She is."

"Has she been informed of this-double bereavement?"

"Not yet," I said. "She has been very ill; perhaps to-night she can be told."

"It is very sad; very sad," he said. "I have a telegram for her, Mrs. Innes. Shall I send it out?"

"Better open it and read it to me," I suggested. "If it is important, that will save time."

There was a pause while Mr. Harton opened the telegram. Then he read it slowly, judicially.

"'Watch for Nina Carrington. Home Monday. Signed F. L. W.'"

"Hum!" I said. "'Watch for Nina Carrington. Home Monday.' Very well, Mr. Harton, I will tell her, but she is not in condition to watch for any one."

"Well, Miss Innes, if you decide to-er-relinquish the lease, let me know," the lawyer said.

"I shall not relinquish it," I replied, and I imagined his irritation from the way he hung up the receiver.

I wrote the telegram down word for word, afraid to trust my memory, and decided to ask Doctor Stewart how soon Louise might be told the truth. The closing of the Traders' Bank I considered unnecessary for her to know, but the death of her stepfather and stepbrother must be broken to her soon, or she might hear it in some unexpected and shocking manner.

Doctor Stewart came about four o'clock, bringing his leather satchel into the house with a great deal of care, and opening it at the foot of the stairs to show me a dozen big yellow eggs nesting among the bottles.

"Real eggs," he said proudly. "None of your anemic store eggs, but the real thing-some of them still warm. Feel them! Egg-nog for Miss Louise."

He was beaming with satisfaction, and before he left, he insisted on going back to the pantry and making an egg-nog with his own hands. Somehow, all the time he was doing it, I had a vision of Doctor Willoughby, my nerve specialist in the city, trying to make an egg-nog. I wondered if he ever prescribed anything so plebeian-and so delicious. And while Doctor Stewart whisked the eggs he talked.

"I said to Mrs. Stewart," he confided, a little red in the face from the exertion, "after I went home the other day, that you would think me an old gossip, for saying what I did about Walker and Miss Louise."

"Nothing of the sort," I protested.

"The fact is," he went on, evidently justifying himself, "I got that piece of information just as we get a lot of things, through the kitchen end of the house. Young Walker's chauffeur-Walker's more fashionable than I am, and he goes around the country in a Stanhope car-well, his chauffeur comes to see our servant girl, and he told her the whole thing. I thought it was probable, because Walker spent a lot of time up here last summer, when the family was here, and besides, Riggs, that's Walker's man, had a very pat little story about the doctor's building a house on this property, just at the foot of the hill. The sugar, please."

The egg-nog was finished. Drop by drop the liquor had cooked the egg, and now, with a final whisk, a last toss in the shaker, it was ready, a symphony in gold and white. The doctor sniffed it.

"Real eggs, real milk, and a touch of real Kentucky whisky," he said.

He insisted on carrying it up himself, but at the foot of the stairs he paused.

"Riggs said the plans were drawn for the house," he said, harking back to the old subject. "Drawn by Huston in town. So I naturally believed him."

When the doctor came down, I was ready with a question.

"Doctor," I asked, "is there any one in the neighborhood named Carrington? Nina Carrington?"

"Carrington?" He wrinkled his forehead. "Carrington? No, I don't remember any such family. There used to be Covingtons down the creek."

"The name was Carrington," I said, and the subject lapsed.

Gertrude and Halsey went for a long walk that afternoon, and Louise slept. Time hung heavy on my hands, and I did as I had fallen into a habit of doing lately—I sat down and thought things over. One result of my meditations was that I got up suddenly and went to the telephone.

I had taken the most intense dislike to this Doctor Walker, whom I had never seen, and who was being talked of in the countryside as the fiancé of Louise Armstrong.

I knew Sam Huston well. There had been a time, when Sam was a good deal younger than he is now, before he had married Anne Endicott, when I knew him even better. So now I felt no hesitation in calling him over the telephone. But when his office boy had given way to his confidential clerk, and that functionary had condescended to connect his employer's desk telephone, I was somewhat at a loss as to how to begin.

"Why, how are you, Rachel?" Sam said sonorously. "Going to build that house at Rock View?" It was a twenty-year-old joke of his.

"Sometime, perhaps," I said. "Just now I want to ask you a question about something which is none of my business."

"I see you haven't changed an iota in a quarter of a century, Rachel." This was intended to be another jest. "Ask ahead: everything but my domestic affairs is at your service."

"Try to be serious," I said. "And tell me this: has your firm made any plans for a house recently, for a Doctor Walker, at Casanova?"

"Yes, we have."

"Where was it to be built? I have a reason for asking."

"It was to be, I believe, on the Armstrong place. Mr. Armstrong himself consulted me, and the inference was-in fact, I am quite certain-the house was to be occupied by Mr. Armstrong's daughter, who was engaged to marry Doctor Walker."

When the architect had inquired for the different members of my family, and had finally rung off, I was certain of one thing. Louise Armstrong was in love with Halsey, and the man she was going to marry was Doctor Walker. Moreover, this decision was not new; marriage had been contemplated for some time. There must certainly be some explanation-but what was it?

That day I repeated to Louise the telegram Mr. Warton had opened. She seemed to understand, but an unhappier face I have never seen. She looked like a criminal whose reprieve is over, and the day of execution approaching.

Liddy Gives the Alarm

The next day, Friday, Gertrude broke the news of her stepfather's death to Louise. She did it as gently as she could, telling her first that he was very ill, and finally that he was dead. Louise received the news in the most unexpected manner, and when Gertrude came out to tell me how she had stood it, I think she was almost shocked.

"She just lay and stared at me, Aunt Ray," she said. "Do you know, I believe she is glad, glad! And she is too honest to pretend anything else. What sort of man was Mr. Paul Armstrong, anyhow?"

"He was a bully as well as a rascal, Gertrude," I said. "But I am convinced of one thing; Louise will send for Halsey now, and they will make it all up."

For Louise had steadily refused to see Halsey all that day, and the boy was frantic.

We had a quiet hour, Halsey and I, that evening, and I told him several things; about the request that we give up the lease to Sunnyside, about the telegram to Louise, about the rumors of an approaching marriage between the girl and Doctor Walker, and, last of all, my own interview with her the day before.

He sat back in a big chair, with his face in the shadow, and my heart fairly ached for him. He was so big and so boyish! When I had finished he drew a long breath.

"Whatever Louise does," he said, "nothing will convince me, Aunt Ray, that she doesn't care for me. And up to two months ago, when she and her mother went west, I was the happiest fellow on earth. Then something made a difference: she wrote me that her people were opposed to the marriage; that her feeling for me was what it had always been, but that something had happened which had changed her ideas as to the future. I was not to write until she wrote me, and whatever occurred, I was to think the best I could of her. It sounded like a puzzle. When I saw her yesterday, it was the same thing, only, perhaps, worse."

"Halsey," I asked, "have you any idea of the nature of the interview between Louise Armstrong and Arnold the night he was murdered?"

"It was stormy. Thomas says once or twice he almost broke into the room, he was so alarmed for Louise."

"Another thing, Halsey," I said, "have you ever heard Louise mention a woman named Carrington, Nina Carrington?"

"Never," he said positively.

For try as we would, our thoughts always came back to that fatal Saturday night, and the murder. Every conversational path led to it, and we all felt that Jamieson was tightening the threads of evidence around John Bailey. The detective's absence was hardly reassuring; he must have had something to work on in town, or he would have returned.

The papers reported that the cashier of the Traders' Bank was ill in his apartments at the Knickerbocker — a condition not surprising, considering everything. The guilt of the defunct president was no longer in doubt; the missing bonds had been advertised and some of them discovered. In every instance they had been used as collateral for large loans, and the belief was current that not less than a million and a half dollars had been realized. Every one connected with the bank had been placed under arrest, and released on heavy bond.

Was he alone in his guilt, or was the cashier his accomplice? Where was the money? The estate of the dead man was comparatively small — a city house on a fashionable street, Sunnyside, a large estate largely mortgaged, an insurance of fifty thousand dollars, and some personal property-this was all. The rest lost in speculation probably, the papers said. There was one thing which looked uncomfortable for Jack Bailey: he and Paul Armstrong together had promoted a railroad company in New Mexico, and it was rumored that together they had sunk large sums of money there. The business alliance between the two men added to the belief that Bailey knew something of the looting. His unexplained absence from the bank on Monday lent color to the suspicion against him. The strange thing seemed to be his surrendering himself on the point of departure. To me, it seemed the shrewd calculation of a clever rascal. I was not actively antagonistic to Gertrude's lover, but I meant to be convinced, one way or the other. I took no one on faith.

That night the Sunnyside ghost began to walk again. Liddy had been sleeping in Louise's dressing-room on a couch, and the approach of dusk was a signal for her to barricade the entire suite. Situated as it was, beyond the circular staircase, nothing but an extremity of excitement would have made her pass it after dark. I confess myself that the place seemed to me to have a sinister appearance, but we kept that wing well lighted, and until the lights went out at midnight it was really cheerful, if one did not know its history.

On Friday night, then, I had gone to bed, resolved to go at once to sleep. Thoughts that insisted on obtruding themselves I pushed resolutely to the back of my mind, and I systematically relaxed every muscle. I fell asleep soon, and was dreaming that Doctor Walker was building his new house immediately in front of my windows: I could hear the thump-thump of the hammers, and then I waked to a knowledge that somebody was pounding on my door.

I was up at once, and with the sound of my footstep on the floor the low knocking ceased, to be followed immediately by sibilant whispering through the keyhole.

"Miss Rachel! Miss Rachel!" somebody was saying, over and over.

"Is that you, Liddy?" I asked, my hand on the knob.

"For the love of mercy, let me in!" she said in a low tone.

She was leaning against the door, for when I opened it, she fell in. She was greenish-white, and she had a red and black barred flannel petticoat over her shoulders.

"Listen," she said, standing in the middle of the floor and holding on to me. "Oh, Miss Rachel, it's the ghost of that dead man hammering to get in!"

Sure enough, there was a dull thud-thud-thud from some place near. It was muffled: one rather felt than heard it, and it was impossible to locate. One moment it seemed to come, three taps and a pause, from the floor under us: the next, thud-thud-thud-it came apparently from the wall.

"It's not a ghost," I said decidedly. "If it was a ghost it wouldn't rap: it would come through the keyhole." Liddy looked at the keyhole. "But it sounds very much as though some one is trying to break into the house."

Liddy was shivering violently. I told her to get me my slippers and she brought me a pair of kid gloves, so I found my things myself, and prepared to call Halsey. As before, the night alarm had found the electric lights gone: the hall, save for its night lamp, was in darkness, as I went across to Halsey's room. I hardly know what I feared, but it was a relief to find him there, very sound asleep, and with his door unlocked.

"Wake up, Halsey," I said, shaking him.

He stirred a little. Liddy was half in and half out of the door, afraid as usual to be left alone, and not quite daring to enter. Her scruples seemed to fade, however, all at once. She gave a suppressed yell, bolted into the room, and stood tightly clutching the foot-board of the bed. Halsey was gradually waking.

"I've seen it," Liddy wailed. "A woman in white down the hall!"

I paid no attention.

"Halsey," I persevered, "some one is breaking into the house. Get up, won't you?"

"It isn't our house," he said sleepily. And then he roused to the exigency of the occasion. "All right, Aunt Ray," he said, still yawning. "If you'll let me get into something—"

It was all I could do to get Liddy out of the room. The demands of the occasion had no influence on her: she had seen the ghost, she persisted, and she wasn't going into the hall. But I got her over to my room at last, more dead than alive, and made her lie down on the bed.

The tappings, which seemed to have ceased for a while, had commenced again, but they were fainter. Halsey came over in a few minutes, and stood listening and trying to locate the sound.

"Give me my revolver, Aunt Ray," he said; and I got it-the one I had found in the tulip bed-and gave it to him. He saw Liddy there and divined at once that Louise was alone.

"You let me attend to this fellow, whoever it is, Aunt Ray, and go to Louise, will you? She may be awake and alarmed."

So in spite of her protests, I left Liddy alone and went back to the east wing. Perhaps I went a little faster past the yawning blackness of the circular staircase; and I could hear Halsey creaking cautiously down the main staircase. The rapping, or pounding, had ceased, and the silence was almost painful. And then suddenly, from apparently under my very feet, there rose a woman's scream, a cry of terror that broke off as suddenly as it came. I stood frozen and still. Every drop of blood in my body seemed to leave the surface and gather around my heart. In the dead silence that followed it throbbed as if it would burst. More dead than alive, I stumbled into Louise's bedroom. She was not there!

In the Early Morning

I stood looking at the empty bed. The coverings had been thrown back, and Louise's pink silk dressing-gown was gone from the foot, where it had lain. The night lamp burned dimly, revealing the emptiness of the place. I picked it up, but my hand shook so that I put it down again, and got somehow to the door.

There were voices in the hall and Gertrude came running toward me.

"What is it?" she cried. "What was that sound? Where is Louise?"

"She is not in her room," I said stupidly. "I think-it was she-who screamed."

Liddy had joined us now, carrying a light. We stood huddled together at the head of the circular staircase, looking down into its shadows. There was nothing to be seen, and it was absolutely quiet down there. Then we heard Halsey running up the main staircase. He came quickly down the hall to where we were standing.

"There's no one trying to get in. I thought I heard some one shriek. Who was it?"

Our stricken faces told him the truth.

"Some one screamed down there," I said. "And-and Louise is not in her room."

With a jerk Halsey took the light from Liddy and ran down the circular staircase. I followed him, more slowly. My nerves seemed to be in a state of paralysis: I could scarcely step. At the foot of the stairs Halsey gave an exclamation and put down the light.

"Aunt Ray," he called sharply.

At the foot of the staircase, huddled in a heap, her head on the lower stair, was Louise Armstrong. She lay limp and white, her dressing-gown dragging loose from one sleeve of her night-dress, and the heavy braid of her dark hair stretching its length a couple of steps above her head, as if she had slipped down.

She was not dead: Halsey put her down on the floor, and began to rub her cold hands, while Gertrude and Liddy ran for stimulants. As for me, I sat there at the foot of that ghostly staircase-sat, because my knees wouldn't hold me-and wondered where it would all end. Louise was still unconscious, but she was breathing better, and I suggested that we get her back to bed before she came to. There was something grisly and horrible to me, seeing her there in almost the same attitude and in the same place where we had found her brother's body. And to add to the similarity, just then the hall clock, far off, struck faintly three o'clock.

It was four before Louise was able to talk, and the first rays of dawn were coming through her windows, which faced the east, before she could tell us coherently what had occurred. I give it as she told it. She lay propped in bed, and Halsey sat beside her, unrebuffed, and held her hand while she talked.

"I was not sleeping well," she began, "partly, I think, because I had slept during the afternoon. Liddy brought me some hot milk at ten o'clock and I slept until twelve. Then I wakened and—I got to thinking about things, and worrying, so I could not go to sleep.

"I was wondering why I had not heard from Arnold since the-since I saw him that night at the lodge. I was afraid he was ill, because-he was to have done something for me, and he had not come back. It must have been three when I heard some one rapping. I sat up and listened, to be quite sure, and the rapping kept up. It was cautious, and I was about to call Liddy. Then suddenly I thought I knew what it was. The east entrance and the circular staircase were always used by Arnold when he was out late, and sometimes, when he forgot his key, he would rap and I would go down and let him in. I thought he had come back to see me —I didn't think about the time, for his hours were always erratic. But I was afraid I was too weak to get down the stairs. The knocking kept up, and just as I was about to call Liddy, she ran through the room and out into the hall. I got up then, feeling weak and dizzy, and put on my dressing-gown. If it was Arnold, I knew I must see him.

"It was very dark everywhere, but, of course, I knew my way. I felt along for the stair-rail, and went down as quickly as I could. The knocking had stopped, and I was afraid I was too late. I got to the foot of the staircase and over to the door on to the east veranda. I had never thought of anything but that it was Arnold, until I reached the door. It was unlocked and opened about an inch. Everything was black: it was perfectly dark outside. I felt very queer and shaky. Then I thought perhaps Arnold had used his key; he did-strange things sometimes, and I turned around. Just as I reached the foot of the staircase I thought I heard some one coming. My nerves were going anyhow, there in the dark, and I could scarcely stand. I got up as far as the third or fourth step; then I felt that some one was coming toward me on the staircase. The next instant a hand met mine on the stair-rail. Some one brushed past me, and I screamed. Then I must have fainted."

That was Louise's story. There could be no doubt of its truth, and the thing that made it inexpressibly awful to me was that the poor girl had crept down to answer the summons of a brother who would never need her kindly offices again. Twice now, without apparent cause, some one had entered the house by means of the east entrance: had apparently gone his way unhindered through the house, and gone out again as he had entered. Had this unknown visitor been there a third time, the night Arnold Armstrong was murdered? Or a fourth, the time Mr. Jamieson had locked some one in the clothes chute?

Sleep was impossible, I think, for any of us. We dispersed finally to bathe and dress, leaving Louise little the worse for her experience. But I determined that before the day was over she must know the true state of affairs. Another decision I made, and I put it into execution immediately after breakfast. I had one of the unused bedrooms in the east wing, back along the small corridor, prepared for occupancy, and from that time on, Alex, the gardener, slept there. One man in that barn of a house was an absurdity, with things happening all the time, and I must say that Alex was as unobjectionable as any one could possibly have been.

The next morning, also, Halsey and I made an exhaustive examination of the circular staircase, the small entry at its foot, and the card-room opening from it. There was no evidence of anything unusual the night before, and had we not ourselves heard the rapping noises, I should have felt that Louise's imagination had run away with her. The outer door was closed and locked, and the staircase curved above us, for all the world like any other staircase.

Halsey, who had never taken seriously my account of the night Liddy and I were there alone, was grave enough now. He examined the paneling of the wainscoting above and below the stairs, evidently looking for a secret door, and suddenly there flashed into my mind the recollection of a scrap of paper that Mr. Jamieson had found among Arnold Armstrong's effects. As nearly as possible I repeated its contents to him, while Halsey took them down in a note-book.

"I wish you had told me that before," he said, as he put the memorandum carefully away. We found nothing at all in the house, and I expected little from any examination of the porch and grounds. But as we opened the outer door something fell into the entry with a clatter. It was a cue from the billiard-room.

Halsey picked it up with an exclamation.

"That's careless enough," he said. "Some of the servants have been amusing themselves."

I was far from convinced. Not one of the servants would go into that wing at night unless driven by dire necessity. And a billiard cue! As a weapon of either offense or defense it was an absurdity, unless one accepted Liddy's hypothesis of a ghost, and even then, as Halsey pointed out, a billiard-playing ghost would be a very modern evolution of an ancient institution.

That afternoon we, Gertrude, Halsey and I, attended the coroner's inquest in town. Doctor Stewart had been summoned also, it transpiring that in that early Sunday morning, when Gertrude and I had gone to our rooms, he had been called to view the body. We went, the four of us, in the machine, preferring the execrable roads to the matinee train, with half of Casanova staring at us. And on the way we decided to say nothing of Louise and her interview with her stepbrother the night he died. The girl was in trouble enough as it was.

A Hint of Scandal

In giving the gist of what happened at the inquest, I have only one excuse-to recall to the reader the events of the night of Arnold Armstrong's murder. Many things had occurred which were not brought out at the inquest and some things were told there that were new to me. Altogether, it was a gloomy affair, and the six men in the corner, who constituted the coroner's jury, were evidently the merest puppets in the hands of that all-powerful gentleman, the coroner.

Gertrude and I sat well back, with our veils down. There were a number of people I knew: Barbara Fitzhugh, in extravagant mourning-she always went into black on the slightest provocation, because it was becoming-and Mr. Jarvis, the man who had come over from the Greenwood Club the night of the murder. Mr. Harton was there, too, looking impatient as the inquest dragged, but alive to every particle of evidence. From a corner Mr. Jamieson was watching the proceedings intently.

Doctor Stewart was called first. His evidence was told briefly, and amounted to this: on the Sunday morning previous, at a quarter before five, he had been called to the telephone. The message was from a Mr. Jarvis, who asked him to come at once to Sunnyside, as there had been an accident there, and Mr. Arnold Armstrong had been shot. He had dressed hastily, gathered up some instruments, and driven to Sunnyside.

He was met by Mr. Jarvis, who took him at once to the east wing. There, just as he had fallen, was the body of Arnold Armstrong. There was no need of the instruments: the man was dead. In answer to the coroner's question—no, the body had not been moved, save to turn it over. It lay at the foot of the circular staircase. Yes, he believed death had been instantaneous. The body was still somewhat warm and *rigor mortis* had not set in. It occurred late in cases of sudden death. No, he believed the probability of suicide might be eliminated; the wounds could have been self-inflicted, but with difficulty, and there had been no weapon found.

The doctor's examination was over, but he hesitated and cleared his throat.

"Mr. Coroner," he said, "at the risk of taking up valuable time, I would like to speak of an incident that may or may not throw some light on this matter."

The audience was alert at once.

"Kindly proceed, Doctor," the coroner said.

"My home is in Englewood, two miles from Casanova," the doctor began. "In the absence of Doctor Walker, a number of Casanova people have been consulting me. A month ago-five weeks, to be exact—a woman whom I had never seen came to my office. She was in deep mourning and kept her veil down, and she brought for examination a child, a boy of six. The little fellow was ill; it looked like typhoid, and the mother was frantic. She wanted a permit to admit the youngster to the Children's Hospital in town here, where I am a member of the staff, and I gave her one. The incident would have escaped me, but for a curious thing. Two days before Mr. Armstrong was shot, I was sent for to go to the Country Club: some one had been struck with a golf-ball that had gone wild. It was late when I left—I was on foot, and about a mile from the club, on the Claysburg road, I met two people. They were disputing violently, and I had no difficulty in recognizing Mr. Armstrong. The woman, beyond doubt, was the one who had consulted me about the child."

At this hint of scandal, Mrs. Ogden Fitzhugh sat up very straight. Jamieson was looking slightly skeptical, and the coroner made a note.

"The Children's Hospital, you say, Doctor?" he asked.

"Yes. But the child, who was entered as Lucien Wallace, was taken away by his mother two weeks ago. I have tried to trace them and failed."

All at once I remembered the telegram sent to Louise by some one signed F. L. W.—presumably Doctor Walker. Could this veiled woman be the Nina Carrington of the message? But it was only idle speculation. I had no way of finding out, and the inquest was proceeding.

The report of the coroner's physician came next. The post-mortem examination showed that the bullet had entered the chest in the fourth left intercostal space and had taken an oblique course downward and backward, piercing both the heart and lungs. The left lung was collapsed, and the exit point of the ball had been found in the muscles of the back to the left of the spinal column. It was improbable that such a wound had been self-inflicted, and its oblique downward course pointed to the fact that the shot had been fired from above. In other words, as the murdered man had been found dead at the foot of a staircase, it was probable that the shot had been fired by some one higher up on the stairs. There were no marks of powder. The bullet, a thirty-eight caliber, had been found in the dead man's clothing, and was shown to the jury.

Mr. Jarvis was called next, but his testimony amounted to little. He had been summoned by telephone to Sunnyside, had come over at once with the steward and Mr. Winthrop, at present out of town. They had been admitted by the housekeeper, and had found the body lying at the foot of the staircase. He had made a search for a weapon, but there was none around. The outer entry door in the east wing had been unfastened and was open about an inch.

I had been growing more and more nervous. When the coroner called Mr. John Bailey, the room was filled with suppressed excitement. Mr. Jamieson went forward and spoke a few words to the coroner, who nodded. Then Halsey was called.

"Mr. Innes," the coroner said, "will you tell under what circumstances you saw Mr. Arnold Armstrong the night he died?"

"I saw him first at the Country Club," Halsey said quietly. He was rather pale, but very composed. "I stopped there with my automobile for gasolene. Mr. Armstrong had been playing cards. When I saw him there, he was coming out of the card-room, talking to Mr. John Bailey."

"The nature of the discussion-was it amicable?"

Halsey hesitated.

"They were having a dispute," he said. "I asked Mr. Bailey to leave the club with me and come to Sunnyside over Sunday."

"Isn't it a fact, Mr. Innes, that you took Mr. Bailey away from the club-house because you were afraid there would be blows?"

"The situation was unpleasant," Halsey said evasively.

"At that time had you any suspicion that the Traders' Bank had been wrecked?"

"No."

"What occurred next?"

"Mr. Bailey and I talked in the billiard-room until two-thirty."

"And Mr. Arnold Armstrong came there, while you were talking?"

"Yes. He came about half-past two. He rapped at the east door, and I admitted him."

The silence in the room was intense. Mr. Jamieson's eyes never left Halsey's face.

"Will you tell us the nature of his errand?"

"He brought a telegram that had come to the club for Mr. Bailey."

"He was sober?"

"Perfectly, at that time. Not earlier."

"Was not his apparent friendliness a change from his former attitude?"

"Yes. I did not understand it."

"How long did he stay?"

"About five minutes. Then he left, by the east entrance."

"What occurred then?"

"We talked for a few minutes, discussing a plan Mr. Bailey had in mind. Then I went to the stables, where I kept my car, and got it out."

"Leaving Mr. Bailey alone in the billiard-room?"

Halsey hesitated.

"My sister was there?"

Mrs. Ogden Fitzhugh had the courage to turn and eye Gertrude through her lorgnon.

"And then?"

"I took the car along the lower road, not to disturb the household. Mr. Bailey came down across the lawn, through the hedge, and got into the car on the road."

"Then you know nothing of Mr. Armstrong's movements after he left the house?"

"Nothing. I read of his death Monday evening for the first time."

"Mr. Bailey did not see him on his way across the lawn?"

"I think not. If he had seen him he would have spoken of it."

"Thank you. That is all. Miss Gertrude Innes."

Gertrude's replies were fully as concise as Halsey's. Mrs. Fitzhugh subjected her to a close inspection, commencing with her hat and ending with her shoes. I flatter myself she found nothing wrong with either her gown or her manner, but poor Gertrude's testimony was the reverse of comforting. She had been summoned, she said, by her brother, after Mr. Armstrong had gone. She had waited in the billiard-room with Mr. Bailey, until the automobile had been ready. Then she had locked the door at the foot of the staircase, and, taking a lamp, had accompanied Mr. Bailey to the main entrance of the house, and had watched him cross the lawn. Instead of going at once to her room, she had gone back to the billiard-room for something which had been left there. The card-room and billiard-room were in darkness. She had groped around, found the article she was looking for, and was on the point of returning to her room, when she had heard some one fumbling at the lock at the east outer door. She had thought it was probably her brother, and had been about to go to the door, when she heard it open. Almost immediately there was a shot, and she had run panic-stricken through the drawing-room and had roused the house.

"You heard no other sound?" the coroner asked. "There was no one with Mr. Armstrong when he entered?"

"It was perfectly dark. There were no voices and I heard nothing. There was just the opening of the door, the shot, and the sound of somebody falling."

"Then, while you went through the drawing-room and up-stairs to alarm the household, the criminal, whoever it was, could have escaped by the east door?"

"Yes."

"Thank you. That will do."

I flatter myself that the coroner got little enough out of me. I saw Mr. Jamieson smiling to himself, and the coroner gave me up, after a time. I admitted I had found the body, said I had not known who it was until Mr. Jarvis told me, and ended by looking up at Barbara Fitzhugh and saying that in renting the house I had not expected to be involved in any family scandal. At which she turned purple.

The verdict was that Arnold Armstrong had met his death at the hands of a person or persons unknown, and we all prepared to leave. Barbara Fitzhugh flounced out without waiting to speak to me, but Mr. Harton came up, as I knew he would.

"You have decided to give up the house, I hope, Miss Innes," he said. "Mrs. Armstrong has wired me again."

"I am not going to give it up," I maintained, "until I understand some things that are puzzling me. The day that the murderer is discovered, I will leave."

"Then, judging by what I have heard, you will be back in the city very soon," he said. And I knew that he suspected the discredited cashier of the Traders' Bank.

Mr. Jamieson came up to me as I was about to leave the coroner's office.

"How is your patient?" he asked with his odd little smile.

"I have no patient," I replied, startled.

"I will put it in a different way, then. How is Miss Armstrong?"

"She-she is doing very well," I stammered.

"Good," cheerfully. "And our ghost? Is it laid?"

"Mr. Jamieson," I said suddenly, "I wish you would do one thing: I wish you would come to Sunnyside and spend a few days there. The ghost is not laid. I want you to spend one night at least watching the circular staircase. The murder of Arnold Armstrong was a beginning, not an end."

He looked serious.

"Perhaps I can do it," he said. "I have been doing something else, but-well, I will come out to-night."

We were very silent during the trip back to Sunnyside. I watched Gertrude closely and somewhat sadly. To me there was one glaring flaw in her story, and it seemed to stand out for every one to see. Arnold Armstrong had had no key, and yet she said she had locked the east door. He must have been admitted from within the house; over and over I repeated it to myself.

That night, as gently as I could, I told Louise the story of her stepbrother's death. She sat in her big, pillow-filled chair, and heard me through without interruption. It was clear that she was shocked beyond words: if I had hoped to learn anything from her expression, I had failed. She was as much in the dark as we were.

A Hole in the Wall

My taking the detective out to Sunnyside raised an unexpected storm of protest from Gertrude and Halsey. I was not prepared for it, and I scarcely knew how to account for it. To me Mr. Jamieson was far less formidable under my eyes where I knew what he was doing, than he was of in the city, twisting circumstances and motives to suit himself and learning what he wished to know, about events at Sunnyside, in some occult way. I was glad enough to have him there, when excitements began to come thick and fast.

A new element was about to enter into affairs: Monday, or Tuesday at the latest, would find Doctor Walker back in his green and white house in the village, and Louise's attitude to him in the immediate future would signify Halsey's happiness or wretchedness, as it might turn out. Then, too, the return of her mother would mean, of course, that she would have to leave us, and I had become greatly attached to her.

From the day Mr. Jamieson came to Sunnyside there was a subtle change in Gertrude's manner to me. It was elusive, difficult to analyze, but it was there. She was no longer frank with me, although I think her affection never wavered. At the time I laid the change to the fact that I had forbidden all communication with John Bailey, and had refused to acknowledge any engagement between the two. Gertrude spent much of her time wandering through the grounds, or taking long cross-country walks. Halsey played golf at the Country Club day after day, and after Louise left, as she did the following week, Mr. Jamieson and I were much together. He played a fair game of cribbage, but he cheated at solitaire.

The night the detective arrived, Saturday, I had a talk with him. I told him of the experience Louise Armstrong had had the night before, on the circular staircase, and about the man who had so frightened Rosie on the drive. I saw that he thought the information was important, and to my suggestion that we put an additional lock on the east wing door he opposed a strong negative.

"I think it probable," he said, "that our visitor will be back again, and the thing to do is to leave things exactly as they are, to avoid rousing suspicion. Then I can watch for at least a part of each night and probably Mr. Innes will help us out. I would say as little to Thomas as possible. The old man knows more than he is willing to admit."

I suggested that Alex, the gardener, would probably be willing to help, and Mr. Jamieson undertook to make the arrangement. For one night, however, Mr. Jamieson preferred to watch alone. Apparently nothing occurred. The detective sat in absolute darkness on the lower step of the stairs, dozing, he said afterwards, now and then. Nothing could pass him in either direction, and the door in the morning remained as securely fastened as it had been the night before. And yet one of the most inexplicable occurrences of the whole affair took place that very night.

Liddy came to my room on Sunday morning with a face as long as the moral law. She laid out my things as usual, but I missed her customary garrulousness. I was not regaled with the new cook's extravagance as to eggs, and she even forbore to mention "that Jamieson," on whose arrival she had looked with silent disfavor.

"What's the matter, Liddy?" I asked at last. "Didn't you sleep last night?"

"No, ma'm," she said stiffly.

"Did you have two cups of coffee at your dinner?" I inquired.

"No, ma'm," indignantly.

I sat up and almost upset my hot water—I always take a cup of hot water with a pinch of salt, before I get up. It tones the stomach.

"Liddy Allen," I said, "stop combing that switch and tell me what is wrong with you."

Liddy heaved a sigh.

"Girl and woman," she said, "I've been with you twenty-five years, Miss Rachel, through good temper and bad—" the idea! and what I have taken from her in the way of sulks!—"but I guess I can't stand it any longer. My trunk's packed."

"Who packed it?" I asked, expecting from her tone to be told she had wakened to find it done by some ghostly hand.

"I did; Miss Rachel, you won't believe me when I tell you this house is haunted. Who was it fell down the clothes chute? Who was it scared Miss Louise almost into her grave?"

"I'm doing my best to find out," I said. "What in the world are you driving at?" She drew a long breath.

"There is a hole in the trunk-room wall, dug out since last night. It's big enough to put your head in, and the plaster's all over the place."

"Nonsense!" I said. "Plaster is always falling."

But Liddy clenched that.

"Just ask Alex," she said. "When he put the new cook's trunk there last night the wall was as smooth as this. This morning it's dug out, and there's plaster on the cook's trunk. Miss Rachel, you can get a dozen detectives and put one on every stair in the house, and you'll never catch anything. There's some things you can't handcuff."

Liddy was right. As soon as I could, I went up to the trunk-room, which was directly over my bedroom. The plan of the upper story of the house was like that of the second floor, in the main. One end, however, over the east wing, had been left only roughly finished, the intention having been to convert it into a ball-room at some future time. The maids' rooms, trunk-room, and various store-rooms, including a large airy linen-room, opened from a long corridor, like that on the second floor. And in the trunk-room, as Liddy had said, was a fresh break in the plaster.

Not only in the plaster, but through the lathing, the aperture extended. I reached into the opening, and three feet away, perhaps, I could touch the bricks of the partition wall. For some reason, the architect, in building the house, had left a space there that struck me, even in the surprise of the discovery, as an excellent place for a conflagration to gain headway.

"You are sure the hole was not here yesterday?" I asked Liddy, whose expression was a mixture of satisfaction and alarm. In answer she pointed to the new cook's trunk-that necessary adjunct of the migratory domestic. The top was covered with fine white plaster, as was the floor. But there were no large pieces of mortar lying around-no bits of lathing. When I mentioned this to Liddy she merely raised her eyebrows. Being quite confident that the gap was of unholy origin, she did not concern herself with such trifles as a bit of mortar and lath. No doubt they were even then heaped neatly on a gravestone in the Casanova churchyard!

I brought Mr. Jamieson up to see the hole in the wall, directly after breakfast. His expression was very odd when he looked at it, and the first thing he did was to try to discover what object, if any, such a hole could have. He got a piece of candle, and by enlarging the aperture a little was able to examine what lay beyond. The result was *nil*. The trunk-room, although heated by steam heat, like the rest of the house, boasted of a fireplace and mantel as well. The opening had been made between the flue and the outer wall of the house. There was revealed, however, on inspection, only the brick of the chimney on one side and the outer wall of the house on the other; in depth the space extended only to the flooring. The breach had been made about four feet from the floor, and inside were all the missing bits of plaster. It had been a methodical ghost.

It was very much of a disappointment. I had expected a secret room, at the very least, and I think even Mr. Jamieson had fancied he might at last have a clue to the mystery. There was evidently nothing more to be discovered: Liddy reported that everything was serene among the servants, and that none of them had been disturbed by the noise. The maddening thing, however, was that the nightly visitor had evidently more than one way of gaining access to the house, and we made arrangements to redouble our vigilance as to windows and doors that night.

Halsey was inclined to pooh-pooh the whole affair. He said a break in the plaster might have occurred months ago and gone unnoticed, and that the dust had probably been stirred up the day before. After all, we had to let it go at that, but we put in an uncomfortable Sunday. Gertrude went to church, and Halsey took a long walk in the morning. Louise was able to sit up, and she allowed Halsey and Liddy to assist her down-stairs late in the afternoon. The east veranda was shady, green with vines and palms, cheerful with cushions and lounging chairs. We put Louise in a steamer chair, and she sat there passively enough, her hands clasped in her lap.

We were very silent. Halsey sat on the rail with a pipe, openly watching Louise, as she looked broodingly across the valley to the hills. There was something baffling in the girl's eyes; and gradually Halsey's boyish features lost their glow at seeing her about again, and settled into grim lines. He was like his father just then.

We sat until late afternoon, Halsey growing more and more moody. Shortly before six, he got up and went into the house, and in a few minutes he came out and called me to the telephone. It was Anna Whitcomb, in town, and she kept me for twenty minutes, telling me the children had had the measles, and how Madame Sweeny had botched her new gown.

When I finished, Liddy was behind me, her mouth a thin line.

"I wish you would try to look cheerful, Liddy," I groaned, "your face would sour milk." But Liddy seldom replied to my gibes. She folded her lips a little tighter.

"He called her up," she said oracularly, "he called her up, and asked her to keep you at the telephone, so he could talk to Miss Louise. *A thankless child is sharper than a serpent's tooth.*"

"Nonsense!" I said bruskly. "I might have known enough to leave them. It's a long time since you and I were in love, Liddy, and-we forget."

Liddy sniffed.

"No man ever made a fool of me," she replied virtuously.

"Well, something did," I retorted.

Concerning Thomas

"Mr. Jamieson," I said, when we found ourselves alone after dinner that night, "the inquest yesterday seemed to me the merest recapitulation of things that were already known. It developed nothing new beyond the story of Doctor Stewart's, and that was volunteered."

"An inquest is only a necessary formality, Miss Innes," he replied. "Unless a crime is committed in the open, the inquest does nothing beyond getting evidence from witnesses while events are still in their minds. The police step in later. You and I both know how many important things never transpired. For instance: the dead man had no key, and yet Miss Gertrude testified to a fumbling at the lock, and then the opening of the door. The piece of evidence you mention, Doctor Stewart's story, is one of those things we have to take cautiously: the doctor has a patient who wears black and does not raise her veil. Why, it is the typical mysterious lady! Then the good doctor comes across Arnold Armstrong, who was a graceless scamp —*de mortuis* —what's the rest of it? —and he is quarreling with a lady in black. Behold, says the doctor, they are one and the same."

"Why was Mr. Bailey not present at the inquest?"

The detective's expression was peculiar.

"Because his physician testified that he is ill, and unable to leave his bed."

"Ill!" I exclaimed. "Why, neither Halsey nor Gertrude has told me that."

"There are more things than that, Miss Innes, that are puzzling. Bailey gives the impression that he knew nothing of the crash at the bank until he read it in the paper Monday night, and that he went back and surrendered himself immediately. I do not believe it. Jonas, the watchman at the Traders' Bank, tells a different story. He says that on the Thursday night before, about eight-thirty, Bailey went back to the bank. Jonas admitted him, and he says the cashier was in a state almost of collapse. Bailey worked until midnight, then he closed the vault and went away. The occurrence was so unusual that the watchman pondered over it an the rest of the night. What did Bailey do when he went back to the Knickerbocker apartments that night? He packed a suit-case ready for instant departure. But he held off too long; he waited for something. My personal opinion is that he waited to see Miss Gertrude before flying from the country. Then, when he had shot down Arnold Armstrong that night, he had to choose between two evils. He did the thing that would immediately turn public opinion in his favor, and surrendered himself, as an innocent man. The strongest thing against him is his preparation for flight, and his deciding to come back after the murder of Arnold Armstrong. He was shrewd enough to disarm suspicion as to the graver charge?"

The evening dragged along slowly. Mrs. Watson came to my bedroom before I went to bed and asked if I had any arnica. She showed me a badly swollen hand, with reddish streaks running toward the elbow; she said it was the hand she had hurt the night of the murder a week before, and that she had not slept well since. It looked to me as if it might be serious, and I told her to let Doctor Stewart see it.

The next morning Mrs. Watson went up to town on the eleven train, and was admitted to the Charity Hospital. She was suffering from blood-poisoning. I fully meant to go up and see her there, but other things drove her entirely from my mind. I telephoned to the hospital that day, however, and ordered a private room for her, and whatever comforts she might be allowed.

Mrs. Armstrong arrived Monday evening with her husband's body, and the services were set for the next day. The house on Chestnut Street, in town, had been opened, and Tuesday morning Louise left us to go home. She sent for me before she went, and I saw she had been crying.

"How can I thank you, Miss Innes?" she said. "You have taken me on faith, and-you have not asked me any questions. Some time, perhaps, I can tell you; and when that time comes, you will all despise me,—Halsey, too."

I tried to tell her how glad I was to have had her but there was something else she wanted to say. She said it finally, when she had bade a constrained good-by to Halsey and the car was waiting at the door.

"Miss Innes," she said in a low tone, "if they-if there is any attempt made to-to have you give up the house, do it, if you possibly can. I am afraid-to have you stay."

That was all. Gertrude went into town with her and saw her safely home. She reported a decided coolness in the greeting between Louise and her mother, and that Doctor Walker was there, apparently in charge of the arrangements for the funeral. Halsey disappeared shortly after Louise left and came home about nine that night, muddy and tired. As for Thomas, he went around dejected and sad, and I saw the detective watching him closely at dinner. Even now I wonder-what did Thomas know? What did he suspect?

At ten o'clock the household had settled down for the night. Liddy, who was taking Mrs. Watson's place, had finished examining the tea-towels and the corners of the shelves in the cooling-room, and had gone to bed. Alex, the gardener, had gone heavily up the circular staircase to his room, and Mr. Jamieson was examining the locks of the windows. Halsey dropped into a chair in the living-room, and stared moodily ahead. Once he roused.

"What sort of a looking chap is that Walker, Gertrude?" he asked!

"Rather tall, very dark, smooth-shaven. Not bad looking," Gertrude said, putting down the book she had been pretending to read. Halsey kicked a taboret viciously.

"Lovely place this village must be in the winter," he said irrelevantly. "A girl would be buried alive here."

It was then some one rapped at the knocker on the heavy front door. Halsey got up leisurely and opened it, admitting Warner. He was out of breath from running, and he looked half abashed.

"I am sorry to disturb you," he said. "But I didn't know what else to do. It's about Thomas."

"What about Thomas?" I asked. Mr. Jamieson had come into the hall and we all stared at Warner.

"He's acting queer," Warner explained. "He's sitting down there on the edge of the porch, and he says he has seen a ghost. The old man looks bad, too; he can scarcely speak."

"He's as full of superstition as an egg is of meat," I said. "Halsey, bring some whisky and we will all go down."

No one moved to get the whisky, from which I judged there were three pocket flasks ready for emergency. Gertrude threw a shawl around my shoulders, and we all started down over the hill:

I had made so many nocturnal excursions around the place that I knew my way perfectly. But Thomas was not on the veranda, nor was he inside the house. The men exchanged significant glances, and Warner got a lantern.

"He can't have gone far," he said. "He was trembling so that he couldn't stand, when I left."

Jamieson and Halsey together made the round of the lodge, occasionally calling the old man by name. But there was no response. No Thomas came, bowing and showing his white teeth through the darkness. I began to be vaguely uneasy, for the first time. Gertrude, who was never nervous in the dark, went alone down the drive to the gate, and stood there, looking along the yellowish line of the road, while I waited on the tiny veranda.

Warner was puzzled. He came around to the edge of the veranda and stood looking at it as if it ought to know and explain.

"He might have stumbled into the house," he said, "but he could not have climbed the stairs. Anyhow, he's not inside or outside, that I can see." The other members of the party had come back now, and no one had found any trace of the old man. His pipe, still warm, rested on the edge of the rail, and inside on the table his old gray hat showed that its owner had not gone far.

He was not far, after all. From the table my eyes traveled around the room, and stopped at the door of a closet. I hardly know what impulse moved me, but I went in and turned the knob. It burst open with the impetus of a weight behind it, and something fell partly forward in a heap on the floor. It was Thomas—Thomas without a mark of injury on him, and dead.

Doctor Walker's Warning

Warner was on his knees in a moment, fumbling at the old man's collar to loosen it, but Halsey caught his hand.

"Let him alone?" he said. "You can't help him; he is dead."

We stood there, each avoiding the other's eyes; we spoke low and reverently in the presence of death, and we tacitly avoided any mention of the suspicion that was in every mind. When Mr. Jamieson had finished his cursory examination, he got up and dusted the knees of his trousers.

"There is no sign of injury," he said, and I know I, for one, drew a long breath of relief. "From what Warner says and from his hiding in the closet, I should say he was scared to death. Fright and a weak heart, together."

"But what could have done it?" Gertrude asked. "He was all right this evening at dinner. Warner, what did he say when you found him on the porch?"

Warner looked shaken: his honest, boyish face was colorless.

"Just what I told you, Miss Innes. He'd been reading the paper down-stairs; I had put up the car, and, feeling sleepy, I came down to the lodge to go to bed. As I went up-stairs, Thomas put down the paper and, taking his pipe, went out on the porch. Then I heard an exclamation from him."

"What did he say?" demanded Jamieson.

"I couldn't hear, but his voice was strange; it sounded startled. I waited for him to call out again, but he did not, so I went down-stairs. He was sitting on the porch step, looking straight ahead, as if he saw something among the trees across the road. And he kept mumbling about having seen a ghost. He looked queer, and I tried to get him inside, but he wouldn't move. Then I thought I'd better go up to the house."

"Didn't he say anything else you could understand?" I asked.

"He said something about the grave giving up its dead."

Mr. Jamieson was going through the old man's pockets, and Gertrude was composing his arms, folding them across his white shirt-bosom, always so spotless.

Mr. Jamieson looked up at me.

"What was that you said to me, Miss Innes, about the murder at the house being a beginning and not an end? By jove, I believe you were right!"

In the course of his investigations the detective had come to the inner pocket of the dead butler's black coat. Here he found some things that interested him. One was a small flat key, with a red cord tied to it, and the other was a bit of white paper, on which was written something in Thomas' cramped hand. Mr. Jamieson read it: then he gave it to me. It was an address in fresh ink —

Lucien Wallace, 14 Elm Street, Richfield.

As the card went around, I think both the detective and I watched for any possible effect it might have, but, beyond perplexity, there seemed to be none.

"Richfield!" Gertrude exclaimed. "Why, Elm Street is the main street; don't you remember, Halsey?"

"Lucien Wallace!" Halsey said. "That is the child Stewart spoke of at the inquest."

Warner, with his mechanic's instinct, had reached for the key. What he said was not a surprise.

"Yale lock," he said. "Probably a key to the east entry."

There was no reason why Thomas, an old and trusted servant, should not have had a key to that particular door, although the servants' entry was in the west wing. But I had not known of this key, and it opened up a new field of conjecture. Just now, however, there were many things to be attended to, and, leaving Warner with the body, we all went back to the house. Mr. Jamieson walked with me, while Halsey and Gertrude followed.

"I suppose I shall have to notify the Armstrongs," I said. "They will know if Thomas had any people and how to reach them. Of course, I expect to defray the expenses of the funeral, but his relatives must be found. What do you think frightened him, Mr. Jamieson?"

"It is hard to say," he replied slowly, "but I think we may be certain it was fright, and that he was hiding from something. I am sorry in more than one way: I have always believed that Thomas knew something, or suspected something, that he would not tell. Do you know how much money there was in that worn-out wallet of his? Nearly a hundred dollars! Almost two months' wages-and yet those darkies seldom have a penny. Well-what Thomas knew will be buried with him."

Halsey suggested that the grounds be searched, but Mr. Jamieson vetoed the suggestion.

"You would find nothing," he said. "A person clever enough to get into Sunnyside and tear a hole in the wall, while I watched down-stairs, is not to be found by going around the shrubbery with a lantern."

With the death of Thomas, I felt that a climax had come in affairs at Sunnyside. The night that followed was quiet enough. Halsey watched at the foot of the staircase, and a complicated system of bolts on the other doors seemed to be effectual.

Once in the night I wakened and thought I heard the tapping again. But all was quiet, and I had reached the stage where I refused to be disturbed for minor occurrences.

The Armstrongs were notified of Thomas' death, and I had my first interview with Doctor Walker as a result. He came up early the next morning, just as we finished breakfast, in a professional looking car with a black hood. I found him striding up and down the living-room, and, in spite of my preconceived dislike, I had to admit that the man was presentable. A big fellow he was, tall and dark, as Gertrude had said, smooth-shaven and erect, with prominent features and a square jaw. He was painfully spruce in his appearance, and his manner was almost obtrusively polite.

"I must make a double excuse for this early visit, Miss Innes," he said as he sat down. The chair was lower than he expected, and his dignity required collecting before he went on. "My professional duties are urgent and long neglected, and"—a fall to the every-day manner—"something must be done about that body."

"Yes," I said, sitting on the edge of my chair. "I merely wished the address of Thomas' people. You might have telephoned, if you were busy."

He smiled.

"I wished to see you about something else," he said. "As for Thomas, it is Mrs. Armstrong's wish that you would allow her to attend to the expense. About his relatives, I have already notified his brother, in the village. It was heart disease, I think. Thomas always had a bad heart."

"Heart disease and fright," I said, still on the edge of my chair. But the doctor had no intention of leaving.

"I understand you have a ghost up here, and that you have the house filled with detectives to exorcise it," he said.

For some reason I felt I was being "pumped," as Halsey says. "You have been misinformed," I replied.

"What, no ghost, no detectives!" he said, still with his smile. "What a disappointment to the village!"

I resented his attempt at playfulness. It had been anything but a joke to us.

"Doctor Walker," I said tartly, "I fail to see any humor in the situation. Since I came here, one man has been shot, and another one has died from shock. There have been intruders in the house, and strange noises. If that is funny, there is something wrong with my sense of humor."

"You miss the point," he said, still good-naturedly. "The thing that is funny, to me, is that you insist on remaining here, under the circumstances. I should think nothing would keep you."

"You are mistaken. Everything that occurs only confirms my resolution to stay until the mystery is cleared."

"I have a message for you, Miss Innes," he said, rising at last. "Mrs. Armstrong asked me to thank you for your kindness to Louise, whose whim, occurring at the time it did, put her to great inconvenience. Also-and this is a delicate matter-she asked me to appeal to your natural sympathy for her, at this time, and to ask you if you will not reconsider your decision about the house. Sunnyside is her home; she loves it dearly, and just now she wishes to retire here for quiet and peace."

"She must have had a change of heart," I said, ungraciously enough. "Louise told me her mother despised the place. Besides, this is no place for quiet and peace just now. Anyhow, doctor, while I don't care to force an issue, I shall certainly remain here, for a time at least."

"For how long?" he asked.

"My lease is for six months. I shall stay until some explanation is found for certain things. My own family is implicated now, and I shall do everything to clear the mystery of Arnold Armstrong's murder."

The doctor stood looking down, slapping his gloves thoughtfully against the palm of a well-looked-after hand.

"You say there have been intruders in the house?" he asked. "You are sure of that, Miss Innes?"

"Certain."

"In what part?"

"In the east wing."

"Can you tell me when these intrusions occurred, and what the purpose seemed to be? Was it robbery?"

"No," I said decidedly. "As to time, once on Friday night a week ago, again the following night, when Arnold Armstrong was murdered, and again last Friday night."

The doctor looked serious. He seemed to be debating some question in his mind, and to reach a decision.

"Miss Innes," he said, "I am in a peculiar position; I understand your attitude, of course; but-do you think you are wise? Ever since you have come here there have been hostile demonstrations against you and your family. I'm not a croaker, but-take a warning. Leave before anything occurs that will cause you a lifelong regret."

"I am willing to take the responsibility," I said coldly.

I think he gave me up then as a poor proposition. He asked to be shown where Arnold Armstrong's body had been found, and I took him there. He scrutinized the whole place carefully, examining the stairs and the lock. When he had taken a formal farewell I was confident of one thing. Doctor Walker would do anything he could to get me away from Sunnyside.

Fourteen Elm Street

It was Monday evening when we found the body of poor old Thomas. Monday night had been uneventful; things were quiet at the house and the peculiar circumstances of the old man's death had been carefully kept from the servants. Rosie took charge of the dining-room and pantry, in the absence of a butler, and, except for the warning of the Casanova doctor, everything breathed of peace.

Affairs at the Traders' Bank were progressing slowly. The failure had hit small stock-holders very hard, the minister of the little Methodist chapel in Casanova among them. He had received as a legacy from an uncle a few shares of stock in the Traders' Bank, and now his joy was turned to bitterness: he had to sacrifice everything he had in the world, and his feeling against Paul Armstrong, dead, as he was, must have been bitter in the extreme. He was asked to officiate at the simple services when the dead banker's body was interred in Casanova churchyard, but the good man providentially took cold, and a substitute was called in.

A few days after the services he called to see me, a kind-faced little man, in a very bad frock-coat and laundered tie. I think he was uncertain as to my connection with the Armstrong family, and dubious whether I considered Mr. Armstrong's taking away a matter for condolence or congratulation. He was not long in doubt.

I liked the little man. He had known Thomas well, and had promised to officiate at the services in the rickety African Zion Church. He told me more of himself than he knew, and before he left, I astonished him-and myself, I admit-by promising a new carpet for his church. He was much affected, and I gathered that he had yearned over his ragged chapel as a mother over a half-clothed child.

"You are laying up treasure, Miss Innes," he said brokenly, "where neither moth nor rust corrupt, nor thieves break through and steal."

"It is certainly a safer place than Sunnyside," I admitted. And the thought of the carpet permitted him to smile. He stood just inside the doorway, looking from the luxury of the house to the beauty of the view.

"The rich ought to be good," he said wistfully. "They have so much that is beautiful, and beauty is ennobling. And yet-while I ought to say nothing but good of the dead-Mr. Armstrong saw nothing of this fair prospect. To him these trees and lawns were not the work of God. They were property, at so much an acre. He loved money, Miss Innes. He offered up everything to his golden calf. Not power, not ambition, was his fetish: it was money." Then he dropped his pulpit manner, and, turning to me with his engaging smile: "In spite of all this luxury," he said, "the country people here have a saying that Mr. Paul Armstrong could sit on a dollar and see all around it. Unlike the summer people, he gave neither to the poor nor to the church. He loved money for its own sake."

"And there are no pockets in shrouds!" I said cynically.

I sent him home in the car, with a bunch of hot-house roses for his wife, and he was quite overwhelmed. As for me, I had a generous glow that was cheap at the price of a church carpet. I received less gratification-and less gratitude-when I presented the new silver communion set to St. Barnabas.

I had a great many things to think about in those days. I made out a list of questions and possible answers, but I seemed only to be working around in a circle. I always ended where I began. The list was something like this:

Who had entered the house the night before the murder?

Thomas claimed it was Mr. Bailey, whom he had seen on the foot-path, and who owned the pearl cuff-link.

Why did Arnold Armstrong come back after he had left the house the night he was killed?

No answer. Was it on the mission Louise had mentioned?

Who admitted him?

Gertrude said she had locked the east entry. There was no key on the dead man or in the door. He must have been admitted from within.

Who had been locked in the clothes chute?

Some one unfamiliar with the house, evidently. Only two people missing from the household, Rosie and Gertrude. Rosie had been at the lodge. Therefore-but was it Gertrude? Might it not have been the mysterious intruder again?

Who had accosted Rosie on the drive?

Again-perhaps the nightly visitor. It seemed more likely some one who suspected a secret at the lodge. Was Louise under surveillance?

Who had passed Louise on the circular staircase?

Could it have been Thomas? The key to the east entry made this a possibility. But why was he there, if it were indeed he?

Who had made the hole in the trunk-room wall?

It was not vandalism. It had been done quietly, and with deliberate purpose. If I had only known how to read the purpose of that gaping aperture what I might have saved in anxiety and mental strain!

Why had Louise left her people and come home to hide at the lodge?

There was no answer, as yet, to this, or to the next questions.

Why did both she and Doctor Walker warn us away from the house?

Who was Lucien Wallace?

What did Thomas see in the shadows the night he died?

What was the meaning of the subtle change in Gertrude?

Was Jack Bailey an accomplice or a victim in the looting of the Traders' Bank?

What all-powerful reason made Louise determine to marry Doctor Walker?

The examiners were still working on the books of the Traders' Bank, and it was probable that several weeks would elapse before everything was cleared up. The firm of expert accountants who had examined the books some two months before testified that every bond, every piece of valuable paper, was there at that time. It had been shortly after their examination that the president, who had been in bad health, had gone to California. Mr. Bailey was still ill at the Knickerbocker, and in this, as in other ways, Gertrude's conduct puzzled me. She seemed indifferent, refused to discuss matters pertaining to the bank, and never, to my knowledge, either wrote to him or went to see him.

Gradually I came to the conclusion that Gertrude, with the rest of the world, believed her lover guilty, and-although I believed it myself, for that matter—I was irritated by her indifference. Girls in my day did not meekly accept the public's verdict as to the man they loved.

But presently something occurred that made me think that under Gertrude's surface calm there was a seething flood of emotions.

Tuesday morning the detective made a careful search of the grounds, but he found nothing. In the afternoon he disappeared, and it was late that night when he came home. He said he would have to go back to the city the following day, and arranged with Halsey and Alex to guard the house.

Liddy came to me on Wednesday morning with her black silk apron held up like a bag, and her eyes big with virtuous wrath. It was the day of Thomas' funeral in the village, and Alex and I were in the conservatory cutting flowers for the old man's casket. Liddy is never so happy as when she is making herself wretched, and now her mouth drooped while her eyes were triumphant.

"I always said there were plenty of things going on here, right under our noses, that we couldn't see," she said, holding out her apron.

"I don't see with my nose," I remarked. "What have you got there?"

Liddy pushed aside a half-dozen geranium pots, and in the space thus cleared she dumped the contents of her apron—a handful of tiny bits of paper. Alex had stepped back, but I saw him watching her curiously.

"Wait a moment, Liddy," I said. "You have been going through the library paper-basket again!"

Liddy was arranging her bits of paper with the skill of long practice and paid no attention.

"Did it ever occur to you," I went on, putting my hand over the scraps, "that when people tear up their correspondence, it is for the express purpose of keeping it from being read?"

"If they wasn't ashamed of it they wouldn't take so much trouble, Miss Rachel," Liddy said oracularly. "More than that, with things happening every day, I consider it my duty. If you don't read and act on this, I shall give it to that Jamieson, and I'll venture he'll not go back to the city to-day."

That decided me. If the scraps had anything to do with the mystery ordinary conventions had no value. So Liddy arranged the scraps, like working out one of the puzzle-pictures children play with, and she did it with much the same eagerness. When it was finished she stepped aside while I read it.

"Wednesday night, nine o'clock. Bridge," I real aloud. Then, aware of Alex's stare, I turned on Liddy.

71

"Some one is to play bridge to-night at nine o'clock," I said. "Is that your business, or mine?"

Liddy was aggrieved. She was about to reply when I scooped up the pieces and left the conservatory.

"Now then," I said, when we got outside, "will you tell me why you choose to take Alex into your confidence? He's no fool. Do you suppose he thinks any one in this house is going to play bridge to-night at nine o'clock, by appointment! I suppose you have shown it in the kitchen, and instead of my being able to slip down to the bridge to-night quietly, and see who is there, the whole household will be going in a procession."

"Nobody knows it," Liddy said humbly. "I found it in the basket in Miss Gertrude's dressing-room. Look at the back of the sheet." I turned over some of the scraps, and, sure enough, it was a blank deposit slip from the Traders' Bank. So Gertrude was going to meet Jack Bailey that night by the bridge! And I had thought he was ill! It hardly seemed like the action of an innocent man-this avoidance of daylight, and of his fiancée's people. I decided to make certain, however, by going to the bridge that night.

After luncheon Mr. Jamieson suggested that I go with him to Richfield, and I consented.

"I am inclined to place more faith in Doctor Stewart's story," he said, "since I found that scrap in old Thomas' pocket. It bears out the statement that the woman with the child, and the woman who quarreled with Armstrong, are the same. It looks as if Thomas had stumbled on to some affair which was more or less discreditable to the dead man, and, with a certain loyalty to the family, had kept it to himself. Then, you see, your story about the woman at the card-room window begins to mean something. It is the nearest approach to anything tangible that we have had yet."

Warner took us to Richfield in the car. It was about twenty-five miles by railroad, but by taking a series of atrociously rough short cuts we got there very quickly. It was a pretty little town, on the river, and back on the hill I could see the Mortons' big country house, where Halsey and Gertrude had been staying until the night of the murder.

Elm Street was almost the only street, and number fourteen was easily found. It was a small white house, dilapidated without having gained anything picturesque, with a low window and a porch only a foot or so above the bit of a lawn. There was a baby-carriage in the path, and from a swing at the side came the sound of conflict. Three small children were disputing vociferously, and a faded young woman with a kindly face was trying to hush the clamor. When she saw us she untied her gingham apron and came around to the porch.

"Good afternoon," I said. Jamieson lifted his hat, without speaking. "I came to inquire about a child named Lucien Wallace."

"I am glad you have come," she said. "In spite of the other children, I think the little fellow is lonely. We thought perhaps his mother would be here to-day."

Mr. Jamieson stepped forward.

"You are Mrs. Tate?" I wondered how the detective knew.

"Yes, sir."

"Mrs. Tate, we want to make some inquiries. Perhaps in the house —"

"Come right in," she said hospitably. And soon we were in the little shabby parlor, exactly like a thousand of its prototypes. Mrs. Tate sat uneasily, her hands folded in her lap.

"How long has Lucien been here?" Mr. Jamieson asked.

"Since a week ago last Friday. His mother paid one week's board in advance; the other has not been paid."

"Was he ill when he came?"

"No, sir, not what you'd call sick. He was getting better of typhoid, she said, and he's picking up fine."

"Will you tell me his mother's name and address?"

"That's the trouble," the young woman said, knitting her brows. "She gave her name as Mrs. Wallace, and said she had no address. She was looking for a boarding-house in town. She said she worked in a department store, and couldn't take care of the child properly, and he needed fresh air and milk. I had three children of my own, and one more didn't make much difference in the work, but —I wish she would pay this week's board."

"Did she say what store it was?"

"No, sir, but all the boy's clothes came from King's. He has far too fine clothes for the country."

There was a chorus of shouts and shrill yells from the front door, followed by the loud stamping of children's feet and a throaty "whoa, whoa!" Into the room came a tandem team of two chubby youngsters, a boy and a girl, harnessed with a clothes-line, and driven by a laughing boy of about seven, in tan overalls and brass buttons. The small driver caught my attention at once: he was a beautiful child, and, although he showed traces of recent severe illness, his skin had now the clear transparency of health.

"Whoa, Flinders," he shouted. "You're goin' to smash the trap."

Mr. Jamieson coaxed him over by holding out a lead-pencil, striped blue and yellow.

"Now, then," he said, when the boy had taken the lead-pencil and was testing its usefulness on the detective's cuff, "now then, I'll bet you don't know what your name is!"

"I do," said the boy. "Lucien Wallace."

"Great! And what's your mother's name?"

"Mother, of course. What's your mother's name?" And he pointed to me! I am going to stop wearing black: it doubles a woman's age.

"And where did you live before you came here?" The detective was polite enough not to smile.

"*Grossmutter*," he said. And I saw Mr. Jamieson's eyebrows go up.

"German," he commented. "Well, young man, you don't seem to know much about yourself."

"I've tried it all week," Mrs. Tate broke in. "The boy knows a word or two of German, but he doesn't know where he lived, or anything about himself."

Mr. Jamieson wrote something on a card and gave it to her.

"Mrs. Tate," he said, "I want you to do something. Here is some money for the telephone call. The instant the boy's mother appears here, call up that number and ask for the person whose name is there. You can run across to the drug-store on an errand and do it quietly. Just say, 'The lady has come.'"

"'The lady has come,'" repeated Mrs. Tate. "Very well, sir, and I hope it will be soon. The milk-bill alone is almost double what it was."

"How much is the child's board?" I asked.

"Three dollars a week, including his washing."

"Very well," I said. "Now, Mrs. Tate, I am going to pay last week's board and a week in advance. If the mother comes, she is to know nothing of this visit-absolutely not a word, and, in return for your silence, you may use this money for-something for your own children."

Her tired, faded face lighted up, and I saw her glance at the little Tates' small feet. Shoes, I divined-the feet of the genteel poor being almost as expensive as their stomachs.

As we went back Mr. Jamieson made only one remark: I think he was laboring under the weight of a great disappointment.

"Is King's a children's outfitting place?" he asked.

"Not especially. It is a general department store."

He was silent after that, but he went to the telephone as soon as we got home, and called up King and Company, in the city.

After a time he got the general manager, and they talked for some time. When Mr. Jamieson hung up the receiver he turned to me.

"The plot thickens," he said with his ready smile. "There are four women named Wallace at King's, none of them married, and none over twenty. I think I shall go up to the city to-night. I want to go to the Children's Hospital. But before I go, Miss Innes, I wish you would be more frank with me than you have been yet. I want you to show me the revolver you picked up in the tulip bed."

So he had known all along!

"It *was* a revolver, Mr. Jamieson," I admitted, cornered at last, "but I can not show it to you. It is not in my possession."

A Ladder Out of Place

At dinner Mr. Jamieson suggested sending a man out in his place for a couple of days, but Halsey was certain there would be nothing more, and felt that he and Alex could manage the situation. The detective went back to town early in the evening, and by nine o'clock Halsey, who had been playing golf-as a man does anything to take his mind away from trouble-was sleeping soundly on the big leather davenport in the living-room.

I sat and knitted, pretending not to notice when Gertrude got up and wandered out into the starlight. As soon as I was satisfied that she had gone, however, I went out cautiously. I had no intention of eavesdropping, but I wanted to be certain that it was Jack Bailey she was meeting. Too many things had occurred in which Gertrude was, or appeared to be, involved, to allow anything to be left in question.

I went slowly across the lawn, skirted the hedge to a break not far from the lodge, and found myself on the open road. Perhaps a hundred feet to the left the path led across the valley to the Country Club, and only a little way off was the foot-bridge over Casanova Creek. But just as I was about to turn down the path I heard steps coming toward me, and I shrank into the bushes. It was Gertrude, going back quickly toward the house.

I was surprised. I waited until she had had time to get almost to the house before I started. And then I stepped back again into the shadows. The reason why Gertrude had not kept her tryst was evident. Leaning on the parapet of the bridge in the moonlight, and smoking a pipe, was Alex, the gardener. I could have throttled Liddy for her carelessness in reading the torn note where he could hear. And I could cheerfully have choked Alex to death for his audacity.

But there was no help for it: I turned and followed Gertrude slowly back to the house.

The frequent invasions of the house had effectually prevented any relaxation after dusk. We had redoubled our vigilance as to bolts and window-locks but, as Mr. Jamieson had suggested, we allowed the door at the east entry to remain as before, locked by the Yale lock only. To provide only one possible entrance for the invader, and to keep a constant guard in the dark at the foot of the circular staircase, seemed to be the only method.

In the absence of the detective, Alex and Halsey arranged to change off, Halsey to be on duty from ten to two, and Alex from two until six. Each man was armed, and, as an additional precaution, the one off duty slept in a room near the head of the circular staircase and kept his door open, to be ready for emergency.

These arrangements were carefully kept from the servants, who were only commencing to sleep at night, and who retired, one and all, with barred doors and lamps that burned full until morning.

The house was quiet again Wednesday night. It was almost a week since Louise had encountered some one on the stairs, and it was four days since the discovery of the hole in the trunk-room wall. Arnold Armstrong and his father rested side by side in the Casanova churchyard, and at the Zion African Church, on the hill, a new mound marked the last resting-place of poor Thomas.

Louise was with her mother in town, and, beyond a polite note of thanks to me, we had heard nothing from her. Doctor Walker had taken up his practice again, and we saw him now and then flying past along the road, always at top speed. The murder of Arnold Armstrong was still unavenged, and I remained firm in the position I had taken-to stay at Sunnyside until the thing was at least partly cleared.

And yet, for all its quiet, it was on Wednesday night that perhaps the boldest attempt was made to enter the house. On Thursday afternoon the laundress sent word she would like to speak to me, and I saw her in my private sitting-room, a small room beyond the dressing-room.

Mary Anne was embarrassed. She had rolled down her sleeves and tied a white apron around her waist, and she stood making folds in it with fingers that were red and shiny from her soap-suds.

"Well, Mary," I said encouragingly, "what's the matter? Don't dare to tell me the soap is out."

"No, ma'm, Miss Innes." She had a nervous habit of looking first at my one eye and then at the other, her own optics shifting ceaselessly, right eye, left eye, right eye, until I found myself doing the same thing. "No, ma'm. I was askin' did you want the ladder left up the clothes chute?"

"The what?" I screeched, and was sorry the next minute. Seeing her suspicions were verified, Mary Anne had gone white, and stood with her eyes shifting more wildly than ever.

"There's a ladder up the clothes chute, Miss Innes," she said. "It's up that tight I can't move it, and I didn't like to ask for help until I spoke to you."

It was useless to dissemble; Mary Anne knew now as well as I did that the ladder had no business to be there. I did the best I could, however. I put her on the defensive at once.

"Then you didn't lock the laundry last night?"

"I locked it tight, and put the key in the kitchen on its nail."

"Very well, then you forgot a window."

Mary Anne hesitated.

"Yes'm," she said at last. "I thought I locked them all, but there was one open this morning."

I went out of the room and down the hall, followed by Mary Anne. The door into the clothes chute was securely bolted, and when I opened it I saw the evidence of the woman's story. A pruning-ladder had been brought from where it had lain against the stable and now stood upright in the clothes shaft, its end resting against the wall between the first and second floors.

I turned to Mary.

"This is due to your carelessness," I said. "If we had all been murdered in our beds it would have been your fault." She shivered. "Now, not a word of this through the house, and send Alex to me."

The effect on Alex was to make him apoplectic with rage, and with it all I fancied there was an element of satisfaction. As I look back, so many things are plain to me that I wonder I could not see at the time. It is all known now, and yet the whole thing was so remarkable that perhaps my stupidity was excusable.

Alex leaned down the chute and examined the ladder carefully.

"It is caught," he said with a grim smile. "The fools, to have left a warning like that! The only trouble is, Miss Innes, they won't be apt to come back for a while."

"I shouldn't regard that in the light of a calamity," I replied.

Until late that evening Halsey and Alex worked at the chute. They forced down the ladder at last, and put a new bolt on the door. As for myself, I sat and wondered if I had a deadly enemy, intent on my destruction.

I was growing more and more nervous. Liddy had given up all pretense at bravery, and slept regularly in my dressing-room on the couch, with a prayer-book and a game knife from the kitchen under her pillow, thus preparing for both the natural and the supernatural. That was the way things stood that Thursday night, when I myself took a hand in the struggle.

While the Stables Burned

About nine o'clock that night Liddy came into the living-room and reported that one of the housemaids declared she had seen two men slip around the corner of the stable. Gertrude had been sitting staring in front of her, jumping at every sound. Now she turned on Liddy pettishly.

"I declare, Liddy," she said, "you are a bundle of nerves. What if Eliza did see some men around the stable? It may have been Warner and Alex."

"Warner is in the kitchen, miss," Liddy said with dignity. "And if you had come through what I have, you would be a bundle of nerves, too. Miss Rachel, I'd be thankful if you'd give me my month's wages to-morrow. I'll be going to my sister's."

"Very well," I said, to her evident amazement. "I will make out the check. Warner can take you down to the noon train."

Liddy's face was really funny.

"You'll have a nice time at your sister's," I went on. "Five children, hasn't she?"

"That's it," Liddy said, suddenly bursting into tears. "Send me away, after all these years, and your new shawl only half done, and nobody knowin' how to fix the water for your bath."

"It's time I learned to prepare my own bath." I was knitting complacently. But Gertrude got up and put her arms around Liddy's shaking shoulders.

"You are two big babies," she said soothingly. "Neither one of you could get along for an hour without the other. So stop quarreling and be good. Liddy, go right up and lay out Aunty's night things. She is going to bed early."

After Liddy had gone I began to think about the men at the stable, and I grew more and more anxious. Halsey was aimlessly knocking the billiard-balls around in the billiard-room, and I called to him.

"Halsey," I said when he sauntered in, "is there a policeman in Casanova?"

"Constable," he said laconically. "Veteran of the war, one arm; in office to conciliate the G. A. R. element. Why?"

"Because I am uneasy to-night." And I told him what Liddy had said. "Is there any one you can think of who could be relied on to watch the outside of the house to-night?"

"We might get Sam Bohannon from the club," he said thoughtfully. "It wouldn't be a bad scheme. He's a smart darky, and with his mouth shut and his shirt-front covered, you couldn't see him a yard off in the dark."

Halsey conferred with Alex, and the result, in an hour, was Sam. His instructions were simple. There had been numerous attempts to break into the house; it was the intention, not to drive intruders away, but to capture them. If Sam saw anything suspicious outside, he was to tap at the east entry, where Alex and Halsey were to alternate in keeping watch through the night.

It was with a comfortable feeling of security that I went to bed that night. The door between Gertrude's rooms and mine had been opened, and, with the doors into the hall bolted, we were safe enough. Although Liddy persisted in her belief that doors would prove no obstacles to our disturbers.

As before, Halsey watched the east entry from ten until two. He had an eye to comfort, and he kept vigil in a heavy oak chair, very large and deep. We went up-stairs rather early, and through the open door Gertrude and I kept up a running fire of conversation. Liddy was brushing my hair, and Gertrude was doing her own, with a long free sweep of her strong round arms.

"Did you know Mrs. Armstrong and Louise are in the village?" she called.

"No," I replied, startled. "How did you hear it?"

"I met the oldest Stewart girl to-day, the doctor's daughter, and she told me they had not gone back to town after the funeral. They went directly to that little yellow house next to Doctor Walker's, and are apparently settled there. They took the house furnished for the summer."

"Why, it's a bandbox," I said. "I can't imagine Fanny Armstrong in such a place."

"It's true, nevertheless. Ella Stewart says Mrs. Armstrong has aged terribly, and looks as if she is hardly able to walk."

I lay and thought over some of these things until midnight. The electric lights went out then, fading slowly until there was only a red-hot loop to be seen in the bulb, and then even that died away and we were embarked on the darkness of another night.

Apparently only a few minutes elapsed, during which my eyes were becoming accustomed to the darkness. Then I noticed that the windows were reflecting a faint pinkish light, Liddy noticed it at the same time, and I heard her jump up. At that moment Sam's deep voice boomed from somewhere just below.

"Fire!" he yelled. "The stable's on fire!"

I could see him in the glare dancing up and down on the drive, and a moment later Halsey joined him. Alex was awake and running down the stairs, and in five minutes from the time the fire was discovered, three of the maids were sitting on their trunks in the drive, although, excepting a few sparks, there was no fire nearer than a hundred yards.

Gertrude seldom loses her presence of mind, and she ran to the telephone. But by the time the Casanova volunteer fire department came toiling up the hill the stable was a furnace, with the Dragon Fly safe but blistered, in the road. Some gasolene exploded just as the volunteer department got to work, which shook their nerves as well as the burning building. The stable, being on a hill, was a torch to attract the population from every direction. Rumor had it that Sunnyside was burning, and it was amazing how many people threw something over their night-clothes and flew to the conflagration. I take it Casanova has few fires, and Sunnyside was furnishing the people, in one way and another, the greatest excitement they had had for years.

The stable was off the west wing. I hardly know how I came to think of the circular staircase and the unguarded door at its foot. Liddy was putting my clothes into sheets, preparatory to tossing them out the window, when I found her, and I could hardly persuade her to stop.

"I want you to come with me, Liddy," I said. "Bring a candle and a couple of blankets."

She lagged behind considerably when she saw me making for the east wing, and at the top of the staircase she balked.

"I am not going down there," she said firmly.

"There is no one guarding the door down there," I explained. "Who knows? —this may be a scheme to draw everybody away from this end of the house, and let some one in here."

The instant I had said it I was convinced I had hit on the explanation, and that perhaps it was already too late. It seemed to me as I listened that I heard stealthy footsteps on the east porch, but there was so much shouting outside that it was impossible to tell. Liddy was on the point of retreat.

"Very well," I said, "then I shall go down alone. Run back to Mr. Halsey's room and get his revolver. Don't shoot down the stairs if you hear a noise: remember —I shall be down there. And hurry."

I put the candle on the floor at the top of the staircase and took off my bedroom slippers. Then I crept down the stairs, going very slowly, and listening with all my ears. I was keyed to such a pitch that I felt no fear: like the condemned who sleep and eat the night before execution, I was no longer able to suffer apprehension. I was past that. Just at the foot of the stairs I stubbed my toe against Halsey's big chair, and had to stand on one foot in a soundless agony until the pain subsided to a dull ache. And then —I knew I was right. Some one had put a key into the lock, and was turning it. For some reason it refused to work, and the key was withdrawn. There was a muttering of voices outside: I had only a second. Another trial, and the door would open. The candle above made a faint gleam down the well-like staircase, and at that moment, with a second, no more, to spare, I thought of a plan.

The heavy oak chair almost filled the space between the newel post and the door. With a crash I had turned it on its side, wedging it against the door, its legs against the stairs. I could hear a faint scream from Liddy, at the crash, and then she came down the stairs on a run, with the revolver held straight out in front of her.

"Thank God," she said, in a shaking voice. "I thought it was you."

I pointed to the door, and she understood.

"Call out the windows at the other end of the house," I whispered. "Run. Tell them not to wait for anything."

She went up the stairs at that, two at a time. Evidently she collided with the candle, for it went out, and I was left in darkness.

I was really astonishingly cool. I remember stepping over the chair and gluing my ear to the door, and I shall never forget feeling it give an inch or two there in the darkness, under a steady pressure from without. But the chair held, although I could hear an ominous cracking of one of the legs. And then, without the slightest warning, the card-room window broke with a crash. I had my finger on the trigger of the revolver, and as I jumped it went off, right through the door. Some one outside swore roundly, and for the first time I could hear what was said.

"Only a scratch.... Men are at the other end of the house.... Have the whole rat's nest on us." And a lot of profanity which I won't write down. The voices were at the broken window now, and although I was trembling violently, I was determined that I would hold them until help came. I moved up the stairs until I could see into the card-room, or rather through it, to the window. As I looked a small man put his leg over the sill and stepped into the room. The curtain confused him for a moment; then he turned, not toward me, but toward the billiard-room door. I fired again, and something that was glass or china crashed to the ground. Then I ran up the stairs and along the corridor to the main staircase. Gertrude was standing there, trying to locate the shots, and I must have been a peculiar figure, with my hair in crimps, my dressing-gown flying, no slippers, and a revolver clutched in my hands I had no time to talk. There was the sound of footsteps in the lower hall, and some one bounded up the stairs.

I had gone Berserk, I think. I leaned over the stair-rail and fired again. Halsey, below, yelled at me.

"What are you doing up there?" he yelled. "You missed me by an inch."

And then I collapsed and fainted. When I came around Liddy was rubbing my temples with *eau de quinine*, and the search was in full blast.

Well, the man was gone. The stable burned to the ground, while the crowd cheered at every falling rafter, and the volunteer fire department sprayed it with a garden hose. And in the house Alex and Halsey searched every corner of the lower floor, finding no one.

The truth of my story was shown by the broken window and the overturned chair. That the unknown had got up-stairs was almost impossible. He had not used the main staircase, there was no way to the upper floor in the east wing, and Liddy had been at the window, in the west wing, where the servants' stair went up. But we did not go to bed at all. Sam Bohannon and Warner helped in the search, and not a closet escaped scrutiny. Even the cellars were given a thorough overhauling, without result. The door in the east entry had a hole through it where my bullet had gone.

The hole slanted downward, and the bullet was embedded in the porch. Some reddish stains showed it had done execution.

"Somebody will walk lame," Halsey said, when he had marked the course of the bullet. "It's too low to have hit anything but a leg or foot."

From that time on I watched every person I met for a limp, and to this day the man who halts in his walk is an object of suspicion to me. But Casanova had no lame men: the nearest approach to it was an old fellow who tended the safety gates at the railroad, and he, I learned on inquiry, had two artificial legs. Our man had gone, and the large and expensive stable at Sunnyside was a heap of smoking rafters and charred boards. Warner swore the fire was incendiary, and in view of the attempt to enter the house, there seemed to be no doubt of it.

Flinders

F Halsey had only taken me fully into his confidence, through the whole affair, it would have been much simpler. If he had been altogether frank about Jack Bailey, and if the day after the fire he had told me what he suspected, there would have been no harrowing period for all of us, with the boy in danger. But young people refuse to profit by the experience of their elders, and sometimes the elders are the ones to suffer.

I was much used up the day after the fire, and Gertrude insisted on my going out. The machine was temporarily out of commission, and the carriage horses had been sent to a farm for the summer. Gertrude finally got a trap from the Casanova liveryman, and we went out. Just as we turned from the drive into the road we passed a woman. She had put down a small valise, and stood inspecting the house and grounds minutely. I should hardly have noticed her, had it not been for the fact that she had been horribly disfigured by smallpox.

"Ugh!" Gertrude said, when we had passed, "what a face! I shall dream of it to-night. Get up, Flinders."

"Flinders?" I asked. "Is that the horse's name?"

"It is." She flicked the horse's stubby mane with the whip. "He didn't look like a livery horse, and the liveryman said he had bought him from the Armstrongs when they purchased a couple of motors and cut down the stable. Nice Flinders-good old boy!"

Flinders was certainly not a common name for a horse, and yet the youngster at Richfield had named his prancing, curly-haired little horse Flinders! It set me to thinking.

At my request Halsey had already sent word of the fire to the agent from whom we had secured the house. Also, he had called Mr. Jamieson by telephone, and somewhat guardedly had told him of the previous night's events. Mr. Jamieson promised to come out that night, and to bring another man with him. I did not consider it necessary to notify Mrs. Armstrong, in the village. No doubt she knew of the fire, and in view of my refusal to give up the house, an interview would probably have been unpleasant enough. But as we passed Doctor Walker's white and green house I thought of something.

"Stop here, Gertrude," I said. "I am going to get out."

"To see Louise?" she asked.

"No, I want to ask this young Walker something."

She was curious, I knew, but I did not wait to explain. I went up the walk to the house, where a brass sign at the side announced the office, and went in. The reception-room was empty, but from the consulting-room beyond came the sound of two voices, not very amicable.

"It is an outrageous figure," some one was storming. Then the doctor's quiet tone, evidently not arguing, merely stating something. But I had not time to listen to some person probably disputing his bill, so I coughed. The voices ceased at once: a door closed somewhere, and the doctor entered from the hall of the house. He looked sufficiently surprised at seeing me.

"Good afternoon, Doctor," I said formally. "I shall not keep you from your patient. I wish merely to ask you a question."

"Won't you sit down?"

"It will not be necessary. Doctor, has any one come to you, either early this morning or to-day, to have you treat a bullet wound?"

"Nothing so startling has happened to me," he said. "A bullet wound! Things must be lively at Sunnyside."

"I didn't say it was at Sunnyside. But as it happens, it was. If any such case comes to you, will it be too much trouble for you to let me know?"

"I shall be only too happy," he said. "I understand you have had a fire up there, too. A fire and shooting in one night is rather lively for a quiet place like that."

"It is as quiet as a boiler-shop," I replied, as I turned to go.

"And you are still going to stay?"

"Until I am burned out," I responded. And then on my way down the steps, I turned around suddenly.

"Doctor," I asked at a venture, "have you ever heard of a child named Lucien Wallace?"

Clever as he was, his face changed and stiffened. He was on his guard again in a moment.

"Lucien Wallace?" he repeated. "No, I think not. There are plenty of Wallaces around, but I don't know any Lucien."

I was as certain as possible that he did. People do not lie readily to me, and this man lied beyond a doubt. But there was nothing to be gained now; his defenses were up, and I left, half irritated and wholly baffled.

Our reception was entirely different at Doctor Stewart's. Taken into the bosom of the family at once, Flinders tied outside and nibbling the grass at the roadside, Gertrude and I drank some home-made elderberry wine and told briefly of the fire. Of the more serious part of the night's experience, of course, we said nothing. But when at last we had left the family on the porch and the good doctor was untying our steed, I asked him the same question I had put to Doctor Walker.

"Shot!" he said. "Bless my soul, no. Why, what have you been doing up at the big house, Miss Innes?"

"Some one tried to enter the house during the fire, and was shot and slightly injured," I said hastily. "Please don't mention it; we wish to make as little of it as possible."

There was one other possibility, and we tried that. At Casanova station I saw the station master, and asked him if any trains left Casanova between one o'clock and daylight. There was none until six a. m. The next question required more diplomacy.

"Did you notice on the six-o'clock train any person-any man-who limped a little?" I asked. "Please try to remember: we are trying to trace a man who was seen loitering around Sunnyside last night before the fire."

He was all attention in a moment.

"I was up there myself at the fire," he said volubly. "I'm a member of the volunteer company. First big fire we've had since the summer house burned over to the club golf links. My wife was sayin' the other day, 'Dave, you might as well 'a' saved the money in that there helmet and shirt.' And here last night they came in handy. Rang that bell so hard I hadn't time scarcely to get 'em on."

"And-did you see a man who limped?" Gertrude put in, as he stopped for breath.

"Not at the train, ma'm," he said. "No such person got on here to-day. But I'll tell you where I did see a man that limped. I didn't wait till the fire company left; there's a fast freight goes through at four forty-five, and I had to get down to the station. I seen there wasn't much more to do anyhow at the fire-we'd got the flames under control" —Gertrude looked at me and smiled —"so I started down the hill. There was folks here and there goin' home, and along by the path to the Country Club I seen two men. One was a short fellow. He was sitting on a big rock, his back to me, and he had something white in his hand, as if he was tying up his foot. After I'd gone on a piece I looked back, and he was hobbling on and-excuse me, miss-he was swearing something sickening."

"Did they go toward the club?" Gertrude asked suddenly, leaning forward.

"No, miss. I think they came into the village. I didn't get a look at their faces, but I know every chick and child in the place, and everybody knows me. When they didn't shout at me-in my uniform, you know —I took it they were strangers."

So all we had for our afternoon's work was this: some one had been shot by the bullet that went through the door; he had not left the village, and he had not called in a physician. Also, Doctor Walker knew who Lucien Wallace was, and his very denial made me confident that, in that one direction at least, we were on the right track.

The thought that the detective would be there that night was the most cheering thing of all, and I think even Gertrude was glad of it. Driving home that afternoon, I saw her in the clear sunlight for the first time in several days, and I was startled to see how ill she looked. She was thin and colorless, and all her bright animation was gone.

"Gertrude," I said, "I have been a very selfish old woman. You are going to leave this miserable house to-night. Annie Morton is going to Scotland next week, and you shall go right with her."

To my surprise, she flushed painfully.

"I don't want to go, Aunt Ray," she said. "Don't make me leave now."

"You are losing your health and your good looks," I said decidedly. "You should have a change."

"I shan't stir a foot." She was equally decided. Then, more lightly: "Why, you and Liddy need me to arbitrate between you every day in the week."

Perhaps I was growing suspicious of every one, but it seemed to me that Gertrude's gaiety was forced and artificial. I watched her covertly during the rest of the drive, and I did not like the two spots of crimson in her pale cheeks. But I said nothing more about sending her to Scotland: I knew she would not go.

A Visit from Louise

That day was destined to be an eventful one, for when I entered the house and found Eliza ensconced in the upper hall on a chair, with Mary Anne doing her best to stifle her with household ammonia, and Liddy rubbing her wrists-whatever good that is supposed to do —I knew that the ghost had been walking again, and this time in daylight.

Eliza was in a frenzy of fear. She clutched at my sleeve when I went close to her, and refused to let go until she had told her story. Coming just after the fire, the household was demoralized, and it was no surprise to me to find Alex and the under-gardener struggling down-stairs with a heavy trunk between them.

"I didn't want to do it, Miss Innes," Alex said. "But she was so excited, I was afraid she would do as she said-drag it down herself, and scratch the staircase."

I was trying to get my bonnet off and to keep the maids quiet at the same time. "Now, Eliza, when you have washed your face and stopped bawling," I said, "come into my sitting-room and tell me what has happened."

Liddy put away my things without speaking. The very set of her shoulders expressed disapproval.

"Well," I said, when the silence became uncomfortable, "things seem to be warming up."

Silence from Liddy, and a long sigh.

"If Eliza goes, I don't know where to look for another cook." More silence.

"Rosie is probably a good cook." Sniff.

"Liddy," I said at last, "don't dare to deny that you are having the time of your life. You positively gloat in this excitement. You never looked better. It's my opinion all this running around, and getting jolted out of a rut, has stirred up that torpid liver of yours."

"It's not myself I'm thinking about," she said, goaded into speech. "Maybe my liver was torpid, and maybe it wasn't; but I know this: I've got some feelings left, and to see you standing at the foot of that staircase shootin' through the door —I'll never be the same woman again."

"Well, I'm glad of that-anything for a change," I said. And in came Eliza, flanked by Rosie and Mary Anne.

Her story, broken with sobs and corrections from the other two, was this: At two o'clock (two-fifteen, Rosie insisted) she had gone up-stairs to get a picture from her room to show Mary Anne. (A picture of a *lady*, Mary Anne interposed.) She went up the servants' staircase and along the corridor to her room, which lay between the trunk-room and the unfinished ball-room. She heard a sound as she went down the corridor, like some one moving furniture, but she was not nervous. She thought it might be men examining the house after the fire the night before, but she looked in the trunk-room and saw nobody.

She went into her room quietly. The noise had ceased, and everything was quiet. Then she sat down on the side of her bed, and, feeling faint-she was subject to spells —("I told you that when I came, didn't I, Rosie?" "Yes'm, indeed she did!") —she put her head down on her pillow and —

"Took a nap. All right!" I said. "Go on."

"When I came to, Miss Innes, sure as I'm sittin' here, I thought I'd die. Somethin' hit me on the face, and I set up, sudden. And then I seen the plaster drop, droppin' from a little hole in the wall. And the first thing I knew, an iron bar that long" (fully two yards by her measure) "shot through that hole and tumbled on the bed. If I'd been still sleeping" ("Fainting," corrected Rosie) "I'd 'a' been hit on the head and killed!"

"I wisht you'd heard her scream," put in Mary Anne. "And her face as white as a pillow-slip when she tumbled down the stairs."

"No doubt there is some natural explanation for it, Eliza," I said. "You may have dreamed it, in your 'fainting' attack. But if it is true, the metal rod and the hole in the wall will show it."

Eliza looked a little bit sheepish.

"The hole's there all right, Miss Innes," she said. "But the bar was gone when Mary Anne and Rosie went up to pack my trunk."

"That wasn't all," Liddy's voice came funereally from a corner. "Eliza said that from the hole in the wall a burning eye looked down at her!"

"The wall must be at least six inches thick," I said with asperity. "Unless the person who drilled the hole carried his eyes on the ends of a stick, Eliza couldn't possibly have seen them."

But the fact remained, and a visit to Eliza's room proved it. I might jeer all I wished: some one had drilled a hole in the unfinished wall of the ball-room, passing between the bricks of the partition, and shooting through the unresisting plaster of Eliza's room with such force as to send the rod flying on to her bed. I had gone up-stairs alone, and I confess the thing puzzled me: in two or three places in the wall small apertures had been made, none of them of any depth. Not the least mysterious thing was the disappearance of the iron implement that had been used.

I remembered a story I read once about an impish dwarf that lived in the spaces between the double walls of an ancient castle. I wondered vaguely if my original idea of a secret entrance to a hidden chamber could be right, after all, and if we were housing some erratic guest, who played pranks on us in the dark, and destroyed the walls that he might listen, hidden safely away, to our amazed investigations.

Mary Anne and Eliza left that afternoon, but Rosie decided to stay. It was about five o'clock when the hack came from the station to get them, and, to my amazement, it had an occupant. Matthew Geist, the driver, asked for me, and explained his errand with pride.

"I've brought you a cook, Miss Innes," he said. "When the message came to come up for two girls and their trunks, I supposed there was something doing, and as this here woman had been looking for work in the village, I thought I'd bring her along."

Already I had acquired the true suburbanite ability to take servants on faith; I no longer demanded written and unimpeachable references. I, Rachel Innes, have learned not to mind if the cook sits down comfortably in my sitting-room when she is taking the orders for the day, and I am grateful if the silver is not cleaned with scouring soap. And so that day I merely told Liddy to send the new applicant in. When she came, however, I could hardly restrain a gasp of surprise. It was the woman with the pitted face.

She stood somewhat awkwardly just inside the door, and she had an air of self-confidence that was inspiring. Yes, she could cook; was not a fancy cook, but could make good soups and desserts if there was any one to take charge of the salads. And so, in the end, I took her. As Halsey said, when we told him, it didn't matter much about the cook's face, if it was clean.

I have spoken of Halsey's restlessness. On that day it seemed to be more than ever a resistless impulse that kept him out until after luncheon. I think he hoped constantly that he might meet Louise driving over the hills in her runabout; possibly he did meet her occasionally, but from his continued gloom I felt sure the situation between them was unchanged.

Part of the afternoon I believe he read-Gertrude and I were out, as I have said, and at dinner we both noticed that something had occurred to distract him. He was disagreeable, which is unlike him, nervous, looking at his watch every few minutes, and he ate almost nothing. He asked twice during the meal on what train Mr. Jamieson and the other detective were coming, and had long periods of abstraction during which he dug his fork into my damask cloth and did not hear when he was spoken to. He refused dessert, and left the table early, excusing himself on the ground that he wanted to see Alex.

Alex, however, was not to be found. It was after eight when Halsey ordered the car, and started down the hill at a pace that, even for him, was unusually reckless. Shortly after, Alex reported that he was ready to go over the house, preparatory to closing it for the night. Sam Bohannon came at a quarter before nine, and began his patrol of the grounds, and with the arrival of the two detectives to look forward to, I was not especially apprehensive.

At half-past nine I heard the sound of a horse driven furiously up the drive. It came to a stop in front of the house, and immediately after there were hurried steps on the veranda. Our nerves were not what they should have been, and Gertrude, always apprehensive lately, was at the door almost instantly. A moment later Louise had burst into the room and stood there bareheaded and breathing hard!

"Where is Halsey?" she demanded. Above her plain black gown her eyes looked big and somber, and the rapid drive had brought no color to her face. I got up and drew forward a chair.

"He has not come back," I said quietly. "Sit down, child; you are not strong enough for this kind of thing."

I don't think she even heard me.

"He has not come back?" she asked, looking from me to Gertrude. "Do you know where he went? Where can I find him?"

"For Heaven's sake, Louise," Gertrude burst out, "tell us what is wrong. Halsey is not here. He has gone to the station for Mr. Jamieson. What has happened?"

"To the station, Gertrude? You are sure?"

"Yes," I said. "Listen. There is the whistle of the train now."

She relaxed a little at our matter-of-fact tone, and allowed herself to sink into a chair.

"Perhaps I was wrong," she said heavily. "He-will be here in a few moments if-everything is right."

We sat there, the three of us, without attempt at conversation. Both Gertrude and I recognized the futility of asking Louise any questions: her reticence was a part of a rôle she had assumed. Our ears were strained for the first throb of the motor as it turned into the drive and commenced the climb to the house. Ten minutes passed, fifteen, twenty. I saw Louise's hands grow rigid as they clutched the arms of her chair. I watched Gertrude's bright color slowly ebbing away, and around my own heart I seemed to feel the grasp of a giant hand.

Twenty-five minutes, and then a sound. But it was not the chug of the motor: it was the unmistakable rumble of the Casanova hack. Gertrude drew aside the curtain and peered into the darkness.

"It's the hack, I am sure," she said, evidently relieved. "Something has gone wrong with the car, and no wonder-the way Halsey went down the hill."

It seemed a long time before the creaking vehicle came to a stop at the door. Louise rose and stood watching, her hand to her throat. And then Gertrude opened the door, admitting Mr. Jamieson and a stocky, middle-aged man. Halsey was not with them. When the door had closed and Louise realized that Halsey had not come, her expression changed. From tense watchfulness to relief, and now again to absolute despair, her face was an open page.

"Halsey?" I asked unceremoniously, ignoring the stranger. "Did he-not meet you?"

"No." Mr. Jamieson looked slightly surprised. "I rather expected the car, but we got up all right."

"You didn't see him at all?" Louise demanded breathlessly.

Mr. Jamieson knew her at once, although he had not seen her before. She had kept to her rooms until the morning she left.

"No, Miss Armstrong," he said. "I saw nothing of him. What is wrong?"

"Then we shall have to find him," she asserted. "Every instant is precious. Mr. Jamieson, I have reason for believing that he is in danger, but I don't know what it is. Only-he must be found."

The stocky man had said nothing. Now, however, he went quickly toward the door.

"I'll catch the hack down the road and hold it," he said. "Is the gentleman down in the town?"

"Mr. Jamieson," Louise said impulsively, "I can use the hack. Take my horse and trap outside and drive like mad. Try to find the Dragon Fly-it ought to be easy to trace. I can think of no other way. Only, don't lose a moment."

The new detective had gone, and a moment later Jamieson went rapidly down the drive, the cob's feet striking fire at every step. Louise stood looking after them. When she turned around she faced Gertrude, who stood indignant, almost tragic, in the hall.

"You *know* what threatens Halsey, Louise," she said accusingly. "I believe you know this whole horrible thing, this mystery that we are struggling with. If anything happens to Halsey, I shall never forgive you."

Louise only raised her hands despairingly and dropped them again.

"He is as dear to me as he is to you," she said sadly. "I tried to warn him."

"Nonsense!" I said, as briskly as I could. "We are making a lot of trouble out of something perhaps very small. Halsey was probably late-he is always late. Any moment we may hear the car coming up the road."

But it did not come. After a half-hour of suspense, Louise went out quietly, and did not come back. I hardly knew she was gone until I heard the station hack moving off. At eleven o'clock the telephone rang. It was Mr. Jamieson.

"I have found the Dragon Fly, Miss Innes," he said. "It has collided with a freight car on the siding above the station. No, Mr. Innes was not there, but we shall probably find him. Send Warner for the car."

But they did not find him. At four o'clock the next morning we were still waiting for news, while Alex watched the house and Sam the grounds. At daylight I dropped into exhausted sleep. Halsey had not come back, and there was no word from the detective

Halsey's Disappearance

Nothing that had gone before had been as bad as this. The murder and Thomas' sudden death we had been able to view in a detached sort of way. But with Halsey's disappearance everything was altered. Our little circle, intact until now, was broken. We were no longer onlookers who saw a battle passing around them. We were the center of action. Of course, there was no time then to voice such an idea. My mind seemed able to hold only one thought: that Halsey had been foully dealt with, and that every minute lost might be fatal.

Mr. Jamieson came back about eight o'clock the next morning: he was covered with mud, and his hat was gone. Altogether, we were a sad-looking trio that gathered around a breakfast that no one could eat. Over a cup of black coffee the detective told us what he had learned of Halsey's movements the night before. Up to a certain point the car had made it easy enough to follow him. And I gathered that Mr. Burns, the other detective, had followed a similar car for miles at dawn, only to find it was a touring car on an endurance run.

"He left here about ten minutes after eight," Mr. Jamieson said. "He went alone, and at eight twenty he stopped at Doctor Walker's. I went to the doctor's about midnight, but he had been called out on a case, and had not come back at four o'clock. From the doctor's it seems Mr. Innes walked across the lawn to the cottage Mrs. Armstrong and her daughter have taken. Mrs. Armstrong had retired, and he said perhaps a dozen words to Miss Louise. She will not say what they were, but the girl evidently suspects what has occurred. That is, she suspects foul play, but she doesn't know of what nature. Then, apparently, he started directly for the station. He was going very fast-the flagman at the Carol Street crossing says he saw the car pass. He knew the siren. Along somewhere in the dark stretch between Carol Street and the depot he evidently swerved suddenly-perhaps some one in the road-and went full into the side of a freight. We found it there last night."

"He might have been thrown under the train by the force of the shock," I said tremulously. Gertrude shuddered.

"We examined every inch of track. There was-no sign."

"But surely-he can't be-gone!" I cried. "Aren't there traces in the mud-anything?"

"There is no mud-only dust. There has been no rain. And the footpath there is of cinders. Miss Innes, I am inclined to think that he has met with bad treatment, in the light of what has gone before. I do not think he has been murdered." I shrank from the word. "Burns is back in the country, on a clue we got from the night clerk at the drug-store. There will be two more men here by noon, and the city office is on the lookout."

"The creek?" Gertrude asked.

"The creek is shallow now. If it were swollen with rain, it would be different. There is hardly any water in it. Now, Miss Innes," he said, turning to me, "I must ask you some questions. Had Mr. Halsey any possible reason for going away like this, without warning?"

"None whatever."

"He went away once before," he persisted. "And you were as sure then."

"He did not leave the Dragon Fly jammed into the side of a freight car before."

"No, but he left it for repairs in a blacksmith shop, a long distance from here. Do you know if he had any enemies? Any one who might wish him out of the way?"

"Not that I know of, unless-no, I can not think of any."

"Was he in the habit of carrying money?"

"He never carried it far. No, he never had more than enough for current expenses."

Mr. Jamieson got up then and began to pace the room. It was an unwonted concession to the occasion.

"Then I think we get at it by elimination. The chances are against flight. If he was hurt, we find no trace of him. It looks almost like an abduction. This young Doctor Walker-have you any idea why Mr. Innes should have gone there last night?"

"I can not understand it," Gertrude said thoughtfully. "I don't think he knew Doctor Walker at all, and-their relations could hardly have been cordial, under the circumstances."

Jamieson pricked up his ears, and little by little he drew from us the unfortunate story of Halsey's love affair, and the fact that Louise was going to marry Doctor Walker.

Mr. Jamieson listened attentively.

"There are some interesting developments here," he said thoughtfully. "The woman who claims to be the mother of Lucien Wallace has not come back. Your nephew has apparently been spirited away. There is an organized attempt being made to enter this house; in fact, it has been entered. Witness the incident with the cook yesterday. And I have a new piece of information." He looked carefully away from Gertrude. "Mr. John Bailey is not at his Knickerbocker apartments, and I don't know where he is. It's a hash, that's what it is. It's a Chinese puzzle. They won't fit together, unless-unless Mr. Bailey and your nephew have again —"

And once again Gertrude surprised me. "They are not together," she said hotly. "I —know where Mr. Bailey is, and my brother is not with him."

The detective turned and looked at her keenly.

"Miss Gertrude," he said, "if you and Miss Louise would only tell me everything you know and surmise about this business, I should be able to do a great many things. I believe I could find your brother, and I might be able to-well, to do some other things." But Gertrude's glance did not falter.

"Nothing that I know could help you to find Halsey," she said stubbornly. "I know absolutely as little of his disappearance as you do, and I can only say this: I do not trust Doctor Walker. I think he hated Halsey, and he would get rid of him if he could."

"Perhaps you are right. In fact, I had some such theory myself. But Doctor Walker went out late last night to a serious case in Summitville, and is still there. Burns traced him there. We have made guarded inquiry at the Greenwood Club, and through the village. There is absolutely nothing to go on but this. On the embankment above the railroad, at the point where we found the machine, is a small house. An old woman and a daughter, who is very lame, live there. They say that they distinctly heard the shock when the Dragon Fly hit the car, and they went to the bottom of their garden and looked over. The automobile was there; they could see the lights, and they thought someone had been injured. It was very dark, but they could make out two figures, standing together. The women were curious, and, leaving the fence, they went back and by a roundabout path down to the road. When they got there the car was still standing, the headlight broken and the bonnet crushed, but there was no one to be seen."

The detective went away immediately, and to Gertrude and me was left the woman's part, to watch and wait. By luncheon nothing had been found, and I was frantic. I went up-stairs to Halsey's room finally, from sheer inability to sit across from Gertrude any longer, and meet her terror-filled eyes.

Liddy was in my dressing-room, suspiciously red-eyed, and trying to put a right sleeve in a left armhole of a new waist for me. I was too much shaken to scold.

"What name did that woman in the kitchen give?" she demanded, viciously ripping out the offending sleeve.

"Bliss. Mattie Bliss," I replied.

"Bliss. M. B. Well, that's not what she has on he suitcase. It is marked N. F. C."

The new cook and her initials troubled me not at all. I put on my bonnet and sent for what the Casanova liveryman called a "stylish turnout." Having once made up my mind to a course of action, I am not one to turn back. Warner drove me; he was plainly disgusted, and he steered the livery horse as he would the Dragon Fly, feeling uneasily with his left foot for the clutch, and working his right elbow at an imaginary horn every time a dog got in the way.

Warner had something on his mind, and after we had turned into the road, he voiced it.

"Miss Innes," he said. "I overheard a part of a conversation yesterday that I didn't understand. It wasn't my business to understand it, for that matter. But I've been thinking all day that I'd better tell you. Yesterday afternoon, while you and Miss Gertrude were out driving, I had got the car in some sort of shape again after the fire, and I went to the library to call Mr. Innes to see it. I went into the living-room, where Miss Liddy said he was, and half-way across to the library I heard him talking to some one. He seemed to be walking up and down, and he was in a rage, I can tell you."

"What did he say?"

"The first thing I heard was-excuse me, Miss Innes, but it's what he said, 'The damned rascal,' he said, 'I'll see him in' —well, in hell was what he said, 'in hell first.' Then somebody else spoke up; it was a woman. She said, 'I warned them, but they thought I would be afraid.'"

"A woman! Did you wait to see who it was?"

"I wasn't spying, Miss Innes," Warner said with dignity. "But the next thing caught my attention. She said, 'I knew there was something wrong from the start. A man isn't well one day, and dead the next, without some reason.' I thought she was speaking of Thomas."

"And you don't know who it was!" I exclaimed. "Warner, you had the key to this whole occurrence in your hands, and did not use it!"

However, there was nothing to be done. I resolved to make inquiry when I got home, and in the meantime, my present errand absorbed me. This was nothing less than to see Louise Armstrong, and to attempt to drag from her what she knew, or suspected, of Halsey's disappearance. But here, as in every direction I turned, I was baffled.

A neat maid answered the bell, but she stood squarely in the doorway, and it was impossible to preserve one's dignity and pass her.

"Miss Armstrong is very ill, and unable to see any one," she said. I did not believe her.

"And Mrs. Armstrong-is she also ill?"

"She is with Miss Louise and can not be disturbed."

"Tell her it is Miss Innes, and that it is a matter of the greatest importance."

"It would be of no use, Miss Innes. My orders are positive."

At that moment a heavy step sounded on the stairs. Past the maid's white-strapped shoulder I could see a familiar thatch of gray hair, and in a moment I was face to face with Doctor Stewart. He was very grave, and his customary geniality was tinged with restraint.

"You are the very woman I want to see," he said promptly. "Send away your trap, and let me drive you home. What is this about your nephew?"

"He has disappeared, doctor. Not only that, but there is every evidence that he has been either abducted, or —" I could not finish. The doctor helped me into his capacious buggy in silence. Until we had got a little distance he did not speak; then he turned and looked at me.

"Now tell me about it," he said. He heard me through without speaking.

"And you think Louise knows something?" he said when I had finished. "I don't—in fact, I am sure of it. The best evidence of it is this: she asked me if he had been heard from, or if anything had been learned. She won't allow Walker in the room, and she made me promise to see you and tell you this: don't give up the search for him. Find him, and find him soon. He is living."

"Well," I said, "if she knows that, she knows more. She is a very cruel and ungrateful girl."

"She is a very sick girl," he said gravely. "Neither you nor I can judge her until we know everything. Both she and her mother are ghosts of their former selves. Under all this, these two sudden deaths, this bank robbery, the invasions at Sunnyside and Halsey's disappearance, there is some mystery that, mark my words, will come out some day. And when it does, we shall find Louise Armstrong a victim."

I had not noticed where we were going, but now I saw we were beside the railroad, and from a knot of men standing beside the track I divined that it was here the car had been found. The siding, however, was empty. Except a few bits of splintered wood on the ground, there was no sign of the accident.

"Where is the freight car that was rammed?" the doctor asked a bystander.

"It was taken away at daylight, when the train was moved."

There was nothing to be gained. He pointed out the house on the embankment where the old lady and her daughter had heard the crash and seen two figures beside the car. Then we drove slowly home. I had the doctor put me down at the gate, and I walked to the house-past the lodge where we had found Louise, and, later, poor Thomas; up the drive where I had seen a man watching the lodge and where, later, Rosie had been frightened; past the east entrance, where so short a time before the most obstinate effort had been made to enter the house, and where, that night two weeks ago, Liddy and I had seen the strange woman. Not far from the west wing lay the blackened ruins of the stables. I felt like a ruin myself, as I paused on the broad veranda before I entered the house.

Two private detectives had arrived in my absence, and it was a relief to turn over to them the responsibility of the house and grounds. Mr. Jamieson, they said, had arranged for more to assist in the search for the missing man, and at that time the country was being scoured in all directions.

The household staff was again depleted that afternoon. Liddy was waiting to tell me that the new cook had gone, bag and baggage, without waiting to be paid. No one had admitted the visitor whom Warner had heard in the library, unless, possibly, the missing cook. Again I was working in a circle.

Who is Nina Carrington?

The four days, from Saturday to the following Tuesday, we lived, or existed, in a state of the most dreadful suspense. We ate only when Liddy brought in a tray, and then very little. The papers, of course, had got hold of the story, and we were besieged by newspaper men. From all over the country false clues came pouring in and raised hopes that crumbled again to nothing. Every morgue within a hundred miles, every hospital, had been visited, without result.

Mr. Jamieson, personally, took charge of the organized search, and every evening, no matter where he happened to be, he called us by long distance telephone. It was the same formula. "Nothing to-day. A new clue to work on. Better luck to-morrow." And heartsick we would put up the receiver and sit down again to our vigil.

The inaction was deadly. Liddy cried all day, and, because she knew I objected to tears, sniffled audibly around the corner.

"For Heaven's sake, smile!" I snapped at her. And her ghastly attempt at a grin, with her swollen nose and red eyes, made me hysterical. I laughed and cried together, and pretty soon, like the two old fools we were, we were sitting together weeping into the same handkerchief.

Things were happening, of course, all the time, but they made little or no impression. The Charity Hospital called up Doctor Stewart and reported that Mrs. Watson was in a critical condition. I understood also that legal steps were being taken to terminate my lease at Sunnyside. Louise was out of danger, but very ill, and a trained nurse guarded her like a gorgon. There was a rumor in the village, brought up by Liddy from the butcher's, that a wedding had already taken place between Louise and Doctor Walkers and this roused me for the first time to action.

On Tuesday, then, I sent for the car, and prepared to go out. As I waited at the porte-cochere I saw the under-gardener, an inoffensive, grayish-haired man, trimming borders near the house. The day detective was watching him, sitting on the carriage block. When he saw me, he got up.

"Miss Innes," he said, taking of his hat, "do you know where Alex, the gardener, is?"

"Why, no. Isn't he here?" I asked.

"He has been gone since yesterday afternoon. Have you employed him long?"

"Only a couple of weeks."

"Is he efficient? A capable man?"

"I hardly know," I said vaguely. "The place looks all right, and I know very little about such things. I know much more about boxes of roses than bushes of them."

"This man," pointing to the assistant, "says Alex isn't a gardener. That he doesn't know anything about plants."

"That's very strange," I said, thinking hard. "Why, he came to me from the Brays, who are in Europe."

"Exactly." The detective smiled. "Every man who cuts grass isn't a gardener, Miss Innes, and just now it is our policy to believe every person around here a rascal until he proves to be the other thing."

Warner came up with the car then, and the conversation stopped. As he helped me in, however, the detective said something further.

"Not a word or sign to Alex, if he comes back," he said cautiously.

I went first to Doctor Walker's. I was tired of beating about the bush, and I felt that the key to Halsey's disappearance was here at Casanova, in spite of Mr. Jamieson's theories.

The doctor was in. He came at once to the door of his consulting-room, and there was no mask of cordiality in his manner.

"Please come in," he said curtly.

"I shall stay here, I think, doctor." I did not like his face or his manner; there was a subtle change in both. He had thrown off the air of friendliness, and I thought, too, that he looked anxious and haggard.

"Doctor Walker," I said, "I have come to you to ask some questions. I hope you will answer them. As you know, my nephew has not yet been found."

"So I understand," stiffly.

"I believe, if you would, you could help us, and that leads to one of my questions. Will you tell me what was the nature of the conversation you held with him the night he was attacked and carried off?"

"Attacked! Carried off!" he said, with pretended surprise. "Really, Miss Innes, don't you think you exaggerate? I understand it is not the first time Mr. Innes has-disappeared."

"You are quibbling, doctor. This is a matter of life and death. Will you answer my question?"

"Certainly. He said his nerves were bad, and I gave him a prescription for them. I am violating professional ethics when I tell you even as much as that."

I could not tell him he lied. I think I looked it. But I hazarded a random shot.

"I thought perhaps," I said, watching him narrowly, "that it might be about-Nina Carrington."

For a moment I thought he was going to strike me. He grew livid, and a small crooked blood-vessel in his temple swelled and throbbed curiously. Then he forced a short laugh.

"Who is Nina Carrington?" he asked.

"I am about to discover that," I replied, and he was quiet at once. It was not difficult to divine that he feared Nina Carrington a good deal more than he did the devil. Our leave-taking was brief; in fact, we merely stared at each other over the waiting-room table, with its litter of year-old magazines. Then I turned and went out.

"To Richfield," I told Warner, and on the way I thought, and thought hard.

"Nina Carrington, Nina Carrington," the roar and rush of the wheels seemed to sing the words. "Nina Carrington, N. C." And I then knew, knew as surely as if I had seen the whole thing. There had been an N. C. on the suit-case belonging to the woman with the pitted face. How simple it all seemed. Mattie Bliss had been Nina Carrington. It was she Warner had heard in the library. It was something she had told Halsey that had taken him frantically to Doctor Walker's office, and from there perhaps to his death. If we could find the woman, we might find what had become of Halsey.

We were almost at Richfield now, so I kept on. My mind was not on my errand there now. It was back with Halsey on that memorable night. What was it he had said to Louise, that had sent her up to Sunnyside, half wild with fear for him? I made up my mind, as the car drew up before the Tate cottage, that I would see Louise if I had to break into the house at night.

Almost exactly the same scene as before greeted my eyes at the cottage. Mrs. Tate, the baby-carriage in the path, the children at the swing-all were the same.

She came forward to meet me, and I noticed that some of the anxious lines had gone out of her face. She looked young, almost pretty.

"I am glad you have come back," she said. "I think I will have to be honest and give you back your money."

"Why?" I asked. "Has the mother come?"

"No, but some one came and paid the boy's board for a month. She talked to him for a long time, but when I asked him afterward he didn't know her name."

"A young woman?"

"Not very young. About forty, I suppose. She was small and fair-haired, just a little bit gray, and very sad. She was in deep mourning, and, I think, when she came, she expected to go at once. But the child, Lucien, interested her. She talked to him for a long time, and, indeed, she looked much happier when she left."

"You are sure this was not the real mother?"

"O mercy, no! Why, she didn't know which of the three was Lucien. I thought perhaps she was a friend of yours, but, of course, I didn't ask."

"She was not-pock-marked?" I asked at a venture.

"No, indeed. A skin like a baby's. But perhaps you will know the initials. She gave Lucien a handkerchief and forgot it. It was very fine, black-bordered, and it had three hand-worked letters in the corner—F. B. A."

"No," I said with truth enough, "she is not a friend of mine." F. B. A. was Fanny Armstrong, without a chance of doubt!

With another warning to Mrs. Tate as to silence, we started back to Sunnyside. So Fanny Armstrong knew of Lucien Wallace, and was sufficiently interested to visit him and pay for his support. Who was the child's mother and where was she? Who was Nina Carrington? Did either of them know where Halsey was or what had happened to him?

On the way home we passed the little cemetery where Thomas had been laid to rest. I wondered if Thomas could have helped us to find Halsey, had he lived. Farther along was the more imposing burial-ground, where Arnold Armstrong and his father lay in the shadow of a tall granite shaft. Of the three, I think Thomas was the only one sincerely mourned.

A Tramp and the Toothache

The bitterness toward the dead president of the Traders' Bank seemed to grow with time. Never popular, his memory was execrated by people who had lost nothing, but who were filled with disgust by constantly hearing new stories of the man's grasping avarice. The Traders' had been a favorite bank for small tradespeople, and in its savings department it had solicited the smallest deposits. People who had thought to be self-supporting to the last found themselves confronting the poorhouse, their two or three hundred dollar savings wiped away. All bank failures have this element, however, and the directors were trying to promise twenty per cent. on deposits.

But, like everything else those days, the bank failure was almost forgotten by Gertrude and myself. We did not mention Jack Bailey: I had found nothing to change my impression of his guilt, and Gertrude knew how I felt. As for the murder of the bank president's son, I was of two minds. One day I thought Gertrude knew or at least suspected that Jack had done it; the next I feared that it had been Gertrude herself, that night alone on the circular staircase. And then the mother of Lucien Wallace would obtrude herself, and an almost equally good case might be made against her. There were times, of course, when I was disposed to throw all those suspicions aside, and fix definitely on the unknown, whoever that might be.

I had my greatest disappointment when it came to tracing Nina Carrington. The woman had gone without leaving a trace. Marked as she was, it should have been easy to follow her, but she was not to be found. A description to one of the detectives, on my arrival at home, had started the ball rolling. But by night she had not been found. I told Gertrude, then, about the telegram to Louise when she had been ill before; about my visit to Doctor Walker, and my suspicions that Mattie Bliss and Nina Carrington were the same. She thought, as I did, that there was little doubt of it.

I said nothing to her, however, of the detective's suspicions about Alex. Little things that I had not noticed at the time now came back to me. I had an uncomfortable feeling that perhaps Alex was a spy, and that by taking him into the house I had played into the enemy's hand. But at eight o'clock that night Alex himself appeared, and with him a strange and repulsive individual. They made a queer pair, for Alex was almost as disreputable as the tramp, and he had a badly swollen eye.

Gertrude had been sitting listlessly waiting for the evening message from Mr. Jamieson, but when the singular pair came in, as they did, without ceremony, she jumped up and stood staring. Winters, the detective who watched the house at night, followed them, and kept his eyes sharply on Alex's prisoner. For that was the situation as it developed.

He was a tall lanky individual, ragged and dirty, and just now he looked both terrified and embarrassed. Alex was too much engrossed to be either, and to this day I don't think I ever asked him why he went off without permission the day before.

"Miss Innes," Alex began abruptly, "this man can tell us something very important about the disappearance of Mr. Innes. I found him trying to sell this watch."

He took a watch from his pocket and put it on the table. It was Halsey's watch. I had given it to him on his twenty-first birthday: I was dumb with apprehension.

"He says he had a pair of cuff-links also, but he sold them—"

"Fer a dollar'n half," put in the disreputable individual hoarsely, with an eye on the detective.

"He is not—dead?" I implored. The tramp cleared his throat.

"No'm," he said huskily. "He was used up pretty bad, but he weren't dead. He was comin' to hisself when I"—he stopped and looked at the detective. "I didn't steal it, Mr. Winters," he whined. "I found it in the road, honest to God, I did."

Mr. Winters paid no attention to him. He was watching Alex.

"I'd better tell what he told me," Alex broke in. "It will be quicker. When Jamieson-when Mr. Jamieson calls up we can start him right. Mr. Winters, I found this man trying to sell that watch on Fifth Street. He offered it to me for three dollars."

"How did you know the watch?" Winters snapped at him.

"I had seen it before, many times. I used it at night when I was watching at the foot of the staircase." The detective was satisfied. "When he offered the watch to me, I knew it, and I pretended I was going to buy it. We went into an alley and I got the watch." The tramp shivered. It was plain how Alex had secured the watch. "Then—I got the story from this fellow. He claims to have seen the whole affair. He says he was in an empty car-in the car the automobile struck."

The tramp broke in here, and told his story, with frequent interpretations by Alex and Mr. Winters. He used a strange medley, in which familiar words took unfamiliar meanings, but it was gradually made clear to us.

On the night in question the tramp had been "pounding his ear"—this stuck to me as being graphic-in an empty box-car along the siding at Casanova. The train was going west, and due to leave at dawn. The tramp and the "brakey" were friendly, and things going well. About ten o'clock, perhaps earlier, a terrific crash against the side of the car roused him. He tried to open the door, but could not move it. He got out of the other side, and just as he did so, he heard some one groan.

The habits of a lifetime made him cautious. He slipped on to the bumper of a car and peered through. An automobile had struck the car, and stood there on two wheels. The tail lights were burning, but the headlights were out. Two men were stooping over some one who lay on the ground. Then the taller of the two started on a dog-trot along the train looking for an empty. He found one four cars away and ran back again. The two lifted the unconscious man into the empty box-car, and, getting in themselves, stayed for three or four minutes. When they came out, after closing the sliding door, they cut up over the railroad embankment toward the town. One, the short one, seemed to limp.

The tramp was wary. He waited for ten minutes or so. Some women came down a path to the road and inspected the automobile. When they had gone, he crawled into the box-car and closed the door again. Then he lighted a match. The figure of a man, unconscious, gagged, and with his hands tied, lay far at the end. The tramp lost no time; he went through his pockets, found a little money and the cuff-links, and took them. Then he loosened the gag-it had been cruelly tight-and went his way, again closing the door of the box-car. Outside on the road he found the watch. He got on the fast freight east, some time after, and rode into the city. He had sold the cuff-links, but on offering the watch to Alex he had been "copped."

The story, with its cold recital of villainy, was done. I hardly knew if I were more anxious, or less. That it was Halsey, there could be no doubt. How badly he was hurt, how far he had been carried, were the questions that demanded immediate answer. But it was the first real information we had had; my boy had not been murdered outright. But instead of vague terrors there was now the real fear that he might be lying in some strange hospital receiving the casual attention commonly given to the charity cases. Even this, had we known it, would have been paradise to the terrible truth. I wake yet and feel myself cold and trembling with the horror of Halsey's situation for three days after his disappearance.

Mr. Winters and Alex disposed of the tramp with a warning. It was evident he had told us all he knew. We had occasion, within a day or two, to be doubly thankful that we had given him his freedom. When Mr. Jamieson telephoned that night we had news for him; he told me what I had not realized before-that it would not be possible to find Halsey at once, even with this clue. The cars by this time, three days, might be scattered over the Union.

But he said to keep on hoping, that it was the best news we had had. And in the meantime, consumed with anxiety as we were, things were happening at the house in rapid succession.

We had one peaceful day-then Liddy took sick in the night. I went in when I heard her groaning, and found her with a hot-water bottle to her face, and her right cheek swollen until it was glassy.

"Toothache?" I asked, not too gently. "You deserve it. A woman of your age, who would rather go around with an exposed nerve in her head than have the tooth pulled! It would be over in a moment."

"So would hanging," Liddy protested, from behind the hot-water bottle.

I was hunting around for cotton and laudanum.

"You have a tooth just like it yourself, Miss Rachel," she whimpered. "And I'm sure Doctor Boyle's been trying to take it out for years."

There was no laudanum, and Liddy made a terrible fuss when I proposed carbolic acid, just because I had put too much on the cotton once and burned her mouth. I'm sure it never did her any permanent harm; indeed, the doctor said afterward that living on liquid diet had been a splendid rest for her stomach. But she would have none of the acid, and she kept me awake groaning, so at last I got up and went to Gertrude's door. To my surprise, it was locked.

I went around by the hall and into her bedroom that way. The bed was turned down, and her dressing-gown and night-dress lay ready in the little room next, but Gertrude was not there. She had not undressed.

I don't know what terrible thoughts came to me in the minute I stood there. Through the door I could hear Liddy grumbling, with a squeal now and then when the pain stabbed harder. Then, automatically, I got the laudanum and went back to her.

It was fully a half-hour before Liddy's groans subsided. At intervals I went to the door into the hall and looked out, but I saw and heard nothing suspicious. Finally, when Liddy had dropped into a doze, I even ventured as far as the head of the circular staircase, but there floated up to me only the even breathing of Winters, the night detective, sleeping just inside the entry. And then, far off, I heard the rapping noise that had lured Louise down the staircase that other night, two weeks before. It was over my head, and very faint-three or four short muffled taps, a pause, and then again, stealthily repeated.

The sound of Mr. Winters' breathing was comforting; with the thought that there was help within call, something kept me from waking him. I did not move for a moment; ridiculous things Liddy had said about a ghost—I am not at all superstitious, except, perhaps, in the middle of the night, with everything dark-things like that came back to me. Almost beside me was the clothes chute. I could feel it, but I could see nothing. As I stood, listening intently, I heard a sound near me. It was vague, indefinite. Then it ceased; there was an uneasy movement and a grunt from the foot of the circular staircase, and silence again.

I stood perfectly still, hardly daring to breathe.

Then I knew I had been right. Some one was stealthily-passing the head of the staircase and coming toward me in the dark. I leaned against the wall for support-my knees were giving way. The steps were close now, and suddenly I thought of Gertrude. Of course it was Gertrude. I put out one hand in front of me, but I touched nothing. My voice almost refused me, but I managed to gasp out, "Gertrude!"

"Good Lord!" a man's voice exclaimed, just beside me. And then I collapsed. I felt myself going, felt some one catch me, a horrible nausea-that was all I remembered.

When I came to it was dawn. I was lying on the bed in Louise's room, with the cherub on the ceiling staring down at me, and there was a blanket from my own bed thrown over me. I felt weak and dizzy, but I managed to get up and totter to the door. At the foot of the circular staircase Mr. Winters was still asleep. Hardly able to stand, I crept back to my room. The door into Gertrude's room was no longer locked: she was sleeping like a tired child. And in my dressing-room Liddy hugged a cold hot-water bottle, and mumbled in her sleep.

"There's some things you can't hold with handcuffs," she was muttering thickly.

A Scrap of Paper

For the first time in twenty years, I kept my bed that day. Liddy was alarmed to the point of hysteria, and sent for Doctor Stewart just after breakfast. Gertrude spent the morning with me, reading something—I forget what. I was too busy with my thoughts to listen. I had said nothing to the two detectives. If Mr. Jamieson had been there, I should have told him everything, but I could not go to these strange men and tell them my niece had been missing in the middle of the night; that she had not gone to bed at all; that while I was searching for her through the house, I had met a stranger who, when I fainted, had carried me into a room and left me there, to get better or not, as it might happen.

The whole situation was terrible: had the issues been less vital, it would have been absurd. Here we were, guarded day and night by private detectives, with an extra man to watch the grounds, and yet we might as well have lived in a Japanese paper house, for all the protection we had.

And there was something else: the man I had met in the darkness had been even more startled than I, and about his voice, when he muttered his muffled exclamation, there was something vaguely familiar. All that morning, while Gertrude read aloud, and Liddy watched for the doctor, I was puzzling over that voice, without result.

And there were other things, too. I wondered what Gertrude's absence from her room had to do with it all, or if it had any connection. I tried to think that she had heard the rapping noises before I did and gone to investigate, but I'm afraid I was a moral coward that day. I could not ask her.

Perhaps the diversion was good for me. It took my mind from Halsey, and the story we had heard the night before. The day, however, was a long vigil, with every ring of the telephone full of possibilities. Doctor Walker came up, some time just after luncheon, and asked for me.

"Go down and see him," I instructed Gertrude. "Tell him I am out-for mercy's sake don't say I'm sick. Find out what he wants, and from this time on, instruct the servants that he is not to be admitted. I loathe that man."

Gertrude came back very soon, her face rather flushed.

"He came to ask us to get out," she said, picking up her book with a jerk. "He says Louise Armstrong wants to come here, now that she is recovering."

"And what did you say?"

"I said we were very sorry we could not leave, but we would be delighted to have Louise come up here with us. He looked daggers at me. And he wanted to know if we would recommend Eliza as a cook. He has brought a patient, a man, out from town, and is increasing his establishment-that's the way he put it."

"I wish him joy of Eliza," I said tartly. "Did he ask for Halsey?"

"Yes. I told him that we were on the track last night, and that it was only a question of time. He said he was glad, although he didn't appear to be, but he said not to be too sanguine."

"Do you know what I believe?" I asked. "I believe, as firmly as I believe anything, that Doctor Walker knows something about Halsey, and that he could put his finger on him, if he wanted to."

There were several things that day that bewildered me. About three o'clock Mr. Jamieson telephoned from the Casanova station and Warner went down to meet him. I got up and dressed hastily, and the detective was shown up to my sitting-room.

"No news?" I asked, as he entered. He tried to look encouraging, without success. I noticed that he looked tired and dusty, and, although he was ordinarily impeccable in his appearance, it was clear that he was at least two days from a razor.

"It won't be long now, Miss Innes," he said. "I have come out here on a peculiar errand, which I will tell you about later. First, I want to ask some questions. Did any one come out here yesterday to repair the telephone, and examine the wires on the roof?"

"Yes," I said promptly; "but it was not the telephone. He said the wiring might have caused the fire at the stable. I went up with him myself, but he only looked around."

Mr. Jamieson smiled.

"Good for you!" he applauded. "Don't allow any one in the house that you don't trust, and don't trust anybody. All are not electricians who wear rubber gloves."

He refused to explain further, but he got a slip of paper out of his pocketbook and opened it carefully.

"Listen," he said. "You heard this before and scoffed. In the light of recent developments I want you to read it again. You are a clever woman, Miss Innes. Just as surely as I sit here, there is something in this house that is wanted very anxiously by a number of people. The lines are closing up, Miss Innes."

The paper was the one he had found among Arnold Armstrong's effects, and I read it again:

> "— —by altering the plans for — —rooms, may be possible. The best way, in my opinion, would be to — —the plan for — — in one of the — —rooms — —chimney."

"I think I understand," I said slowly. "Some one is searching for the secret room, and the invaders —"

"And the holes in the plaster —"

"Have been in the progress of his —"

"Or her-investigations."

"Her?" I asked.

"Miss Innes," the detective said, getting up, "I believe that somewhere in the walls of this house is hidden some of the money, at least, from the Traders' Bank. I believe, just as surely, that young Walker brought home from California the knowledge of something of the sort and, failing in his effort to reinstall Mrs. Armstrong and her daughter here, he, or a confederate, has tried to break into the house. On two occasions I think he succeeded."

"On three, at least," I corrected. And then I told him about the night before. "I have been thinking hard," I concluded, "and I do not believe the man at the head of the circular staircase was Doctor Walker. I don't think he could have got in, and the voice was not his."

Mr. Jamieson got up and paced the floor, his hands behind him.

"There is something else that puzzles me," he said, stepping before me. "Who and what is the woman Nina Carrington? If it was she who came here as Mattie Bliss, what did she tell Halsey that sent him racing to Doctor Walker's, and then to Miss Armstrong? If we could find that woman we would have the whole thing."

"Mr. Jamieson, did you ever think that Paul Armstrong might not have died a natural death?"

"That is the thing we are going to try to find out," he replied. And then Gertrude came in, announcing a man below to see Mr. Jamieson.

"I want you present at this interview, Miss Innes," he said. "May Riggs come up? He has left Doctor Walker and he has something he wants to tell us."

Riggs came into the room diffidently, but Mr. Jamieson put him at his ease. He kept a careful eye on me, however, and slid into a chair by the door when he was asked to sit down.

"Now, Riggs," began Mr. Jamieson kindly. "You are to say what you have to say before this lady."

"You promised you'd keep it quiet, Mr. Jamieson." Riggs plainly did not trust me. There was nothing friendly in the glance he turned on me.

"Yes, yes. You will be protected. But, first of all, did you bring what you promised?"

Riggs produced a roll of papers from under his coat, and handed them over. Mr. Jamieson examined them with lively satisfaction, and passed them to me. "The blue-prints of Sunnyside," he said. "What did I tell you? Now, Riggs, we are ready."

"I'd never have come to you, Mr. Jamieson," he began, "if it hadn't been for Miss Armstrong. When Mr. Innes was spirited away, like, and Miss Louise got sick because of it, I thought things had gone far enough. I'd done some things for the doctor before that wouldn't just bear looking into, but I turned a bit squeamish."

"Did you help with that?" I asked, leaning forward.

"No, ma'm. I didn't even know of it until the next day, when it came out in the Casanova *Weekly Ledger*. But I know who did it, all right. I'd better start at the beginning.

"When Doctor Walker went away to California with the Armstrong family, there was talk in the town that when he came back he would be married to Miss Armstrong, and we all expected it. First thing I knew, I got a letter from him, in the west. He seemed to be excited, and he said Miss Armstrong had taken a sudden notion to go home and he sent me some money. I was to watch for her, to see if she went to Sunnyside, and wherever she was, not to lose sight of her until he got home. I traced her to the lodge, and I guess I scared you on the drive one night, Miss Innes."

"And Rosie!" I ejaculated.

Riggs grinned sheepishly.

"I only wanted to make sure Miss Louise was there. Rosie started to run, and I tried to stop her and tell her some sort of a story to account for my being there. But she wouldn't wait."

"And the broken china-in the basket?"

"Well, broken china's death to rubber tires," he said. "I hadn't any complaint against you people here, and the Dragon Fly was a good car."

So Rosie's highwayman was explained.

"Well, I telegraphed the doctor where Miss Louise was and I kept an eye on her. Just a day or so before they came home with the body, I got another letter, telling me to watch for a woman who had been pitted with smallpox. Her name was Carrington, and the doctor made things pretty strong. If I found any such woman loafing around, I was not to lose sight of her for a minute until the doctor got back.

"Well, I would have had my hands full, but the other woman didn't show up for a good while, and when she did the doctor was home."

"Riggs," I asked suddenly, "did you get into this house a day or two after I took it, at night?"

"I did not, Miss Innes. I have never been in the house before. Well, the Carrington woman didn't show up until the night Mr. Halsey disappeared. She came to the office late, and the doctor was out. She waited around, walking the floor and working herself into a passion. When the doctor didn't come back, she was in an awful way. She wanted me to hunt him, and when he didn't appear, she called him names; said he couldn't fool her. There was murder being done, and she would see him swing for it.

"She struck me as being an ugly customer, and when she left, about eleven o'clock, and went across to the Armstrong place, I was not far behind her. She walked all around the house first, looking up at the windows. Then she rang the bell, and the minute the door was opened she was through it, and into the hall."

"How long did she stay?"

"That's the queer part of it," Riggs said eagerly. "She didn't come out that night at all. I went to bed at daylight, and that was the last I heard of her until the next day, when I saw her on a truck at the station, covered with a sheet. She'd been struck by the express and you would hardly have known her-dead, of course. I think she stayed all night in the Armstrong house, and the agent said she was crossing the track to take the up-train to town when the express struck her."

"Another circle!" I exclaimed. "Then we are just where we started."

"Not so bad as that, Miss Innes," Riggs said eagerly. "Nina Carrington came from the town in California where Mr. Armstrong died. Why was the doctor so afraid of her? The Carrington woman knew something. I lived with Doctor Walker seven years, and I know him well. There are few things he is afraid of. I think he killed Mr. Armstrong out in the west somewhere, that's what I think. What else he did I don't know-but he dismissed me and pretty nearly throttled me-for telling Mr. Jamieson here about Mr. Innes' having been at his office the night he disappeared, and about my hearing them quarreling."

"What was it Warner overheard the woman say to Mr. Innes, in the library?" the detective asked me.

"She said 'I knew there was something wrong from the start. A man isn't well one day and dead the next without some reason.'"

How perfectly it all seemed to fit!

When Churchyards Yawn

It was on Wednesday Riggs told us the story of his connection with some incidents that had been previously unexplained. Halsey had been gone since the Friday night before, and with the passage of each day I felt that his chances were lessening. I knew well enough that he might be carried thousands of miles in the box-car, locked in, perhaps, without water or food. I had read of cases where bodies had been found locked in cars on isolated sidings in the west, and my spirits went down with every hour.

His recovery was destined to be almost as sudden as his disappearance, and was due directly to the tramp Alex had brought to Sunnyside. It seems the man was grateful for his release, and when he learned some thing of Halsey's whereabouts from another member of his fraternity-for it is a fraternity-he was prompt in letting us know.

On Wednesday evening Mr. Jamieson, who had been down at the Armstrong house trying to see Louise-and failing-was met near the gate at Sunnyside by an individual precisely as repulsive and unkempt as the one Alex had captured. The man knew the detective, and he gave him a piece of dirty paper, on which was scrawled the words —"He's at City Hospital, Johnsville." The tramp who brought the paper pretended to know nothing, except this: the paper had been passed along from a "hobo" in Johnsville, who seemed to know the information would be valuable to us.

Again the long distance telephone came into requisition. Mr. Jamieson called the hospital, while we crowded around him. And when there was no longer any doubt that it was Halsey, and that he would probably recover, we all laughed and cried together. I am sure I kissed Liddy, and I have had terrible moments since when I seem to remember kissing Mr. Jamieson, too, in the excitement.

Anyhow, by eleven o'clock that night Gertrude was on her way to Johnsville, three hundred and eighty miles away, accompanied by Rosie. The domestic force was now down to Mary Anne and Liddy, with the under-gardener's wife coming every day to help out. Fortunately, Warner and the detectives were keeping bachelor hall in the lodge. Out of deference to Liddy they washed their dishes once a day, and they concocted queer messes, according to their several abilities. They had one triumph that they ate regularly for breakfast, and that clung to their clothes and their hair the rest of the day. It was bacon, hardtack and onions, fried together. They were almost pathetically grateful, however, I noticed, for an occasional broiled tenderloin.

It was not until Gertrude and Rosie had gone and Sunnyside had settled down for the night, with Winters at the foot of the staircase, that Mr. Jamieson broached a subject he had evidently planned before he came.

"Miss Innes," he said, stopping me as I was about to go to my room up-stairs, "how are your nerves tonight?"

"I have none," I said happily. "With Halsey found, my troubles have gone."

"I mean," he persisted, "do you feel as though you could go through with something rather unusual?"

"The most unusual thing I can think of would be a peaceful night. But if anything is going to occur, don't dare to let me miss it."

"Something is going to occur," he said. "And you're the only woman I can think of that I can take along." He looked at his watch. "Don't ask me any questions, Miss Innes. Put on heavy shoes, and some old dark clothes, and make up your mind not to be surprised at anything."

Liddy was sleeping the sleep of the just when I went up-stairs, and I hunted out my things cautiously. The detective was waiting in the hall, and I was astonished to see Doctor Stewart with him. They were talking confidentially together, but when I came down they ceased. There were a few preparations to be made: the locks to be gone over, Winters to be instructed as to renewed vigilance, and then, after extinguishing the hall light, we crept, in the darkness, through the front door, and into the night.

I asked no questions. I felt that they were doing me honor in making me one of the party, and I would show them I could be as silent as they. We went across the fields, passing through the woods that reached almost to the ruins of the stable, going over stiles now and then, and sometimes stepping over low fences. Once only somebody spoke, and then it was an emphatic bit of profanity from Doctor Stewart when he ran into a wire fence.

We were joined at the end of five minutes by another man, who fell into step with the doctor silently. He carried something over his shoulder which I could not make out. In this way we walked for perhaps twenty minutes. I had lost all sense of direction: I merely stumbled along in silence, allowing Mr. Jamieson to guide me this way or that as the path demanded. I hardly know what I expected. Once, when through a miscalculation I jumped a little short over a ditch and landed above my shoe-tops in the water and ooze, I remember wondering if this were really I, and if I had ever tasted life until that summer. I walked along with the water sloshing in my boots, and I was actually cheerful. I remember whispering to Mr. Jamieson that I had never seen the stars so lovely, and that it was a mistake, when the Lord had made the night so beautiful, to sleep through it!

The doctor was puffing somewhat when we finally came to a halt. I confess that just at that minute even Sunnyside seemed a cheerful spot. We had paused at the edge of a level cleared place, bordered all around with primly trimmed evergreen trees. Between them I caught a glimpse of starlight shining down on rows of white headstones and an occasional more imposing monument, or towering shaft. In spite of myself, I drew my breath in sharply. We were on the edge of the Casanova churchyard.

I saw now both the man who had joined the party and the implements he carried. It was Alex, armed with two long-handled spades. After the first shock of surprise, I flatter myself I was both cool and quiet. We went in single file between the rows of headstones, and although, when I found myself last, I had an instinctive desire to keep looking back over my shoulder, I found that, the first uneasiness past, a cemetery at night is much the same as any other country place, filled with vague shadows and unexpected noises. Once, indeed—but Mr. Jamieson said it was an owl, and I tried to believe him.

In the shadow of the Armstrong granite shaft we stopped. I think the doctor wanted to send me back.

"It's no place for a woman," I heard him protesting angrily. But the detective said something about witnesses, and the doctor only came over and felt my pulse.

"Anyhow, I don't believe you're any worse off here than you would be in that nightmare of a house," he said finally, and put his coat on the steps of the shaft for me to sit on.

There is an air of finality about a grave: one watches the earth thrown in, with the feeling that this is the end. Whatever has gone before, whatever is to come in eternity, that particular temple of the soul has been given back to the elements from which it came. Thus, there is a sense of desecration, of a reversal of the everlasting fitness of things, in resurrecting a body from its mother clay. And yet that night, in the Casanova churchyard, I sat quietly by, and watched Alex and Mr. Jamieson steaming over their work, without a single qualm, except the fear of detection.

The doctor kept a keen lookout, but no one appeared. Once in a while he came over to me, and gave me a reassuring pat on the shoulder.

"I never expected to come to this," he said once. "There's one thing sure —I'll not be suspected of complicity. A doctor is generally supposed to be handier at burying folks than at digging them up."

The uncanny moment came when Alex and Jamieson tossed the spades on the grass, and I confess I hid my face. There was a period of stress, I think, while the heavy coffin was being raised. I felt that my composure was going, and, for fear I would shriek, I tried to think of something else-what time Gertrude would reach Halsey-anything but the grisly reality that lay just beyond me on the grass.

And then I heard a low exclamation from the detective and I felt the pressure of the doctor's fingers on my arm.

"Now, Miss Innes," he said gently. "If you will come over—"

I held on to him frantically, and somehow I got there and looked down. The lid of the casket had been raised and a silver plate on it proved we had made no mistake. But the face that showed in the light of the lantern was a face I had never seen before. The man who lay before us was not Paul Armstrong!

Between Two Fireplaces

What with the excitement of the discovery, the walk home under the stars in wet shoes and draggled skirts, and getting up-stairs and undressed without rousing Liddy, I was completely used up. What to do with my boots was the greatest puzzle of all, there being no place in the house safe from Liddy, until I decided to slip upstairs the next morning and drop them into the hole the "ghost" had made in the trunk-room wall.

I went asleep as soon as I reached this decision, and in my dreams I lived over again the events of the night. Again I saw the group around the silent figure on the grass, and again, as had happened at the grave, I heard Alex's voice, tense and triumphant:

"Then we've got them," he said. Only, in my dreams, he said it over and over until he seemed to shriek it in my ears.

I wakened early, in spite of my fatigue, and lay there thinking. Who was Alex? I no longer believed that he was a gardener. Who was the man whose body we had resurrected? And where was Paul Armstrong? Probably living safely in some extraditionless country on the fortune he had stolen. Did Louise and her mother know of the shameful and wicked deception? What had Thomas known, and Mrs. Watson? Who was Nina Carrington?

This last question, it seemed to me, was answered. In some way the woman had learned of the substitution, and had tried to use her knowledge for blackmail. Nina Carrington's own story died with her, but, however it happened, it was clear that she had carried her knowledge to Halsey the afternoon Gertrude and I were looking for clues to the man I had shot on the east veranda. Halsey had been half crazed by what he heard; it was evident that Louise was marrying Doctor Walker to keep the shameful secret, for her mother's sake. Halsey, always reckless, had gone at once to Doctor Walker and denounced him. There had been a scene, and he left on his way to the station to meet and notify Mr. Jamieson of what he had learned. The doctor was active mentally and physically. Accompanied perhaps by Riggs, who had shown himself not overscrupulous until he quarreled with his employer, he had gone across to the railroad embankment, and, by jumping in front of the car, had caused Halsey to swerve. The rest of the story we knew.

That was my reconstructed theory of that afternoon and evening: it was almost correct-not quite.

There was a telegram that morning from Gertrude.

"Halsey conscious and improving. Probably home in day or so.

Gertrude."

With Halsey found and improving in health, and with at last something to work on, I began that day, Thursday, with fresh courage. As Mr. Jamieson had said, the lines were closing up. That I was to be caught and almost finished in the closing was happily unknown to us all.

It was late when I got up. I lay in my bed, looking around the four walls of the room, and trying to imagine behind what one of them a secret chamber might lie. Certainly, in daylight, Sunnyside deserved its name: never was a house more cheery and open, less sinister in general appearance. There was not a corner apparently that was not open and above-board, and yet, somewhere behind its handsomely papered walls I believed firmly that there lay a hidden room, with all the possibilities it would involve.

I made a mental note to have the house measured during the day, to discover any discrepancy between the outer and inner walls, and I tried to recall again the exact wording of the paper Jamieson had found.

The slip had said "chimney." It was the only clue, and a house as large as Sunnyside was full of them. There was an open fireplace in my dressing-room, but none in the bedroom, and as I lay there, looking around, I thought of something that made me sit up suddenly. The trunk-room, just over my head, had an open fireplace and a brick chimney, and yet, there was nothing of the kind in my room. I got out of bed and examined the opposite wall closely. There was apparently no flue, and I knew there was none in the hall just beneath. The house was heated by steam, as I have said before. In the living-room was a huge open fireplace, but it was on the other side.

Why did the trunk-room have both a radiator and an open fireplace? Architects were not usually erratic! It was not fifteen minutes before I was up-stairs, armed with a tape-measure in lieu of a foot-rule, eager to justify Mr. Jamieson's opinion of my intelligence, and firmly resolved not to tell him of my suspicion until I had more than theory to go on. The hole in the trunk-room wall still yawned there, between the chimney and the outer wall. I examined it again, with no new result. The space between the brick wall and the plaster and lath one, however, had a new significance. The hole showed only one side of the chimney, and I determined to investigate what lay in the space on the other side of the mantel.

I worked feverishly. Liddy had gone to the village to market, it being her firm belief that the store people sent short measure unless she watched the scales, and that, since the failure of the Traders' Bank, we must watch the corners; and I knew that what I wanted to do must be done before she came back. I had no tools, but after rummaging around I found a pair of garden scissors and a hatchet, and thus armed, I set to work. The plaster came out easily: the lathing was more obstinate. It gave under the blows, only to spring back into place again, and the necessity for caution made it doubly hard.

I had a blister on my palm when at last the hatchet went through and fell with what sounded like the report of a gun to my overstrained nerves. I sat on a trunk, waiting to hear Liddy fly up the stairs, with the household behind her, like the tail of a comet. But nothing happened, and with a growing feeling of uncanniness I set to work enlarging the opening.

The result was absolutely *nil*. When I could hold a lighted candle in the opening, I saw precisely what I had seen on the other side of the chimney—a space between the true wall and the false one, possibly seven feet long and about three feet wide. It was in no sense of the word a secret chamber, and it was evident it had not been disturbed since the house was built. It was a supreme disappointment.

It had been Mr. Jamieson's idea that the hidden room, if there was one, would be found somewhere near the circular staircase. In fact, I knew that he had once investigated the entire length of the clothes chute, hanging to a rope, with this in view. I was reluctantly about to concede that he had been right, when my eyes fell on the mantel and fireplace. The latter had evidently never been used: it was closed with a metal fire front, and only when the front refused to move, and investigation showed that it was not intended to be moved, did my spirits revive.

I hurried into the next room. Yes, sure enough, there was a similar mantel and fireplace there, similarly closed. In both rooms the chimney flue extended well out from the wall. I measured with the tape-line, my hands trembling so that I could scarcely hold it. They extended two feet and a half into each room, which, with the three feet of space between the two partitions, made eight feet to be accounted for. Eight feet in one direction and almost seven in the other-what a chimney it was!

But I had only located the hidden room. I was not in it, and no amount of pressing on the carving of the wooden mantels, no search of the floors for loose boards, none of the customary methods availed at all. That there was a means of entrance, and probably a simple one, I could be certain. But what? What would I find if I did get in? Was the detective right, and were the bonds and money from the Traders' Bank there? Or was our whole theory wrong? Would not Paul Armstrong have taken his booty with him? If he had not, and if Doctor Walker was in the secret, he would have known how to enter the chimney room. Then-who had dug the other hole in the false partition?

Anne Watson's Story

Liddy discovered the fresh break in the trunk-room wall while we were at luncheon, and ran shrieking down the stairs. She maintained that, as she entered, unseen hands had been digging at the plaster; that they had stopped when she went in, and she had felt a gust of cold air. In support of her story she carried in my wet and muddy boots, that I had unluckily forgotten to hide, and held them out to the detective and myself.

"What did I tell you?" she said dramatically. "Look at 'em. They're yours, Miss Rachel-and covered with mud and soaked to the tops. I tell you, you can scoff all you like; something has been wearing your shoes. As sure as you sit there, there's the smell of the graveyard on them. How do we know they weren't tramping through the Casanova churchyard last night, and sitting on the graves!"

Mr. Jamieson almost choked to death. "I wouldn't be at all surprised if they were doing that very thing, Liddy," he said, when he got his breath. "They certainly look like it."

I think the detective had a plan, on which he was working, and which was meant to be a *coup*. But things went so fast there was no time to carry it into effect. The first thing that occurred was a message from the Charity Hospital that Mrs. Watson was dying, and had asked for me. I did not care much about going. There is a sort of melancholy pleasure to be had out of a funeral, with its pomp and ceremony, but I shrank from a death-bed. However, Liddy got out the black things and the crape veil I keep for such occasions, and I went. I left Mr. Jamieson and the day detective going over every inch of the circular staircase, pounding, probing and measuring. I was inwardly elated to think of the surprise I was going to give them that night; as it turned out, I *did* surprise them almost into spasms.

I drove from the train to the Charity Hospital, and was at once taken to a ward. There, in a gray-walled room in a high iron bed, lay Mrs. Watson. She was very weak, and she only opened her eyes and looked at me when I sat down beside her. I was conscience-stricken. We had been so engrossed that I had left this poor creature to die without even a word of sympathy.

The nurse gave her a stimulant, and in a little while she was able to talk. So broken and half-coherent, however, was her story that I shall tell it in my own way. In an hour from the time I entered the Charity Hospital, I had heard a sad and pitiful narrative, and had seen a woman slip into the unconsciousness that is only a step from death.

Briefly, then, the housekeeper's story was this:

She was almost forty years old, and had been the sister-mother of a large family of children. One by one they had died, and been buried beside their parents in a little town in the Middle West. There was only one sister left, the baby, Lucy. On her the older girl had lavished all the love of an impulsive and emotional nature. When Anne, the elder, was thirty-two and Lucy was nineteen, a young man had come to the town. He was going east, after spending the summer at a celebrated ranch in Wyoming-one of those places where wealthy men send worthless and dissipated sons, for a season of temperance, fresh air and hunting. The sisters, of course, knew nothing of this, and the young man's ardor rather carried them away. In a word, seven years before, Lucy Haswell had married a young man whose name was given as Aubrey Wallace.

Anne Haswell had married a carpenter in her native town, and was a widow. For three months everything went fairly well. Aubrey took his bride to Chicago, where they lived at a hotel. Perhaps the very unsophistication that had charmed him in Valley Mill jarred on him in the city. He had been far from a model husband, even for the three months, and when he disappeared Anne was almost thankful. It was different with the young wife, however. She drooped and fretted, and on the birth of her baby boy, she had died. Anne took the child, and named him Lucien.

Anne had had no children of her own, and on Lucien she had lavished all her aborted maternal instinct. On one thing she was determined, however: that was that Aubrey Wallace should educate his boy. It was a part of her devotion to the child that she should be ambitious for him: he must have every opportunity. And so she came east. She drifted around, doing plain sewing and keeping a home somewhere always for the boy. Finally, however, she realized that her only training had been domestic, and she put the boy in an Episcopalian home, and secured the position of housekeeper to the Armstrongs. There she found Lucien's father, this time under his own name. It was Arnold Armstrong.

I gathered that there was no particular enmity at that time in Anne's mind. She told him of the boy, and threatened exposure if he did not provide for him. Indeed, for a time, he did so. Then he realized that Lucien was the ruling passion in this lonely woman's life. He found out where the child was hidden, and threatened to take him away. Anne was frantic. The positions became reversed. Where Arnold had given money for Lucien's support, as the years went on he forced money from Anne Watson instead until she was always penniless. The lower Arnold sank in the scale, the heavier his demands became. With the rupture between him and his family, things were worse. Anne took the child from the home and hid him in a farmhouse near Casanova, on the Claysburg road. There she went sometimes to see the boy, and there he had taken fever. The people were Germans, and he called the farmer's wife *Grossmutter*. He had grown into a beautiful boy, and he was all Anne had to live for.

The Armstrongs left for California, and Arnold's persecutions began anew. He was furious over the child's disappearance and she was afraid he would do her some hurt. She left the big house and went down to the lodge. When I had rented Sunnyside, however, she had thought the persecutions would stop. She had applied for the position of housekeeper, and secured it.

That had been on Saturday. That night Louise arrived unexpectedly. Thomas sent for Mrs. Watson and then went for Arnold Armstrong at the Greenwood Club. Anne had been fond of Louise-she reminded her of Lucy. She did not know what the trouble was, but Louise had been in a state of terrible excitement. Mrs. Watson tried to hide from Arnold, but he was ugly. He left the lodge and went up to the house about two-thirty, was admitted at the east entrance and came out again very soon. Something had occurred, she didn't know what; but very soon Mr. Innes and another gentleman left, using the car.

Thomas and she had got Louise quiet, and a little before three, Mrs. Watson started up to the house. Thomas had a key to the east entry, and gave it to her.

On the way across the lawn she was confronted by Arnold, who for some reason was determined to get into the house. He had a golf-stick in his hand, that he had picked up somewhere, and on her refusal he had struck her with it. One hand had been badly cut, and it was that, poisoning having set in, which was killing her. She broke away in a frenzy of rage and fear, and got into the house while Gertrude and Jack Bailey were at the front door. She went up-stairs, hardly knowing what she was doing. Gertrude's door was open, and Halsey's revolver lay there on the bed. She picked it up and turning, ran part way down the circular staircase. She could hear Arnold fumbling at the lock outside. She slipped down quietly and opened the door: he was inside before she had got back to the stairs. It was quite dark, but she could see his white shirt-bosom. From the fourth step she fired. As he fell, somebody in the billiard-room screamed and ran. When the alarm was raised, she had had no time to get up-stairs: she hid in the west wing until every one was down on the lower floor. Then she slipped upstairs, and threw the revolver out of an upper window, going down again in time to admit the men from the Greenwood Club.

If Thomas had suspected, he had never told. When she found the hand Arnold had injured was growing worse, she gave the address of Lucien at Richfield to the old man, and almost a hundred dollars. The money was for Lucien's board until she recovered. She had sent for me to ask me if I would try to interest the Armstrongs in the child. When she found herself growing worse, she had written to Mrs. Armstrong, telling her nothing but that Arnold's legitimate child was at Richfield, and imploring her to recognize him. She was dying: the boy was an Armstrong, and entitled to his father's share of the estate. The papers were in her trunk at Sunnyside, with letters from the dead man that would prove what she said. She was going; she would not be judged by earthly laws; and somewhere else perhaps Lucy would plead for her. It was she who had crept down the circular staircase, drawn by a magnet, that night Mr. Jamieson had heard some one there. Pursued, she had fled madly, anywhere-through the first door she came to. She had fallen down the clothes chute, and been saved by the basket beneath. I could have cried with relief; then it had not been Gertrude, after all!

That was the story. Sad and tragic though it was, the very telling of it seemed to relieve the dying woman. She did not know that Thomas was dead, and I did not tell her. I promised to look after little Lucien, and sat with her until the intervals of consciousness grew shorter and finally ceased altogether. She died that night.

At the Foot of the Stairs

As I drove rapidly up to the house from Casanova Station in the hack, I saw the detective Burns loitering across the street from the Walker place. So Jamieson was putting the screws on-lightly now, but ready to give them a twist or two, I felt certain, very soon.

The house was quiet. Two steps of the circular staircase had been pried off, without result, and beyond a second message from Gertrude, that Halsey insisted on coming home and they would arrive that night, there was nothing new. Mr. Jamieson, having failed to locate the secret room, had gone to the village. I learned afterwards that he called at Doctor Walker's, under pretense of an attack of acute indigestion, and before he left, had inquired about the evening trains to the city. He said he had wasted a lot of time on the case, and a good bit of the mystery was in my imagination! The doctor was under the impression that the house was guarded day and night. Well, give a place a reputation like that, and you don't need a guard at all, —thus Jamieson. And sure enough, late in the afternoon, the two private detectives, accompanied by Mr. Jamieson, walked down the main street of Casanova and took a city-bound train.

That they got off at the next station and walked back again to Sunnyside at dusk, was not known at the time. Personally, I knew nothing of either move; I had other things to absorb me at that time.

Liddy brought me some tea while I rested after my trip, and on the tray was a small book from the Casanova library. It was called *The Unseen World* and had a cheerful cover on which a half-dozen sheeted figures linked hands around a headstone.

At this point in my story, Halsey always says: "Trust a woman to add two and two together, and make six." To which I retort that if two and two plus X make six, then to discover the unknown quantity is the simplest thing in the world. That a houseful of detectives missed it entirely was because they were busy trying to prove that two and two make four.

The depression due to my visit to the hospital left me at the prospect of seeing Halsey again that night. It was about five o'clock when Liddy left me for a nap before dinner, having put me into a gray silk dressing-gown and a pair of slippers. I listened to her retreating footsteps, and as soon as she was safely below stairs, I went up to the trunk-room. The place had not been disturbed, and I proceeded at once to try to discover the entrance to the hidden room. The openings on either side, as I have said, showed nothing but perhaps three feet of brick wall. There was no sign of an entrance-no levers, no hinges, to give a hint. Either the mantel or the roof, I decided, and after a half-hour at the mantel, productive of absolutely no result, I decided to try the roof.

I am not fond of a height. The few occasions on which I have climbed a step-ladder have always left me dizzy and weak in the knees. The top of the Washington monument is as impossible to me as the elevation of the presidential chair. And yet—I climbed out on to the Sunnyside roof without a second's hesitation. Like a dog on a scent, like my bearskin progenitor, with his spear and his wild boar, to me now there was the lust of the chase, the frenzy of pursuit, the dust of battle. I got quite a little of the latter on me as I climbed from the unfinished ball-room out through a window to the roof of the east wing of the building, which was only two stories in height.

Once out there, access to the top of the main building was rendered easy-at least it looked easy-by a small vertical iron ladder, fastened to the wall outside of the ball-room, and perhaps twelve feet high. The twelve feet looked short from below, but they were difficult to climb. I gathered my silk gown around me, and succeeded finally in making the top of the ladder. Once there, however, I was completely out of breath. I sat down, my feet on the top rung, and put my hair pins in more securely, while the wind bellowed my dressing-gown out like a sail. I had torn a great strip of the silk loose, and now I ruthlessly finished the destruction of my gown by jerking it free and tying it around my head.

From far below the smallest sounds came up with peculiar distinctness. I could hear the paper boy whistling down the drive, and I heard something else. I heard the thud of a stone, and a spit, followed by a long and startled *meiou* from Beulah. I forgot my fear of a height, and advanced boldly almost to the edge of the roof.

It was half-past six by that time, and growing dusk.

"You boy, down there!" I called.

The paper boy turned and looked around. Then, seeing nobody, he raised his eyes. It was a moment before he located me: when he did, he stood for one moment as if paralyzed, then he gave a horrible yell, and dropping his papers, bolted across the lawn to the road without stopping to look around. Once he fell, and his impetus was so great that he turned an involuntary somersault. He was up and off again without any perceptible pause, and he leaped the hedge-which I am sure under ordinary stress would have been a feat for a man.

I am glad in this way to settle the Gray Lady story, which is still a choice morsel in Casanova. I believe the moral deduced by the village was that it is always unlucky to throw a stone at a black cat.

With Johnny Sweeny a cloud of dust down the road, and the dinner-hour approaching, I hurried on with my investigations. Luckily, the roof was flat, and I was able to go over every inch of it. But the result was disappointing; no trap-door revealed itself, no glass window; nothing but a couple of pipes two inches across, and standing perhaps eighteen inches high and three feet apart, with a cap to prevent rain from entering and raised to permit the passage of air. I picked up a pebble from the roof and dropped it down, listening with my ear at one of the pipes. I could hear it strike on something with a sharp, metallic sound, but it was impossible for me to tell how far it had gone.

I gave up finally and went down the ladder again, getting in through the ball-room window without being observed. I went back at once to the trunk-room, and, sitting down on a box, I gave my mind, as consistently as I could, to the problem before me. If the pipes in the roof were ventilators to the secret room, and there was no trap-door above, the entrance was probably in one of the two rooms between which it lay-unless, indeed, the room had been built, and the opening then closed with a brick and mortar wall.

The mantel fascinated me. Made of wood and carved, the more I looked the more I wondered that I had not noticed before the absurdity of such a mantel in such a place. It was covered with scrolls and panels, and finally, by the merest accident, I pushed one of the panels to the side. It moved easily, revealing a small brass knob.

It is not necessary to detail the fluctuations of hope and despair, and not a little fear of what lay beyond, with which I twisted and turned the knob. It moved, but nothing seemed to happen, and then I discovered the trouble. I pushed the knob vigorously to one side, and the whole mantel swung loose from the wall almost a foot, revealing a cavernous space beyond.

I took a long breath, closed the door from the trunk-room into the hall-thank Heaven, I did not lock it-and pulling the mantel-door wide open, I stepped into the chimney-room. I had time to get a hazy view of a small portable safe, a common wooden table and a chair-then the mantel door swung to, and clicked behind me. I stood quite still for a moment, in the darkness, unable to comprehend what had happened. Then I turned and beat furiously at the door with my fists. It was closed and locked again, and my fingers in the darkness slid over a smooth wooden surface without a sign of a knob.

I was furiously angry-at myself, at the mantel door, at everything. I did not fear suffocation; before the thought had come to me I had already seen a gleam of light from the two small ventilating pipes in the roof. They supplied air, but nothing else. The room itself was shrouded in blackness.

I sat down in the stiff-backed chair and tried to remember how many days one could live without food and water. When that grew monotonous and rather painful, I got up and, according to the time-honored rule for people shut in unknown and ink-black prisons, I felt my way around-it was small enough, goodness knows. I felt nothing but a splintery surface of boards, and in endeavoring to get back to the chair, something struck me full in the face, and fell with the noise of a thousand explosions to the ground. When I had gathered up my nerves again, I found it had been the bulb of a swinging electric light, and that had it not been for the accident, I might have starved to death in an illuminated sepulcher.

I must have dozed off. I am sure I did not faint. I was never more composed in my life. I remember planning, if I were not discovered, who would have my things. I knew Liddy would want my heliotrope poplin, and she's a fright in lavender. Once or twice I heard mice in the partitions, and so I sat on the table, with my feet on the chair. I imagined I could hear the search going on through the house, and once some one came into the trunk-room; I could distinctly hear footsteps.

"In the chimney! In the chimney!" I called with all my might, and was rewarded by a piercing shriek from Liddy and the slam of the trunk-room door.

I felt easier after that, although the room was oppressively hot and enervating. I had no doubt the search for me would now come in the right direction, and after a little, I dropped into a doze. How long I slept I do not know.

It must have been several hours, for I had been tired from a busy day, and I wakened stiff from my awkward position. I could not remember where I was for a few minutes, and my head felt heavy and congested. Gradually I roused to my surroundings, and to the fact that in spite of the ventilators, the air was bad and growing worse. I was breathing long, gasping respirations, and my face was damp and clammy. I must have been there a long time, and the searchers were probably hunting outside the house, dredging the creek, or beating the woodland. I knew that another hour or two would find me unconscious, and with my inability to cry out would go my only chance of rescue. It was the combination of bad air and heat, probably, for some inadequate ventilation was coming through the pipes. I tried to retain my consciousness by walking the length of the room and back, over and over, but I had not the strength to keep it up, so I sat down on the table again, my back against the wall.

The house was very still. Once my straining ears seemed to catch a footfall beneath me, possibly in my own room. I groped for the chair from the table, and pounded with it frantically on the floor. But nothing happened: I realized bitterly that if the sound was heard at all, no doubt it was classed with the other rappings that had so alarmed us recently.

It was impossible to judge the flight of time. I measured five minutes by counting my pulse, allowing seventy-two beats to the minute. But it took eternities, and toward the last I found it hard to count; my head was confused.

And then —I heard sounds from below me, in the house. There was a peculiar throbbing, vibrating noise that I felt rather than heard, much like the pulsing beat of fire engines in the city. For one awful moment I thought the house was on fire, and every drop of blood in my body gathered around my heart; then I knew. It was the engine of the automobile, and Halsey had come back. Hope sprang up afresh. Halsey's clear head and Gertrude's intuition might do what Liddy's hysteria and three detectives had failed in.

After a time I thought I had been right. There was certainly something going on down below; doors were slamming, people were hurrying through the halls, and certain high notes of excited voices penetrated to me shrilly. I hoped they were coming closer, but after a time the sounds died away below, and I was left to the silence and heat, to the weight of the darkness, to the oppression of walls that seemed to close in on me and stifle me.

The first warning I had was a stealthy fumbling at the lock of the mantel-door. With my mouth open to scream, I stopped. Perhaps the situation had rendered me acute, perhaps it was instinctive. Whatever it was, I sat without moving, and some one outside, in absolute stillness, ran his fingers over the carving of the mantel and-found the panel.

Now the sounds below redoubled: from the clatter and jarring I knew that several people were running up the stairs, and as the sounds approached, I could even hear what they said.

"Watch the end staircases!" Jamieson was shouting. "Damnation-there's no light here!" And then a second later. "All together now. One-two-three —"

The door into the trunk-room had been locked from the inside. At the second that it gave, opening against the wall with a crash and evidently tumbling somebody into the room, the stealthy fingers beyond the mantel-door gave the knob the proper impetus, and-the door swung open, and closed again. Only-and Liddy always screams and puts her fingers in her ears at this point-only now I was not alone in the chimney room. There was some one else in the darkness, some one who breathed hard, and who was so close I could have touched him with my hand.

I was in a paralysis of terror. Outside there were excited voices and incredulous oaths. The trunks were being jerked around in a frantic search, the windows were thrown open, only to show a sheer drop of forty feet. And the man in the room with me leaned against the mantel-door and listened. His pursuers were plainly baffled: I heard him draw a long breath, and turn to grope his way through the blackness. Then-he touched my hand, cold, clammy, death-like.

A hand in an empty room! He drew in his breath, the sharp intaking of horror that fills lungs suddenly collapsed. Beyond jerking his hand away instantly, he made no movement. I think absolute terror had him by the throat. Then he stepped back, without turning, retreating foot by foot from The Dread in the corner, and I do not think he breathed.

Then, with the relief of space between us, I screamed, ear-splittingly, madly, and they heard me outside.

"In the chimney!" I shrieked. "Behind the mantel! The mantel!"

With an oath the figure hurled itself across the room at me, and I screamed again. In his blind fury he had missed me; I heard him strike the wall. That one time I eluded him; I was across the room, and I had got the chair. He stood for a second, listening, then-he made another rush, and I struck out with my weapon. I think it stunned him, for I had a second's respite when I could hear him breathing, and some one shouted outside:

"We-can't —get-in. How-does-it-open?"

105

But the man in the room had changed his tactics. I knew he was creeping on me, inch by inch, and I could not tell from where. And then-he caught me. He held his hand over my mouth, and I bit him. I was helpless, strangling, —and some one was trying to break in the mantel from outside. It began to yield somewhere, for a thin wedge of yellowish light was reflected on the opposite wall. When he saw that, my assailant dropped me with a curse; then-the opposite wall swung open noiselessly, closed again without a sound, and I was alone. The intruder was gone.

"In the next room!" I called wildly. "The next room!" But the sound of blows on the mantel drowned my voice. By the time I had made them understand, a couple of minutes had elapsed. The pursuit was taken up then, by all except Alex, who was determined to liberate me. When I stepped out into the trunk-room, a free woman again, I could hear the chase far below.

I must say, for all Alex's anxiety to set me free, he paid little enough attention to my plight. He jumped through the opening into the secret room, and picked up the portable safe.

"I am going to put this in Mr. Halsey's room, Miss Innes," he said, "and I shall send one of the detectives to guard it."

I hardly heard him. I wanted to laugh and cry in the same breath-to crawl into bed and have a cup of tea, and scold Liddy, and do any of the thousand natural things that I had never expected to do again. And the air! The touch of the cool night air on my face!

As Alex and I reached the second floor, Mr. Jamieson met us. He was grave and quiet, and he nodded comprehendingly when he saw the safe.

"Will you come with me for a moment, Miss Innes?" he asked soberly, and on my assenting, he led the way to the east wing. There were lights moving around below, and some of the maids were standing gaping down. They screamed when they saw me, and drew back to let me pass. There was a sort of hush over the scene; Alex, behind me, muttered something I could not hear, and brushed past me without ceremony. Then I realized that a man was lying doubled up at the foot of the staircase, and that Alex was stooping over him.

As I came slowly down, Winters stepped back, and Alex straightened himself, looking at me across the body with impenetrable eyes. In his hand he held a shaggy gray wig, and before me on the floor lay the man whose headstone stood in Casanova churchyard-Paul Armstrong.

Winters told the story in a dozen words. In his headlong flight down the circular staircase, with Winters just behind, Paul Armstrong had pitched forward violently, struck his head against the door to the east veranda, and probably broken his neck. He had died as Winters reached him.

As the detective finished, I saw Halsey, pale and shaken, in the card-room doorway, and for the first time that night I lost my self-control. I put my arms around my boy, and for a moment he had to support me. A second later, over Halsey's shoulder, I saw something that turned my emotion into other channels, for, behind him, in the shadowy card-room, were Gertrude and Alex, the gardener, and-there is no use mincing matters-he was kissing her!

I was unable to speak. Twice I opened my mouth: then I turned Halsey around and pointed. They were quite unconscious of us; her head was on his shoulder, his face against her hair. As it happened, it was Mr. Jamieson who broke up the tableau.

He stepped over to Alex and touched him on the arm.

"And now," he said quietly, "how long are you and I to play *our* little comedy, Mr. Bailey?"

The Odds and Ends

Of Doctor Walker's sensational escape that night to South America, of the recovery of over a million dollars in cash and securities in the safe from the chimney room-the papers have kept the public well informed. Of my share in discovering the secret chamber they have been singularly silent. The inner history has never been told. Mr. Jamieson got all kinds of credit, and some of it he deserved, but if Jack Bailey, as Alex, had not traced Halsey and insisted on the disinterring of Paul Armstrong's casket, if he had not suspected the truth from the start, where would the detective have been?

When Halsey learned the truth, he insisted on going the next morning, weak as he was, to Louise, and by night she was at Sunnyside, under Gertrude's particular care, while her mother had gone to Barbara Fitzhugh's.

What Halsey said to Mrs. Armstrong I never knew, but that he was considerate and chivalrous I feel confident. It was Halsey's way always with women.

He and Louise had no conversation together until that night. Gertrude and Alex—I mean Jack-had gone for a walk, although it was nine o'clock, and anybody but a pair of young geese would have known that dew was falling, and that it is next to impossible to get rid of a summer cold.

At half after nine, growing weary of my own company, I went down-stairs to find the young people. At the door of the living-room I paused. Gertrude and Jack had returned and were there, sitting together on a divan, with only one lamp lighted. They did not see or hear me, and I beat a hasty retreat to the library. But here again I was driven back. Louise was sitting in a deep chair, looking the happiest I had ever seen her, with Halsey on the arm of the chair, holding her close.

It was no place for an elderly spinster. I retired to my up-stairs sitting-room and got out Eliza Klinefelter's lavender slippers. Ah, well, the foster motherhood would soon have to be put away in camphor again.

The next day, by degrees, I got the whole story.

Paul Armstrong had a besetting evil-the love of money. Common enough, but he loved money, not for what it would buy, but for its own sake. An examination of the books showed no irregularities in the past year since John had been cashier, but before that, in the time of Anderson, the old cashier, who had died, much strange juggling had been done with the records. The railroad in New Mexico had apparently drained the banker's private fortune, and he determined to retrieve it by one stroke. This was nothing less than the looting of the bank's securities, turning them into money, and making his escape.

But the law has long arms. Paul Armstrong evidently studied the situation carefully. Just as the only good Indian is a dead Indian, so the only safe defaulter is a dead defaulter. He decided to die, to all appearances, and when the hue and cry subsided, he would be able to enjoy his money almost anywhere he wished.

The first necessity was an accomplice. The connivance of Doctor Walker was suggested by his love for Louise. The man was unscrupulous, and with the girl as a bait, Paul Armstrong soon had him fast. The plan was apparently the acme of simplicity: a small town in the west, an attack of heart disease, a body from a medical college dissecting-room shipped in a trunk to Doctor Walker by a colleague in San Francisco, and palmed off for the supposed dead banker. What was simpler?

The woman, Nina Carrington, was the cog that slipped. What she only suspected, what she really knew, we never learned. She was a chambermaid in the hotel at C—, and it was evidently her intention to blackmail Doctor Walker. His position at that time was uncomfortable: to pay the woman to keep quiet would be confession. He denied the whole thing, and she went to Halsey.

It was this that had taken Halsey to the doctor the night he disappeared. He accused the doctor of the deception, and, crossing the lawn, had said something cruel to Louise. Then, furious at her apparent connivance, he had started for the station. Doctor Walker and Paul Armstrong-the latter still lame where I had shot him-hurried across to the embankment, certain only of one thing. Halsey must not tell the detective what he suspected until the money had been removed from the chimney-room. They stepped into the road in front of the car to stop it, and fate played into their hands. The car struck the train, and they had only to dispose of the unconscious figure in the road. This they did as I have told. For three days Halsey lay in the box car, tied hand and foot, suffering tortures of thirst, delirious at times, and discovered by a tramp at Johnsville only in time to save his life.

To go back to Paul Armstrong. At the last moment his plans had been frustrated. Sunnyside, with its hoard in the chimney-room, had been rented without his knowledge! Attempts to dislodge me having failed, he was driven to breaking into his own house. The ladder in the chute, the burning of the stable and the entrance through the card-room window-all were in the course of a desperate attempt to get into the chimney-room.

Louise and her mother had, from the first, been the great stumbling-blocks. The plan had been to send Louise away until it was too late for her to interfere, but she came back to the hotel at C — just at the wrong time. There was a terrible scene. The girl was told that something of the kind was necessary, that the bank was about to close and her stepfather would either avoid arrest and disgrace in this way, or kill himself. Fanny Armstrong was a weakling, but Louise was more difficult to manage. She had no love for her stepfather, but her devotion to her mother was entire, self-sacrificing. Forced into acquiescence by her mother's appeals, overwhelmed by the situation, the girl consented and fled.

From somewhere in Colorado she sent an anonymous telegram to Jack Bailey at the Traders' Bank. Trapped as she was, she did not want to see an innocent man arrested. The telegram, received on Thursday, had sent the cashier to the bank that night in a frenzy.

Louise arrived at Sunnyside and found the house rented. Not knowing what to do, she sent for Arnold at the Greenwood Club, and told him a little, not all. She told him that there was something wrong, and that the bank was about to close. That his father was responsible. Of the conspiracy she said nothing. To her surprise, Arnold already knew, through Bailey that night, that things were not right. Moreover, he suspected what Louise did not, that the money was hidden at Sunnyside. He had a scrap of paper that indicated a concealed room somewhere.

His inherited cupidity was aroused. Eager to get Halsey and Jack Bailey out of the house, he went up to the east entry, and in the billiard-room gave the cashier what he had refused earlier in the evening-the address of Paul Armstrong in California and a telegram which had been forwarded to the club for Bailey, from Doctor Walker. It was in response to one Bailey had sent, and it said that Paul Armstrong was very ill.

Bailey was almost desperate. He decided to go west and find Paul Armstrong, and to force him to disgorge. But the catastrophe at the bank occurred sooner than he had expected. On the moment of starting west, at Andrews Station, where Mr. Jamieson had located the car, he read that the bank had closed, and, going back, surrendered himself.

John Bailey had known Paul Armstrong intimately. He did not believe that the money was gone; in fact, it was hardly possible in the interval since the securities had been taken. Where was it? And from some chance remark let fall some months earlier by Arnold Armstrong at a dinner, Bailey felt sure there was a hidden room at Sunnyside. He tried to see the architect of the building, but, like the contractor, if he knew of the such a room he refused any information. It was Halsey's idea that John Bailey come to the house as a gardener, and pursue his investigations as he could. His smooth upper lip had been sufficient disguise, with his change of clothes, and a hair-cut by a country barber.

So it was Alex, Jack Bailey, who had been our ghost. Not only had he alarmed Louise-and himself, he admitted-on the circular staircase, but he had dug the hole in the trunk-room wall, and later sent Eliza into hysteria. The note Liddy had found in Gertrude's scrap-basket was from him, and it was he who had startled me into unconsciousness by the clothes chute, and, with Gertrude's help, had carried me to Louise's room. Gertrude, I learned, had watched all night beside me, in an extremity of anxiety about me.

That old Thomas had seen his master, and thought he had seen the Sunnyside ghost, there could be no doubt. Of that story of Thomas', about seeing Jack Bailey in the footpath between the club and Sunnyside, the night Liddy and I heard the noise on the circular staircase-that, too, was right. On the night before Arnold Armstrong was murdered, Jack Bailey had made his first attempt to search for the secret room. He secured Arnold's keys from his room at the club and got into the house, armed with a golf-stick for sounding the walls. He ran against the hamper at the head of the stairs, caught his cuff-link in it, and dropped the golf-stick with a crash. He was glad enough to get away without an alarm being raised, and he took the "owl" train to town.

The oddest thing to me was that Mr. Jamieson had known for some time that Alex was Jack Bailey. But the face of the pseudo-gardener was very queer indeed, when that night, in the card-room, the detective turned to him and said:

"How long are you and I going to play our little comedy, *Mr. Bailey?*"

Well, it is all over now. Paul Armstrong rests in Casanova churchyard, and this time there is no mistake. I went to the funeral, because I wanted to be sure he was really buried, and I looked at the step of the shaft where I had sat that night, and wondered if it was all real. Sunnyside is for sale-no, I shall not buy it. Little Lucien Armstrong is living with his step-grandmother, and she is recovering gradually from troubles that had extended over the entire period of her second marriage. Anne Watson lies not far from the man she killed, and who as surely caused her death. Thomas, the fourth victim of the conspiracy, is buried on the hill. With Nina Carrington, five lives were sacrificed in the course of this grim conspiracy.

There will be two weddings before long, and Liddy has asked for my heliotrope poplin to wear to the church. I knew she would. She has wanted it for three years, and she was quite ugly the time I spilled coffee on it. We are very quiet, just the two of us. Liddy still clings to her ghost theory, and points to my wet and muddy boots in the trunk-room as proof. I am gray, I admit, but I haven't felt as well in a dozen years. Sometimes, when I am bored, I ring for Liddy, and we talk things over. When Warner married Rosie, Liddy sniffed and said what I took for faithfulness in Rosie had been nothing but mawkishness. I have not yet outlived Liddy's contempt because I gave them silver knives and forks as a wedding gift.

So we sit and talk, and sometimes Liddy threatens to leave, and often I discharge her, but we stay together somehow. I am talking of renting a house next year, and Liddy says to be sure there is no ghost. To be perfectly frank, I never really lived until that summer. Time has passed since I began this story. My neighbors are packing up for another summer. Liddy is having the awnings put up, and the window boxes filled. Liddy or no Liddy, I shall advertise to-morrow for a house in the country, and I don't care if it has a Circular Staircase.

THE END

The Bat

by Mary Roberts Rinehart

Chapter One
The Shadow of the Bat

"You've got to get him, boys-get him or bust!" said a tired police chief, pounding a heavy fist on a table. The detectives he bellowed the words at looked at the floor. They had done their best and failed. Failure meant "resignation" for the police chief, return to the hated work of pounding the pavements for them-they knew it, and, knowing it, could summon no gesture of bravado to answer their chief's. Gunmen, thugs, hi-jackers, loft-robbers, murderers, they could get them all in time-but they could not get the man he wanted.

"Get him-to hell with expense—I'll give you carte blanche-but get him!" said a haggard millionaire in the sedate inner offices of the best private detective firm in the country. The man on the other side of the desk, man hunter extraordinary, old servant of Government and State, sleuthhound without a peer, threw up his hands in a gesture of odd hopelessness. "It isn't the money, Mr. De Courcy—I'd give every cent I've made to get the man you want-but I can't promise you results-for the first time in my life." The conversation was ended.

"Get him? Huh! I'll get him, watch my smoke!" It was young ambition speaking in a certain set of rooms in Washington. Three days later young ambition lay in a New York gutter with a bullet in his heart and a look of such horror and surprise on his dead face that even the ambulance-Doctor who found him felt shaken. "We've lost the most promising man I've had in ten years," said his chief when the news came in. He swore helplessly, "Damn the luck!"

"Get him-get him-get him-get him!" From a thousand sources now the clamor arose-press, police, and public alike crying out for the capture of the master criminal of a century-lost voices hounding a specter down the alleyways of the wind. And still the meshes broke and the quarry slipped away before the hounds were well on the scent-leaving behind a trail of shattered safes and rifled jewel cases-while ever the clamor rose higher to "Get him-get him-get —"

Get whom, in God's name-get what? Beast, man, or devil? A specter—a flying shadow-the shadow of a Bat.

From thieves' hangout to thieves' hangout the word passed along stirring the underworld like the passage of an electric spark. "There's a bigger guy than Pete Flynn shooting the works, a guy that could have Jim Gunderson for breakfast and not notice he'd et." The underworld heard and waited to be shown; after a little while the underworld began to whisper to itself in tones of awed respect. There were bright stars and flashing comets in the sky of the world of crime-but this new planet rose with the portent of an evil moon.

The Bat-they called him the Bat. Like a bat he chose the night hours for his work of rapine; like a bat he struck and vanished, pouncingly, noiselessly; like a bat he never showed himself to the face of the day. He'd never been in stir, the bulls had never mugged him, he didn't run with a mob, he played a lone hand, and fenced his stuff so that even the fence couldn't swear he knew his face. Most lone wolves had a moll at any rate-women were their ruin-but if the Bat had a moll, not even the grapevine telegraph could locate her.

Rat-faced gunmen in the dingy back rooms of saloons muttered over his exploits with bated breath. In tawdrily gorgeous apartments, where gathered the larger figures, the proconsuls of the world of crime, cold, conscienceless brains dissected the work of a colder and swifter brain than theirs, with suave and bitter envy. Evil's Four Hundred chattered, discussed, debated-sent out a thousand invisible tentacles to clutch at a shadow-to turn this shadow and its distorted genius to their own ends. The tentacles recoiled, baffled-the Bat worked alone-not even Evil's Four Hundred could bend him into a willing instrument to execute another's plan.

The men higher up waited. They had dealt with lone wolves before and broken them. Some day the Bat would slip and falter; then they would have him. But the weeks passed into months and still the Bat flew free, solitary, untamed, and deadly. At last even his own kind turned upon him; the underworld is like the upper in its fear and distrust of genius that flies alone. But when they turned against him, they turned against a spook—a shadow. A cold and bodiless laughter from a pit of darkness answered and mocked at their bungling gestures of hate-and went on, flouting Law and Lawless alike.

Where official trailer and private sleuth had failed, the newspapers might succeed-or so thought the disillusioned young men of the Fourth Estate-the tireless foxes, nose-down on the trail of news-the trackers, who never gave up until that news was run to earth. Star reporter, leg-man, cub, veteran gray in the trade-one and all they tried to pin the Bat like a caught butterfly to the front page of their respective journals-soon or late each gave up, beaten. He was news-bigger news each week—a thousand ticking typewriters clicked his adventures-the brief, staccato recital of his career in the morgues of the great dailies grew longer and more incredible each day. But the big news-the scoop of the century-the yearned-for headline, "Bat Nabbed Red-Handed", "Bat Slain in Gun Duel with Police"—still eluded the ravenous maw of the Linotypes. And meanwhile, the red-scored list of his felonies lengthened and the rewards offered from various sources for any clue which might lead to his apprehension mounted and mounted till they totaled a small fortune.

Columnists took him up, played with the name and the terror, used the name and the terror as a starting point from which to exhibit their own particular opinions on everything and anything. Ministers mentioned him in sermons; cranks wrote fanatic letters denouncing him as one of the even-headed beasts of the Apocalypse and a forerunner of the end of the world; a popular revue put on a special Bat number wherein eighteen beautiful chorus girls appeared masked and black-winged in costumes of Brazilian bat fur; there were Bat club sandwiches, Bat cigarettes, and a new shade of hosiery called simply and succinctly Bat. He became a fad—a catchword—a national figure. And yet-he was walking Death-cold-remorseless. But Death itself had become a toy of publicity in these days of limelight and jazz.

A city editor, at lunch with a colleague, pulled at his cigarette and talked. "See that Sunday story we had on the Bat?" he asked. "Pretty tidy-huh-and yet we didn't have to play it up. It's an amazing list-the Marshall jewels-the Allison murder-the mail truck thing-two hundred thousand he got out of that, all negotiable, and two men dead. I wonder how many people he's really killed. We made it six murders and nearly a million in loot-didn't even have room for the small stuff-but there must be more —"

His companion whistled.

"And when is the Universe's Finest Newspaper going to burst forth with 'Bat Captured by BLADE Reporter?'" he queried sardonically.

"Oh, for-lay off it, will you?" said the city editor peevishly. "The Old Man's been hopping around about it for two months till everybody's plumb cuckoo. Even offered a bonus—a big one-and that shows how crazy he is-he doesn't love a nickel any better than his right eye-for any sort of exclusive story. Bonus-huh!" and he crushed out his cigarette. "It won't be a Blade reporter that gets that bonus-or any reporter. It'll be Sherlock Holmes from the spirit world!"

"Well-can't you dig up a Sherlock?"

The editor spread out his hands. "Now, look here," he said. "We've got the best staff of any paper in the country, if I do say it. We've got boys that could get a personal signed story from Delilah on how she barbered Samson-and find out who struck Billy Patterson and who was the Man in the Iron Mask. But the Bat's something else again. Oh, of course, we've panned the police for not getting him; that's always the game. But, personally, I won't pan them;

they've done their damnedest. They're up against something new. Scotland Yard wouldn't do any better-or any other bunch of cops that I know about."

"But look here, Bill, you don't mean to tell me he'll keep on getting away with it indefinitely?"

The editor frowned. "Confidentially —I don't know," he said with a chuckle: "The situation's this: for the first time the super-crook —the super-crook of fiction-the kind that never makes a mistake-has come to life-real life. And it'll take a cleverer man than any Central Office dick I've ever met to catch him!"

"Then you don't think he's just an ordinary crook with a lot of luck?"

"I do not." The editor was emphatic. "He's much brainier. Got a ghastly sense of humor, too. Look at the way he leaves his calling card after every job —a black paper bat inside the Marshall safe —a bat drawn on the wall with a burnt match where he'd jimmied the Cedarburg Bank —a real bat, dead, tacked to the mantelpiece over poor old Allison's body. Oh, he's in a class by himself-and I very much doubt if he was a crook at all for most of his life."

"You mean?"

"I mean this. The police have been combing the underworld for him; I don't think he comes from there. I think they've got to look higher, up in our world, for a brilliant man with a kink in the brain. He may be a Doctor, a lawyer, a merchant, honored in his community by day-good line that, I'll use it some time-and at night, a bloodthirsty assassin. Deacon Brodie-ever hear of him-the Scotch deacon that burgled his parishioners' houses on the quiet? Well-that's our man."

"But my Lord, Bill —"

"I know. I've been going around the last month, looking at everybody I knew and thinking-are you the Bat? Try it for a while. You'll want to sleep with a light in your room after a few days of it. Look around the University Club-that white-haired man over there-dignified-respectable-is he the Bat? Your own lawyer-your own Doctor-your own best friend. Can happen you know-look at those Chicago boys-the thrill-killers. Just brilliant students-likeable boys-to the people that taught them-and cold-blooded murderers all the same."

"Bill! You're giving me the shivers!"

"Am I?" The editor laughed grimly. "Think it over. No, it isn't so pleasant. —But that's my theory-and I swear I think I'm right." He rose.

His companion laughed uncertainly.

"How about you, Bill-are you the Bat?"

The editor smiled. "See," he said, "it's got you already. No, I can prove an alibi. The Bat's been laying off the city recently-taking a fling at some of the swell suburbs. Besides I haven't the brains —I'm free to admit it." He struggled into his coat. "Well, let's talk about something else. I'm sick of the Bat and his murders."

His companion rose as well, but it was evident that the editor's theory had taken firm hold on his mind. As they went out the door together he recurred to the subject.

"Honestly, though, Bill-were you serious, really serious-when you said you didn't know of a single detective with brains enough to trap this devil?"

The editor paused in the doorway. "Serious enough," he said. "And yet there's one man —I don't know him myself but from what I've heard of him, he might be able-but what's the use of speculating?"

"I'd like to know all the same," insisted the other, and laughed nervously. "We're moving out to the country next week ourselves-right in the Bat's new territory."

"We-el," said the editor, "you won't let it go any further? Of course it's just an idea of mine, but if the Bat ever came prowling around our place, the detective I'd try to get in touch with would be —" He put his lips close to his companion's ear and whispered a name.

The man whose name he whispered, oddly enough, was at that moment standing before his official superior in a quiet room not very far away. Tall, reticently good-looking and well, if inconspicuously, clothed and groomed, he by no means seemed the typical detective that the editor had spoken of so scornfully. He looked something like a college athlete who had kept

113

up his training, something like a pillar of one of the more sedate financial houses. He could assume and discard a dozen manners in as many minutes, but, to the casual observer, the one thing certain about him would probably seem his utter lack of connection with the seamier side of existence. The key to his real secret of life, however, lay in his eyes. When in repose, as now, they were veiled and without unusual quality-but they were the eyes of a man who can wait and a man who can strike.

He stood perfectly easy before his chief for several moments before the latter looked up from his papers.

"Well, Anderson," he said at last, looking up, "I got your report on the Wilhenry burglary this morning. I'll tell you this about it-if you do a neater and quicker job in the next ten years, you can take this desk away from me. I'll give it to you. As it is, your name's gone up for promotion today; you deserved it long ago."

"Thank you, sir," replied the tall man quietly, "but I had luck with that case."

"Of course you had luck," said the chief. "Sit down, won't you, and have a cigar-if you can stand my brand. Of course you had luck, Anderson, but that isn't the point. It takes a man with brains to use a piece of luck as you used it. I've waited a long time here for a man with your sort of brains and, by Judas, for a while I thought they were all as dead as Pinkerton. But now I know there's one of them alive at any rate-and it's a hell of a relief."

"Thank you, sir," said the tall man, smiling and sitting down. He took a cigar and lit it. "That makes it easier, sir-your telling me that. Because —I've come to ask a favor."

"All right," responded the chief promptly. "Whatever it is, it's granted."

Anderson smiled again. "You'd better hear what it is first, sir. I don't want to put anything over on you."

"Try it!" said the chief. "What is it-vacation? Take as long as you like-within reason-you've earned it—I'll put it through today."

Anderson shook his head, "No sir—I don't want a vacation."

"Well," said the chief impatiently. "Promotion? I've told you about that. Expense money for anything-fill out a voucher and I'll O.K. it-be best man at your wedding-by Judas, I'll even do that!"

Anderson laughed. "No, sir—I'm not getting married and —I'm pleased about the promotion, of course-but it's not that. I want to be assigned to a certain case-that's all."

The chief's look grew searching. "H'm," he said. "Well, as I say, anything within reason. What case do you want to be assigned to?"

The muscles of Anderson's left hand tensed on the arm of his chair. He looked squarely at the chief. "I want a chance at the Bat!" he replied slowly.

The chief's face became expressionless. "I said-anything within reason," he responded softly, regarding Anderson keenly.

"I want a chance at the Bat!" repeated Anderson stubbornly. "If I've done good work so far—I want a chance at the Bat!"

The chief drummed on the desk. Annoyance and surprise were in his voice when he spoke.

"But look here, Anderson," he burst out finally. "Anything else and I'll-but what's the use? I said a minute ago, you had brains-but now, by Judas, I doubt it! If anyone else wanted a chance at the Bat, I'd give it to them and gladly —I'm hard-boiled. But you're too valuable a man to be thrown away!"

"I'm no more valuable than Wentworth would have been."

"Maybe not-and look what happened to him! A bullet hole in his heart-and thirty years of work that he might have done thrown away! No, Anderson, I've found two first-class men since I've been at this desk-Wentworth and you. He asked for his chance; I gave it to him-turned him over to the Government-and lost him. Good detectives aren't so plentiful that I can afford to lose you both."

"Wentworth was a friend of mine," said Anderson softly. His knuckles were white dints in the hand that gripped the chair. "Ever since the Bat got him I've wanted my chance. Now my other work's cleaned up-and I still want it."

"But I tell you —" began the chief in tones of high exasperation. Then he stopped and looked at his protege. There was a silence for a time.

"Oh, well —" said the chief finally in a hopeless voice. "Go ahead-commit suicide —I'll send you a 'Gates Ajar' and a card, 'Here lies a damn fool who would have been a great detective if he hadn't been so pig-headed.' Go ahead!"

Anderson rose. "Thank you, sir," he said in a deep voice. His eyes had light in them now. "I can't thank you enough, sir."

"Don't try," grumbled the chief. "If I weren't as much of a damn fool as you are I wouldn't let you do it. And if I weren't so damn old, I'd go after the slippery devil myself and let you sit here and watch me get brought in with an infernal paper bat pinned where my shield ought to be. The Bat's supernatural, Anderson. You haven't a chance in the world but it does me good all the same to shake hands with a man with brains and nerve," and he solemnly wrung Anderson's hand in an iron grip.

Anderson smiled. "The cagiest bat flies once too often," he said. "I'm not promising anything, chief, but —"

"Maybe," said the chief. "Now wait a minute, keep your shirt on, you're not going out bat hunting this minute, you know —"

"Sir? I thought I —"

"Well, you're not," said the chief decidedly. "I've still some little respect for my own intelligence and it tells me to get all the work out of you I can, before you start wild-goose chasing after this-this bat out of hell. The first time he's heard of again-and it shouldn't be long from the fast way he works-you're assigned to the case. That's understood. Till then, you do what I tell you-and it'll be work, believe me!"

"All right, sir," Anderson laughed and turned to the door. "And-thank you again."

He went out. The door closed. The chief remained for some minutes looking at the door and shaking his head. "The best man I've had in years-except Wentworth," he murmured to himself. "And throwing himself away-to be killed by a cold-blooded devil that nothing human can catch-you're getting old, John Grogan-but, by Judas, you can't blame him, can you? If you were a man in the prime like him, by Judas, you'd be doing it yourself. And yet it'll go hard-losing him —"

He turned back to his desk and his papers. But for some minutes he could not pay attention to the papers. There was a shadow on them —a shadow that blurred the typed letters-the shadow of bat's wings.

Chapter Two
The Indomitable Miss Van Gorder

Miss Cornelis Van Gorder, indomitable spinster, last bearer of a name which had been great in New York when New York was a red-roofed Nieuw Amsterdam and Peter Stuyvesant a parvenu, sat propped up in bed in the green room of her newly rented country house reading the morning newspaper. Thus seen, with an old soft Paisley shawl tucked in about her thin shoulders and without the stately gray transformation that adorned her on less intimate occasions, —she looked much less formidable and more innocently placid than those could ever have imagined who had only felt the bite of her tart wit at such functions as the state Van Gorder dinners. Patrician to her finger tips, independent to the roots of her hair, she preserved, at sixty-five, a humorous and quenchless curiosity in regard to every side of life, which even the full and crowded years that already lay behind her had not entirely satisfied. She was an Age and an Attitude, but she was more than that; she had grown old without growing dull or losing touch with youth-her face had the delicate strength of a fine cameo and her mild and youthful heart preserved an innocent zest for adventure.

Wide travel, social leadership, the world of art and books, a dozen charities, an existence rich with diverse experience-all these she had enjoyed energetically and to the full-but she felt, with ingenious vanity, that there were still sides to her character which even these had not brought to light. As a little girl she had hesitated between wishing to be a locomotive engineer or a famous bandit-and when she had found, at seven, that the accident of sex would probably debar her from either occupation, she had resolved fiercely that some time before she died she would show the world in general and the Van Gorder clan in particular that a woman was quite as capable of dangerous exploits as a man. So far her life, while exciting enough at moments, had never actually been dangerous and time was slipping away without giving her an opportunity to prove her hardiness of heart. Whenever she thought of this the fact annoyed her extremely-and she thought of it now.

She threw down the morning paper disgustedly. Here she was at 65 —rich, safe, settled for the summer in a delightful country place with a good cook, excellent servants, beautiful gardens and grounds-everything as respectable and comfortable as-as a limousine! And out in the world people were murdering and robbing each other, floating over Niagara Falls in barrels, rescuing children from burning houses, taming tigers, going to Africa to hunt gorillas, doing all sorts of exciting things! She could not float over Niagara Falls in a barrel; Lizzie Allen, her faithful old maid, would never let her! She could not go to Africa to hunt gorillas; Sally Ogden, her sister, would never let her hear the last of it. She could not even, as she certainly would if she were a man, try and track down this terrible creature, the Bat!

She sniffed disgruntledly. Things came to her much too easily. Take this very house she was living in. Ten days ago she had decided on the spur of the moment —a decision suddenly crystallized by a weariness of charitable committees and the noise and heat of New York-to take a place in the country for the summer. It was late in the renting season-even the ordinary difficulties of finding a suitable spot would have added some spice to the quest-but this ideal place had practically fallen into her lap, with no trouble or search at all. Courtleigh Fleming, president of the Union Bank, who had built the house on a scale of comfortable magnificence-Courtleigh Fleming had died suddenly in the West when Miss Van Gorder was beginning her house hunting. The day after his death her agent had called her up. Richard Fleming, Courtleigh Fleming's nephew and heir, was anxious to rent the Fleming house at once. If she made a quick decision it was hers for the summer, at a bargain. Miss Van Gorder had decided at once; she took an innocent pleasure in bargains. The next day the keys were hers-the servants engaged to stay on-within a week she had moved. All very pleasant and easy no doubt-adventure-pooh!

And yet she could not really say that her move to the country had brought her no adventures at all. There had been-things. Last night the lights had gone off unexpectedly and Billy, the Japanese butler and handy man, had said that he had seen a face at one of the kitchen windows — a face that vanished when he went to the window. Servants' nonsense, probably, but the servants seemed unusually nervous for people who were used to the country. And Lizzie, of course, had sworn that she had seen a man trying to get up the stairs but Lizzie could grow hysterical over a creaking door. Still-it was queer! And what had that affable Doctor Wells said to her —"I respect your courage, Miss Van Gorder-moving out into the Bat's home country, you know!" She picked up the paper again. There was a map of the scene of the Bat's most recent exploits and, yes, three of his recent crimes had been within a twenty-mile radius of this very spot. She thought it over and gave a little shudder of pleasurable fear. Then she dismissed the thought with a shrug. No chance! She might live in a lonely house, two miles from the railroad station, all summer long-and the Bat would never disturb her. Nothing ever did.

She had skimmed through the paper hurriedly; now a headline caught her eye. Failure of Union Bank-wasn't that the bank of which Courtleigh Fleming had been president? She settled down to read the article but it was disappointingly brief. The Union Bank had closed its doors; the cashier, a young man named Bailey, was apparently under suspicion; the article mentioned

Courtleigh Fleming's recent and tragic death in the best vein of newspaperese. She laid down the paper and thought-Bailey-Bailey-she seemed to have a vague recollection of hearing about a young man named Bailey who worked in a bank-but she could not remember where or by whom his name had been mentioned.

Well-it didn't matter. She had other things to think about. She must ring for Lizzie-get up and dress. The bright morning sun, streaming in through the long window, made lying in bed an old woman's luxury and she refused to be an old woman.

"Though the worst old woman I ever knew was a man!" she thought with a satiric twinkle. She was glad Sally's daughter-young Dale Ogden-was here in the house with her. The companionship of Dale's bright youth would keep her from getting old-womanish if anything could.

She smiled, thinking of Dale. Dale was a nice child-her favorite niece. Sally didn't understand her, of course-but Sally wouldn't. Sally read magazine articles on the younger generation and its wild ways. "Sally doesn't remember when she was a younger generation herself," thought Miss Cornelia. "But I do-and if we didn't have automobiles, we had buggies-and youth doesn't change its ways just because it has cut its hair." Before Mr. and Mrs. Ogden left for Europe, Sally had talked to her sister Cornelia...long and weightily, on the problem of Dale. "Problem of Dale, indeed!" thought Miss Cornelia scornfully. "Dale's the nicest thing I've seen in some time. She'd be ten times happier if Sally wasn't always trying to marry her off to some young snip with more of what fools call 'eligibility' than brains! But there, Cornelia Van Gorder-Sally's given you your innings by rampaging off to Europe and leaving Dale with you all summer and you've a lot less sense than I flatter myself you have, if you can't give your favorite niece a happy vacation from all her immediate family-and maybe find her someone who'll make her happy for good and all in the bargain." Miss Cornelia was an incorrigible matchmaker.

Nevertheless, she was more concerned with "the problem of Dale" than she would have admitted. Dale, at her age, with her charm and beauty-why, she ought to behave as if she were walking on air, thought her aunt worriedly. "And instead she acts more as if she were walking on pins and needles. She seems to like being here —I know she likes me —I'm pretty sure she's just as pleased to get a little holiday from Sally and Harry-she amuses herself-she falls in with any plan I want to make, and yet —" And yet Dale was not happy-Miss Cornelia felt sure of it. "It isn't natural for a girl to seem so lackluster and-and quiet-at her age and she's nervous, too-as if something were preying on her mind-particularly these last few days. If she were in love with somebody-somebody Sally didn't approve of particularly-well, that would account for it, of course-but Sally didn't say anything that would make me think that-or Dale either-though I don't suppose Dale would, yet, even to me. I haven't seen so much of her in these last two years ——"

Then Miss Cornelia's mind seized upon a sentence in a hurried flow of her sister's last instructions —a sentence that had passed almost unnoticed at the time-something about Dale and "an unfortunate attachment-but of course, Cornelia, dear, she's so young-and I'm sure it will come to nothing now her father and I have made our attitude plain!"

"Pshaw—I bet that's it," thought Miss Cornelia shrewdly. "Dale's fallen in love, or thinks she has, with some decent young man without a penny or an 'eligibility' to his name-and now she's unhappy because her parents don'"'t approve-or because she's trying to give him up and finds she can't. Well—" and Miss Cornelia's tight little gray curls trembled with the vehemence of her decision, "if the young thing ever comes to me for advice I'll give her a piece of my mind that will surprise her and scandalize Sally Van Gorder Ogden out of her seven senses. Sally thinks nobody's worth looking at if they didn't come over to America when our family did-she hasn't gumption enough to realize that if some people hadn't come over later, we'd all still be living on crullers and Dutch punch!"

She was just stretching out her hand to ring for Lizzie when a knock came at the door. She gathered her Paisley shawl more tightly about her shoulders. "Who is it-oh, it's only you, Lizzie," as a pleasant Irish face, crowned by an old-fashioned pompadour of graying hair, peeped in at the door. "Good morning, Lizzie—I was just going to ring for you. Has Miss Dale had breakfast—I know it's shamefully late."

"Good morning, Miss Neily," said Lizzie, "and a lovely morning it is, too-if that was all of it," she added somewhat tartly as she came into the room with a little silver tray whereupon the morning mail reposed.

We have not yet described Lizzie Allen-and she deserves description. A fixture in the Van Gorder household since her sixteenth year, she had long ere now attained the dignity of a Tradition. The slip of a colleen fresh from Kerry had grown old with her mistress, until the casual bond between mistress and servant had changed into something deeper; more in keeping with a better-mannered age than ours. One could not imagine Miss Cornelia without a Lizzie to grumble at and cherish-or Lizzie without a Miss Cornelia to baby and scold with the privileged frankness of such old family servitors. The two were at once a contrast and a complement. Fifty years of American ways had not shaken Lizzie's firm belief in banshees and leprechauns or tamed her wild Irish tongue; fifty years of Lizzie had not altered Miss Cornelia's attitude of fond exasperation with some of Lizzie's more startling eccentricities. Together they may have been, as one of the younger Van Gorder cousins had, irreverently put it, "a scream," but apart each would have felt lost without the other.

"Now what do you mean-if that were all of it, Lizzie?" queried Miss Cornelia sharply as she took her letters from the tray.

Lizzie's face assumed an expression of doleful reticence.

"It's not my place to speak," she said with a grim shake of her head, "but I saw my grandmother last night, God rest her-plain as life she was, the way she looked when they waked her-and if it was my doing we'd be leaving this house this hour!"

"Cheese-pudding for supper-of course you saw your grandmother!" said Miss Cornelia crisply, slitting open the first of her letters with a paper knife. "Nonsense, Lizzie, I'm not going to be scared away from an ideal country place because you happen to have a bad dream!"

"Was it a bad dream I saw on the stairs last night when the lights went out and I was looking for the candles?" said Lizzie heatedly. "Was it a bad dream that ran away from me and out the back door, as fast as Paddy's pig? No, Miss Neily, it was a man-Seven feet tall he was, and eyes that shone in the dark and——"

"Lizzie Allen!"

"Well, it's true for all that," insisted Lizzie stubbornly. "And why did the lights go out-tell me that, Miss Neily? They never go out in the city."

"Well, this isn't the city," said Miss Cornelia decisively. "It's the country, and very nice it is, and we're staying here all summer. I suppose I may be thankful," she went on ironically, "that it was only your grandmother you saw last night. It might have been the Bat-and then where would you be this morning?"

"I'd be stiff and stark with candles at me head and feet," said Lizzie gloomily. "Oh, Miss Neily, don't talk of that terrible creature, the Bat!" She came nearer to her mistress. "There's bats in this house, too-real bats," she whispered impressively. "I saw one yesterday in the trunk room-the creature! It flew in the window and nearly had the switch off me before I could get away!"

Miss Cornelia chuckled. "Of course there are bats," she said. "There are always bats in the country. They're perfectly harmless,—except to switches."

"And the Bat ye were talking of just then-he's harmless too, I suppose?" said Lizzie with mournful satire. "Oh, Miss Neily, Miss Neily-do let's go back to the city before he flies away with us all!"

"Nonsense, Lizzie," said Miss Cornelia again, but this time less firmly. Her face grew serious. "If I thought for an instant that there was any real possibility of our being in danger here—" she said slowly. "But-oh, look at the map, Lizzie! The Bat has been flying in this district-that's true enough-but he hasn't come within ten miles of us yet!"

"What's ten miles to the Bat?" the obdurate Lizzie sighed. "And what of the letter ye had when ye first moved in here? 'The Fleming house is unhealthy for strangers,' it said. Leave it while ye can."

"Some silly boy or some crank." Miss Cornelia's voice was firm. "I never pay any attention to anonymous letters."

"And there's a funny-lookin' letter this mornin', down at the bottom of the pile —" persisted Lizzie. "It looked like the other one. I'd half a mind to throw it away before you saw it!"

"Now, Lizzie, that's quite enough!" Miss Cornelia had the Van Gorder manner on now. "I don't care to discuss your ridiculous fears any further. Where is Miss Dale?"

Lizzie assumed an attitude of prim rebuff, "Miss Dale's gone into the city, ma'am."

"Gone into the city?"

"Yes, ma'am. She got a telephone call this morning, early-long distance it was. I don't know who it was called her."

"Lizzie! You didn't listen?"

"Of course not, Miss Neily." Lizzie's face was a study in injured virtue. "Miss Dale took the call in her own room and shut the door."

"And you were outside the door?"

"Where else would I be dustin' that time in the mornin'?" said Lizzie fiercely. "But it's yourself knows well enough the doors in this house is thick and not a sound goes past them."

"I should hope not," said Miss Cornelia rebukingly. "But-tell me, Lizzie, did Miss Dale seem-well-this morning?"

"That she did not," said Lizzie promptly. "When she came down to breakfast, after the call, she looked like a ghost. I made her the eggs she likes, too-but she wouldn't eat 'em."

"H'm," Miss Cornelia pondered. "I'm sorry if-well, Lizzie, we mustn't meddle in Miss Dale's affairs."

"No, ma'am."

"But-did she say when she would be back?"

"Yes, Miss Neily. On the two o'clock train. Oh, and I was almost forgettin'—she told me to tell you, particular-she said while she was in the city she'd be after engagin' the gardener you spoke of."

"The gardener? Oh, yes—I spoke to her about that the other night. The place is beginning to look run down-so many flowers to attend to. Well-that's very kind of Miss Dale."

"Yes, Miss Neily." Lizzie hesitated, obviously with some weighty news on her mind which she wished to impart. Finally she took the plunge. "I might have told Miss Dale she could have been lookin' for a cook as well-and a housemaid —" she muttered at last, "but they hadn't spoken to me then."

Miss Cornelia sat bolt upright in bed. "A cook-and a housemaid? But we have a cook and a housemaid, Lizzie! You don't mean to tell me — —"

Lizzie nodded her head. "Yes'm. They're leaving. Both of 'em. Today."

"But good heav — — Lizzie, why on earth didn't you tell me before?"

Lizzie spoke soothingly, all the blarney of Kerry in her voice. "Now, Miss Neily, as if I'd wake you first thing in the morning with bad news like that! And thinks I, well, maybe 'tis all for the best after all-for when Miss Neily hears they're leavin'—and her so particular-maybe she'll go back to the city for just a little and leave this house to its haunts and its bats and —"

"Go back to the city? I shall do nothing of the sort. I rented this house to live in and live in it I will, with servants or without them. You should have told me at once, Lizzie. I'm really very much annoyed with you because you didn't. I shall get up immediately—I want to give those two a piece of my mind. Is Billy leaving too?"

"Not that I know of-the heathern Japanese!" said Lizzie sorrowfully. "And yet he'd be better riddance than cook or housemaid."

"Now, Lizzie, how many times have I told you that you must conquer your prejudices? Billy is an excellent butler-he'd been with Mr. Fleming ten years and has the very highest recommendations. I am very glad that he is staying, if he is. With you to help him, we shall do very well until I can get other servants." Miss Cornelia had risen now and Lizzie was helping her with the intricacies of her toilet. "But it's too annoying," she went on, in the pauses of Lizzie's deft ministrations. "What did they say to you, Lizzie-did they give any reason? It isn't as if they were new to the country like you. They'd been with Mr. Fleming for some time, though not as long as Billy."

"Oh, yes, Miss Neily-they had reasons you could choke a goat with," said Lizzie viciously as she arranged Miss Cornelia's transformation. "Cook was the first of them-she was up late—I think they'd been talking it over together. She comes into the kitchen with her hat on and her bag in her hand. 'Good morning,' says I, pleasant enough, 'you've got your hat on,' says I. 'I'm leaving,' says she. 'Leaving, are you?' says I. 'Leaving,' says she. 'My sister has twins,' says she. 'I just got word—I must go to her right away.' 'What?' says I, all struck in a heap. 'Twins,' says she, 'you've heard of such things as twins.' 'That I have,' says I, 'and I know a lie on a face when I see it, too.'"

"Lizzie!"

"Well, it made me sick at heart, Miss Neily. Her with her hat and her bag and her talk about twins-and no consideration for you. Well, I'll go on. 'You're a clever woman, aren't you?' says she-the impudence! 'I can see through a millstone as far as most,' says I—I wouldn't put up with her sauce. 'Well!' says she, 'you can see that Annie the housemaid's leaving, too.' 'Has her sister got twins as well?' says I and looked at her. 'No,' says she as bold as brass, 'but Annie's got a pain in her side and she's feared it's appendycitis-so she's leaving to go back to her family.' 'Oh,' says I, 'and what about Miss Van Gorder?' 'I'm sorry for Miss Van Gorder,' says she-the falseness of her!—'But she'll have to do the best she can for twins and appendycitis is acts of God and not to be put aside for even the best of wages.' 'Is that so?' says I and with that I left her, for I knew if I listened to her a minute longer I'd be giving her bonnet a shake and that wouldn't be respectable. So there you are, Miss Neily, and that's the gist of the matter."

Miss Cornelia laughed. "Lizzie-you're unique," she said. "But I'm glad you didn't give her bonnet a shake-though I've no doubt you could."

"Humph!" said Lizzie snorting, the fire of battle in her eye. "And is it any Black Irish from Ulster would play impudence to a Kerrywoman without getting the flat of a hand in-but that's neither here nor there. The truth of it is, Miss Neily," her voice grew solemn, "it's my belief they're scared-both of them-by the haunts and the banshees here-and that's all."

"If they are they're very silly," said Miss Cornelia practically. "No, they may have heard of a better place, though it would seem as if when one pays the present extortionate wages and asks as little as we do here-but it doesn't matter. If they want to go, they may. Am I ready, Lizzie?"

"You look like an angel, ma'am," said Lizzie, clasping her hands.

"Well, I feel very little like one," said Miss Cornelia, rising. "As cook and housemaid may discover before I'm through with them. Send them into the livingroom, Lizzie, when I've gone down. I'll talk to them there."

An hour or so later, Miss Cornelia sat in a deep chintz chair in the comfortable living-room of the Fleming house going through the pile of letters which Lizzie's news of domestic revolt had prevented her reading earlier. Cook and housemaid had come and gone-civil enough, but so obviously determined upon leaving the house at once that Miss Cornelia had sighed and let them go, though not without caustic comment. Since then, she had devoted herself to calling up various employment agencies without entirely satisfactory results. A new cook and housemaid were promised for the end of the week-but for the next three days the Japanese butler, Billy, and Lizzie between them would have to bear the brunt of the service. Oh, yes-and then there's Dale's gardener, if she gets one, thought Miss, Cornelia. "I wish he could cook-but I don't suppose gardeners can-and Billy's a treasure. Still, its inconvenient-now, stop-Cornelia Van

Gorder-you were asking for an adventure only this morning and the moment the littlest sort of one comes along, you want to crawl out of it."

She had reached the bottom of her pile of letters-these to be thrown away, these to be answered-ah, here was one she had overlooked somehow. She took it up. It must be the one Lizzie had wanted to throw away-she smiled at Lizzie's fears. The address was badly typed, on cheap paper-she tore the envelope open and drew out a single unsigned sheet.

> If you stay in this house any longer-DEATH. Go back to the city at once and save your life.

Her fingers trembled a little as she turned the missive over but her face remained calm. She looked at the envelope-at the postmark-while her heart thudded uncomfortably for a moment and then resumed its normal beat. It had come at last-the adventure-and she was not afraid!

Chapter Three
Pistol Practice

She knew who it was, of course. The Bat! No doubt of it. And yet-did the Bat ever threaten before he struck? She could not remember. But it didn't matter. The Bat was unprecedented-unique. At any rate, Bat or no Bat, she must think out a course of action. The defection of cook and housemaid left her alone in the house with Lizzie and Billy-and Dale, of course, if Dale returned. Two old women, a young girl, and a Japanese butler to face the most dangerous criminal in America, she thought grimly. And yet-one couldn't be sure. The threatening letter might be only a joke —a letter from a crank-after all. Still, she must take precautions; look for aid somewhere. But where could she look for aid?

She ran over in her mind the new acquaintances she had made since she moved to the country. There was Doctor Wells, the local physician, who had joked with her about moving into the Bat's home territory-He seemed an intelligent man-but she knew him only slightly-she couldn't call a busy Doctor away from his patients to investigate something which might only prove to be a mare's-nest. The boys Dale had met at the country club —"Humph!" she sniffed, "I'd rather trust my gumption than any of theirs." The logical person to call on, of course, was Richard Fleming, Courtleigh Fleming's nephew and heir, who had rented her the house. He lived at the country club-she could probably reach him now. She was just on the point of doing so when she decided against it-partly from delicacy, partly from an indefinable feeling that he would not be of much help. Besides, she thought sturdily, it's my house now, not his. He didn't guarantee burglar protection in the lease.

As for the local police-her independence revolted at summoning them. They would bombard her with ponderous questions and undoubtedly think she was merely a nervous old spinster. If it was just me, she thought, I swear I wouldn't say a word to anybody-and if the Bat flew in he mightn't find it so easy to fly out again, if I am sixty-five and never shot a burglar in my life! But there's Dale-and Lizzie. I've got to be fair to them.

For a moment she felt very helpless, very much alone. Then her courage returned.

"Pshaw, Cornelia, if you have got to get help-get the help you want and hang the consequences!" she adjured herself. "You've always hankered to see a first-class detective do his detecting-well, get one-or decide to do the job yourself. I'll bet you could at that."

She tiptoed to the main door of the living-room and closed it cautiously, smiling as she did so. Lizzie might be about and Lizzie would promptly go into hysterics if she got an inkling of her mistress's present intentions. Then she went to the city telephone and asked for long distance.

When she had finished her telephoning, she looked at once relieved and a little naughty-like a demure child who has carried out some piece of innocent mischief unobserved. "My stars!"

she muttered to herself. "You never can tell what you can do till you try." Then she sat down again and tried to think of other measures of defense.

Now if I were the Bat, or any criminal, she mused, how would I get into this house? Well, that's it—I might get in 'most any way-it's so big and rambling. All the grounds you want to lurk in, too; it'd take a company of police to shut them off. Then there's the house itself. Let's see-third floor-trunk room, servants' rooms-couldn't get in there very well except with a pretty long ladder-that's all right. Second floor-well, I suppose a man could get into my bedroom from the porch if he were an acrobat, but he'd need to be a very good acrobat and there's no use borrowing trouble. Downstairs is the problem, Cornelia, downstairs is the problem.

"Take this room now." She rose and examined it carefully. "There's the door over there on the right that leads into the billiard room. There's this door over here that leads into the hall. Then there's that other door by the alcove, and all those French windows-whew!" She shook her head.

It was true. The room in which she stood, while comfortable and charming, seemed unusually accessible to the night prowler. A row of French windows at the rear gave upon a little terrace; below the terrace, the drive curved about and beneath the billiard-room windows in a hairpin loop, drawing up again at the main entrance on the other side of the house. At the left of the French windows (if one faced the terrace as Miss Cornelia was doing) was the alcove door of which she spoke. When open, it disclosed a little alcove, almost entirely devoted to the foot of a flight of stairs that gave direct access to the upper regions of the house. The alcove itself opened on one side upon the terrace and upon the other into a large butler's pantry. The arrangement was obviously designed so that, if necessary, one could pass directly from the terrace to the downstairs service quarters or the second floor of the house without going through the living-room, and so that trays could be carried up from the pantry by the side stairs without using the main staircase.

The middle pair of French windows were open, forming a double door. Miss Cornelia went over to them-shut them-tried the locks. Humph! Flimsy enough! she thought. Then she turned toward the billiard room.

The billiard room, as has been said, was the last room to the right in the main wing of the house. A single door led to it from the living-room. Miss Cornelia passed through this door, glanced about the billiard room, noting that most of its windows were too high from the ground to greatly encourage a marauder. She locked the only one that seemed to her particularly tempting-the billiard-room window on the terrace side of the house. Then she returned to the living-room and again considered her defenses.

Three points of access from the terrace to the house-the door that led into the alcove, the French windows of the living room-the billiard-room window. On the other side of the house there was the main entrance, the porch, the library and dining-room windows. The main entrance led into a hall-living-room, and the main door of the living-room was on the right as one entered, the dining-room and library on the left, main staircase in front. "My mind is starting to go round like a pinwheel, thinking of all those windows and doors," she murmured to herself. She sat down once more, and taking a pencil and a piece of paper drew a plan of the lower floor of the house.

And now I've studied it, she thought after a while, I'm no further than if I hadn't. As far as I can figure out, there are so many ways for a clever man to get into this house that I'd have to be a couple of Siamese twins to watch it properly. The next house I rent in the country, she decided, just isn't going to have any windows and doors-or I'll know the reason why.

But of course she was not entirely shut off from the world, even if the worst developed. She considered the telephone instruments on a table near the wall, one the general phone, the other connecting a house line which also connected with the garage and the greenhouses. The garage would not be helpful, since Slocum, her chauffeur for many years, had gone back to England for a visit. Dale had been driving the car. But with an able-bodied man in the gardener's house — —

She pulled herself together with a jerk.

"Cornelia Van Gorder, you're going to go crazy before nightfall if you don't take hold of yourself. What you need is lunch and a nap in the afternoon if you can make yourself take it. You'd better look up that revolver of yours, too, that you bought when you thought you were going to take a trip to China. You've never fired it off yet, but you've got to sometime today-there's no other way of telling if it will work. You can shut your eyes when you do it-no, you can't either-that's silly.

"Call you a spirited old lady, do they? Well, you never had a better time to show your spirit than now!"

And Miss Van Gorder, sighing, left the living-room to reach the kitchen just in time to calm a heated argument between Lizzie and Billy on the relative merits of Japanese and Irish-American cooking.

Dale Ogden, taxiing up from the two o'clock train some time later, to her surprise discovered the front door locked and rang for some time before she could get an answer. At last, Billy appeared, white-coated, with an inscrutable expression on his face.

"Will you take my bag, Billy-thanks. Where is Miss Van Gorder-taking a nap?"

"No," said Billy succinctly. "She take no nap. She out in srubbery shotting."

Dale stared at him incredulously. "Shooting, Billy?"

"Yes, ma'am. At least-she not shoot yet but she say she going to soon."

"But, good heavens, Billy-shooting what?"

"Shotting pistol," said Billy, his yellow mask of a face preserving its impish repose. He waved his hand. "You go srubbery. You see."

The scene that met Dale's eyes when she finally found the "srubbery" was indeed a singular one. Miss Van Gorder, her back firmly planted against the trunk of a large elm tree and an expression of ineffable distaste on her features, was holding out a blunt, deadly looking revolver at arm's length. Its muzzle wavered, now pointing at the ground, now at the sky. Behind the tree Lizzie sat in a heap, moaning quietly to herself, and now and then appealing to the saints to avert a visioned calamity.

As Dale approached, unseen, the climax came. The revolver steadied, pointed ferociously at an inoffensive grass-blade some 10 yards from Miss Van Gorder and went off. Lizzie promptly gave vent to a shrill Irish scream. Miss Van Gorder dropped the revolver like a hot potato and opened her mouth to tell Lizzie not to be such a fool. Then she saw Dale-her mouth went into a round O of horror and her hand clutched weakly at her heart.

"Good heavens, child!" she gasped. "Didn't Billy tell you what I was doing? I might have shot you like a rabbit!" and, overcome with emotion, she sat down on the ground and started to fan herself mechanically with a cartridge.

Dale couldn't help laughing-and the longer she looked at her aunt the more she laughed-until that dignified lady joined in the mirth herself.

"Aunt Cornelia-Aunt Cornelia!" said Dale when she could get her breath. "That I've lived to see the day-and they call *us* the wild generation! Why on earth were you having pistol practice, darling-has Billy turned into a Japanese spy or what?"

Miss Van Gorder rose from the ground with as much stateliness as she could muster under the circumstances.

"No, my dear-but there's no fool like an old fool-that's all," she stated. "I've wanted to fire that infernal revolver off ever since I bought it two years ago, and now I have and I'm satisfied. Still," she went on thoughtfully, picking up the weapon, "it seems a very good revolver-and shooting people must be much easier than I supposed. All you have to do is to point the-the front of it-like this and — —"

"Oh, Miss Dale, dear Miss Dale!" came in woebegone accents from the other side of the tree. "For the love of heaven, Miss Dale, say no more but take it away from her-she'll have herself all riddled through with bullets like a kitchen sieve-and me too-if she's let to have it again."

"Lizzie, I'm ashamed of you!" said Lizzie's mistress. "Come out from behind that tree and stop wailing like a siren. This weapon is perfectly safe in competent hands and —" She seemed on the verge of another demonstration of its powers.

"Miss Dale, for the dear love o' God will you make her put it away?"

Dale laughed again. "I really think you'd better, Aunt Cornelia. Or both of us will have to put Lizzie to bed with a case of acute hysteria."

"Well," said Miss Van Gorder, "perhaps you're right, dear." Her eyes gleamed. "I should have liked to try it just once more though," she confided. "I feel certain that I could hit that tree over there if my eye wouldn't wink so when the thing goes off."

"Now, it's winking eyes," said Lizzie on a note of tragic chant, "but next time it'll be bleeding corpses and ———"

Dale added her own protestations to Lizzie's. "Please, darling, if you really want to practice, Billy can fix up some sort of target range-but I don't want my favorite aunt assassinated by a ricocheted bullet before my eyes!"

"Well, perhaps it would be best to try again another time," admitted Miss Van Gorder. But there was a wistful look in her eyes as she gave the revolver to Dale and the three started back to the house.

"I should never have allowed Lizzie to know what I was doing," she confided in a whisper, on the way. "A woman is perfectly capable of managing firearms-but Lizzie is really too nervous to live, sometimes."

"I know just how you feel, darling," Dale agreed, suppressed mirth shaking her as the little procession reached the terrace. "But-oh," she could keep it no longer, "oh-you did look funny, darling-sitting under that tree, with Lizzie on the other side of it making banshee noises and —"

Miss Van Gorder laughed too, a little shamefacedly.

"I must have," she said. "But-oh, you needn't shake your head, Lizzie Allen—I am going to practice with it. There's no reason I shouldn't and you never can tell when things like that might be useful," she ended rather vaguely. She did not wish to alarm Dale with her suspicions yet.

"There, Dale-yes, put it in the drawer of the table-that will reassure Lizzie. Lizzie, you might make us some lemonade, I think-Miss Dale must be thirsty after her long, hot ride."

"Yes, Miss Cornelia," said Lizzie, recovering her normal calm as the revolver was shut away in the drawer of the large table in the living-room. But she could not resist one parting shot. "And thank God it's lemonade I'll be making-and not bandages for bullet wounds!" she muttered darkly as she went toward the service quarters.

Miss Van Gorder glared after her departing back. "Lizzie is really impossible sometimes!" she said with stately ire. Then her voice softened. "Though of course I couldn't do without her," she added.

Dale stretched out on the settee opposite her aunt's chair. "I know you couldn't, darling. Thanks for thinking of the lemonade." She passed her hand over her forehead in a gesture of fatigue. "I *am* hot-and tired."

Miss Van Gorder looked at her keenly. The young face seemed curiously worn and haggard in the clear afternoon light.

"You-you don't really feel very well, do you, Dale?"

"Oh-it's nothing. I feel all right-really."

"I could send for Doctor Wells if———"

"Oh, heavens, no, Aunt Cornelia." She managed a wan smile. "It isn't as bad as all that. I'm just tired and the city was terribly hot and noisy and ———" She stole a glance at her aunt from between lowered lids. "I got your gardener, by the way," she said casually.

"Did you, dear? That's splendid, though-but I'll tell you about that later. Where did you get him?"

"That good agency, I can't remember its name." Dale's hand moved restlessly over her eyes, as if remembering details were too great an effort. "But I'm sure he'll be satisfactory. He'll be out here this evening-he-he couldn't get away before, I believe. What have you been doing all day, darling?"

Miss Cornelia hesitated. Now that Dale had returned she suddenly wanted very much to talk over the various odd happenings of the day with her-get the support of her youth and her common sense. Then that independence which was so firmly rooted a characteristic of hers restrained her. No use worrying the child unnecessarily; they all might have to worry enough before tomorrow morning.

She compromised. "We have had a domestic upheaval," she said. "The cook and the housemaid have left-if you'd only waited till the next train you could have had the pleasure of their company into town."

"Aunt Cornelia-how exciting! I'm so sorry! Why did they leave?"

"Why do servants ever leave a good place?" asked Miss Cornelia grimly. "Because if they had sense enough to know when they were well off, they wouldn't be servants. Anyhow, they've gone-we'll have to depend on Lizzie and Billy the rest of this week. I telephoned-but they couldn't promise me any others before Monday."

"And I was in town and could have seen people for you-if I'd only known!" said Dale remorsefully. "Only," she hesitated, "I mightn't have had time-at least I mean there were some other things I had to do, besides getting the gardener and —" She rose. "I think I will go and lie down for a little if you don't mind, darling."

Miss Van Gorder was concerned. "Of course I don't mind but-won't you even have your lemonade?"

"Oh, I'll get some from Lizzie in the pantry before I go up," Dale managed to laugh. "I think I must have a headache after all," she said. "Maybe I'll take an aspirin. Don't worry, darling."

"I shan't. I only wish there were something I could do for you, my dear."

Dale stopped in the alcove doorway. "There's nothing anybody can do for me, really," she said soberly. "At least-oh, I don't know what I'm saying! But don't worry. I'm quite all right. I may go over to the country club after dinner-and dance. Won't you come with me, Aunt Cornelia?"

"Depends on your escort," said Miss Cornelia tartly. "If our landlord, Mr. Richard Fleming, is taking you I certainly shall —I don't like his looks and never did!"

Dale laughed. "Oh, he's all right," she said. "Drinks a good deal and wastes a lot of money, but harmless enough. No, this is a very sedate party; I'll be home early."

"Well, in that case," said her aunt, "I shall stay here with my Lizzie and my ouija-board. Lizzie deserves some punishment for the very cowardly way she behaved this afternoon-and the ouija-board will furnish it. She's scared to death to touch the thing. I think she believes it's alive."

"Well, maybe I'll send you a message on it from the country club," said Dale lightly. She had paused, half-way up the flight of side stairs in the alcove, and her aunt noticed how her shoulders drooped, belying the lightness of her voice. "Oh," she went on, "by the way-have the afternoon papers come yet? I didn't have time to get one when I was rushing for the train."

"I don't think so, dear, but I'll ask Lizzie." Miss Cornelia moved toward a bell push.

"Oh, don't bother; it doesn't matter. Only if they have, would you ask Lizzie to bring me one when she brings up the lemonade? I want to read about-about the Bat-he fascinates me."

"There was something else in the paper this morning," said Miss Cornelia idly. "Oh, yes-the Union Bank-the bank Mr. Fleming, Senior, was president of has failed. They seem to think the cashier robbed it. Did you see that, Dale?"

The shoulders of the girl on the staircase straightened suddenly. Then they drooped again. "Yes —I saw it," she said in a queerly colorless voice. "Too bad. It must be terrible to-to have everyone suspect you-and hunt you-as I suppose they're hunting that poor cashier."

"Well," said Miss Cornelia, "a man who wrecks a bank deserves very little sympathy to my way of thinking. But then I'm old-fashioned. Well, dear, I won't keep you. Run along-and if you want an aspirin, there's a box in my top bureau-drawer."

"Thanks, darling. Maybe I'll take one and maybe I won't—all I really need is to lie down for a while."

She moved on up the staircase and disappeared from the range of Miss Cornelia's vision, leaving Miss Cornelia to ponder many things. Her trip to the city had done Dale no good, of a certainty. If not actually ill, she was obviously under some considerable mental strain. And why this sudden interest, first in the Bat, then in the failure of the Union Bank? Was it possible that Dale, too, had been receiving threatening letters?

I'll be glad when that gardener comes, she thought to herself. He'll make a *man* in the house at any rate.

When Lizzie at last came in with the lemonade she found her mistress shaking her head.

"Cornelia, Cornelia," she was murmuring to herself, "you should have taken to pistol practice when you were younger; it just shows how children waste their opportunities."

Chapter Four
The Storm Gathers

The long summer afternoon wore away, sunset came, red and angry, a sunset presaging storm. A chill crept into the air with the twilight. When night fell, it was not a night of silver patterns enskied, but a dark and cloudy cloak where a few stars glittered fitfully. Miss Cornelia, at dinner, saw a bat swoop past the window of the dining room in its scurrying flight, and narrowly escaped oversetting her glass of water with a nervous start. The tension of waiting-waiting-for some vague menace which might not materialize after all-had begun to prey on her nerves. She saw Dale off to the country club with relief-the girl looked a little better after her nap but she was still not her normal self. When Dale was gone, she wandered restlessly for some time between living-room and library, now giving an unnecessary dusting to a piece of bric-a-brac with her handkerchief, now taking a book from one of the shelves in the library only to throw it down before she read a page.

This house was queer. She would not have admitted it to Lizzie, for her soul's salvation-but, for the first time in her sensible life, she listened for creakings of woodwork, rustling of leaves, stealthy steps outside, beyond the safe, bright squares of the windows-for anything that was actual, tangible, not merely formless fear.

"There's too much *room* in the country for things to happen to you!" she confided to herself with a shiver. "Even the night-whenever I look out, it seems to me as if the night were ten times bigger and blacker than it ever is in New York!"

To comfort herself she mentally rehearsed her telephone conversation of the morning, the conversation she had not mentioned to her household. At the time it had seemed to her most reassuring-the plans she had based upon it adequate and sensible in the normal light of day. But now the light of day had been blotted out and with it her security. Her plans seemed weapons of paper against the sinister might of the darkness beyond her windows. A little wind wailed somewhere in that darkness like a beaten child-beyond the hills thunder rumbled, drawing near, and with it lightning and the storm.

She made herself sit down in the chair beside her favorite lamp on the center table and take up her knitting with stiff fingers. Knit two-purl two-Her hands fell into the accustomed rhythm mechanically—a spy, peering in through the French windows, would have deemed her the picture of calm. But she had never felt less calm in all the long years of her life.

She wouldn't ring for Lizzie to come and sit with her, she simply wouldn't. But she was very glad, nevertheless, when Lizzie appeared at the door.

"Miss Neily."

"Yes, Lizzie?" Miss Cornelia's voice was composed but her heart felt a throb of relief.

"Can I—can I sit in here with you, Miss Neily, just a minute?" Lizzie's voice was plaintive. "I've been sitting out in the kitchen watching that Jap read his funny newspaper the wrong way and listening for ghosts till I'm nearly crazy!"

"Why, certainly, Lizzie," said Miss Cornelia primly. "Though," she added doubtfully, "I really shouldn't pamper your absurd fears, I suppose, but——"

"Oh, please, Miss Neily!"

"Very well," said Miss Cornelia brightly. "You can sit here, Lizzie-and help me work the ouija-board. That will take your mind off listening for things!"

Lizzie groaned. "You know I'd rather be shot than touch that uncanny ouijie!" she said dolefully. "It gives me the creeps every time I put my hands on it!"

"Well, of course, if you'd rather sit in the kitchen, Lizzie——"

"Oh, give me the ouijie!" said Lizzie in tones of heartbreak. "I'd rather be shot and stabbed than stay in the kitchen any more."

"Very well," said Miss Cornelia, "it's your own decision, Lizzie-remember that." Her needles clicked on. "I'll just finish this row before we start," she said. "You might call up the light company in the meantime, Lizzie-there seems to be a storm coming up and I want to find out if they intend to turn out the lights tonight as they did last night. Tell them I find it most inconvenient to be left without light that way."

"It's worse than inconvenient," muttered Lizzie, "it's criminal-that's what it is-turning off all the lights in a haunted house, like this one. As if spooks wasn't bad enough with the lights on——"

"Lizzie!"

"Yes, Miss Neily—I wasn't going to say another word." She went to the telephone. Miss Cornelia knitted on-knit two-purl two — In spite of her experiments with the ouija-board she didn't believe in ghosts-and yet-there were things one couldn't explain by logic. Was there something like that in this house—a shadow walking the corridors—a vague shape of evil, drifting like mist from room to room, till its cold breath whispered on one's back and-there! She had ruined her knitting, the last two rows would have to be ripped out. That came of mooning about ghosts like a ninny.

She put down the knitting with an exasperated little gesture. Lizzie had just finished her telephoning and was hanging up the receiver.

"Well, Lizzie?"

"Yes'm," said the latter, glaring at the phone. "That's what he says-they turned off the lights last night because there was a storm threatening. He says it burns out their fuses if they leave 'em on in a storm."

A louder roll of thunder punctuated her words.

"There!" said Lizzie. "They'll be going off again to-night." She took an uncertain step toward the French windows.

"Humph!" said Miss Cornelia, "I hope it will be a dry summer." Her hands tightened on each other. Darkness-darkness inside this house of whispers to match with the darkness outside! She forced herself to speak in a normal voice.

"Ask Billy to bring some candles, Lizzie-and have them ready."

Lizzie had been staring fixedly at the French windows. At Miss Cornelia's command she gave a little jump of terror and moved closer to her mistress.

"You're not going to ask me to go out in that hall alone?" she said in a hurt voice.

It was too much. Miss Cornelia found vent for her feelings in crisp exasperation.

"What's the matter with you anyhow, Lizzie Allen?"

The nervousness in her own tones infected Lizzie's. She shivered frankly.

"Oh, Miss Neily-Miss Neily!" she pleaded. "I don't like it! I want to go back to the city!"

Miss Cornelia braced herself. "I have rented this house for four months and I am going to stay," she said firmly. Her eyes sought Lizzie's, striving to pour some of her own inflexible courage into the latter's quaking form. But Lizzie would not look at her. Suddenly she started and gave a low scream;

"There's somebody on the terrace!" she breathed in a ghastly whisper, clutching at Miss Cornelia's arm.

For a second Miss Cornelia sat frozen. Then, "Don't do that!" she said sharply. "What nonsense!" but she, looked over her shoulder as she said it and Lizzie saw the look. Both waited, in pulsing stillness-one second-two.

"I guess it was the wind," said Lizzie at last, relieved, her grip on Miss Cornelia relaxing. She began to look a trifle ashamed of herself and Miss Cornelia seized the opportunity.

"You were born on a brick pavement," she said crushingly. "You get nervous out here at night whenever a cricket begins to sing-or scrape his legs-or whatever it is they do!"

Lizzie bowed before the blast of her mistress's scorn and began to move gingerly toward the alcove door. But obviously she was not entirely convinced.

"Oh, it's more than that, Miss Neily," she mumbled. "I ——"

Miss Cornelia turned to her fiercely. If Lizzie was going to behave like this, they might as well have it out now between them-before Dale came home.

"What did you really see last night?" she said in a minatory voice.

The instant relief on Lizzie's face was ludicrous; she so obviously preferred discussing any subject at any length to braving the dangers of the other part of the house unaccompanied.

"I was standing right there at the top of that there staircase," she began, gesticulating toward the alcove stairs in the manner of one who embarks upon the narration of an epic. "Standing there with your switch in my hand, Miss Neily-and then I looked down and," her voice dropped, "I saw a gleaming eye! It looked at me and winked! I tell you this house is haunted!"

"A flirtatious ghost?" queried Miss Cornelia skeptically. She snorted. "Humph! Why didn't you yell?"

"I was too scared to yell! And I'm not the only one." She started to back away from the alcove, her eyes still fixed upon its haunted stairs. "Why do you think the servants left so sudden this morning?" she went on. "Do you really believe the housemaid had appendicitis? Or the cook's sister had twins?"

She turned and gestured at her mistress with a long, pointed forefinger. Her voice had a note of doom.

"I bet a cent the cook never had any sister-and the sister never had any twins," she said impressively. "No, Miss Neily, they couldn't put it over on me like that! They were scared away. They saw-It!"

She concluded her epic and stood nodding her head, an Irish Cassandra who had prophesied the evil to come.

"Fiddlesticks!" said Miss Cornelia briskly, more shaken by the recital than she would have admitted. She tried to think of another topic of conversation.

"What time is it?" she asked.

Lizzie glanced at the mantel clock. "Half-past ten, Miss Neily."

Miss Cornelia yawned, a little dismally. She felt as if the last two hours had not been hours but years.

"Miss Dale won't be home for half an hour," she said reflectively. And if I have to spend another thirty minutes listening to Lizzie shiver, she thought, Dale will find me a nervous wreck when she does come home. She rolled up her knitting and put it back in her knitting-bag; it was no use going on, doing work that would have to be ripped out again and yet she must do something to occupy her thoughts. She raised her head and discovered Lizzie returning toward the alcove stairs with the stealthy tread of a panther. The sight exasperated her.

"Now, Lizzie Allen!" she said sharply, "you forget all that superstitious nonsense and stop looking for ghosts! There's nothing in that sort of thing." She smiled-she would punish Lizzie for her obdurate timorousness. "Where's that ouija-board?" she questioned, rising, with determination in her eye.

Lizzie shuddered violently. "It's up there-with a prayer book on it to keep it quiet!" she groaned, jerking her thumb in the direction of the farther bookcase.

"Bring it here!" said Miss Cornelia implacably; then as Lizzie still hesitated, "Lizzie!"

Shivering, every movement of her body a conscious protest, Lizzie slowly went over to the bookcase, lifted off the prayer book, and took down the ouija-board. Even then she would not carry it normally but bore it over to Miss Cornelia at arms'-length, as if any closer contact would blast her with lightning, her face a comic mask of loathing and repulsion.

She placed the lettered board in Miss Cornelia's lap with a sigh of relief. "You can do it yourself! I'll have none of it!" she said firmly.

"It takes two people and you know it, Lizzie Allen!" Miss Cornelia's voice was stern but-it was also amused.

Lizzie groaned, but she knew her mistress. She obeyed. She carefully chose the farthest chair in the room and took a long time bringing it over to where her mistress sat waiting.

"I've been working for you for twenty years," she muttered. "I've been your goat for twenty years and I've got a right to speak my mind ——"

Miss Cornelia cut her off. "You haven't got a mind. Sit down," she commanded.

Lizzie sat-her hands at her sides. With a sigh of tried patience, Miss Cornelia put her unwilling fingers on the little moving table that is used to point to the letters on the board itself. Then she placed her own hands on it, too, the tips of the fingers just touching Lizzie's.

"Now make your mind a blank!" she commanded her factotum.

"You just said I haven't got any mind," complained the latter.

"Well," said Miss Cornelia magnificently, "make what you haven't got a blank."

The repartee silenced Lizzie for the moment, but only for the moment. As soon as Miss Cornelia had settled herself comfortably and tried to make her mind a suitable receiving station for ouija messages, Lizzie began to mumble the sorrows of her heart.

"I've stood by you through thick and thin," she mourned in a low voice. "I stood by you when you were a vegetarian—I stood by you when you were a theosophist-and I seen you through socialism, Fletcherism and rheumatism-but when it comes to carrying on with ghosts ——"

"Be still!" ordered Miss Cornelia. "Nothing will come if you keep chattering!"

"That's why I'm chattering!" said Lizzie, driven to the wall. "My teeth are, too," she added. "I can hardly keep my upper set in," and a desolate clicking of artificial molars attested the truth of the remark. Then, to Miss Cornelia's relief, she was silent for nearly two minutes, only to start so violently at the end of the time that she nearly upset the ouija-board on her mistress's toes.

"I've got a queer feeling in my fingers-all the way up my arms," she whispered in awed accents, wriggling the arms she spoke of violently.

"Hush!" said Miss Cornelia indignantly. Lizzie always exaggerated, of course-yet now her own fingers felt prickly, uncanny. There was a little pause while both sat tense, staring at the board.

"Now, Ouija," said Miss Cornelia defiantly, "is Lizzie Allen right about this house or is it all stuff and nonsense?"

For one second-two-the ouija remained anchored to its resting place in the center of the board. Then—

"My Gawd! It's moving!" said Lizzie in tones of pure horror as the little pointer began to wander among the letters.

"You shoved it!"

"I did not-cross my heart, Miss Neily—I—" Lizzie's eyes were round, her fingers glued rigidly and awkwardly to the ouija. As the movements of the pointer grew more rapid her mouth dropped open-wider and wider-prepared for an ear-piercing scream.

"Keep quiet!" said Miss Cornelia tensely. There was a pause of a few seconds while the pointer darted from one letter to another wildly.

"B—M—C—X—P—R—S—K—Z—" murmured Miss Cornelia trying to follow the spelled letters.

"It's Russian!" gasped Lizzie breathlessly and Miss Cornelia nearly disgraced herself in the eyes of any spirits that might be present by inappropriate laughter. The ouija continued to move-more letters-what was it spelling? —it couldn't be-good heavens —"B —A —T —Bat!" said Miss Cornelia with a tiny catch in her voice.

The pointer stopped moving: She took her hands from the board.

"That's queer," she said with a forced laugh. She glanced at Lizzie to see how Lizzie was taking it. But the latter seemed too relieved to have her hands off the ouija-board to make the mental connection that her mistress had feared.

All she said was, "Bats indeed! That shows it's spirits. There's been a bat flying around this house all evening."

She got up from her chair tentatively, obviously hoping that the seance was over.

"Oh, Miss Neily," she burst out. "Please let me sleep in your room tonight! It's only when my jaw drops that I snore —I can tie it up with a handkerchief!"

"I wish you'd tie it up with a handkerchief now," said her mistress absent-mindedly, still pondering the message that the pointer had spelled. "B —A —T —Bat!" she murmured. Thought-transference —warning-accident? Whatever it was, it was-nerve-shaking. She put the ouija-board aside. Accident or not, she was done with it for the evening. But she could not so easily dispose of the Bat. Sending a protesting Lizzie off for her reading glasses, Miss Cornelia got the evening paper and settled down to what by now had become her obsession. She had not far to search for a long black streamer ran across the front page —"Bat Baffles Police Again."

She skimmed through the article with eerie fascination, reading bits of it aloud for Lizzie's benefit.

"'Unique criminal-long baffled the police-record of his crimes shows him to be endowed with an almost diabolical ingenuity-so far there is no clue to his identity —'" Pleasant reading for an old woman who's just received a threatening letter, she thought ironically-ah, here was something new in a black-bordered box on the front page —a statement by the paper.

She read it aloud. "'We must cease combing the criminal world for the Bat and look higher. He may be a merchant —a lawyer —a Doctor-honored in his community by day and at night a bloodthirsty assassin ——'" The print blurred before her eyes, she could read no more for the moment. She thought of the revolver in the drawer of the table close at hand and felt glad that it was there, loaded.

"I'm going to take the butcher knife to bed with me!" Lizzie was saying.

Miss Cornelia touched the ouija-board. "That thing certainly spelled Bat," she remarked. "I wish I were a man. I'd like to see any lawyer, Doctor, or merchant of my acquaintance leading a double life without my suspecting it."

"Every man leads a double life and some more than that," Lizzie observed. "I guess it rests them, like it does me to take off my corset."

Miss Cornelia opened her mouth to rebuke her but just at that moment there, was a clink of ice from the hall, and Billy, the Japanese, entered carrying a tray with a pitcher of water and some glasses on it. Miss Cornelia watched his impassive progress, wondering if the Oriental races ever felt terror-she could not imagine all Lizzie's banshees and kelpies producing a single shiver from Billy. He set down the tray and was about to go as silently as he had come when Miss Cornelia spoke to him on impulse.

"Billy, what's all this about the cook's sister not having twins?" she said in an offhand voice. She had not really discussed the departure of the other servants with Billy before. "Did you happen to know that this interesting event was anticipated?"

Billy drew in his breath with a polite hiss. "Maybe she have twins," he admitted. "It happen sometime. Mostly not expected."

"Do you think there was any other reason for her leaving?"

"Maybe," said Billy blandly.

"Well, what was the reason?"

"All say the same thing-house haunted." Billy's reply was prompt as it was calm.

130

Miss Cornelia gave a slight laugh. "You know better than that, though, don't you?"

Billy's Oriental placidity remained unruffled. He neither admitted nor denied. He shrugged his shoulders.

"Funny house," he said laconically. "Find window open-nobody there. Door slam-nobody there!"

On the heels of his words came a single, startling bang from the kitchen quarters-the bang of a slammed door!

Chapter Five
Alopecia and Rubeola

Miss Cornelia dropped her newspaper. Lizzie, frankly frightened, gave a little squeal and moved closer to her mistress. Only Billy remained impassive but even he looked sharply in the direction whence the sound had come.

Miss Cornelia was the first of the others to recover her poise.

"Stop that! It was the wind!" she said, a little irritably-the "Stop that!" addressed to Lizzie who seemed on the point of squealing again.

"I think not wind," said Billy. His very lack of perturbation added weight to the statement. It made Miss Cornelia uneasy. She took out her knitting again.

"How long have you lived in this house, Billy?"

"Since Mr. Fleming built."

"H'm." Miss Cornelia pondered. "And this is the first time you have been disturbed?"

"Last two days only." Billy would have made an ideal witness in a courtroom. He restricted himself so precisely to answering what was asked of him in as few words as possible.

Miss Cornelia ripped out a row in her knitting. She took a deep breath.

"What about that face Lizzie said you saw last night at the window?" she asked in a steady voice.

Billy grinned, as if slightly embarrassed. "Just face-that's all."

"A —man's face?"

He shrugged again.

"Don't know-maybe. It there! It gone!"

Miss Cornelia did not want to believe him-but she did. "Did you go out after it?" she persisted.

Billy's yellow grin grew wider. "No thanks," he said cheerfully with ideal succinctness.

Lizzie, meanwhile, had stood first on one foot and then on the other during the interrogation, terror and morbid interest fighting in her for mastery. Now she could hold herself in no longer.

"Oh, Miss Neily!" she exploded in a graveyard moan, "last night when the lights went out I had a token! My oil lamp was full of oil but, do what I would, it kept going out, too-the minute I shut my eyes out that lamp would go. There ain't a surer token of death! The Bible says, 'Let your light shine' —and when a hand you can't see puts your lights out-good night!"

She ended in a hushed whisper and even Billy looked a trifle uncomfortable after her climax.

"Well, now that you've cheered us up," began Miss Cornelia undauntedly, but a long, ominous roll of thunder that rattled the panes in the French windows drowned out the end of her sentence. Nevertheless she welcomed the thunder as a diversion. At least its menace was a physical one-to be guarded against by physical means.

She rose and went over to the French windows. That flimsy bolt! She parted the curtains and looked out —a flicker of lightning stabbed the night-the storm must be almost upon them.

"Bring some candles, Billy," she said. "The lights may be going out any moment-and Billy," as he started to leave, "there's a gentleman arriving on the last train. After he comes you may go to bed. I'll wait up for Miss Dale-oh, and Billy," arresting him at the door, "see that all the outer doors on this floor are locked and bring the keys here."

Billy nodded and departed. Miss Cornelia took a long breath. Now that the moment for waiting had passed-the moment for action come-she felt suddenly indomitable, prepared to face a dozen Bats!

Her feelings were not shared by her maid. "I know what all this means," moaned Lizzie. "I tell you there's going to be a death, sure!"

"There certainly will be if you don't keep quiet," said her mistress acidly. "Lock the billiard-room windows and go to bed."

But this was the last straw for Lizzie. A picture of the two long, dark flights of stairs up which she had to pass to reach her bedchamber rose before her-and she spoke her mind.

"I am not going to bed!" she said wildly. "I'm going to pack up tomorrow and leave this house." That such a threat would never be carried out while she lived made little difference to her-she was beyond the need of Truth's consolations. "I asked you on my bended knees not to take this place two miles from a railroad," she went on heatedly. "For mercy's sake, Miss Neily, let's go back to the city before it's too late!"

Miss Cornelia was inflexible.

"I'm not going. You can make up your mind to that. I'm going to find out what's wrong with this place if it takes all summer. I came out to the country for a rest and I'm going to get it."

"You'll get your heavenly rest!" mourned Lizzie, giving it up. She looked pitifully at her mistress's face for a sign that the latter might be weakening-but no such sign came. Instead, Miss Cornelia seemed to grow more determined.

"Besides," she said, suddenly deciding to share the secret she had hugged to herself all day, "I might as well tell you, Lizzie. I'm having a detective sent down tonight from police headquarters in the city."

"A detective?" Lizzie's face was horrified. "Miss Neily, you're keeping something from me! You know something I don't know."

"I hope so. I daresay he will be stupid enough. Most of them are. But at least we can have one proper night's sleep."

"Not I. I trust no man," said Lizzie. But Miss Cornelia had picked up the paper again.

"'The Bat's last crime was a particularly atrocious one,'" she read. "'The body of the murdered man...'"

But Lizzie could bear no more.

"Why don't you read the funny page once in a while?" she wailed and hurried to close the windows in the billiard room. The door leading into the billiard room shut behind her.

Miss Cornelia remained reading for a moment. Then-was that a sound from the alcove? She dropped the paper, went into the alcove and stood for a moment at the foot of the stairs, listening. No-it must have been imagination. But, while she was here, she might as well put on the spring lock that bolted the door from the alcove to the terrace. She did so, returned to the living-room and switched off the lights for a moment to look out at the coming storm. It was closer now-the lightning flashes more continuous. She turned on the lights again as Billy re-entered with three candles and a box of matches.

He put them down on a side table.

"New gardener come," he said briefly to Miss Cornelia's back.

Miss Cornelia turned. "Nice hour for him to get here. What's his name?"

"Say his name Brook," said Billy, a little doubtful. English names still bothered him-he was never quite sure of them at first.

Miss Cornelia thought. "Ask him to come in," she said. "And Billy-where are the keys?"

Billy silently took two keys from his pocket and laid them on the table. Then he pointed to the terrace door which Miss Cornelia had just bolted.

"Door up there-spring lock," he said.

"Yes." She nodded. "And the new bolt you put on today makes it fairly secure. One thing is fairly sure, Billy. If anyone tries to get in tonight, he will have to break a window and make a certain amount of noise."

But he only smiled his curious enigmatic smile and went out. And no sooner had Miss Cornelia seated herself when the door of the billiard room slammed open suddenly and Lizzie burst into the room as if she had been shot from a gun-her hair wild-her face stricken with fear.

"I heard somebody yell out in the grounds-away down by the gate!" she informed her mistress in a loud stage whisper which had a curious note of pride in it, as if she were not too displeased at seeing her doleful predictions so swiftly coming to pass.

Miss Cornelia took her by the shoulder-half-startled, half-dubious.

"What did they yell?"

"Just yelled a yell!"

"Lizzie!"

"I heard them!"

But she had cried "Wolf!" too often.

"You take a liver pill," said her mistress disgustedly, "and go to bed."

Lizzie was about to protest both the verdict on her story and the judgment on herself when the door in the hall was opened by Billy to admit the new gardener. A handsome young fellow, in his late twenties, he came two steps into the room and then stood there respectfully with his cap in his hand, waiting for Miss Cornelia to speak to him.

After a swift glance of observation that gave her food for thought she did so.

"You are Brooks, the new gardener?"

The young man inclined his head.

"Yes, madam. The butler said you wanted to speak to me."

Miss Cornelia regarded him anew. His hands look soft-for a gardener's, she thought. And his manners seem much too good for one — Still — —

"Come in," she said briskly. The young man advanced another two steps. "You're the man my niece engaged in the city this afternoon?"

"Yes, madam." He seemed a little uneasy under her searching scrutiny. She dropped her eyes.

"I could not verify your references as the Brays are in Canada —" she proceeded.

The young man took an eager step forward. "I am sure if Mrs. Bray were here — —" he began, then flushed and stopped, twisting his cap.

"Were here?" said Miss Cornelia in a curious voice. "Are you a professional gardener?"

"Yes." The young man's manner had grown a trifle defiant but Miss Cornelia's next question followed remorselessly.

"Know anything about hardy perennials?" she said in a soothing voice, while Lizzie regarded the interview with wondering eyes.

"Oh, yes," but the young man seemed curiously lacking in confidence. "They-they're the ones that keep their leaves during the winter, aren't they?"

"Come over here-closer — —" said Miss Cornelia imperiously. Once more she scrutinized him and this time there was no doubt of his discomfort under her stare.

"Have you had any experience with rubeola?" she queried finally.

"Oh, yes-yes-yes, indeed," the gardener stammered. "Yes."

"And-alopecia?" pursued Miss Cornelia.

The young man seemed to fumble in his mind for the characteristics of such a flower or shrub.

"The dry weather is very hard on alopecia," he asserted finally, and was evidently relieved to see Miss Cornelia receive the statement with a pleasant smile.

"What do you think is the best treatment for urticaria?" she propounded with a highly professional manner.

It appeared to be a catch-question. The young man knotted his brows. Finally a gleam of light seemed to come to him.

"Urticaria frequently needs-er-thinning," he announced decisively.

"Needs scratching you mean!" Miss Cornelia rose with a snort of disdain and faced him. "Young man, urticaria is hives, rubeola is measles, and alopecia is baldness!" she thundered. She waited a moment for his defense. None came.

"Why did you tell me you were a professional gardener?" she went on accusingly. "Why have you come here at this hour of night pretending to be something you're not?"

By all standards of drama the young man should have wilted before her wrath, Instead he suddenly smiled at her, boyishly, and threw up his hands in a gesture of defeat.

"I know I shouldn't have done it!" he confessed with appealing frankness. "You'd have found me out anyhow! I don't know anything about gardening. The truth is," his tone grew somber, "I was desperate! I *had* to have work!"

The candor of his smile would have disarmed a stonier-hearted person than Miss Cornelia. But her suspicions were still awake.

"'That's all, is it?"

"That's enough when you're down and out." His words had an unmistakable accent of finality. She couldn't help wanting to believe him, and yet, he wasn't what he had pretended to be-and this night of all nights was no time to take people on trust!

"How do I know you won't steal the spoons?" she queried, her voice still gruff.

"Are they nice spoons?" he asked with absurd seriousness.

She couldn't help smiling at his tone. "Beautiful spoons."

Again that engaging, boyish manner of his touched something in her heart.

"Spoons are a great temptation to me, Miss Van Gorder-but if you'll take me, I'll promise to leave them alone."

"That's extremely kind of you," she answered with grim humor, knowing herself beaten. She went over to ring for Billy.

Lizzie took the opportunity to gain her ear.

"I don't trust him, Miss Neily! He's too smooth!" she whispered warningly.

Miss Cornelia stiffened. "I haven't asked for your opinion, Lizzie," she said.

But Lizzie was not to be put off by the Van Gorder manner.

"Oh," she whispered, "you're just as bad as all the rest of 'em. A good-looking man comes in the door and your brains fly out the window!"

Miss Cornelia quelled her with a gesture and turned back to the young man. He was standing just where she had left him, his cap in his hands-but, while her back had been turned, his eyes had made a stealthy survey of the living-room —a survey that would have made it plain to Miss Cornelia, if she had seen him, that his interest in the Fleming establishment was not merely the casual interest of a servant in his new place of abode. But she had not seen and she could have told nothing from his present expression.

"Have you had anything to eat lately?" she asked in a kindly voice.

He looked down at his cap. "Not since this morning," he admitted as Billy answered the bell.

Miss Cornelia turned to the impassive Japanese. "Billy, give this man something to eat and then show him where he is to sleep."

She hesitated. The gardener's house was some distance from the main building, and with the night and the approaching storm she felt her own courage weakening. Into the bargain, whether this stranger had lied about his gardening or not, she was curiously attracted to him.

"I think," she said slowly, "that I'll have you sleep in the house here, at least for tonight. Tomorrow we can-the housemaid's room, Billy," she told the butler. And before their departure she held out a candle and a box of matches.

"Better take these with you, Brooks," she said. "The local light company crawls under its bed every time there is a thunderstorm. Good night, Brooks."

"Good night, ma'am," said the young man smiling. Following Billy to the door, he paused. "You're being mighty good to me," he said diffidently, smiled again, and disappeared after Billy.

As the door closed behind them, Miss Cornelia found herself smiling too. "That's a pleasant young fellow-no matter what he is," she said to herself decidedly, and not even Lizzie's feverish "Haven't you any sense taking strange men into the house? How do you know he isn't the Bat?" could draw a reply from her.

Again the thunder rolled as she straightened the papers and magazines on the table and Lizzie gingerly took up the ouija-board to replace it on the bookcase with the prayer book firmly on top of it. And this time, with the roll of the thunder, the lights in the living-room blinked uncertainly for an instant before they recovered their normal brilliance.

"There go the lights!" grumbled Lizzie, her fingers still touching the prayer book, as if for protection. Miss Cornelia did not answer her directly.

"We'll put the detective in the blue room when he comes," she said. "You'd better go up and see if it's all ready."

Lizzie started to obey, going toward the alcove to ascend to the second floor by the alcove stairs. But Miss Cornelia stopped her.

"Lizzie-you know that stair rail's just been varnished. Miss Dale got a stain on her sleeve there this afternoon-and Lizzie ———"

"Yes'm?"

"No one is to know that he is a detective. Not even Billy." Miss Cornelia was very firm.

"Well, what'll I say he is?"

"It's nobody's business."

"A detective," moaned Lizzie, opening the hall door to go by the main staircase. "Tiptoeing around with his eye to all the keyholes. A body won't be safe in the bathtub." She shut the door with a little slap and disappeared. Miss Cornelia sat down-she had many things to think over —"if I ever get time really to think of anything again," she thought, because with gardeners coming who aren't gardeners-and Lizzie hearing yells in the grounds and ———"

She started slightly. The front door bell was ringing—a long trill, uncannily loud in the quiet house. She sat rigid in her chair, waiting. Billy came in.

"Front door key, please?" he asked urbanely. She gave him the key.

"Find out who it is before you unlock the door," she said. He nodded. She heard him at the door, then a murmur of voices-Dale's voice and another's —"Won't you come in for a few minutes? Oh, thank you." She relaxed.

The door opened; it was Dale. "How lovely she looks in that evening wrap!" thought Miss Cornelia. But how tired, too. I wish I knew what was worrying her.

She smiled. "Aren't you back early, Dale?"

Dale threw off her wrap and stood for a moment patting back into its smooth, smart bob, hair ruffled by the wind.

"I was tired," she said, sinking into a chair.

"Not worried about anything?" Miss Cornelia's eyes were sharp.

"No," said Dale without conviction, "but I've come here to be company for you and I don't want to run away all the time." She picked up the evening paper and looked at it without apparently seeing it. Miss Cornelia heard voices in the hall—a man's voice-affable—"How have you been, Billy?"—Billy's voice in answer, "Very well, sir."

"Who's out there, Dale?" she queried.

Dale looked up from the paper. "Doctor Wells, darling," she said in a listless voice. "He brought me over from the club; I asked him to come in for a few minutes. Billy's just taking his coat." She rose, threw the paper aside, came over and kissed Miss Cornelia suddenly and passionately-then before Miss Cornelia, a little startled, could return the kiss, went over and sat on the settee by the fireplace near the door of the billiard room.

Miss Cornelia turned to her with a thousand questions on her tongue, but before she could ask any of them, Billy was ushering in Doctor Wells.

As she shook hands with the Doctor, Miss Cornelia observed him with casual interest-wondering why such a good-looking man, in his early forties, apparently built for success, should be content with the comparative rustication of his local practice. That shrewd, rather aquiline face, with its keen gray eyes, would have found itself more at home in a wider sphere of action, she thought-there was just that touch of ruthlessness about it which makes or mars a captain in the world's affairs. She found herself murmuring the usual conventionalities of greeting.

"Oh, I'm very well, Doctor, thank you. Well, many people at the country club?"

"Not very many," he said, with a shake of his head. "This failure of the Union Bank has knocked a good many of the club members sky high."

"Just how did it happen?" Miss Cornelia was making conversation.

"Oh, the usual thing." The Doctor took out his cigarette case. "The cashier, a young chap named Bailey, looted the bank to the tune of over a million."

Dale turned sharply toward them from her seat by the fireplace.

"How do you know the cashier did it?" she said in a low voice.

The Doctor laughed. "Well-he's run away, for one thing. The bank examiners found the deficit. Bailey, the cashier, went out on an errand-and didn't come back. The method was simple enough-worthless bonds substituted for good ones-with a good bond on the top and bottom of each package, so the packages would pass a casual inspection. Probably been going on for some time."

The fingers of Dale's right hand drummed restlessly on the edge of her settee.

"Couldn't somebody else have done it?" she queried tensely.

The Doctor smiled, a trifle patronizingly.

"Of course the president of the bank had access to the vaults," he said. "But, as you know, Mr. Courtleigh Fleming, the late president, was buried last Monday."

Miss Cornelia had seen her niece's face light up oddly at the beginning of the Doctor's statement-to relapse into lassitude again at its conclusion. Bailey-Bailey-she was sure she remembered that name-on Dale's lips.

"Dale, dear, did you know this young Bailey?" she asked point-blank.

The girl had started to light a cigarette. The flame wavered in her fingers, the match went out.

"Yes-slightly," she said. She bent to strike another match, averting her face. Miss Cornelia did not press her.

"What with bank robberies and communism and the income tax," she said, turning the subject, "the only way to keep your money these days is to spend it."

"Or not to have any-like myself!" the Doctor agreed.

"It seems strange," Miss Cornelia went on, "living in Courtleigh Fleming's house. A month ago I'd never even heard of Mr. Fleming-though I suppose I should have-and now-why, I'm as interested in the failure of his bank as if I were a depositor!"

The Doctor regarded the end of his cigarette.

"As a matter of fact," he said pleasantly, "Dick Fleming had no right to rent you the property before the estate was settled. He must have done it the moment he received my telegram announcing his uncle's death."

"Were you with him when he died?"

"Yes-in Colorado. He had angina pectoris and took me with him for that reason. But with care he might have lived a considerable time. The trouble was that he wouldn't use ordinary care. He ate and drank more than he should, and so —"

"I suppose," pursued Miss Cornelia, watching Dale out of the corner of her eye, "that there is no suspicion that Courtleigh Fleming robbed his own bank?"

"Well, if he did," said the Doctor amicably, "I can testify that he didn't have the loot with him." His tone grew more serious. "No! He had his faults-but not that."

Miss Cornelia made up her mind. She had resolved before not to summon the Doctor for aid in her difficulties, but now that chance had brought him here the opportunity seemed too good a one to let slip.

"Doctor," she said, "I think I ought to tell you something. Last night and the night before, attempts were made to enter this house. Once an intruder actually got in and was frightened away by Lizzie at the top of that staircase." She indicated the alcove stairs. "And twice I have received anonymous communications threatening my life if I did not leave the house and go back to the city."

Dale rose from her settee, startled.

"I didn't know that, Auntie! How dreadful!" she gasped.

Instantly Miss Cornelia regretted her impulse of confidence. She tried to pass the matter off with tart humor.

"Don't tell Lizzie," she said. "She'd yell like a siren. It's the only thing she does like a siren, but she does it superbly!"

For a moment it seemed as if Miss Cornelia had succeeded. The Doctor smiled; Dale sat down again, her expression altering from one of anxiety to one of amusement. Miss Cornelia opened her lips to dilate further upon Lizzie's eccentricities.

But just then there was a splintering crash of glass from one of the French windows behind her!

Chapter Six
Detective Anderson Takes Charge

"What's that?"

"Somebody smashed a windowpane!"

"And threw in a stone!"

"Wait a minute, I'll—" The Doctor, all alert at once, ran into the alcove and jerked at the terrace door.

"It's bolted at the top, too," called Miss Cornelia. He nodded, without wasting words on a reply, unbolted the door and dashed out into the darkness of the terrace. Miss Cornelia saw him run past the French windows and disappear into blackness. Meanwhile Dale, her listlessness vanished before the shock of the strange occurrence, had gone to the broken window and picked up the stone. It was wrapped in paper; there seemed to be writing on the paper. She closed the terrace door and brought the stone to her aunt.

Miss Cornelia unwrapped the paper and smoothed out the sheet.

Two lines of coarse, round handwriting sprawled across it:

> Take warning! Leave this house at once! It is threatened with disaster which will involve you if you remain!

There was no signature.

"Who do you think wrote it?" asked Dale breathlessly.

Miss Cornelia straightened up like a ramrod-indomitable.

"A fool-that's who! If anything was calculated to make me stay here forever, this sort of thing would do it!"

She twitched the sheet of paper angrily.

"But-something may happen, darling!"

"I hope so! That's the reason I——"

She stopped. The doorbell was ringing again-thrilling, insistent. Her niece started at the sound.

"Oh, don't let anybody in!" she besought Miss Cornelia as Billy came in from the hall with his usual air of walking on velvet.

"Key, front door please-bell ring," he explained tersely, taking the key from the table.

Miss Cornelia issued instructions.

"See that the chain is on the door, Billy. Don't open it all the way. And get the visitor's name before you let him in."

She lowered her voice.

"If he says he is Mr. Anderson, let him in and take him to the library."

Billy nodded and disappeared. Dale turned to her aunt, the color out of her cheeks.

"Anderson? Who is Mr. ——"

137

Miss Cornelia did not answer. She thought for a moment. Then she put her hand on Dale's shoulder in a gesture of protective affection.

"Dale, dear-you know how I love having you here-but it might be better if you went back to the city."

"Tonight, darling?" Dale managed a wan smile. But Miss Cornelia seemed serious.

"There's something behind all this disturbance-something I don't understand. But I mean to."

She glanced about to see if the Doctor was returning. She lowered her voice. She drew Dale closer to her.

"The man in the library is a detective from police headquarters," she said.

She had expected Dale to show surprise-excitement-but the white mask of horror which the girl turned toward her appalled her. The young body trembled under her hand for a moment like a leaf in the storm.

"Not-the police!" breathed Dale in tones of utter consternation. Miss Cornelia could not understand why the news had stirred her niece so deeply. But there was no time to puzzle it out, she heard crunching steps on the terrace, the Doctor was returning.

"Ssh!" she whispered. "It isn't necessary to tell the Doctor. I think he's a sort of perambulating bedside gossip-and once it's known the police are here we'll *never* catch the criminals!"

When the Doctor entered from the terrace, brushing drops of rain from his no longer immaculate evening clothes, Dale was back on her favorite settee and Miss Cornelia was poring over the mysterious missive that had been wrapped about the stone.

"He got away in the shrubbery," said the Doctor disgustedly, taking out a handkerchief to fleck the spots of mud from his shoes.

Miss Cornelia gave him the letter of warning. "Read this," she said.

The Doctor adjusted a pair of pince-nez—read the two crude sentences over-once-twice. Then he looked shrewdly at Miss Cornelia.

"Were the others like this?" he queried.

She nodded. "Practically."

He hesitated for a moment like a man with an unpleasant social duty to face.

"Miss Van Gorder, may I speak frankly?"

"Generally speaking, I detest frankness," said that lady grimly. "But-go on!"

The Doctor tapped the letter. His face was wholly serious.

"I think you ought to leave this house," he said bluntly.

"Because of that letter? Humph!" His very seriousness, perversely enough, made her suddenly wish to treat the whole matter as lightly as possible.

The Doctor repressed the obvious annoyance of a man who sees a warning, given in all sobriety, unexpectedly taken as a quip.

"There is some deviltry afoot," he persisted. "You are not safe here, Miss Van Gorder."

But if he was persistent in his attitude, so was she in hers.

"I've been safe in all kinds of houses for sixty-odd years," she said lightly. "It's time I had a bit of a change. Besides," she gestured toward her defenses, "this house is as nearly impregnable as I can make it. The window locks are sound enough, the doors are locked, and the keys are there," she pointed to the keys lying on the table. "As for the terrace door you just used," she went on, "I had Billy put an extra bolt on it today. By the way, did you bolt that door again?" She moved toward the alcove.

"Yes, I did," said the Doctor quickly, still seeming unconvinced of the wisdom of her attitude.

"Miss Van Gorder, I confess—I'm very anxious for you," he continued. "This letter is-ominous. Have you any enemies?"

"Don't insult me! Of course I have. Enemies are an indication of character."

The Doctor's smile held both masculine pity and equally masculine exasperation. He went on more gently.

"Why not accept my hospitality in the village to-night?" he proposed reasonably. "It's a little house but I'll make you comfortable. Or," he threw out his hands in the gesture of one who reasons with a willful child, "if you won't come to me, let me stay here!"

Miss Cornelia hesitated for an instant. The proposition seemed logical enough-more than that-sensible, safe. And yet, some indefinable feeling-hardly strong enough to be called a premonition-kept her from accepting it. Besides, she knew what the Doctor did not, that help was waiting across the hall in the library.

"Thank you, no, Doctor," she said briskly, before she had time to change her mind. "I'm not easily frightened. And tomorrow I intend to equip this entire house with burglar alarms on doors and windows!" she went on defiantly. The incident, as far as she was concerned, was closed. She moved on into the alcove. The Doctor stared at her, shaking his head.

She tried the terrace door. "There, I knew it!" she said triumphantly. "Doctor-you didn't fasten that bolt!"

The Doctor seemed a little taken aback. "Oh —I'm sorry ——" he said.

"You only pushed it part of the way," she explained. She completed the task and stepped back into the living-room. "The only thing that worries me now is that broken French window," she said thoughtfully. "Anyone can reach a hand through it and open the latch." She came down toward the settee where Dale was sitting. "Please, Doctor!"

"Oh-what are you going to do?" said the Doctor, coming out of a brown study.

"I'm going to barricade that window!" said Miss Cornelia firmly, already struggling to lift one end of the settee. But now Dale came to her rescue.

"Oh, darling, you'll hurt yourself. Let me ——" and between them, the Doctor and Dale moved the heavy settee along until it stood in front of the window in question.

The Doctor stood up when the dusty task was finished, wiping his hands.

"It would take a furniture mover to get in there now!" he said airily.

Miss Cornelia smiled.

"Well, Doctor —I'll say good night now-and thank you very much," she said, extending her hand to the Doctor, who bowed over it silently. "Don't keep this young lady up too late; she looks tired." She flashed a look at Dale who stood staring out at the night.

"I'll only smoke a cigarette," promised the Doctor. Once again his voice had a note of plea in it. "You won't change your mind?" he asked anew.

Miss Van Gorder's smile was obdurate. "I have a great deal of mind," she said. "It takes a long time to change it."

Then, having exercised her feminine privilege of the last word, she sailed out of the room, still smiling, and closed the door behind her.

The Doctor seemed a little nettled by her abrupt departure.

"It may be mind," he said, turning back toward Dale, "but forgive me if I say I think it seems more like foolhardy stubbornness!"

Dale turned away from the window. "Then you think there is really danger?"

The Doctor's eyes were grave.

"Well-those letters—" he dropped the letter on the table. "They mean something. Here you are-isolated the village two miles away-and enough shrubbery round the place to hide a dozen assassins —"

If his manner had been in the slightest degree melodramatic, Dale would have found the ominous sentences more easy to discount. But this calm, intent statement of fact was a chill touch at her heart. And yet—

"But what enemies can Aunt Cornelia have?" she asked helplessly.

"Any man will tell you what I do," said the Doctor with increasing seriousness. He took a cigarette from his case and tapped it on the case to emphasize his words. "This is no place for two women, practically alone."

Dale moved away from him restlessly, to warm her hands at the fire. The Doctor gave a quick glance around the room. Then, unseen by her, he stepped noiselessly over to the table, took the matchbox there off its holder and slipped it into his pocket. It seemed a curiously useless and meaningless gesture, but his next words evinced that the action had been deliberate.

"I don't seem to be able to find any matches — —" he said with assumed carelessness, fiddling with the matchbox holder.

Dale turned away from the fire. "Oh, aren't there any? I'll get you some," she said with automatic politeness, and departed to search for them.

The Doctor watched her go-saw the door close behind her. Instantly his face set into tense and wary lines. He glanced about-then ran lightly into the alcove and noiselessly unfastened the bolt on the terrace door which he had pretended to fasten after his search of the shrubbery. When Dale returned with the matches, he was back where he had been when she had left him, glancing at a magazine on the table.

He thanked her urbanely as she offered him the box. "So sorry to trouble you-but tobacco is the one drug every Doctor forbids his patients and prescribes for himself."

Dale smiled at the little joke. He lit his cigarette and drew in the fragrant smoke with apparent gusto. But a moment later he had crushed out the glowing end in an ash tray.

"By the way, has Miss Van Gorder a revolver?" he queried casually, glancing at his wrist watch.

"Yes-she fired it off this afternoon to see if it would work." Dale smiled at the memory.

The Doctor, too, seemed amused. "If she tries to shoot anything-for goodness' sake stand behind her!" he advised. He glanced at the wrist watch again. "Well—I must be going — —"

"If anything happens," said Dale slowly, "I shall telephone you at once."

Her words seemed to disturb the Doctor slightly-but only for a second. He grew even more urbane.

"I'll be home shortly after midnight," he said. "I'm stopping at the Johnsons' on my way-one of their children is ill-or supposed to be." He took a step toward the door, then he turned toward Dale again.

"Take a parting word of advice," he said. "The thing to do with a midnight prowler is-let him alone. Lock your bedroom doors and don't let anything bring you out till morning." He glanced at Dale to see how she took the advice, his hand on the knob of the door.

"Thank you," said Dale seriously. "Good night, Doctor-Billy will let you out, he has the key."

"By Jove!" laughed the Doctor, "you are careful, aren't you! The place is like a fortress! Well-good night, Miss Dale — —"

"Good night." The door closed behind him-Dale was left alone. Suddenly her composure left her, the fixed smile died. She stood gazing ahead at nothing, her face a mask of terror and apprehension. But it was like a curtain that had lifted for a moment on some secret tragedy and then fallen again. When Billy returned with the front door key she was as impassive as he was.

"Has the new gardener come yet?"

"He here," said Billy stolidly. "Name Brook."

She was entirely herself once more when Billy, departing, held the door open wide-to admit Miss Cornelia Van Gorder and a tall, strong-featured man, quietly dressed, with reticent, piercing eyes-the detective!

Dale's first conscious emotion was one of complete surprise. She had expected a heavy-set, blue-jowled vulgarian with a black cigar, a battered derby, and stubby policeman's shoes. "Why this man's a gentleman!" she thought. "At least he looks like one-and yet-you can tell from his face he'd have as little mercy as a steel trap for anyone he had to-catch — —" She shuddered uncontrollably.

"Dale, dear," said Miss Cornelia with triumph in her voice. "This is Mr. Anderson."

The newcomer bowed politely, glancing at her casually and then looking away. Miss Cornelia, however, was obviously in fine feather and relishing to the utmost the presence of a real detective in the house.

"This is the room I spoke of," she said briskly. "All the disturbances have taken place around that terrace door."

The detective took three swift steps into the alcove, glanced about it searchingly. He indicated the stairs.

"That is not the main staircase?"

"No, the main staircase is out there," Miss Cornelia waved her hand in the direction of the hall.

The detective came out of the alcove and paused by the French windows.

"I think there must be a conspiracy between the Architects' Association and the Housebreakers' Union these days," he said grimly. "Look at all that glass. All a burglar needs is a piece of putty and a diamond-cutter to break in."

"But the curious thing is," continued Miss Cornelia, "that whoever got into the house evidently had a key to that door." Again she indicated the terrace door, but Anderson did not seem to be listening to her.

"Hello-what's this?" he said sharply, his eye lighting on the broken glass below the shattered French window. He picked up a piece of glass and examined it.

Dale cleared her throat. "It was broken from the outside a few minutes ago," she said.

"The outside?" Instantly the detective had pulled aside a blind and was staring out into the darkness.

"Yes. And then that letter was thrown in." She pointed to the threatening missive on the center table.

Anderson picked it up, glanced through it, laid it down. All his movements were quick and sure-each executed with the minimum expense of effort.

"H'm," he said in a calm voice that held a glint of humor. "Curious, the anonymous letter complex! Apparently someone considers you an undesirable tenant!"

Miss Cornelia took up the tale.

"There are some things I haven't told you yet," she said. "This house belonged to the late Courtleigh Fleming." He glanced at her sharply.

"The Union Bank?"

"Yes. I rented it for the summer and moved in last Monday. We have not had a really quiet night since I came. The very first night I saw a man with an electric flashlight making his way through the shrubbery!"

"You poor dear!" from Dale sympathetically. "And you were here alone!"

"Well, I had Lizzie. And," said Miss Cornelia with enormous importance, opening the drawer of the center table, "I had my revolver. I know so little about these things, Mr. Anderson, that if I didn't hit a burglar, I knew I'd hit somebody or something!" and she gazed with innocent awe directly down the muzzle of her beloved weapon, then waved it with an airy gesture beneath the detective's nose.

Anderson gave an involuntary start, then his eyes lit up with grim mirth.

"Would you mind putting that away?" he said suavely. "I like to get in the papers as much as anybody, but I don't want to have them say-omit flowers."

Miss Cornelia gave him a glare of offended pride, but he endured it with such quiet equanimity that she merely replaced the revolver in the drawer, with a hurt expression, and waited for him to open the next topic of conversation.

He finished his preliminary survey of the room and returned to her.

"Now you say you don't think anybody has got upstairs yet?" he queried.

Miss Cornelia regarded the alcove stairs.

"I think not. I'm a very light sleeper, especially since the papers have been so full of the exploits of this criminal they call the Bat. He's in them again tonight." She nodded toward the evening paper.

The detective smiled faintly.

"Yes, he's contrived to surround himself with such an air of mystery that it verges on the supernatural-or seems that way to newspapermen."

"I confess," admitted Miss Cornelia, "I've thought of him in this connection." She looked at Anderson to see how he would take the suggestion but the latter merely smiled again, this time more broadly.

"That's going rather a long way for a theory," he said. "And the Bat is not in the habit of giving warnings."

"Nevertheless," she insisted, "somebody has been trying to get into this house, night after night."

Anderson seemed to be revolving a theory in his mind.

"Any liquor stored here?" he asked.

Miss Cornelia nodded. "Yes."

"What?"

Miss Cornelia beamed at him maliciously. "Eleven bottles of home-made elderberry wine."

"You're safe." The detective smiled ruefully. He picked up the evening paper, glanced at it, shook his head. "I'd forget the Bat in all this. You can always tell when the Bat has had anything to do with a crime. When he's through, he signs his name to it."

Miss Cornelia sat bolt upright. "His name? I thought nobody knew his name?"

The detective made a little gesture of apology. "That was a figure of speech. The newspapers named him the Bat because he moved with incredible rapidity, always at night, and by signing his name I mean he leaves the symbol of his identity-the Bat, which can see in the dark."

"I wish I could," said Miss Cornelia, striving to seem unimpressed. "These country lights are always going out."

Anderson's face grew stern. "Sometimes he draws the outline of a bat at the scene of the crime. Once, in some way, he got hold of a real bat, and nailed it to the wall."

Dale, listening, could not repress a shudder at the gruesome picture-and Miss Cornelia's hands gave an involuntary twitch as her knitting needles clicked together. Anderson seemed by no means unconscious of the effect he had created.

"How many people in this house, Miss Van Gorder?"

"My niece and myself." Miss Cornelia indicated Dale, who had picked up her wrap and was starting to leave the room. "Lizzie Allen-who has been my personal maid ever since I was a child-the Japanese butler, and the gardener. The cook and the housemaid left this morning-frightened away."

She smiled as she finished her description. Dale reached the door and passed slowly out into the hall. The detective gave her a single, sharp glance as she made her exit. He seemed to think over the factors Miss Cornelia had mentioned.

"Well," he said, after a slight pause, "you can have a good night's sleep tonight. I'll stay right here in the dark and watch."

"Would you like some coffee to keep you awake?"

Anderson nodded. "Thank you." His voice sank lower. "Do the servants know who I am?"

"Only Lizzie, my maid."

His eyes fixed hers. "I wouldn't tell anyone I'm remaining up all night," he said.

A formless fear rose in Miss Cornelia's mind. "You don't suspect my household?" she said in a low voice.

He spoke with emphasis-all the more pronounced because of the quietude of his tone.

"I'm not taking any chances," he said determinedly.

Chapter Seven
Cross-Questions and Crooked Answers

All unconscious of the slur just cast upon her forty years of single-minded devotion to the Van Gorder family, Lizzie chose that particular moment to open the door and make a little bob at her mistress and the detective.

"The gentleman's room is ready," she said meekly. In her mind she was already beseeching her patron saint that she would not have to show the gentleman to his room. Her ideas of detectives were entirely drawn from sensational magazines and her private opinion was that Anderson might have anything in his pocket from a set of terrifying false whiskers to a bomb!

Miss Cornelia, obedient to the detective's instructions, promptly told the whitest of fibs for Lizzie's benefit.

"The maid will show you to your room now and you can make yourself comfortable for the night." There-that would mislead Lizzie, without being quite a lie.

"My toilet is made for an occasion like this when I've got my gun loaded," answered Anderson carelessly. The allusion to the gun made Lizzie start nervously, unhappily for her, for it drew his attention to her and he now transfixed her with a stare.

"This is the maid you referred to?" he inquired. Miss Cornelia assented. He drew nearer to the unhappy Lizzie.

"What's your name?" he asked, turning to her.

"E-Elizabeth Allen," stammered Lizzie, feeling like a small and distrustful sparrow in the toils of an officious python.

Anderson seemed to run through a mental rogues gallery of other criminals named Elizabeth Allen that he had known.

"How old are you?" he proceeded.

Lizzie looked at her mistress despairingly. "Have I got to answer that?" she wailed. Miss Cornelia nodded-inexorably.

Lizzie braced herself. "Thirty-two," she said, with an arch toss of her head.

The detective looked surprised and slightly amused.

"She's fifty if she's a day," said Miss Cornelia treacherously in spite of a look from Lizzie that would have melted a stone.

The trace of a smile appeared and vanished on the detective's face.

"Now, Lizzie," he said sternly, "do you ever walk in your sleep?"

"I do not," said Lizzie indignantly.

"Don't care for the country, I suppose?"

"I do not!"

"Or detectives?" Anderson deigned to be facetious.

"*I do not!*" There could be no doubt as to the sincerity of Lizzie's answer.

"All right, Lizzie. Be calm. I can stand it," said the detective with treacherous suavity. But he favored her with a long and careful scrutiny before he moved to the table and picked up the note that had been thrown through the window. Quietly he extended it beneath Lizzie's nose.

"Ever see this before?" he said crisply, watching her face.

Lizzie read the note with bulging eyes, her face horror-stricken. When she had finished, she made a gesture of wild disclaimer that nearly removed a portion of Anderson's left ear.

"Mercy on us!" she moaned, mentally invoking not only her patron saint but all the rosary of heaven to protect herself and her mistress.

But the detective still kept his eye on her.

"Didn't write it yourself, did you?" he queried curtly.

"I did not!" said Lizzie angrily. "I did not!"

"And-you're sure you don't walk in your sleep?" The bare idea strained Lizzie's nerves to the breaking point.

"When I get into bed in this house I wouldn't put my feet out for a million dollars!" she said with heartfelt candor. Even Anderson was compelled to grin at this.

"Then I won't ask you to," he said, relaxing considerably; "That's more money than I'm worth, Lizzie."

"Well, I'll say it is!" quoth Lizzie, now thoroughly aroused, and flounced out of the room in high dudgeon, her pompadour bristling, before he had time to interrogate her further.

He replaced the note on the table and turned back to Miss Cornelia. If he had found any clue to the mystery in Lizzie's demeanor, she could not read it in his manner.

"Now, what about the butler?" he said.

"Nothing about him-except that he was Courtleigh Fleming's servant."

Anderson paused. "Do you consider that significant?"

A shadow appeared behind him deep in the alcove —a vague, listening figure-Dale-on tiptoe, conspiratorial, taking pains not to draw the attention of the others to her presence. But both Miss Cornelia and Anderson were too engrossed in their conversation to notice her.

Miss Cornelia hesitated.

"Isn't it possible that there is a connection between the colossal theft at the Union Bank and these disturbances?" she said.

Anderson seemed to think over the question.

"What do you mean?" he asked as Dale slowly moved into the room from the alcove, silently closing the alcove doors behind her, and still unobserved.

"Suppose," said Miss Cornelia slowly, "that Courtleigh Fleming took that money from his own bank and concealed it in this house?" The eavesdropper grew rigid.

"That's the theory you gave headquarters, isn't it?" said Anderson. "But I'll tell you how headquarters figures it out. In the first place, the cashier is missing. In the second place, if Courtleigh Fleming did it and got as far as Colorado, he had it with him when he died, and the facts apparently don't bear that out. In the third place, suppose he had hidden the money in or around this house. Why did he rent it to you?"

"But he didn't," said Miss Cornelia obstinately, "I leased this house from his nephew, his heir."

The detective smiled tolerantly.

"Well, I wouldn't struggle like that for a theory," he said, the professional note coming back to his voice. "The cashier's missing-that's the answer."

Miss Cornelia resented his offhand demolition of the mental card-castle she had erected with such pride.

"I have read a great deal on the detection of crime," she said hotly, "and —"

"Well, we all have our little hobbies," he said tolerantly. "A good many people rather fancy themselves as detectives and run around looking for clues under the impression that a clue is a big and vital factor that sticks up like-well, like a sore thumb. The fact is that the criminal takes care of the big and important factors. It's only the little ones he may overlook. To go back to your friend the Bat, it's because of his skill in little things that he's still at large."

"Then you don't think there's a chance that the money from the Union Bank is in this house?" persisted Miss Cornelia.

"I think it very unlikely."

Miss Cornelia put her knitting away and rose. She still clung tenaciously to her own theories but her belief in them had been badly shaken.

"If you'll come with me, I'll show you to your room," she said a little stiffly. The detective stepped back to let her pass.

"Sorry to spoil your little theory," he said, and followed her to the door. If either had noticed the unobtrusive listener to their conversation, neither made a sign.

The moment the door had closed on them Dale sprang into action. She seemed a different girl from the one who had left the room so inconspicuously such a short time before. There were two bright spots of color in her cheeks and she was obviously laboring under great excitement. She went quickly to the alcove doors-they opened softly-disclosing the young man who had said that he was Brooks the new gardener-and yet not the same young man-for his assumed air of servitude had dropped from him like a cloak, revealing him as a young fellow at least of the same general social class as Dale's if not a fellow-inhabitant of the select circle where Van Gorders revolved about Van Gorders, and a man's great-grandfather was more important than the man himself.

Dale cautioned him with a warning finger as he advanced into the room.

"Sh! Sh!" she whispered. "Be careful! That man's a detective!"

Brooks gave a hunted glance at the door into the hall.

"Then they've traced me here," he said in a dejected voice.

"I don't think so."

He made a gesture of helplessness.

"I couldn't get back to my rooms," he said in a whisper. "If they've searched them," he paused, "as they're sure to-they'll find your letters to me." He paused again. "Your aunt doesn't suspect anything?"

"No, I told her I'd engaged a gardener-and that's all there was about it."

He came nearer to her. "Dale!" he murmured in a tense voice. "You know I didn't take that money!" he said with boyish simplicity.

All the loyalty of first-love was in her answer.

"Of course! I believe in you absolutely!" she said. He caught her in his arms and kissed her-gratefully, passionately. Then the galling memory of the predicament in which he stood, the hunt already on his trail, came back to him. He released her gently, still holding one of her hands.

"But-the police here!" he stammered, turning away. "What does that mean?"

Dale swiftly informed him of the situation.

"Aunt Cornelia says people have been trying to break into this house for days-at night."

Brooks ran his hand through his hair in a gesture of bewilderment. Then he seemed to catch at a hope.

"What sort of people?" he queried sharply.

Dale was puzzled. "She doesn't know."

The excitement in her lover's manner came to a head. "That proves exactly what I've contended right along," he said, thudding one fist softly in the palm of the other. "Through some underneath channel old Fleming has been selling those securities for months, turning them into cash. And somebody knows about it, and knows that that money is hidden here. Don't you see? Your Aunt Cornelia has crabbed the game by coming here."

"Why didn't you tell the police that? Now they think, because you ran away ——"

"Ran away! The only chance I had was a few hours to myself to try to prove what actually happened."

"Why don't you tell the detective what you think?" said Dale at her wits' end. "That Courtleigh Fleming took the money and that it is still here?"

Her lover's face grew somber.

"He'd take me into custody at once and I'd have no chance to search."

He was searching now-his eyes roved about the living-room —walls-ceiling-hopefully-desperately-looking for a clue-the tiniest clue to support his theory.

"Why are you so sure it is here?" queried Dale.

Brooks explained. "You must remember Fleming was no ordinary defaulter and he had no intention of being exiled to a foreign country. He wanted to come back here and take his place in the community while I was in the pen."

"But even then——"

He interrupted her. "Listen, dear——" He crossed to the billiard-room door, closed it firmly, returned.

"The architect that built this house was an old friend of mine," he said in hushed accents. "We were together in France and you know the way fellows get to talking when they're far away and cut off—" He paused, seeing the cruel gleam of the flame throwers-two figures huddled in a foxhole, whiling away the terrible hours of waiting by muttered talk.

"Just an hour or two before—a shell got this friend of mine," he resumed, "he told me he had built a hidden room in this house."

"Where?" gasped Dale.

Brooks shook his head. "I don't know. We never got to finish that conversation. But I remember what he said. He said, 'You watch old Fleming. If I get mine over here it won't break his heart. He didn't want any living being to know about that room.'"

Now Dale was as excited as he.

"Then you think the money is in this hidden room?"

"I do," said Brooks decidedly. "I don't think Fleming took it away with him. He was too shrewd for that. No, he meant to come back all right, the minute he got the word the bank had been looted. And he'd fixed things so I'd be railroaded to prison-you wouldn't understand, but it was pretty neat. And then the fool nephew rents this house the minute he's dead, and whoever knows about the money ——"

"Jack! Why isn't it the nephew who is trying to break in?"

"He wouldn't have to break in. He could make an excuse and come in any time."

He clenched his hands despairingly.

"If I could only get hold of a blue-print of this place!" he muttered.

Dale's face fell. It was sickening to be so close to the secret-and yet not find it. "Oh, Jack, I'm so confused and worried!" she confessed, with a little sob.

Brooks put his hands on her shoulders in an effort to cheer her spirits.

"Now listen, dear," he said firmly, "this isn't as hard as it sounds. I've got a clear night to work in-and as true as I'm standing here, that money's in this house. Listen, honey-it's like this." He pantomimed the old nursery rhyme of The House that Jack Built, "Here's the house that Courtleigh Fleming built-here, somewhere, is the Hidden Room in the house that Courtleigh Fleming built-and here-somewhere-pray Heaven-is the money-in the Hidden Room-in the house that Courtleigh Fleming built. When you're low in your mind, just say that over!"

She managed a faint smile. "I've forgotten it already," she said, drooping.

He still strove for an offhand gaiety that he did not feel.

"Why, look here!" and she followed the play of his hands obediently, like a tired child, "it's a sort of game, dearest. 'Money, money-who's got the money?' You know!" For the dozenth time he stared at the unrevealing walls of the room. "For that matter," he added, "the Hidden Room may be behind these very walls."

He looked about for a tool, a poker, anything that would sound the walls and test them for hollow spaces. Ah, he had it-that driver in the bag of golf clubs over in the corner. He got the driver and stood wondering where he had best begin. That blank wall above the fireplace looked as promising as any. He tapped it gently with the golf club-afraid to make too much noise and yet anxious to test the wall as thoroughly as possible. A dull, heavy reverberation answered his stroke-nothing hollow there apparently.

As he tried another spot, again thunder beat the long roll on its iron drum outside, in the night. The lights blinked-wavered-recovered.

"The lights are going out again," said Dale dully, her excitement sunk into a stupefied calm.

"Let them go! The less light the better for me. The only thing to do is to go over this house room by room." He pointed to the billiard room door. "What's in there?"

"The billiard room." She was thinking hard. "Jack! Perhaps Courtleigh Fleming's nephew would know where the blue-prints are!"

He looked dubious. "It's a chance, but not a very good one," he said. "Well—" He led the way into the billiard room and began to rap at random upon its walls while Dale listened intently for any echo that might betray the presence of a hidden chamber or sliding panel.

Thus it happened that Lizzie received the first real thrill of what was to prove to her-and to others—a sensational and hideous night. For, coming into the living-room to lay a cloth for Mr. Anderson's night suppers not only did the lights blink threateningly and the thunder roll, but a series of spirit raps was certainly to be heard coming from the region of the billiard room.

"Oh, my God!" she wailed, and the next instant the lights went out, leaving her in inky darkness. With a loud shriek she bolted out of the room.

Thunder-lightning-dashing of rain on the streaming glass of the windows-the storm hallooing its hounds. Dale huddled close to her lover as they groped their way back to the living-room, cautiously, doing their best to keep from stumbling against some heavy piece of furniture whose fall would arouse the house.

"There's a candle on the table, Jack, if I can find the table." Her outstretched hands touched a familiar object. "Here it is." She fumbled for a moment. "Have you any matches?"

"Yes." He struck one-another-lit the candle-set it down on the table. In the weak glow of the little taper, whose tiny flame illuminated but a portion of the living-room, his face looked tense and strained.

"It's pretty nearly hopeless," he said, "if all the walls are paneled like that."

As if in mockery of his words and his quest, a muffled knocking that seemed to come from the ceiling of the very room he stood in answered his despair.

"What's that?" gasped Dale.

They listened. The knocking was repeated-knock-knock-knock-knock.

"Someone else is looking for the Hidden Room!" muttered Brooks, gazing up at the ceiling intently, as if he could tear from it the secret of this new mystery by sheer strength of will.

Chapter Eight
The Gleaming Eye

"It's upstairs!" Dale took a step toward the alcove stairs. Brooks halted her.

"Who's in this house besides ourselves?" he queried.

"Only the detective, Aunt Cornelia, Lizzie, and Billy."

"Billy's the Jap?"

"Yes."

Brooks paused an instant. "Does he belong to your aunt?"

"No. He was Courtleigh Fleming's butler."

Knock-knock-knock-knock the dull, methodical rapping on the ceiling of the living-room began again.

"Courtleigh Fleming's butler, eh?" muttered Brooks. He put down his candle and stole noiselessly into the alcove. "It may be the Jap!" he whispered.

Knock-knock-knock-knock! This time the mysterious rapping seemed to come from the upper hall.

"If it is the Jap, I'll get him!" Brooks's voice was tense with resolution. He hesitated-made for the hall door-tiptoed out into the darkness around the main staircase, leaving Dale alone in the living-room beset by shadowy terrors.

Utter silence succeeded his noiseless departure. Even the storm lulled for a moment. Dale stood thinking, wondering, searching desperately for some way to help her lover.

At last a resolution formed in her mind. She went to the city telephone.

"Hello," she said in a low voice, glancing over her shoulder now and then to make sure she was not overheard. "1-2-4—please-yes, that's right. Hello-is that the country club? Is Mr. Richard Fleming there? Yes, I'll hold the wire."

She looked about nervously. Had something moved in that corner of blackness where her candle did not pierce? No! How silly of her!

Buzz-buzz on the telephone. She picked up the receiver again.

"Hello-is this Mr. Fleming? This is Miss Ogden-Dale Ogden. I know it must seem odd my calling you this late, but —I wonder if you could come over here for a few minutes. Yes-tonight." Her voice grew stronger. "I wouldn't trouble you but-it's awfully important. Hold the wire a moment." She put down the phone and made another swift survey of the room, listened furtively at the door-all clear! She returned to the phone.

"Hello-Mr. Fleming —I'll wait outside the house on the drive. It-it's a confidential matter. Thank you so much."

She hung up the phone, relieved-not an instant too soon, for, as she crossed toward the fireplace to add a new log to the dying glow of the fire, the hall door opened and Anderson, the detective, came softly in with an unlighted candle in his hand.

Her composure almost deserted her. How much had he heard? What deduction would he draw if he had heard? An assignation, perhaps! Well, she could stand that; she could stand anything to secure the next few hours of liberty for Jack. For that length of time she and the law were at war; she and this man were at war.

But his first words relieved her fears.

"Spooky sort of place in the dark, isn't it?" he said casually.

"Yes-rather." If he would only go away before Brooks came back or Richard Fleming arrived! But he seemed in a distressingly chatty frame of mind.

"Left me upstairs without a match," continued Anderson. "I found my way down by walking part of the way and falling the rest. Don't suppose I'll ever find the room I left my toothbrush in!" He laughed, lighting the candle in his hand from the candle on the table.

"You're not going to stay up all night, are you?" said Dale nervously, hoping he would take the hint. But he seemed entirely oblivious of such minor considerations as sleep. He took out a cigar.

"Oh, I may doze a bit," he said. He eyed her with a certain approval. She was a darned pretty girl and she looked intelligent. "I suppose you have a theory of your own about these intrusions you've been having here? Or apparently having."

"I knew nothing about them until tonight."

"Still," he persisted conversationally, "you know about them now." But when she remained silent, "Is Miss Van Gorder usually-of a nervous temperament? Imagines she sees things, and all that?"

"I don't think so." Dale's voice was strained. Where was Brooks? What had happened to him?

Anderson puffed on his cigar, pondering. "Know the Flemings?" he asked.

"I've met Mr. Richard Fleming once or twice."

Something in her tone caused him to glance at her. "Nice fellow?"

"I don't know him at all well."

"Know the cashier of the Union Bank?" he shot at her suddenly.

"No!" She strove desperately to make the denial convincing but she could not hide the little tremor in her voice.

The detective mused.

"Fellow of good family, I understand," he said, eyeing her. "Very popular. That's what's behind most of these bank embezzlements-men getting into society and spending more than they make."

Dale hailed the tinkle of the city telephone with an inward sigh of relief. The detective moved to answer the house phone on the wall by the alcove, mistaking the direction of the ring. Dale corrected him quickly.

"No, the other one. That's the house phone." Anderson looked the apparatus over.

"No connection with the outside, eh?"

"No," said Dale absent-mindedly. "Just from room to room in the house."

He accepted her explanation and answered the other telephone.

"Hello-hello-what the —" He moved the receiver hook up and down, without result, and gave it up. "This line sounds dead," he said.

"It was all right a few minutes ago," said Dale without thinking.

"You were using it a few minutes ago?"

She hesitated-what use to deny what she had already admitted, for all practical purposes.

"Yes."

The city telephone rang again. The detective pounced upon it.

"Hello-yes-yes-this is Anderson-go ahead." He paused, while the tiny voice in the receiver buzzed for some seconds. Then he interrupted it impatiently.

"You're sure of that, are you? I see. All right. 'By."

He hung up the receiver and turned swiftly on Dale. "Did I understand you to say that you were not acquainted with the cashier of the Union Bank?" he said to her with a new note in his voice.

Dale stared ahead of her blankly. It had come! She did not reply.

Anderson went on ruthlessly.

"That was headquarters, Miss Ogden. They have found some letters in Bailey's room which seem to indicate that you were not telling the entire truth just now."

He paused, waiting for her answer. "What letters?" she said wearily.

"From you to Jack Bailey-showing that you had recently become engaged to him."

Dale decided to make a clean breast of it, or as clean a one as she dared.

"Very well," she said in an even voice, "that's true."

"Why didn't you say so before?" There was menace beneath his suavity.

She thought swiftly. Apparent frankness seemed to be the only resource left her. She gave him a candid smile.

"It's been a secret. I haven't even told my aunt yet." Now she let indignation color her tones. "How can the police be so stupid as to accuse Jack Bailey, a young man and about to be married? Do you think he would wreck his future like that?"

"Some people wouldn't call it wrecking a future to lay away a million dollars," said Anderson ominously. He came closer to Dale, fixing her with his eyes. "Do you know where Bailey is now?" He spoke slowly and menacingly.

She did not flinch.

"No."

The detective paused.

"Miss Ogden," he said, still with that hidden threat in his voice, "in the last minute or so the Union Bank case and certain things in this house have begun to tie up pretty close together. Bailey disappeared this morning. Have you heard from him since?"

Her eyes met his without weakening, her voice was cool and composed.

"No."

The detective did not comment on her answer. She could not tell from his face whether he thought she had told the truth or lied. He turned away from her brusquely.

"I'll ask you to bring Miss Van Gorder here," he said in his professional voice.

"Why do you want her?" Dale blazed at him rebelliously.

He was quiet. "Because this case is taking on a new phase."

"You don't think I know anything about that money?" she said, a little wildly, hoping that a display of sham anger might throw him off the trail he seemed to be following.

He seemed to accept her words, cynically, at their face value.

"No," he said, "but you know somebody who does." Dale hesitated, sought for a biting retort, found none. It did not matter; any respite, no matter how momentary, from these probing questions, would be a relief. She silently took one of the lighted candles and left the living-room to search for her aunt.

Left alone, the detective reflected for a moment, then picking up the one lighted candle that remained, commenced a systematic examination of the living-room. His methods were thorough, but if, when he came to the end of his quest, he had made any new discoveries, the reticent composure of his face did not betray the fact. When he had finished he turned patiently toward the billiard room-the little flame of his candle was swallowed up in its dark recesses-he closed the door of the living-room behind him. The storm was dying away now, but a few flashes of lightning still flickered, lighting up the darkness of the deserted living-room now and then with a harsh, brief glare.

A lightning flash —a shadow cast abruptly on the shade of one of the French windows, to disappear as abruptly as the flash was blotted out-the shadow of a man —a prowler-feeling his way through the lightning-slashed darkness to the terrace door. The detective? Brooks? The Bat? The lightning flash was too brief for any observer to have recognized the stealing shape-if any observer had been there.

But the lack of an observer was promptly remedied. Just as the shadowy shape reached the terrace door and its shadow-fingers closed over the knob, Lizzie entered the deserted living-room on stumbling feet. She was carrying a tray of dishes and food-some cold meat on a platter, a cup and saucer, a roll, a butter pat-and she walked slowly, with terror only one leap behind her and blank darkness ahead.

She had only reached the table and was preparing to deposit her tray and beat a shameful retreat, when a sound behind her made her turn. The key in the door from the terrace to the alcove had clicked. Paralyzed with fright she stared and waited, and the next moment a formless thing, a blacker shadow in a world of shadows, passed swiftly in and up the small staircase.

But not only a shadow. To Lizzie's terrified eyes it bore an eye, a single gleaming eye, just above the level of the stair rail, and this eye was turned on her.

It was too much. She dropped the tray on the table with a crash and gave vent to a piercing shriek that would have shamed the siren of a fire engine.

Miss Cornelia and Anderson, rushing in from the hall and the billiard room respectively, each with a lighted candle, found her gasping and clutching at the table for support.

"For the love of heaven, what's wrong?" cried Miss Cornelia irritatedly. The coffeepot she was carrying in her other hand spilled a portion of its boiling contents on Lizzie's shoe and Lizzie screamed anew and began to dance up and down on the uninjured foot.

"Oh, my foot-my foot!" she squealed hysterically. "My foot!"

Miss Cornelia tried to shake her back to her senses.

"My patience! Did you yell like that because you stubbed your toe?"

"You scalded it!" cried Lizzie wildly. "It went up the staircase!"

"Your toe went up the staircase?"

"No, no! An eye-an eye as big as a saucer! It ran right up that staircase —" She indicated the alcove with a trembling forefinger. Miss Cornelia put her coffeepot and her candle down on the table and opened her mouth to express her frank opinion of her factotum's sanity. But here the detective took charge.

"Now see here," he said with some sternness to the quaking Lizzie, "stop this racket and tell me what you saw!"

"A ghost!" persisted Lizzie, still hopping around on one leg. "It came right through that door and ran up the stairs-oh —" and she seemed prepared to scream again as Dale, white-faced, came in from the hall, followed by Billy and Brooks, the latter holding still another candle.

"Who screamed?" said Dale tensely.

"I did!" Lizzie wailed, "I saw a ghost!" She turned to Miss Cornelia. "I begged you not to come here," she vociferated. "I begged you on my bended knees. There's a graveyard not a quarter of a mile away."

"Yes, and one more scare like that, Lizzie Allen, and you'll have me lying in it," said her mistress unsympathetically. She moved up to examine the scene of Lizzie's ghostly misadventure, while Anderson began to interrogate its heroine.

"Now, Lizzie," he said, forcing himself to urbanity, "what did you really see?"

"I told you what I saw."

His manner grew somewhat threatening.

"You're not trying to frighten Miss Van Gorder into leaving this house and going back to the city?"

"Well, if I am," said Lizzie with grim, unconscious humor, "I'm giving myself an awful good scare, too, ain't I?"

The two glared at each other as Miss Cornelia returned from her survey of the alcove.

"Somebody who had a key could have got in here, Mr. Anderson," she said annoyedly. "That terrace door's been unbolted from the inside."

Lizzie groaned. "I told you so," she wailed. "I knew something was going to happen tonight. I heard rappings all over the house today, and the ouija-board spelled Bat!"

The detective recovered his poise. "I think I see the answer to your puzzle, Miss Van Gorder," he said, with a scornful glance at Lizzie. "A hysterical and not very reliable woman, anxious to go back to the city and terrified over and over by the shutting off of the electric lights."

If looks could slay, his characterization of Lizzie would have laid him dead at her feet at that instant. Miss Van Gorder considered his theory.

"I wonder," she said.

The detective rubbed his hands together more cheerfully.

"A good night's sleep and —— —" he began, but the irrepressible Lizzie interrupted him.

"My God, we're not going to bed, are we?" she said, with her eyes as big as saucers.

He gave her a kindly pat on the shoulder, which she obviously resented.

"You'll feel better in the morning," he said. "Lock your door and say your prayers, and leave the rest to me."

Lizzie muttered something inaudible and rebellious, but now Miss Cornelia added her protestations to his.

"That's very good advice," she said decisively. "You take her, Dale."

Reluctantly, with a dragging of feet and scared glances cast back over her shoulder, Lizzie allowed herself to be drawn toward the door and the main staircase by Dale. But she did not depart without one Parthian shot.

"I'm not going to bed!" she wailed as Dale's strong young arm helped her out into the hall. "Do you think I want to wake up in the morning with my throat cut?" Then the creaking of the stairs, and Dale's soothing voice reassuring her as she painfully clambered toward the third floor, announced that Lizzie, for some time at least, had been removed as an active factor from the puzzling equation of Cedarcrest.

Anderson confronted Miss Cornelia with certain relief.

"There are certain things I want to discuss with you, Miss Van Gorder," he said. "But they can wait until tomorrow morning."

Miss Cornelia glanced about the room. His manner was reassuring.

"Do you think all this-pure imagination?" she said.

"Don't you?"

She hesitated. "I'm not sure."

He laughed. "I'll tell you what I'll do. You go upstairs and go to bed comfortably. I'll make a careful search of the house before I settle down, and if I find anything at all suspicious, I'll promise to let you know."

She agreed to that, and after sending the Jap out for more coffee prepared to go upstairs.

Never had the thought of her own comfortable bed appealed to her so much. But, in spite of her weariness, she could not quite resign herself to take Lizzie's story as lightly as the detective seemed to.

"If what Lizzie says is true," she said, taking her candle, "the upper floors of the house are even less safe than this one."

"I imagine Lizzie's account just now is about as reliable as her previous one as to her age," Anderson assured her. "I'm certain you need not worry. Just go on up and get your beauty sleep; I'm sure you need it."

On which ambiguous remark Miss Van Gorder took her leave, rather grimly smiling.

It was after she had gone that Anderson's glance fell on Brooks, standing warily in the doorway.

"What are you? The gardener?"

But Brooks was prepared for him.

"Ordinarily I drive a car," he said. "Just now I'm working on the place here."

Anderson was observing him closely, with the eyes of a man ransacking his memory for a name—a picture. "I've seen you somewhere—" he went on slowly. "And I'll-place you before long." There was a little threat in his shrewd scrutiny. He took a step toward Brooks.

"Not in the portrait gallery at headquarters, are you?"

"Not yet." Brooks's voice was resentful. Then he remembered his pose and his back grew supple, his whole attitude that of the respectful servant.

"Well, we slip up now and then," said the detective slowly. Then, apparently, he gave up his search for the name-the pictured face. But his manner was still suspicious.

"All right, Brooks," he said tersely, "if you're needed in the night, you'll be called!"

Brooks bowed. "Very well, sir." He closed the door softly behind him, glad to have escaped as well as he had.

But that he had not entirely lulled the detective's watchfulness to rest was evident as soon as he had gone. Anderson waited a few seconds, then moved noiselessly over to the hall door-listened-opened it suddenly-closed it again. Then he proceeded to examine the alcove-the stairs, where the gleaming eye had wavered like a corpse-candle before Lizzie's affrighted vision. He tested the terrace door and bolted it. How much truth had there been in her story? He could not decide, but he drew out his revolver nevertheless and gave it a quick inspection to see if it was in working order. A smile crept over his face-the smile of a man who has dangerous work to do and does not shrink from the prospect. He put the revolver back in his pocket and, taking the one lighted candle remaining, went out by the hall door, as the storm burst forth in fresh fury and the window-panes of the living-room rattled before a new reverberation of thunder.

For a moment, in the living-room, except for the thunder, all was silence. Then the creak of surreptitious footsteps broke the stillness-light footsteps descending the alcove stairs where the gleaming eye had passed.

It was Dale slipping out of the house to keep her appointment with Richard Fleming. She carried a raincoat over her arm and a pair of rubbers in one hand. Her other hand held a candle. By the terrace door she paused, unbolted it, glanced out into the streaming night with a shiver. Then she came into the living-room and sat down to put on her rubbers.

Hardly had she begun to do so when she started up again. A muffled knocking sounded at the terrace door. It was ominous and determined, and in a panic of terror she rose to her feet. If it was the law, come after Jack, what should she do? Or again, suppose it was the Unknown who had threatened them with death? Not coherent thoughts these, but chaotic, bringing panic with them. Almost unconscious of what she was doing, she reached into the drawer beside her, secured the revolver there and leveled it at the door.

Chapter Nine
A Shot in the Dark

A key clicked in the terrace door—a voice swore muffledly at the rain. Dale lowered her revolver slowly. It was Richard Fleming-come to meet her here, instead of down by the drive.

She had telephoned him on an impulse. But now, as she looked at him in the light of her single candle, she wondered if this rather dissipated, rather foppish young man about town, in his early thirties, could possibly understand and appreciate the motives that had driven her to seek his aid. Still, it was for Jack! She clenched her teeth and resolved to go through with the plan mapped out in her mind. It might be a desperate expedient but she had nowhere else to turn!

Fleming shut the terrace door behind him and moved down from the alcove, trying to shake the rain from his coat.

"Did I frighten you?"

"Oh, Mr. Fleming-yes!" Dale laid her aunt's revolver down on the table. Fleming perceived her nervousness and made a gesture of apology.

"I'm sorry," he said, "I rapped but nobody seemed to hear me, so I used my key."

"You're wet through —I'm sorry," said Dale with mechanical politeness.

He smiled. "Oh, no." He stripped off his cap and raincoat and placed them on a chair, brushing himself off as he did so with finicky little movements of his hands.

"Reggie Beresford brought me over in his car," he said. "He's waiting down the drive."

Dale decided not to waste words in the usual commonplaces of social greeting.

"Mr. Fleming, I'm in dreadful trouble!" she said, facing him squarely, with a courageous appeal in her eyes.

He made a polite movement. "Oh, I say! That's too bad."

She plunged on. "You know the Union Bank closed today."

He laughed lightly.

"Yes, I know it! I didn't have anything in it-or any other bank for that matter," he admitted ruefully, "but I hate to see the old thing go to smash."

Dale wondered which angle was best from which to present her appeal.

"Well, even if you haven't lost anything in this bank failure, a lot of your friends have-surely?" she went on.

"I'll say so!" said Fleming, debonairly. "Beresford is sitting down the road in his Packard now writhing with pain!"

Dale hesitated; Fleming's lightness seemed so incorrigible that, for a moment, she was on the verge of giving her project up entirely. Then, "Waster or not-he's the only man who can help us!" she told herself and continued.

"Lots of awfully poor people are going to suffer, too," she said wistfully.

Fleming chuckled, dismissing the poor with a wave of his hand.

"Oh, well, the poor are always in trouble," he said with airy heartlessness. "They specialize in suffering."

He extracted a monogrammed cigarette from a thin gold case.

"But look here," he went on, moving closer to Dale, "you didn't send for me to discuss this hypothetical poor depositor, did you? Mind if I smoke?"

"No." He lit his cigarette and puffed at it with enjoyment while Dale paused, summoning up her courage. Finally the words came in a rush.

"Mr. Fleming, I'm going to say something rather brutal. Please don't mind. I'm merely-desperate! You see, I happen to be engaged to the cashier, Jack Bailey— —"

Fleming whistled. "I see! And he's beat it!"

Dale blazed with indignation.

"He has not! I'm going to tell you something. He's here, now, in this house —" she continued fierily, all her defenses thrown aside. "My aunt thinks he's a new gardener. He is here, Mr. Fleming, because he knows he didn't take the money, and the only person who could have done it was-your uncle!"

Dick Fleming dropped his cigarette in a convenient ash tray and crushed it out there, absently, not seeming to notice whether it scorched his fingers or not. He rose and took a turn about the room. Then he came back to Dale.

"That's a pretty strong indictment to bring against a dead man," he said slowly, seriously.

"It's true!" Dale insisted stubbornly, giving him glance for glance.

Fleming nodded. "All right."

He smiled —a smile that Dale didn't like.

"Suppose it's true-where do I come in?" he said. "You don't think I know where the money is?"

"No," admitted Dale, "but I think you might help to find it."

She went swiftly over to the hall door and listened tensely for an instant. Then she came back to Fleming.

"If anybody comes in-you've just come to get something of yours," she said in a low voice. He nodded understandingly. She dropped her voice still lower.

"Do you know anything about a Hidden Room in this house?" she asked.

Dick Fleming stared at her for a moment. Then he burst into laughter.

"A Hidden Room-that's rich!" he said, still laughing. "Never heard of it! Now, let me get this straight. The idea is—a Hidden Room-and the money is in it-is that it?"

Dale nodded a "Yes."

"The architect who built this house told Jack Bailey that he had built a Hidden Room in it," she persisted.

For a moment Dick Fleming stared at her as if he could not believe his ears. Then, slowly, his expression changed. Beneath the well-fed, debonair mask of the clubman about town, other lines appeared-lines of avarice and calculation-wolf-marks, betokening the craft and petty ruthlessness of the small soul within the gentlemanly shell. His eyes took on a shifty, uncertain stare-they no longer looked at Dale-their gaze seemed turned inward, beholding a visioned treasure, a glittering pile of gold. And yet, the change in his look was not so pronounced as to give Dale pause-she felt a vague uneasiness steal over her, true-but it would have taken a shrewd and long-experienced woman of the world to read the secret behind Fleming's eyes at first glance-and Dale, for all her courage and common sense, was a young and headstrong girl.

She watched him, puzzled, wondering why he made no comment on her last statement.

"Do you know where there are any blue-prints of the house?" she asked at last.

An odd light glittered in Fleming's eyes for a moment. Then it vanished-he held himself in check-the casual idler again.

"Blue-prints?" He seemed to think it over. "Why-there may be some. Have you looked in the old secretary in the library? My uncle used to keep all sorts of papers there," he said with apparent helpfulness.

"Why, don't you remember-you locked it when we took the house."

"So I did." Fleming took out his key ring, selected a key. "Suppose you go and look," he said. "Don't you think I'd better stay here?"

"Oh, yes—" said Dale, blinded to everything else by the rising hope in her heart. "Oh, I can hardly thank you enough!" and before he could even reply, she had taken the key and was hurrying toward the hall door.

He watched her leave the room, a bleak smile on his face. As soon as she had closed the door behind her, his languor dropped from him. He became a hound—a ferret-questing for its prey. He ran lightly over to the bookcase by the hall door—a moment's inspection-he shook his head. Perhaps the other bookcase near the French windows-no-it wasn't there. Ah, the bookcase over the fireplace! He remembered now! He made for it, hastily swept the books from the top shelf, reached groping fingers into the space behind the second row of books. There! A dusty roll of three blue-prints! He unrolled them hurriedly and tried to make out the white tracings by the light of the fire-no-better take them over to the candle on the table.

He peered at them hungrily in the little spot of light thrown by the candle. The first one-no-nor the second-but the third-the bottom one-good heavens! He took in the significance of the blurred white lines with greedy eyes, his lips opening in a silent exclamation of triumph. Then he pondered for an instant, the blue-print itself-was an awkward size-bulky-good, he had it! He carefully tore a small portion from the third blue-print and was about to stuff it in the inside pocket of his dinner jacket when Dale, returning, caught him before he had time to conceal his find. She took in the situation at once.

"Oh, you found it!" she said in tones of rejoicing, giving him back the key to the secretary. Then, as he still made no move to transfer the scrap of blue paper to her, "Please let me have it, Mr. Fleming. I know that's it."

Dick Fleming's lips set in a thin line. "Just a moment," he said, putting the table between them with a swift movement. Once more he stole a glance at the scrap of paper in his hand by the flickering light of the candle. Then he faced Dale boldly.

154

"Do you suppose, if that money is actually here, that I can simply turn this over to you and let you give it to Bailey?" he said. "Every man has his price. How do I know that Bailey's isn't a million dollars?"

Dale felt as if he had dashed cold water in her face. "What do you mean to do with it then?" she said.

Fleming turned the blue-print over in his hand.

"I don't know," he said. "What is it you want me to do?"

But by now Dale's vague distrust in him had grown very definite.

"Aren't you going to give it to me?"

He put her off. "I'll have to think about that." He looked at the blue-print again. "So the missing cashier is in this house posing as a gardener?" he said with a sneer in his tones.

Dale's temper was rising.

"If you won't give it to me-there's a detective in this house," she said, with a stamp of her foot. She made a movement as if to call Anderson-then, remembering Jack, turned back to Fleming.

"Give it to the detective and let him search," she pleaded.

"A detective?" said Fleming startled. "What's a detective doing here?"

"People have been trying to break in."

"What people?"

"I don't know."

Fleming stared out beyond Dale, into the night.

"Then it is here," he muttered to himself.

Behind his back-was it a gust of air that moved them? —the double doors of the alcove swung open just a crack. Was a listener crouched behind those doors-or was it only a trick of carpentry —a gesture of chance?

The mask of the clubman dropped from Fleming completely. His lips drew back from his teeth in the snarl of a predatory animal that clings to its prey at the cost of life or death.

Before Dale could stop him, he picked up the discarded blue-prints and threw them on the fire, retaining only the precious scrap in his hand. The roll blackened and burst into flame. He watched it, smiling.

"I'm not going to give this to any detective," he said quietly, tapping the piece of paper in his hand.

Dale's heart pounded sickeningly but she kept her courage up.

"What do you mean?" she said fiercely. "What are you going to do?"

He faced her across the fireplace, his airy manner coming back to him just enough to add an additional touch of the sinister to the cold self-revelation of his words.

"Let us suppose a few things, Miss Ogden," he said. "Suppose my price is a million dollars. Suppose I need money very badly and my uncle has left me a house containing that amount in cash. Suppose I choose to consider that that money is mine-then it wouldn't be hard to suppose, would it, that I'd make a pretty sincere attempt to get away with it?"

Dale summoned all her fortitude.

"If you go out of this room with that paper I'll scream for help!" she said defiantly.

Fleming made a little mock-bow of courtesy. He smiled.

"To carry on our little game of supposing," he said easily, "suppose there is a detective in this house-and that, if I were cornered, I should tell him where to lay his hands on Jack Bailey. Do you suppose you would scream?"

Dale's hands dropped, powerless, at her sides. If only she hadn't told him-too late! —she was helpless. She could not call the detective without ruining Jack-and yet, if Fleming escaped with the money-how could Jack ever prove his innocence?

Fleming watched her for an instant, smiling. Then, seeing she made no move, he darted hastily toward the double doors of the alcove, flung them open, seemed about to dash up the alcove stairs. The sight of him escaping with the only existing clue to the hidden room galvanized Dale into action. She followed him, hurriedly snatching up Miss Cornelia's revolver from the table as she did so, in a last gesture of desperation.

"No! No! Give it to me! Give it to me!" and she sprang after him, clutching the revolver. He waited for her on the bottom step of the stairs, the slight smile still on his face.

Panting breaths in the darkness of the alcove —a short, furious scuffle-he had wrested the revolver away from her, but in doing so had unguarded the precious blue-print —she snatched at it desperately, tearing most of it away, leaving only a corner in his hand. He swore-tried to get it back-she jerked away.

Then suddenly a bright shaft of light split the darkness of the alcove stairs like a sword, a spot of brilliance centered on Fleming's face like the glare of a flashlight focused from above by an invisible hand. For an instant it revealed him-his features distorted with fury-about to rush down the stairs again and attack the trembling girl at their foot.

A single shot rang out. For a second, the fury on Fleming's face seemed to change to a strange look of bewilderment and surprise.

Then the shaft of light was extinguished as suddenly as the snuffing of a candle, and he crumpled forward to the foot of the stairs-struck-lay on his face in the darkness, just inside the double doors.

Dale gave a little whimpering cry of horror.

"Oh, no, no, no," she whispered from a dry throat, automatically stuffing her portion of the precious scrap of blue-print into the bosom of her dress. She stood frozen, not daring to move, not daring even to reach down with her hand and touch the body of Fleming to see if he was dead or alive.

A murmur of excited voices sounded from the hall. The door flew open, feet stumbled through the darkness —"The noise came from this room!" that was Anderson's voice —"Holy Virgin!" that must be Lizzie — —"

Even as Dale turned to face the assembled household, the house lights, extinguished since the storm, came on in full brilliance-revealing her to them, standing beside Fleming's body with Miss Cornelia's revolver between them.

She shuddered, seeing Fleming's arm flung out awkwardly by his side. No living man could lie in such a posture.

"I didn't do it! I didn't do it!" she stammered, after a tense silence that followed the sudden reillumining of the lights. Her eyes wandered from figure to figure idly, noting unimportant details. Billy was still in his white coat and his face, impassive as ever, showed not the slightest surprise. Brooks and Anderson were likewise completely dressed-but Miss Cornelia had evidently begun to retire for the night when she had heard the shot-her transformation was askew and she wore a dressing-gown. As for Lizzie, that worthy shivered in a gaudy wrapper adorned with incredible orange flowers, with her hair done up in curlers. Dale saw it all and was never after to forget one single detail of it.

The detective was beside her now, examining Fleming's body with professional thoroughness. At last he rose.

"He's dead," he said quietly. A shiver ran through the watching group. Dale felt a stifling hand constrict about her heart.

There was a pause. Anderson picked up the revolver beside Fleming's body and examined it swiftly, careful not to confuse his own fingerprints with any that might already be on the polished steel. Then he looked at Dale. "Who is he?" he said bluntly.

Dale fought hysteria for some seconds before she could speak.

"Richard Fleming-somebody shot him!" she managed to whisper at last.

Anderson took a step toward her.

"What do you mean by somebody?" he said.

The world to Dale turned into a crowd of threatening, accusing eyes —a multitude of shadowy voices, shouting, Guilty! Guilty! Prove that you're innocent-you can't!

"I don't know," she said wildly. "Somebody on the staircase."

"Did you see anybody?" Anderson's voice was as passionless and cold as a bar of steel.

"No-but there was a light from somewhere-like a pocket-flash —" She could not go on. She saw Fleming's face before her-furious at first-then changing to that strange look of bewildered surprise-she put her hands over her eyes to shut the vision out.

Lizzie made a welcome interruption.

"I told you I saw a man go up that staircase!" she wailed, jabbing her forefinger in the direction of the alcove stairs.

Miss Cornelia, now recovered from the first shock of the discovery, supported her gallantly.

"That's the only explanation, Mr. Anderson," she said decidedly.

The detective looked at the stairs-at the terrace door. His eyes made a circuit of the room and came back to Fleming's body. "I've been all over the house," he said. "There's nobody there."

A pause followed. Dale found herself helplessly looking toward her lover for comfort-comfort he could not give without revealing his own secret.

Eerily, through the tense silence, a sudden tinkling sounded-the sharp, persistent ringing of a telephone bell.

Miss Cornelia rose to answer it automatically. "The house phone!" she said. Then she stopped. "But we're all here."

They looked attach other aghast. It was true. And yet-somehow-somewhere-one of the other phones on the circuit was calling the living-room.

Miss Cornelia summoned every ounce of inherited Van Gorder pride she possessed and went to the phone. She took off the receiver. The ringing stopped.

"Hello-hello —" she said, while the others stood rigid, listening. Then she gasped. An expression of wondering horror came over her face.

Chapter Ten
The Phone Call from Nowhere

"Somebody groaning!" gasped Miss Cornelia. "It's horrible!"

The detective stepped up and took the receiver from her. He listened anxiously for a moment.

"I don't hear anything," he said.

"I heard it! I couldn't imagine such a dreadful sound! I tell you-somebody in this house is in terrible distress."

"Where does this phone connect?" queried Anderson practically.

Miss Cornelia made a hopeless little gesture. "Practically every room in this house!"

The detective put the receiver to his ear again.

"Just what did you hear?" he said stolidly.

Miss Cornelia's voice shook.

"Dreadful groans-and what seemed to be an inarticulate effort to speak!"

Lizzie drew her gaudy wrapper closer about her shuddering form.

"I'd go somewhere," she wailed in the voice of a lost soul, "if I only had somewhere to go!"

Miss Cornelia quelled her with a glare and turned back to the detective.

"Won't you send these men to investigate-or go yourself?" she said, indicating Brooks and Billy. The detective thought swiftly.

"My place is here," he said. "You two men," Brooks and Billy moved forward to take his orders, "take another look through the house-don't leave the building—I'll want you pretty soon."

Brooks-or Jack Bailey, as we may as well call him through the remainder of this narrative-started to obey. Then his eye fell on Miss Cornelia's revolver which Anderson had taken from beside Fleming's body and still held clasped in his hand.

"If you'll give me that revolver —" he began in an offhand tone, hoping Anderson would not see through his little ruse. Once wiped clean of fingerprints, the revolver would not be such telling evidence against Dale Ogden.

But Anderson was not to be caught napping. "That revolver will stay where it is," he said with a grim smile.

Jack Bailey knew better than to try and argue the point, he followed Billy reluctantly out of the door, giving Dale a surreptitious glance of encouragement and faith as he did so. The Japanese and he mounted to the second floor as stealthily as possible, prying into dark corners and searching unused rooms for any clue that might betray the source of the startling phone call from nowhere. But Bailey's heart was not in the search. His mind kept going back to the figure of Dale-nervous, shaken, undergoing the terrors of the third degree at Anderson's hands. She couldn't have shot Fleming of course, and yet, unless he and Billy found something to substantiate her story of how the killing had happened, it was her own, unsupported word against a damning mass of circumstantial evidence. He plunged with renewed vigor into his quest.

Back in the living-room, as he had feared, Anderson was subjecting Dale to a merciless interrogation.

"Now I want the real story!" he began with calculated brutality. "You lied before!"

"That's no tone to use! You'll only terrify her," cried Miss Cornelia indignantly. The detective paid no attention, his face had hardened, he seemed every inch the remorseless sleuthhound of the law. He turned on Miss Cornelia for a moment.

"Where were you when this happened?" he said.

"Upstairs in my room." Miss Cornelia's tones were icy.

"And you?" badgeringly, to Lizzie.

"In my room," said the latter pertly, "brushing Miss Cornelia's hair."

Anderson broke open the revolver and gave a swift glance at the bullet chambers.

"One shot has been fired from this revolver!"

Miss Cornelia sprang to her niece's defense.

"I fired it myself this afternoon," she said.

The detective regarded her with grudging admiration.

"You're a quick thinker," he said with obvious unbelief in his voice. He put the revolver down on the table.

Miss Cornelia followed up her advantage.

"I demand that you get the coroner here," she said.

"Doctor Wells is the coroner," offered Lizzie eagerly. Anderson brushed their suggestions aside.

"I'm going to ask you some questions!" he said menacingly to Dale.

But Miss Cornelia stuck to her guns. Dale was not going to be bullied into any sort of confession, true or false, if she could help it-and from the way that the girl's eyes returned with fascinated horror to the ghastly heap on the floor that had been Fleming, she knew that Dale was on the edge of violent hysteria.

"Do you mind covering that body first?" she asked crisply. The detective eyed her for a moment in a rather ugly fashion-then grunted ungraciously and, taking Fleming's raincoat from the chair, threw it over the body. Dale's eyes telegraphed her aunt a silent message of gratitude.

"Now-shall I telephone for the coroner?" persisted Miss Cornelia. The detective obviously resented her interference with his methods but he could not well refuse such a customary request.

"I'll do it," he said with a snort, going over to the city telephone. "What's his number?"

"He's not at his office; he's at the Johnsons'," murmured Dale.

Miss Cornelia took the telephone from Anderson's hands.

"I'll get the Johnsons', Mr. Anderson," she said firmly. The detective seemed about to rebuke her. Then his manner recovered some of its former suavity. He relinquished the telephone and turned back toward his prey.

"Now, what was Fleming doing here?" he asked Dale in a gentler voice.

Should she tell him the truth? No-Jack Bailey's safety was too inextricably bound up with the whole sinister business. She must lie, and lie again, while there was any chance of a lie's being believed.

"I don't know," she said weakly, trying to avoid the detective's eyes.

Anderson took thought.

"Well, I'll ask that question another way," he said. "How did he get into the house?"

Dale brightened-no need for a lie here.

"He had a key."

"Key to what door?"

"That door over there." Dale indicated the terrace door of the alcove.

The detective was about to ask another question-then he paused. Miss Cornelia was talking on the phone.

"Hello-is that Mr. Johnson's residence? Is Doctor Wells there? No?" Her expression was puzzled. "Oh-all right-thank you-good night——"

Meanwhile Anderson had been listening-but thinking as well. Dale saw his sharp glance travel over to the fireplace-rest for a moment, with an air of discovery, on the fragments of the roll of blue-prints that remained unburned among ashes-return. She shut her eyes for a moment, trying tensely to summon every atom of shrewdness she possessed to aid her.

He was hammering at her with questions again. "When did you take that revolver out of the table drawer?"

"When I heard him outside on the terrace," said Dale promptly and truthfully. "I was frightened."

Lizzie tiptoed over to Miss Cornelia.

"You wanted a detective!" she said in an ironic whisper. "I hope you're happy now you've got one!"

Miss Cornelia gave her a look that sent her scuttling back to her former post by the door. But nevertheless, internally, she felt thoroughly in accord with Lizzie.

Again Anderson's questions pounded at the rigid Dale, striving to pierce her armor of mingled truth and falsehood.

"When Fleming came in, what did he say to you?"

"Just-something about the weather," said Dale weakly. The whole scene was, still too horribly vivid before her eyes for her to furnish a more convincing alibi.

"You didn't have any quarrel with him?"

Dale hesitated.

"No."

"He just came in that door-said something about the weather-and was shot from that staircase. Is that it?" said the detective in tones of utter incredulity.

Dale hesitated again. Thus baldly put, her story seemed too flimsy for words; she could not even blame Anderson for disbelieving it. And yet-what other story could she tell that would not bring ruin on Jack?

Her face whitened. She put her hand on the back of a chair for support.

"Yes-that's it," she said at last, and swayed where she stood.

Again Miss Cornelia tried to come to the rescue. "Are all these questions necessary?" she queried sharply. "You can't for a moment believe that Miss Ogden shot that man!" But by now, though she did not show it, she too began to realize the strength of the appalling net of circumstances that drew with each minute tighter around the unhappy girl. Dale gratefully seized the momentary respite and sank into a chair. The detective looked at her.

"I think she knows more than she's telling. She's concealing something!" he said with deadly intentness. "The nephew of the president of the Union Bank-shot in his own house the day the bank has failed-that's queer enough —" Now he turned back to Miss Cornelia. "But when the only person present at his murder is the girl who's engaged to the guilty cashier," he continued, watching Miss Cornelia's face as the full force of his words sank into her mind, "I want to know more about it!"

He stopped. His right hand moved idly over the edge of the table-halted beside an ash tray-closed upon something.

Miss Cornelia rose.

"Is that true, Dale?" she said sorrowfully.

Dale nodded. "Yes." She could not trust herself to explain at greater length.

Then Miss Cornelia made one of the most magnificent gestures of her life.

"Well, even if it is-what has that got to do with it?" she said, turning upon Anderson fiercely, all her protective instinct for those whom she loved aroused.

Anderson seemed somewhat impressed by the fierceness of her query. When he went on it was with less harshness in his manner.

"I'm not accusing this girl," he said more gently. "But behind every crime there is a motive. When we've found the motive for this crime, we'll have found the criminal."

Unobserved, Dale's hand instinctively went to her bosom. There it lay-the motive-the precious fragment of blue-print which she had torn from Fleming's grasp but an instant before he was shot down. Once Anderson found it in her possession the case was closed, the evidence against her overwhelming. She could not destroy it-it was the only clue to the Hidden Room and the truth that might clear Jack Bailey. But, somehow, she must hide it-get it out of her hands-before Anderson's third-degree methods broke her down or he insisted on a search of her person. Her eyes roved wildly about the room, looking for a hiding place.

The rain of Anderson's questions began anew.

"What papers did Fleming burn in that grate?" he asked abruptly, turning back to Dale.

"Papers!" she faltered.

"Papers! The ashes are still there."

Miss Cornelia made an unavailing interruption.

"Miss Ogden has said he didn't come into this room."

The detective smiled.

"I hold in my hand proof that he was in this room for some time," he said coldly, displaying the half-burned cigarette he had taken from the ash tray a moment before.

"His cigarette-with his monogram on it." He put the fragment of tobacco and paper carefully away in an envelope and marched over to the fireplace. There he rummaged among the ashes for a moment, like a dog uncovering a bone. He returned to the center of the room with a fragment of blackened blue paper fluttering between his fingers.

"A fragment of what is technically known as a blue-print," he announced. "What were you and Richard Fleming doing with a blue-print?" His eyes bored into Dale's.

Dale hesitated-shut her lips.

"Now think it over!" he warned. "The truth will come out, sooner or later! Better be frank *now!*"

If he only knew how I wanted to be-he wouldn't be so cruel, thought Dale wearily. But I can't —I can't! Then her heart gave a throb of relief. Jack had come back into the room-Jack and Billy-Jack would protect her! But even as she thought of this her heart sank again. Protect her, indeed! Poor Jack! He would find it hard enough to protect himself if once this terrible man with the cold smile and steely eyes started questioning him. She looked up anxiously.

Bailey made his report breathlessly.

"Nothing in the house, sir."

Billy's impassive lips confirmed him.

"We go all over house-nobody!"

Nobody-nobody in the house! And yet-the mysterious ringing of the phone-the groans Miss Cornelia had heard! Were old wives' tales and witches' fables true after all? Did a power-merciless-evil-exists outside the barriers of the flesh-blasting that trembling flesh with a cold breath from beyond the portals of the grave? There seemed to be no other explanation.

"You men stay here!" said the detective. "I want to ask you some questions." He doggedly returned to his third-degreeing of Dale.

"Now what about this blue-print?" he queried sharply.

Dale stiffened in her chair. Her lies had failed. Now she would tell a portion of the truth, as much of it as she could without menacing Jack.

"I'll tell you just what happened," she began. "I sent for Richard Fleming-and when he came, I asked him if he knew where there were any blue-prints of the house."

The detective pounced eagerly upon her admission.

"Why did you want blue-prints?" he thundered.

"Because," Dale took a long breath, "I believe old Mr. Fleming took the money himself from the Union Bank and hid it here."

"Where did you get that idea?"

Dale's jaw set. "I won't tell you."

"What had the blue-prints to do with it?"

She could think of no plausible explanation but the true one.

"Because I'd heard there was a Hidden Room in this house."

The detective leaned forward intently. "Did you locate that room?"

Dale hesitated. "No."

"Then why did you burn the blue-prints?"

Dale's nerve was crumbling-breaking-under the repeated, monotonous impact of his questions.

"He burned them!" she cried wildly. "I don't know why!"

The detective paused an instant, then returned to a previous query.

"Then you didn't locate this Hidden Room?"

Dale's lips formed a pale "No."

"Did he?" went on Anderson inexorably.

Dale stared at him, dully-the breaking point had come. Another question-another-and she would no longer be able to control herself. She would sob out the truth hysterically-that Brooks, the gardener, was Jack Bailey, the missing cashier-that the scrap of blue-print hidden in the bosom of her dress might unravel the secret of the Hidden Room-that—

But just as she felt herself, sucked of strength, beginning to slide toward a black, tingling pit of merciful oblivion, Miss Cornelia provided a diversion.

"What's that?" she said in a startled voice.

The detective turned away from his quarry for an instant.

"What's what?"

"I heard something," averred Miss Cornelia, staring toward the French windows.

All eyes followed the direction of her stare. There was an instant of silence.

Then, suddenly, traveling swiftly from right to left across the shades of the French windows, there appeared a glowing circle of brilliant white light. Inside the circle was a black, distorted shadow—a shadow like the shadow of a gigantic black Bat! It was there-then a second later, it was gone!

"Oh, my God!" wailed Lizzie from her corner. "It's the Bat-that's his sign!"

Jack Bailey made a dash for the terrace door. But Miss Cornelia halted him peremptorily.

"Wait, Brooks!" She turned to the detective. "Mr. Anderson, you are familiar with the sign of the Bat. Did that look like it?"

The detective seemed both puzzled and disturbed. "Well, it looked like the shadow of a bat. I'll say that for it," he said finally.

On the heels of his words the front door bell began to ring. All turned in the direction of the hall.

"I'll answer that!" said Jack Bailey eagerly.

Miss Cornelia gave him the key to the front door.

"Don't admit anyone till you know who it is," she said. Bailey nodded and disappeared into the hall. The others waited tensely. Miss Cornelia's hand crept toward the revolver lying on the table where Anderson had put it down.

There was the click of an opening door, the noise of a little scuffle-then men's voices raised in an angry dispute. "What do I know about a flashlight?" cried an irritated voice. "I haven't got a pocket-flash—take your hands off me!" Bailey's voice answered the other voice, grim, threatening. The scuffle resumed.

Then Doctor Wells burst suddenly into the room, closely followed by Bailey. The Doctor's tie was askew-he looked ruffled and enraged. Bailey followed him vigilantly, seeming not quite sure whether to allow him to enter or not.

"My dear Miss Van Gorder," began the Doctor in tones of high dudgeon, "won't you instruct your servants that even if I do make a late call, I am not to be received with violence?"

"I asked you if you had a pocket-flash about you!" answered Bailey indignantly. "If you call a question like that violence —" He seemed about to restrain the Doctor by physical force.

Miss Cornelia quelled the teapot-tempest.

"It's all right, Brooks," she said, taking the front door key from his hand and putting it back on the table. She turned to Doctor Wells.

"You see, Doctor Wells," she explained, "just a moment before you rang the doorbell a circle of white light was thrown on those window shades."

The Doctor laughed with a certain relief.

"Why, that was probably the searchlight from my car!" he said. "I noticed as I drove up that it fell directly on that window."

His explanation seemed to satisfy all present but Lizzie. She regarded him with a deep suspicion. "'He may be a lawyer, a merchant, a Doctor...'" she chanted ominously to herself.

Miss Cornelia, too, was not entirely at ease.

"In the center of this ring of light," she proceeded, her eyes on the Doctor's calm countenance, "was an almost perfect silhouette of a bat."

"A bat!" The Doctor seemed at sea. "Ah, I see-the symbol of the criminal of that name." He laughed again.

"I think I can explain what you saw. Quite often my headlights collect insects at night and a large moth, spread on the glass, would give precisely the effect you speak of. Just to satisfy you, I'll go out and take a look."

He turned to do so. Then he caught sight of the raincoat-covered huddle on the floor.

"Why——" he said in a voice that mingled astonishment with horror. He paused. His glance slowly traversed the circle of silent faces.

Chapter Eleven
Billy Practices Jiu-Jitsu

"We have had a very sad occurrence here, Doctor," said Miss Cornelia gently.

The Doctor braced himself.

"Who?"

"Richard Fleming."

"Richard Fleming?" gasped the Doctor in tones of incredulous horror.

"Shot and killed from that staircase," said Miss Cornelia tonelessly.

The detective demurred.

"Shot and killed, anyhow," he said in accents of significant omission.

The Doctor knelt beside the huddle on the floor. He removed the fold of the raincoat that covered the face of the corpse and stared at the dead, blank mask. Till a moment ago, even at the height of his irritation with Bailey, he had been blithe and offhand —a man who seemed comparatively young for his years. Now Age seemed to fall upon him, suddenly, like a gray, clinging dust-he looked stricken and feeble under the impact of this unexpected shock.

"Shot and killed from that stairway," he repeated dully. He rose from his knees and glanced at the fatal stairs.

"What was Richard Fleming doing in this house at this hour?" he said.

He spoke to Miss Cornelia but Anderson answered the question.

"That's what I'm trying to find out," he said with a saturnine smile.

The Doctor gave him a look of astonished inquiry. Miss Cornelia remembered her manners.

"Doctor, this is Mr. Anderson."

"Headquarters," said Anderson tersely, shaking hands.

It was Lizzie's turn to play her part in the tangled game of mutual suspicion that by now made each member of the party at Cedarcrest watch every other member with nervous distrust. She crossed to her mistress on tiptoe.

"Don't you let him fool you with any of that moth business!" she said in a thrilling whisper, jerking her thumb in the direction of the Doctor. "He's the Bat."

Ordinarily Miss Cornelia would have dismissed her words with a smile. But by now her brain felt as if it had begun to revolve like a pinwheel in her efforts to fathom the uncanny mystery of the various events of the night.

She addressed Doctor Wells.

"I didn't tell you, Doctor—I sent for a detective this afternoon." Then, with mounting suspicion, "You happened in very opportunely!"

"After I left the Johnsons' I felt very uneasy," he explained. "I determined to make one more effort to get you away from this house. As this shows-my fears were justified!"

He shook his head sadly. Miss Cornelia sat down. His last words had given her food for thought. She wanted to mull them over for a moment.

The Doctor removed muffler and topcoat-stuffed the former in his topcoat pocket and threw the latter on the settee. He took out his handkerchief and began to mop his face, as if to wipe away some strain of mental excitement under which he was laboring. His breath came quickly-the muscles of his jaw stood out.

"Died instantly, I suppose?" he said, looking over at the body. "Didn't have time to say anything?"

"Ask the young lady," said Anderson, with a jerk of his head. "She was here when it happened."

The Doctor gave Dale a feverish glance of inquiry.

"He just fell over," said the latter pitifully. Her answer seemed to relieve the Doctor of some unseen weight on his mind. He drew a long breath and turned back toward Fleming's body with comparative calm.

"Poor Dick has proved my case for me better than I expected," he said, regarding the still, unbreathing heap beneath the raincoat. He swerved toward the detective.

"Mr. Anderson," he said with dignified pleading, "I ask you to use your influence, to see that these two ladies find some safer spot than this for the night."

Lizzie bounced up from her chair, instanter.

"Two?" she wailed. "If you know any safe spot, lead me to it!"

The Doctor overlooked her sudden eruption into the scene. He wandered back again toward the huddle under the raincoat, as if still unable to believe that it was-or rather had been-Richard Fleming.

Miss Cornelia spoke suddenly in a low voice, without moving a muscle of her body.

"I have a strange feeling that I'm being watched by unfriendly eyes," she said.

Lizzie clutched at her across the table.

"I wish the lights would go out again!" she pattered. "No, I don't neither!" as Miss Cornelia gave the clutching hand a nervous little slap.

During the little interlude of comedy, Billy, the Japanese, unwatched by the others, had stolen to the French windows, pulled aside a blind, looked out. When he turned back to the room his face had lost a portion of its Oriental calm-there was suspicion in his eyes. Softly, under cover of pretending to arrange the tray of food that lay untouched on the table, he possessed himself of the key to the front door, unperceived by the rest, and slipped out of the room like a ghost.

Meanwhile the detective confronted Doctor Wells.

"You say, Doctor, that you came back to take these women away from the house. Why?"

The Doctor gave him a dignified stare.

"Miss Van Gorder has already explained."

Miss Cornelia elucidated. "Mr. Anderson has already formed a theory of the crime," she said with a trace of sarcasm in her tones.

The detective turned on her quickly. "I haven't said that." He started.

It had come again-tinkling-persistent. —the phone call from nowhere-the ringing of the bell of the house telephone!

"The house telephone-again!" breathed Dale. Miss Cornelia made a movement to answer the tinkling, inexplicable bell. But Anderson was before her.

"I'll answer that!" he barked. He sprang to the phone.

"Hello-hello —"

All eyes were bent on him nervously-the Doctor's face, in particular, seemed a very study in fear and amazement. He clutched the back of a chair to support himself, his hand was the trembling hand of a sick, old man.

"Hello-hello —" Anderson swore impatiently. He hung up the phone.

"There's nobody there!"

Again, a chill breath from another world than ours seemed to brush across the faces of the little group in the living-room. Dale, sensitive, impressionable, felt a cold, uncanny prickling at the roots of her hair.

A light came into Anderson's eyes. "Where's that Jap?" he almost shouted.

"He just went out," said Miss Cornelia. The cold fear, the fear of the unearthly, subsided from around Dale's heart, leaving her shaken but more at peace.

The detective turned swiftly to the Doctor, as if to put his case before the eyes of an unprejudiced witness.

"That Jap rang the phone," he said decisively. "Miss Van Gorder believes that this murder is the culmination of the series of mysterious happenings that caused her to send for me. I do not."

"Then what is the significance of the anonymous letters?" broke in Miss Cornelia heatedly. "Of the man Lizzie saw going up the stairs, of the attempt to break into this house-of the ringing of that telephone bell?"

Anderson replied with one deliberate word.

"Terrorization," he said.

The Doctor moistened his dry lips in an effort to speak.

"By whom?" he asked.

Anderson's voice was an icicle.

"I imagine by Miss Van Gorder's servants. By that woman there —" he pointed at Lizzie, who rose indignantly to deny the charge. But he gave her no time for denial. He rushed on, " —who probably writes the letters," he continued. "By the gardener —" his pointing finger found Bailey " —who may have been the man Lizzie saw slipping up the stairs. By the Jap, who goes out and rings the telephone," he concluded triumphantly.

Miss Cornelia seemed unimpressed by his fervor.

"With what object?" she queried smoothly.

"That's what I'm going to find out!" There was determination in Anderson's reply.

Miss Cornelia sniffed. "Absurd! The butler was in this room when the telephone rang for the first time."

The thrust pierced Anderson's armor. For once he seemed at a loss. Here was something he had omitted from his calculations. But he did not give up. He was about to retort when-crash! thud! —the noise of a violent struggle in the hall outside drew all eyes to the hall door.

An instant later the door slammed open and a disheveled young man in evening clothes was catapulted into the living-room as if slung there by a giant's arm. He tripped and fell to the floor in the center of the room. Billy stood in the doorway behind him, inscrutable, arms folded, on his face an expression of mild satisfaction as if he were demurely pleased with a neat piece of housework, neatly carried out.

The young man picked himself up, brushed off his clothes, sought for his hat, which had rolled under the table. Then he turned on Billy furiously.

"Damn you-what do you mean by this?"

"Jiu-jitsu," said Billy, his yellow face quite untroubled. "Pretty good stuff. Found on terrace with searchlight," he added.

"With searchlight?" barked Anderson.

The young man turned to face this new enemy.

"Well, why shouldn't I be on the terrace with a searchlight?" he demanded.

The detective moved toward him menacingly.

"Who are you?"

"Who are you?" said the young man with cool impertinence, giving him stare for stare.

Anderson did not deign to reply, in so many words. Instead he displayed the police badge which glittered on the inside of the right lapel of his coat. The young man examined it coolly.

"H'm," he said. "Very pretty-nice neat design-very chaste!" He took out a cigarette case and opened it, seemingly entirely unimpressed by both the badge and Anderson. The detective chafed.

"If you've finished admiring my badge," he said with heavy sarcasm, "I'd like to know what you were doing on the terrace."

The young man hesitated-shot an odd, swift glance at Dale who ever since his abrupt entrance into the room, had been sitting rigid in her chair with her hands clenched tightly together.

"I've had some trouble with my car down the road," he said finally. He glanced at Dale again. "I came to ask if I might telephone."

"Did it require a flashlight to find the house?" Miss Cornelia asked suspiciously.

"Look here," the young man blustered, "why are you asking me all these questions?" He tapped his cigarette case with an irritated air.

Miss Cornelia stepped closer to him.

"Do you mind letting me see that flashlight?" she said.

The young man gave it to her with a little, mocking bow. She turned it over, examined it, passed it to Anderson, who examined it also, seeming to devote particular attention to the lens. The young man stood puffing his cigarette a little nervously while the examination was in progress. He did not look at Dale again.

Anderson handed back the flashlight to its owner.

"Now-what's your name?" he said sternly.

"Beresford-Reginald Beresford," said the young man sulkily. "If you doubt it I've probably got a card somewhere —" He began to search through his pockets.

"What's your business?" went on the detective.

"What's my business here?" queried the young man, obviously fencing with his interrogator.

"No-how do you earn your living?" said Anderson sharply.

"I don't," said the young man flippantly. "I may have to begin now, if that is of any interest to you. As a matter of fact, I've studied law but ——"

The one word was enough to start Lizzie off on another trail of distrust. "He may be a *lawyer* —" she quoted to herself sepulchrally from the evening newspaper article that had dealt with the mysterious identity of the Bat.

"And you came here to telephone about your car?" persisted the detective.

Dale rose from her chair with a hopeless little sigh. "Oh, don't you see-he's trying to protect me," she said wearily. She turned to the young man. "It's no use, Mr. Beresford."

Beresford's air of flippancy vanished.

"I see," he said. He turned to the other, frankly. "Well, the plain truth is—I didn't know the situation and I thought I'd play safe for Miss Ogden's sake."

Miss Cornelia moved over to her niece protectingly. She put a hand on Dale's shoulder to reassure her. But Dale was quite composed now-she had gone through so many shocks already that one more or less seemed to make very little difference to her overwearied nerves. She turned to Anderson calmly.

"He doesn't know anything about-this," she said, indicating Beresford. "He brought Mr. Fleming here in his car-that's all."

Anderson looked to Beresford for confirmation.

"Is that true?"

"Yes," said Beresford. He started to explain. "I got tired of waiting and so I——"

The detective broke in curtly.

"All right."

He took a step toward the alcove.

"Now, Doctor." He nodded at the huddle beneath the raincoat. Beresford followed his glance-and saw the ominous heap for the first time.

"What's that?" he said tensely. No one answered him. The Doctor was already on his knees beside the body, drawing the raincoat gently aside. Beresford stared at the shape thus revealed with frightened eyes. The color left his face.

"That's not-Dick Fleming-is it?" he said thickly. Anderson slowly nodded his head. Beresford seemed unable to believe his eyes.

"If you've looked over the ground," said the Doctor in a low voice to Anderson, "I'll move the body where we can have a better light." His right hand fluttered swiftly over Fleming's still, clenched fist-extracted from it a torn corner of paper....

Still Beresford did not seem to be able to take in what had happened. He took another step toward the body.

"Do you mean to say that Dick Fleming——" he began. Anderson silenced him with an uplifted hand.

"What have you got there, Doctor?" he said in a still voice.

The Doctor, still on his knees beside the corpse, lifted his head.

"What do you mean?"

"You took something, just then, out of Fleming's hand," said the detective.

"I took nothing out of his hand," said the Doctor firmly.

Anderson's manner grew peremptory.

"I warn you not to obstruct the course of justice!" he said forcibly. "Give it here!"

The Doctor rose slowly, dusting off his knees. His eyes tried to meet Anderson's and failed. He produced a torn corner of blue-print.

"Why, it's only a scrap of paper, nothing at all," he said evasively.

Anderson looked at him meaningly.

"Scraps of paper are sometimes very important," said with a side glance at Dale.

Beresford approached the two angrily.

"Look here!" he burst out, "I've got a right to know about this thing. I brought Fleming over here-and I want to know what happened to him!"

"You don't have to be a mind reader to know that!" moaned Lizzie, overcome.

As usual, her comment went unanswered. Beresford persisted in his questions.

"Who killed him? That's what I want to know!" he continued, nervously puffing his cigarette.

"Well, you're not alone in that," said Anderson in his grimly humorous vein.

The Doctor motioned nervously to them both.

"As the coroner-if Mr. Anderson is satisfied —I suggest that the body be taken where I can make a thorough examination," he said haltingly.

Once more Anderson bent over the shell that had been Richard Fleming. He turned the body half-over —let it sink back on its face. For a moment he glanced at the corner of the blue-print in his hand, then at the Doctor. Then he stood aside.

"All right," he said laconically.

So Richard Fleming left the room where he had been struck down so suddenly and strangely-borne out by Beresford, the Doctor, and Jack Bailey. The little procession moved as swiftly and softly as circumstances would permit-Anderson followed its passage with watchful eyes. Billy went mechanically to pick up the stained rug which the detective had kicked aside and carried it off after the body. When the burden and its bearers, with Anderson in the rear, reached the doorway into the hall, Lizzie shrank before the sight, affrighted, and turned toward the alcove while Miss Cornelia stared unseeingly out toward the front windows. So, for perhaps a dozen ticks of time Dale was left unwatched-and she made the most of her opportunity.

Her fingers fumbled at the bosom of her dress-she took out the precious, dangerous fragment of blue-print that Anderson must not find in her possession-but where to hide it, before her chance had passed? Her eyes fell on the bread roll that had fallen from the detective's supper tray to the floor when Lizzie had seen the gleaming eye on the stairs and had lain there unnoticed ever since. She bent over swiftly and secreted the tantalizing scrap of blue paper in the body of the roll, smoothing the crust back above it with trembling fingers. Then she replaced the roll where it had fallen originally and straightened up just as Billy and the detective returned.

Billy went immediately to the tray, picked it up, and started to go out again. Then he noticed the roll on the floor, stooped for it, and replaced it upon the tray. He looked at Miss Cornelia for instructions.

"Take that tray out to the dining-room," she said mechanically. But Anderson's attention had already been drawn to the tiny incident.

"Wait —I'll look at that tray," he said briskly. Dale, her heart in her mouth, watched him examine the knives, the plates, even shake out the napkin to see that nothing was hidden in its folds. At last he seemed satisfied.

"All right-take it away," he commanded. Billy nodded and vanished toward the dining-room with tray and roll. Dale breathed again.

The sight of the tray had made Miss Cornelia's thoughts return to practical affairs.

"Lizzie," she commanded now, "go out in the kitchen and make some coffee. I'm sure we all need it," she sighed.

Lizzie bristled at once.

"Go out in that kitchen alone?"

"Billy's there," said Miss Cornelia wearily.

The thought of Billy seemed to bring little solace to Lizzie's heart.

"That Jap and his jooy-jitsu," she muttered viciously. "One twist and I'd be folded up like a pretzel."

But Miss Cornelia's manner was imperative, and Lizzie slowly dragged herself kitchenward, yawning and promising the saints repentance of every sin she had or had not committed if she were allowed to get there without something grabbing at her ankles in the dark corner of the hall.

When the door had shut behind her, Anderson turned to Dale, the corner of blue-print which he had taken from the Doctor in his hand.

"Now, Miss Ogden," he said tensely, "I have here a scrap of blue-print which was in Dick Fleming's hand when he was killed. I'll trouble you for the rest of it, if you please!"

Chapter Twelve

"I Didn't Kill Him."

"The rest of it?" queried Dale with a show of bewilderment, silently thanking her stars that, for the moment at least, the incriminating fragment had passed out of her possession.

Her reply seemed only to infuriate the detective.

"Don't tell me Fleming started to go out of this house with a blank scrap of paper in his hand," he threatened. "He didn't start to go out at all!"

Dale rose. Was Anderson trying a chance shot in the dark-or had he stumbled upon some fresh evidence against her? She could not tell from his manner.

"Why do you say that?" she feinted.

"His cap's there on that table," said the detective with crushing terseness. Dale started. She had not remembered the cap-why hadn't she burned it, concealed it-as she had concealed the blue-print? She passed a hand over her forehead wearily.

Miss Cornelia watched her niece.

"It you're keeping anything back, Dale-tell him," she said.

"She's keeping something back all right," he said. "She's told part of the truth, but not all." He hammered at Dale again. "You and Fleming located that room by means of a blue-print of the house. He started-not to go out-but, probably, to go up that staircase. And he had in his hand the rest of this!" Again he displayed the blank corner of blue paper.

Dale knew herself cornered at last. The detective's deductions were too shrewd; do what she would, she could keep him away from the truth no longer.

"He was going to take the money and go away with it!" she said rather pitifully, feeling a certain relief of despair steal over her, now that she no longer needed to go on lying-lying-involving herself in an inextricable web of falsehood.

"Dale!" gasped Miss Cornelia, alarmed. But Dale went on, reckless of consequences to herself, though still warily shielding Jack.

"He changed the minute he heard about it. He was all kindness before that-but afterward —" She shuddered, closing her eyes. Fleming's face rose before her again, furious, distorted with passion and greed-then, suddenly, quenched of life.

Anderson turned to Miss Cornelia triumphantly.

"She started to find the money-and save Bailey," he explained, building up his theory of the crime. "But to do it she had to take Fleming into her confidence-and he turned yellow. Rather than let him get away with it, she —" He made an expressive gesture toward his hip pocket.

Dale trembled, feeling herself already in the toils. She had not quite realized, until now, how damningly plausible such an explanation of Fleming's death could sound. It fitted the evidence perfectly-it took account of every factor but one-the factor left unaccounted for was one which even she herself could not explain.

"Isn't that true?" demanded Anderson. Dale already felt the cold clasp of handcuffs on her slim wrists. What use of denial when every tiny circumstance was so leagued against her? And yet she must deny.

"I didn't kill him," she repeated perplexedly, weakly.

"Why didn't you call for help? You-you knew I was here."

Dale hesitated. "I—I couldn't." The moment the words were out of her mouth she knew from his expression that they had only cemented his growing certainty of her guilt.

"Dale! Be careful what you say!" warned Miss Cornelia agitatedly. Dale looked dumbly at her aunt. Her answers must seem the height of reckless folly to Miss Cornelia-oh, if there were only someone who understood!

Anderson resumed his grilling.

"Now I mean to find out two things," he said, advancing upon Dale. "Why you did not call for help-and what you have done with that blue-print."

"Suppose I could find that piece of blue-print for you?" said Dale desperately. "Would that establish Jack Bailey's innocence?"

The detective stared at her keenly for a moment.

"If the money's there-yes."

Dale opened her lips to reveal the secret, reckless of what might follow. As long as Jack was cleared-what matter what happened to herself? But Miss Cornelia nipped the heroic attempt at self-sacrifice in the bud.

She put herself between her niece and the detective, shielding Dale from his eager gaze.

"But her own guilt!" she said in tones of great dignity. "No, Mr. Anderson, granting that she knows where that paper is-and she has not said that she does—I shall want more time and much legal advice before I allow her to turn it over to you."

All the unconscious note of command that long-inherited wealth and the pride of a great name can give was in her voice, and the detective, for the moment, bowed before it, defeated. Perhaps he thought of men who had been broken from the Force for injudicious arrests, perhaps he merely bided his time. At any rate, he gave up his grilling of Dale for the present and turned to question the Doctor and Beresford who had just returned, with Jack Bailey, from their grim task of placing Fleming's body in a temporary resting place in the library.

"Well, Doctor?" he grunted.

The Doctor shook his head

"Poor fellow-straight through the heart."

"Were there any powder marks?" queried Miss Cornelia.

"No-and the clothing was not burned. He was apparently shot from some little distance-and I should say from above."

The detective received this information without the change of a muscle in his face. He turned to Beresford-resuming his attack on Dale from another angle.

"Beresford, did Fleming tell you why he came here tonight?"

Beresford considered the question.

"No. He seemed in a great hurry, said Miss Ogden had telephoned him, and asked me to drive him over."

"Why did you come up to the house?"

"We-el," said Beresford with seeming candor, "I thought it was putting rather a premium on friendship to keep me sitting out in the rain all night, so I came up the drive-and, by the way!" He snapped his fingers irritatedly, as if recalling some significant incident that had slipped his memory, and drew a battered object from his pocket. "I picked this up, about a hundred feet from the house," he explained. "A man's watch. It was partly crushed into the ground, and, as you see, it's stopped running."

The detective took the object and examined it carefully. A man's open-face gold watch, crushed and battered in as if it had been trampled upon by a heavy heel.

"Yes," he said thoughtfully. "Stopped running at ten-thirty."

Beresford went on, with mounting excitement.

"I was using my pocket-flash to find my way and what first attracted my attention was the ground-torn up, you know, all around it. Then I saw the watch itself. Anybody here recognize it?"

The detective silently held up the watch so that all present could examine it. He waited. But if anyone in the party recognized the watch-no one moved forward to claim it.

"You didn't hear any evidence of a struggle, did you?" went on Beresford. "The ground looked as if a fight had taken place. Of course it might have been a dozen other things."

Miss Cornelia started.

"Just about ten-thirty Lizzie heard somebody cry out, in the grounds," she said.

The detective looked Beresford over till the latter grew a little uncomfortable.

"I don't suppose it has any bearing on the case," admitted the latter uneasily. "But it's interesting."

The detective seemed to agree. At least he slipped the watch in his pocket.

"Do you always carry a flashlight, Mr. Beresford?" asked Miss Cornelia a trifle suspiciously.

"Always at night, in the car." His reply was prompt and certain.

"This is all you found?" queried the detective, a curious note in his voice.

"Yes." Beresford sat down, relieved. Miss Cornelia followed his example. Another clue had led into a blind alley, leaving the mystery of the night's affairs as impenetrable as ever.

"Some day I hope to meet the real estate agent who promised me that I would sleep here as I never slept before!" she murmured acridly. "He's right! I've slept with my clothes on every night since I came!"

As she ended, Billy darted in from the hall, his beady little black eyes gleaming with excitement, a long, wicked-looking butcher knife in his hand.

"Key, kitchen door, please!" he said, addressing his mistress.

"Key?" said Miss Cornelia, startled. "What for?"

For once Billy's polite little grin was absent from his countenance.

"Somebody outside trying to get in," he chattered. "I see knob turn, so," he illustrated with the butcher knife, "and so-three times."

The detective's hand went at once to his revolver.

"You're sure of that, are you?" he said roughly to Billy.

"Sure, I sure!"

"Where's that hysterical woman Lizzie?" queried Anderson. "She may get a bullet in her if she's not careful."

"She see too. She shut in closet-say prayers, maybe," said Billy, without a smile.

The picture was a ludicrous one but not one of the little group laughed.

"Doctor, have you a revolver?" Anderson seemed to be going over the possible means of defense against this new peril.

"No."

"How about you, Beresford?"

Beresford hesitated.

"Yes," he admitted finally. "Always carry one at night in the country." The statement seemed reasonable enough but Miss Cornelia gave him a sharp glance of mistrust, nevertheless.

The detective seemed to have more confidence in the young idler.

"Beresford, will you go with this Jap to the kitchen?" as Billy, grimly clutching his butcher knife, retraced his steps toward the hall. "If anyone's working at the knob-shoot through the door. I'm going round to take a look outside."

Beresford started to obey. Then he paused.

"I advise you not to turn the doorknob yourself, then," he said flippantly.

The detective nodded. "Much obliged," he said, with a grin. He ran lightly into the alcove and tiptoed out of the terrace door, closing the door behind him. Beresford and Billy departed to take up their posts in the kitchen. "I'll go with you, if you don't mind —" and Jack Bailey had followed them, leaving Miss Cornelia and Dale alone with the Doctor. Miss Cornelia, glad of the opportunity to get the Doctor's theories on the mystery without Anderson's interference, started to question him at once.

"Doctor."

"Yes." The Doctor turned, politely.

"Have you any theory about this occurrence to-night?" She watched him eagerly as she asked the question.

He made a gesture of bafflement.

"None whatever-it's beyond me," he confessed.

"And yet you warned me to leave this house," said Miss Cornelia cannily. "You didn't have any reason to believe that the situation was even as serious as it has proved to be?"

"I did the perfectly obvious thing when I warned you," said the Doctor easily. "Those letters made a distinct threat."

Miss Cornelia could not deny the truth in his words. And yet she felt decidedly unsatisfied with the way things were progressing.

"You said Fleming had probably been shot from above?" she queried, thinking hard.

The Doctor nodded. "Yes."

"Have you a pocket-flash, Doctor?" she asked him suddenly.

"Why-yes —" The Doctor did not seem to perceive the significance of the query. "A flashlight is more important to a country Doctor than-castor oil," he added, with a little smile.

Miss Cornelia decided upon an experiment. She turned to Dale.

"Dale, you said you saw a white light shining down from above?"

"Yes," said Dale in a minor voice.

Miss Cornelia rose.

"May I borrow your flashlight, Doctor? Now that fool detective is out of the way," she continued some what acidly, "I want to do something."

The Doctor gave her his flashlight with a stare of bewilderment. She took it and moved into the alcove.

"Doctor, I shall ask you to stand at the foot of the small staircase, facing up."

"Now?" queried the Doctor with some reluctance.

"Now, please."

The Doctor slowly followed her into the alcove and took up the position she assigned him at the foot of the stairs.

"Now, Dale," said Miss Cornelia briskly, "when I give the word, you put out the lights here-and then tell me when I have reached the point on the staircase from which the flashlight seemed to come. All ready?"

Two silent nods gave assent. Miss Cornelia left the room to seek the second floor by the main staircase and then slowly return by the alcove stairs, her flashlight poised, in her reconstruction of the events of the crime. At the foot of the alcove stairs the Doctor waited uneasily for her arrival. He glanced up the stairs-were those her footsteps now? He peered more closely into the darkness.

An expression of surprise and apprehension came over his face.

He glanced swiftly at Dale-was she watching him? No-she sat in her chair, musing. He turned back toward the stairs and made a frantic, insistent gesture —"Go back, go back!" it said, plainer than words, to-Something-in the darkness by the head of the stairs. Then his face relaxed, he gave a noiseless sigh of relief.

Dale, rousing from her brown study, turned out the floor lamp by the table and went over to the main light switch, awaiting Miss Cornelia's signal to plunge the room in darkness. The Doctor stole, another glance at her-had his gestures been observed? —apparently not.

Unobserved by either, as both waited tensely for Miss Cornelia's signal, a hand stole through the broken pane of the shattered French window behind their backs and fumbled for the knob which unlocked the window-door. It found the catch-unlocked it-the window-door swung open, noiselessly-just enough to admit a crouching figure that cramped itself uncomfortably behind the settee which Dale and the Doctor had placed to barricade those very doors. When it had settled itself, unperceived, in its lurking place-the Hand stole out again-closed the window-door, relocked it.

Hand or claw? Hand of man or woman or paw of beast? In the name of God —*whose hand?*

Miss Cornelia's voice from the head of the stairs broke the silence.

"All right! Put out the lights!"

Dale pressed the switch. Heavy darkness. The sound of her own breathing. A mutter from the Doctor. Then, abruptly, a white, piercing shaft of light cut the darkness of the stairs-horribly reminiscent of that other light-shaft that had signaled Fleming's doom.

"Was it here?" Miss Cornelia's voice came muffledly from the head of the stairs.

Dale considered. "Come down a little," she said. The white spot of light wavered, settled on the Doctor's face.

"I hope you haven't a weapon," the Doctor called up the stairs with an unsuccessful attempt at jocularity.

Miss Cornelia descended another step.

"How's this?"

"That's about right," said Dale uncertainly. Miss Cornelia was satisfied.

"Lights, please." She went up the stairs again to see if she could puzzle out what course of escape the man who had shot Fleming had taken after his crime-if it had been a man.

Dale switched on the living-room lights with a sense of relief. The reconstruction of the crime had tried her sorely. She sat down to recover her poise.

"Doctor! I'm so frightened!" she confessed.

The Doctor at once assumed his best manner of professional reassurance.

"Why, my dear child?" he asked lightly. "Because you happened to be in the room when a crime was committed?"

"But he has a perfect case against me," sighed Dale.

"That's absurd!"

"No."

"*You don't mean?*" said the Doctor aghast.

Dale looked at him with horror in her face.

"I didn't kill him!" she insisted anew. "But, you know the piece of blue-print you found in his hand?"

"Yes," from the Doctor tensely.

Dale's nerves, too bitterly tested, gave way at last under the strain of keeping her secret. She felt that she must confide in someone or perish. The Doctor was kind and thoughtful-more than that, he was an experienced man of the world-if he could not advise her, who could? Besides, a Doctor was in many ways like a priest-both sworn to keep inviolate the secrets of their respective confessionals.

"There was another piece of blue-print, a larger piece —" said Dale slowly, "I tore it from him just before — —"

The Doctor seemed greatly excited by her words. But he controlled himself swiftly.

"Why did you do such a thing?"

"Oh, I'll explain that later," said Dale tiredly, only too glad to be talking the matter out at last, to pay attention to the logic of her sentences. "It's not safe where it is," she went on, as if the Doctor already knew the whole story. "Billy may throw it out or burn it without knowing — —"

"Let me understand this," said the Doctor. "The butler has the paper now?"

"He doesn't know he has it. It was in one of the rolls that went out on the tray."

The Doctor's eyes gleamed. He gave Dale's shoulder a sympathetic pat.

"Now don't you worry about it —I'll get it," he said. Then, on the point of going toward the dining-room, he turned.

"But-you oughtn't to have it in your possession," he said thoughtfully. "Why not let it be burned?"

Dale was on the defensive at once.

"Oh, no! It's important, it's vital!" she said decidedly.

The Doctor seemed to consider ways and means of getting the paper.

"The tray is in the dining-room?" he asked.

"Yes," said Dale.

He thought a moment, then left the room by the hall door. Dale sank back in her chair and felt a sense of overpowering relief steal over her whole body, as if new life had been poured into her veins. The Doctor had been so helpful-why had she not confided in him before? He would know what to do with the paper-she would have the benefit of his counsel through the rest of this troubled time. For a moment she saw herself and Jack, exonerated, their worries at an end, wandering hand in hand over the green lawns of Cedarcrest in the cheerful sunlight of morning.

Behind her, mockingly, the head of the Unknown concealed behind the settee lifted cautiously until, if she had turned, she would have just been able to perceive the top of its skull.

Chapter Thirteen
The Blackened Bag

As it chanced, she did not turn. The hall door opened-the head behind the settee sank down again. Jack Bailey entered, carrying a couple of logs of firewood.

Dale moved toward him as soon as he had shut the door.

"Oh, things have gone awfully wrong, haven't they?" she said with a little break in her voice.

He put his finger to his lips.

"Be careful!" he whispered. He glanced about the room cautiously.

"I don't trust even the furniture in this house to-night!" he said. He took Dale hungrily in his arms and kissed her once, swiftly, on the lips. Then they parted-his voice changed to the formal voice of a servant.

"Miss Van Gorder wishes the fire kept burning," he announced, with a whispered "Play up!" to Dale.

Dale caught his meaning at once.

"Put some logs on the fire, please," she said loudly, for the benefit of any listening ears. Then in an undertone to Bailey, "Jack —I'm nearly distracted!"

Bailey threw his wood on the fire, which received it with appreciative crackles and sputterings. Then again, for a moment, he clasped his sweetheart closely to him.

"Dale, pull yourself together!" he whispered warningly. "We've got a fight ahead of us!"

He released her and turned back toward the fire.

"These old-fashioned fireplaces eat up a lot of wood," he said in casual tones, pretending to arrange the logs with the poker so the fire would draw more cleanly.

But Dale felt that she must settle one point between them before they took up their game of pretense again.

"You know why I sent for Richard Fleming, don't you?" she said, her eyes fixed beseechingly on her lover. The rest of the world might interpret her action as it pleased-she couldn't bear to have Jack misunderstand.

But there was no danger of that. His faith in her was too complete.

"Yes-of course —" he said, with a look of gratitude. Then his mind reverted to the ever-present problem before them. "But who in God's name killed him?" he muttered, kneeling before the fire.

"You don't think it was-Billy?" Dale saw Billy's face before her for a moment, calm, impassive. But he was an Oriental-an alien-his face might be just as calm, just as impassive while his hands were still red with blood. She shuddered at the thought.

Bailey considered the matter.

"More likely the man Lizzie saw going upstairs," he said finally. "But —I've been all over the upper floors."

"And-nothing?" breathed Dale.

"Nothing." Bailey's voice had an accent of dour finality. "Dale, do you think that — —" he began.

Some instinct warned the girl that they were not to continue their conversation uninterrupted. "Be careful!" she breathed, as footsteps sounded in the hall. Bailey nodded and turned back to his pretense of mending the fire. Dale moved away from him slowly.

The door opened and Miss Cornelia entered, her black knitting-bag in her hand, on her face a demure little smile of triumph. She closed the door carefully behind her and began to speak at once.

"Well, Mr. Alopecia-Urticaria-Rubeola-otherwise *Bailey!*" she said in tones of the greatest satisfaction, addressing herself to Bailey's rigid back. Bailey jumped to his feet mechanically at her mention of his name. He and Dale exchanged one swift and hopeless glance of utter defeat.

"I wish," proceeded Miss Cornelia, obviously enjoying the situation to the full, "I wish you young people would remember that even if hair and teeth have fallen out at sixty the mind still functions."

She pulled out a cabinet photograph from the depths of her knitting-bag.

"His photograph-sitting on your dresser!" she chided Dale. "Burn it and be quick about it!"

Dale took the photograph but continued to stare at her aunt with incredulous eyes.

"Then-you knew?" she stammered.

Miss Cornelia, the effective little tableau she had planned now accomplished to her most humorous satisfaction, relapsed into a chair.

"My dear child," said the indomitable lady, with a sharp glance at Bailey's bewildered face, "I have employed many gardeners in my time and never before had one who manicured his fingernails, wore silk socks, and regarded baldness as a plant instead of a calamity."

An unwilling smile began to break on the faces of both Dale and her lover. The former crossed to the fireplace and threw the damning photograph of Bailey on the flames. She watched it shrivel-curl up-be reduced to ash. She stirred the ashes with a poker till they were well scattered.

Bailey, recovering from the shock of finding that Miss Cornelia's sharp eyes had pierced his disguise without his even suspecting it, now threw himself on her mercy.

"Then you know why I'm here?" he stammered.

"I still have a certain amount of imagination! I may think you are a fool for taking the risk, but I can see what that idiot of a detective might not-that if you had looted the Union Bank you wouldn't be trying to discover if the money is in this house. You would at least presumably know where it is."

The knowledge that he had an ally in this brisk and indomitable spinster lady cheered him greatly. But she did not wait for any comment from him. She turned abruptly to Dale.

"Now I want to ask you something," she said more gravely. "Was there a blue-print, and did you get it from Richard Fleming?"

It was Dale's turn now to bow her head.

"Yes," she confessed.

Bailey felt a thrill of horror run through him. She hadn't told him this!

"Dale!" he said uncomprehendingly, "don't you see where this places you? If you had it, why didn't you give it to Anderson when he asked for it?"

"Because," said Miss Cornelia uncompromisingly, "she had sense enough to see that Mr. Anderson considered that piece of paper the final link in the evidence against her!"

"But she could have no motive!" stammered Bailey, distraught, still failing to grasp the significance of Dale's refusal.

"Couldn't she?" queried Miss Cornelia pityingly. "The detective thinks she could-to save you!"

Now the full light of revelation broke upon Bailey. He took a step back.

"Good God!" he said.

Miss Cornelia would have liked to comment tartly upon the singular lack of intelligence displayed by even the nicest young men in trying circumstances. But there was no time. They might be interrupted at any moment and before they were, there were things she must find out.

"Where is that paper, now?" she asked Dale sharply.

"Why-the Doctor is getting it for me." Dale seemed puzzled by the intensity of her aunt's manner.

"What?" almost shouted Miss Cornelia. Dale explained.

"It was on the tray Billy took out," she said, still wondering why so simple an answer should disturb Miss Cornelia so greatly.

"Then I'm afraid everything's over," Miss Cornelia said despairingly, and made her first gesture of defeat. She turned away. Dale followed her, still unable to fathom her course of reasoning.

"I didn't know what else to do," she said rather plaintively, wondering if again, as with Fleming, she had misplaced her confidence at a moment critical for them all.

But Miss Cornelia seemed to have no great patience with her dejection.

"One of two things will happen now," she said, with acrid, logic. "Either the Doctor's an honest man-in which case, as coroner, he will hand that paper to the detective —" Dale gasped. "Or he is not an honest man," went on Miss Cornelia, "and he will keep it for himself. I don't think he's an honest man."

The frank expression of her distrust seemed to calm her a little. She resumed her interrogation of Dale more gently.

"Now, let's be clear about this. Had Richard Fleming ascertained that there was a concealed room in this house?"

"He was starting up to it!" said Dale in the voice of a ghost, remembering.

"Just what did you tell him?"

"That I believed there was a Hidden Room in the house-and that the money from the Union Bank might be in it."

Again, for the millionth time, indeed it seemed to her, she reviewed the circumstances of the crime.

"Could anyone have overheard?" asked Miss Cornelia.

The question had rung in Dale's ears ever since she had come to her senses after the firing of the shot and seen Fleming's body stark on the floor of the alcove.

"I don't know," she said. "We were very cautious."

"You don't know where this room is?"

"No, I never saw the print. Upstairs somewhere, for he ——"

"Upstairs! Then the thing to do, if we can get that paper from the Doctor, is to locate the room at once."

Jack Bailey did not recognize the direction where her thoughts were tending. It seemed terrible to him that anyone should devote a thought to the money while Dale was still in danger.

"What does the money matter now?" he broke in somewhat irritably. "We've got to save her!" and his eyes went to Dale.

Miss Cornelia gave him an ineffable look of weary patience.

"The money matters a great deal," she said, sensibly. "Someone was in this house on the same errand as Richard Fleming. After all," she went on with a tinge of irony, "the course of reasoning that you followed, Mr. Bailey, is not necessarily unique."

She rose.

"Somebody else may have suspected that Courtleigh Fleming robbed his own bank," she said thoughtfully. Her eye fell on the Doctor's professional bag-she seemed to consider it as if it were a strange sort of animal.

"Find the man who followed your course of reasoning," she ended, with a stare at Bailey, "and you have found the murderer."

"With that reasoning you might suspect me!" said the latter a trifle touchily.

Miss Cornelia did not give an inch.

"I have," she said. Dale shot a swift, sympathetic glance at her lover, another less sympathetic and more indignant at her aunt. Miss Cornelia smiled.

"However, I now suspect somebody else," she said. They waited for her to reveal the name of the suspect but she kept her own counsel. By now she had entirely given up confidence if not in the probity at least in the intelligence of all persons, male or female, under the age of sixty-five.

She rang the bell for Billy. But Dale was still worrying over the possible effects of the confidence she had given Doctor Wells.

"Then you think the Doctor may give this paper to Mr. Anderson?" she asked.

"He may or he may not. It is entirely possible that he may elect to search for this room himself! He may even already have gone upstairs!"

She moved quickly to the door and glanced across toward the dining-room, but so far apparently all was safe. The Doctor was at the table making a pretense of drinking a cup of coffee and Billy was in close attendance. That the Doctor already had the paper she was certain; it was the use he intended to make of it that was her concern.

She signaled to the Jap and he came out into the hall. Beresford, she learned, was still in the kitchen with his revolver, waiting for another attempt on the door and the detective was still outside in his search. To Billy she gave her order in a low voice.

"If the Doctor attempts to go upstairs," she said, "let me know at once. Don't seem to be watching. You can be in the pantry. But let me know instantly."

Once back in the living-room the vague outlines of a plan—a test-formed slowly in Miss Cornelia's mind, grew more definite.

"Dale, watch that door and warn me if anyone is coming!" she commanded, indicating the door into the hall. Dale obeyed, marveling silently at her aunt's extraordinary force of character. Most of Miss Cornelia's contemporaries would have called for a quiet ambulance to take them to a sanatorium some hours ere this-but Miss Cornelia was not merely, comparatively speaking, as fresh as a daisy; her manner bore every evidence of a firm intention to play Sherlock Holmes to the mysteries that surrounded her, in spite of Doctors, detectives, dubious noises, or even the Bat himself.

The last of the Van Gorder spinsters turned to Bailey now.

"Get some soot from that fireplace," she ordered. "Be quick. Scrape it off with a knife or a piece of paper. Anything."

Bailey wondered and obeyed. As he was engaged in his grimy task, Miss Cornelia got out a piece of writing paper from a drawer and placed it on the center table, with a lead pencil beside it.

Bailey emerged from the fireplace with a handful of sooty flakes.

"Is this all right?"

"Yes. Now rub it on the handle of that bag." She indicated the little black bag in which Doctor Wells carried the usual paraphernalia of a country Doctor.

A private suspicion grew in Bailey's mind as to whether Miss Cornelia's fine but eccentric brain had not suffered too sorely under the shocks of the night. But he did not dare disobey. He blackened the handle of the Doctor's bag with painstaking thoroughness and awaited further instructions.

"Somebody's coming!" Dale whispered, warning from her post by the door.

Bailey quickly went to the fireplace and resumed his pretended labors with the fire. Miss Cornelia moved away from the Doctor's bag and spoke for the benefit of whoever might be coming.

"We all need sleep," she began, as if ending a conversation with Dale, "and I think——"

The door opened, admitting Billy.

"Doctor just go upstairs," he said, and went out again leaving the door open.

A flash passed across Miss Cornelia's face. She stepped to the door. She called.

"Doctor! Oh, Doctor!"

"Yes?" answered the Doctor's voice from the main staircase. His steps clattered down the stairs-he entered the room. Perhaps he read something in Miss Cornelia's manner that demanded an explanation of his action. At any rate, he forestalled her, just as she was about to question him.

"I was about to look around above," he said. "I don't like to leave if there is the possibility of some assassin still hidden in the house."

"That is very considerate of you. But we are well protected now. And besides, why should this person remain in the house? The murder is done, the police are here."

"True," he said. "I only thought——"

But a knocking at the terrace door interrupted him. While the attention of the others was turned in that direction Dale, less cynical than her aunt, made a small plea to him and realized before she had finished with it that the Doctor too had his price.

"Doctor-did you get it?" she repeated, drawing the Doctor aside.

The Doctor gave her a look of apparent bewilderment.

"My dear child," he said softly, "are you sure that you put it there?"

Dale felt as if she had received a blow in the face.

"Why, yes—I—" she began in tones of utter dismay. Then she stopped. The Doctor's seeming bewilderment was too pat-too plausible. Of course she was sure-and, though possible, it seemed extremely unlikely that anyone else could have discovered the hiding-place of the blue-print in the few moments that had elapsed between the time when Billy took the tray from the room and the time when the Doctor ostensibly went to find it. A cold wave of distrust swept over her-she turned away from the Doctor silently.

Meanwhile Anderson had entered, slamming the terrace-door behind him.

"I couldn't find anybody!" he said in an irritated voice. "I think that Jap's crazy."

The Doctor began to struggle into his topcoat, avoiding any look at Dale.

"Well," he said, "I believe I've fulfilled all the legal requirements—I think I must be going." He turned toward the door but the detective halted him.

"Doctor," he said, "did you ever hear Courtleigh Fleming mention a Hidden Room in this house?"

If the Doctor started, the movement passed apparently unnoted by Anderson. And his reply was coolly made.

"No-and I knew him rather well."

"You don't think then," persisted the detective, "that such a room and the money in it could be the motive for this crime?"

The Doctor's voice grew a little curt.

"I don't believe Courtleigh Fleming robbed his own bank, if that's what you mean," he said with nicely calculated emphasis, real or feigned. He crossed over to get his bag and spoke to Miss Cornelia.

"Well, Miss Van Gorder," he said, picking up the bag by its blackened handle, "I can't wish you a comfortable night but I can wish you a quiet one."

Miss Cornelia watched him silently. As he turned to go, she spoke.

"We're all of us a little upset, naturally," she confessed. "Perhaps you could write a prescription—a sleeping-powder or a bromide of some sort."

"Why, certainly," agreed the Doctor at once. He turned back. Miss Cornelia seemed pleased.

"I hoped you would," she said with a little tremble in her voice such as might easily occur in the voice of a nervous old lady. "Oh, yes, here's paper and a pencil," as the Doctor fumbled in a pocket.

The Doctor took the sheet of paper she proffered and, using the side of his bag as a pad, began to write out the prescription.

"I don't generally advise these drugs," he said, looking up for a moment. "Still——"

He paused. "What time is it?"

Miss Cornelia glanced at the clock. "Half-past eleven."

"Then I'd better bring you the powders myself," decided the Doctor. "The pharmacy closes at eleven. I shall have to make them up myself."

"That seems a lot of trouble."

"Nothing is any trouble if I can be helpful," he assured her, smilingly. And Miss Cornelia also smiled, took the piece of paper from his hand, glanced at it once, as if out of idle curiosity about the unfinished prescription, and then laid it down on the table with a careless little gesture. Dale gave her aunt a glance of dumb entreaty. Miss Cornelia read her wish for another moment alone with the Doctor.

"Dale will let you out, Doctor," said she, giving the girl the key to the front door.

The Doctor approved her watchfulness.

"That's right," he said smilingly. "Keep things locked up. Discretion is the better part of valor!"

But Miss Cornelia failed to agree with him.

"I've been discreet for sixty-five years," she said with a sniff, "and sometimes I think it was a mistake!"

The Doctor laughed easily and followed Dale out of the room, with a nod of farewell to the others in passing. The detective, seeking for some object upon whom to vent the growing irritation which seemed to possess him, made Bailey the scapegoat of his wrath.

"I guess we can do without you for the present!" he said, with an angry frown at the latter. Bailey flushed, then remembered himself, and left the room submissively, with the air of a well-trained servant accepting an unmerited rebuke. The detective turned at once to Miss Cornelia.

"Now I want a few words with you!"

"Which means that you mean to do all the talking!" said Miss Cornelia acidly. "Very well! But first I want to show you something. Will you come here, please, Mr. Anderson?"

She started for the alcove.

"I've examined that staircase," said the detective.

"Not with me!" insisted Miss Cornelia. "I have something to show you."

He followed her unwillingly up the stairs, his whole manner seeming to betray a complete lack of confidence in the theories of all amateur sleuths in general and spinster detectives of sixty-five in particular. Their footsteps died away up the alcove stairs. The living-room was left vacant for an instant.

Vacant? Only in seeming. The moment that Miss Cornelia and the detective had passed up the stairs, the crouching, mysterious Unknown, behind the settee, began to move. The French window-door opened —a stealthy figure passed through it silently to be swallowed up in the darkness of the terrace.

And poor Lizzie, entering the room at that moment, saw a hand covered with blood reach back and gropingly, horribly, through the broken pane, refasten the lock.

She shrieked madly.

Chapter Fourteen
Handcuffs

Dale had failed with the Doctor. When Lizzie's screams once more had called the startled household to the living-room, she knew she had failed. She followed in mechanically, watched an irritated Anderson send the Pride of Kerry to bed and threaten to lock her up, and listened vaguely to the conversation between her aunt and the detective that followed it, without more than casual interest.

Nevertheless, that conversation was to have vital results later on.

"Your point about that thumbprint on the stair rail is very interesting," Anderson said with a certain respect. "But just what does it prove?"

"It points down," said Miss Cornelia, still glowing with the memory of the whistle of surprise the detective had given when she had shown him the strange thumbprint on the rail of the alcove stairs.

"It does," he admitted. "But what then?"

Miss Cornelia tried to put her case as clearly and tersely as possible.

"It shows that somebody stood there for some time, listening to my niece and Richard Fleming in this room below," she said.

"All right —I'll grant that to save argument," retorted the detective. "But the moment that shot was fired the lights came on. If somebody on that staircase shot him, and then came down and took the blue-print, Miss Ogden would have seen him."

He turned upon Dale.

"Did you?"

She hesitated. Why hadn't she thought of such an explanation before? But now-it would sound too flimsy!

"No, nobody came down," she admitted candidly. The detective's face altered, grew menacing. Miss Cornelia once more had put herself between him and Dale.

"Now, Mr. Anderson——" she warned.

The detective was obviously trying to keep his temper.

"I'm not hounding this girl!" he said doggedly. "I haven't said yet that she committed the murder-but she took that blue-print and I want it!"

"You want it to connect her with the murder," parried Miss Cornelia.

The detective threw up his hands.

"It's rather reasonable to suppose that I might want to return the funds to the Union Bank, isn't it?" he queried in tones of heavy sarcasm. "Provided they're here," he added doubtfully.

Miss Cornelia resolved upon comparative frankness.

"I see," she said. "Well, I'll tell you this much, Mr. Anderson, and I'll ask you to believe me as a lady. Granting that at one time my niece knew something of that blue-print—at this moment we do not know where it is or who has it."

Her words had the unmistakable ring of truth. The very oath from the detective that succeeded them showed his recognition of the fact.

"Damnation," he muttered. "That's true, is it?"

"That's true," said Miss Cornelia firmly. A silence of troubled thoughts fell upon the three. Miss Cornelia took out her knitting.

"Did you ever try knitting when you wanted to think?" she queried sweetly, after a pause in which the detective tramped from one side of the room to the other, brows knotted, eyes bent on the floor.

"No," grunted the detective. He took out a cigar-bit off the end with a savage snap of teeth-lit it-resumed his pacing.

"You should, sometimes," continued Miss Cornelia, watching his troubled movements with a faint light of mockery in her eyes. "I find it very helpful."

"I don't need knitting to think straight," rasped Anderson indignantly. Miss Cornelia's eyes danced.

"I wonder!" she said with caustic affability. "You seem to have so much evidence left over."

The detective paused and glared at her helplessly.

"Did you ever hear of the man who took a clock apart-and when he put it together again, he had enough left over to make another clock?" she twitted.

The detective, ignoring the taunt, crossed quickly to Dale.

"What do you mean by saying that paper isn't where you put it?" he demanded in tones of extreme severity. Miss Cornelia replied for her niece.

"She hasn't said that."

The detective made an impatient movement of his hand and walked away-as if to get out of the reach of the indefatigable spinster's tongue. But Miss Cornelia had not finished with him yet, by any means.

"Do you believe in circumstantial evidence?" she asked him with seeming ingenuousness.

"It's my business," said the detective stolidly. Miss Cornelia smiled.

"While you have been investigating," she announced, "I, too, have not been idle."

The detective gave a barking laugh. She let it pass. "To me," she continued, "it is perfectly obvious that one intelligence has been at work behind many of the things that have occurred in this house."

Now Anderson observed her with a new respect.

"Who?" he grunted tersely.

Her eyes flashed.

"I'll ask you that! Some one person who, knowing Courtleigh Fleming well, probably knows of the existence of a Hidden Room in this house and who, finding us in occupation of the house, has tried to get rid of me in two ways. First, by frightening me with anonymous threats-and, second, by urging me to leave. Someone, who very possibly entered this house tonight shortly before the murder and slipped up that staircase!"

The detective had listened to her outburst with unusual thoughtfulness. A certain wonder-perhaps at her shrewdness, perhaps at an unexpected confirmation of certain ideas of his own-grew upon his face. Now he jerked out two words.

"The Doctor?"

Miss Cornelia knitted on as if every movement of her needles added one more link to the strong chain of probabilities she was piecing together.

"When Doctor Wells said he was leaving here earlier in the evening for the Johnsons' he did not go there," she observed. "He was not expected to go there. I found that out when I telephoned."

"The Doctor!" repeated the detective, his eyes narrowing, his head beginning to sway from side to side like the head of some great cat just before a spring.

"As you know," Miss Cornelia went on, "I had a supplementary bolt placed on that terrace door today." She nodded toward the door that gave access into the alcove from the terrace. "Earlier this evening Doctor Wells said that he had bolted it, when he had left it open-purposely, as I now realize, in order that he might return later. You may also recall that Doctor Wells took a scrap of paper from Richard Fleming's hand and tried to conceal it-why did he do that?"

She paused for a second. Then she changed her tone a little.

"May I ask you to look at this?"

She displayed the piece of paper on which Doctor Wells had started to write the prescription for her sleeping-powders —and now her strategy with the doctor's bag and the soot Jack Bailey had got from the fireplace stood revealed. A sharp, black imprint of a man's right thumb-the Doctor's —stood out on the paper below the broken line of writing. The Doctor had not noticed the staining of his hand by the blackened bag handle, or, noticing, had thought nothing of it-but the blackened bag handle had been a trap, and he had left an indelible piece of evidence behind him. It now remained to test the value of this evidence.

Miss Cornelia handed the paper to Anderson silently. But her eyes were bright with pardonable vanity at the success of her little piece of strategy.

"A thumb-print," muttered Anderson. "Whose is it?"

"Doctor Wells," said Miss Cornelia with what might have been a little crow of triumph in anyone not a Van Gorder.

Anderson looked thoughtful. Then he felt in his pocket for a magnifying glass, failed to find it, muttered, and took the reading glass Miss Cornelia offered him.

"Try this," she said. "My whole case hangs on my conviction that that print and the one out there on the stair rail are the same."

He put down the paper and smiled at her ironically. "Your case!" he said. "You don't really believe you need a detective at all, do you?"

"I will only say that so far your views and mine have failed to coincide. If I am right about that fingerprint, then you may be right about my private opinion."

And on that he went out, rather grimly, paper and reading glass in hand, to make his comparison.

It was then that Beresford came in, a new and slightly rigid Beresford, and crossed to her at once.

"Miss Van Gorder," he said, all the flippancy gone from his voice, "may I ask you to make an excuse and call your gardener here?"

Dale started uncontrollably at the ominous words, but Miss Cornelia betrayed no emotion except in the increased rapidity of her knitting.

"The gardener? Certainly, if you'll touch that bell," she said pleasantly.

Beresford stalked to the bell and rang it. The three waited-Dale in an agony of suspense.

The detective re-entered the room by the alcove stairs, his mien unfathomable by any of the anxious glances that sought him out at once.

"It's no good, Miss Van Gorder," he said quietly. "The prints are not the same."

"Not the same!" gasped Miss Cornelia, unwilling to believe her ears.

Anderson laid down the paper and the reading glass with a little gesture of dismissal.

"If you think I'm mistaken, I'll leave it to any unprejudiced person or your own eyesight. Thumbprints never lie," he said in a flat, convincing voice. Miss Cornelia stared at him-disappointment written large on her features. He allowed himself a little ironic smile.

"Did you ever try a good cigar when you wanted to think?" he queried suavely, puffing upon his own.

But Miss Cornelia's spirit was too broken by the collapse of her dearly loved and adroitly managed scheme for her to take up the gauge of battle he offered.

"I still believe it was the Doctor," she said stubbornly. But her tones were not the tones of utter conviction which she had used before.

"And yet," said the detective, ruthlessly demolishing another link in her broken chain of evidence, "the Doctor was in this room tonight, according to your own statement, when the anonymous letter came through the window."

Miss Cornelia gazed at him blankly, for the first time in her life at a loss for an appropriately sharp retort. It was true-the Doctor had been here in the room beside her when the stone bearing the last anonymous warning had crashed through the windowpane. And yet —

Billy's entrance in answer to Beresford's ring made her mind turn to other matters for the moment. Why had Beresford's manner changed so, and what was he saying to Billy now?

"Tell the gardener Miss Van Gorder wants him and don't say we're all here," the young lawyer commanded the butler sharply. Billy nodded and disappeared. Miss Cornelia's back began to stiffen-she didn't like other people ordering her servants around like that.

The detective, apparently, had somewhat of the same feeling.

"I seem to have plenty of help in this case!" he said with obvious sarcasm, turning to Beresford.

The latter made no reply. Dale rose anxiously from her chair, her lips quivering.

"Why have you sent for the gardener?" she inquired haltingly.

Beresford deigned to answer at last.

"I'll tell you that in a moment," he said with a grim tightening of his lips.

There was a fateful pause, for an instant, while Dale roved nervously from one side of the room to the other. Then Jack Bailey came into the room-alone.

He seemed to sense danger in the air. His hands clenched at his sides, but except for that tiny betrayal of emotion, he still kept his servant's pose.

"You sent for me?" he queried of Miss Cornelia submissively, ignoring the glowering Beresford.

But Beresford would be ignored no longer. He came between them before Miss Cornelia had time to answer.

"How long has this man been in your employ?" he asked brusquely, manner tense.

Miss Cornelia made one final attempt at evasion. "Why should that interest you?" she parried, answering his question with an icy question of her own.

It was too late. Already Bailey had read the truth in Beresford's eyes.

"I came this evening," he admitted, still hoping against hope that his cringing posture of the servitor might give Beresford pause for the moment.

But the promptness of his answer only crystallized Beresford's suspicions.

"Exactly," he said with terse finality. He turned to the detective.

"I've been trying to recall this man's face ever since I came in tonight —" he said with grim triumph. "Now, I know who he is."

"Who is he?"

181

Bailey straightened up. He had lost his game with Chance-and the loss, coming when it did, seemed bitterer than even he had thought it could be, but before they took him away he would speak his mind.

"It's all right, Beresford," he said with a fatigue so deep that it colored his voice like flakes of iron-rust. "I know you think you're doing your duty-but I wish to God you could have restrained your sense of duty for about three hours more!"

"To let you get away?" the young lawyer sneered, unconvinced.

"No," said Bailey with quiet defiance. "To let me finish what I came here to do."

"Don't you think you have done enough?" Beresford's voice flicked him with righteous scorn, no less telling because of its youthfulness. He turned back to the detective soberly enough.

"This man has imposed upon the credulity of these women, I am quite sure without their knowledge," he said with a trace of his former gallantry. "He is Bailey of the Union Bank, the missing cashier."

The detective slowly put down his cigar on an ash tray.

"That's the truth, is it?" he demanded.

Dale's hand flew to her breast. If Jack would only deny it-even now! But even as she thought this, she realized the uselessness of any such denial.

Bailey realized it, too.

"It's true, all right," he admitted hopelessly. He closed his eyes for a moment. Let them come with the handcuffs now and get it over-every moment the scene dragged out was a moment of unnecessary torture for Dale.

But Beresford had not finished with his indictment. "I accuse him not only of the thing he is wanted for, but of the murder of Richard Fleming!" he said fiercely, glaring at Bailey as if only a youthful horror of making a scene before Dale and Miss Cornelia held him back from striking the latter down where he stood.

Bailey's eyes snapped open. He took a threatening step toward his accuser. "You lie!" he said in a hoarse, violent voice.

Anderson crossed between them, just as conflict seemed inevitable.

"You knew this?" he queried sharply in Dale's direction.

Dale set her lips in a line. She did not answer.

He turned to Miss Cornelia.

"Did you?"

"Yes," admitted the latter quietly, her knitting needles at last at rest. "I knew he was Mr. Bailey if that is all you mean."

The quietness of her answer seemed to infuriate the detective.

"Quite a pretty little conspiracy," he said. "How in the name of God do you expect me to do anything with the entire household united against me? Tell me that."

"Exactly," said Miss Cornelia. "And if we are united against you, why should I have sent for you? You might tell me that, too."

He turned on Bailey savagely.

"What did you mean by that 'three hours more'?" he demanded.

"I could have cleared myself in three hours," said Bailey with calm despair.

Beresford laughed mockingly —a laugh that seemed to sear into Bailey's consciousness like the touch of a hot iron. Again he turned frenziedly upon the young lawyer-and Anderson was just preparing to hold them away from each other, by force if necessary, when the doorbell rang.

For an instant the ringing of the bell held the various figures of the little scene in the rigid postures of a waxworks tableau-Bailey, one foot advanced toward Beresford, his hands balled up into fists-Beresford already in an attitude of defense-the detective about to step in between them-Miss Cornelia stiff in her chair-Dale over by the fireplace, her hand at her heart. Then they relaxed, but not, at least on the part of Bailey and Beresford, to resume their interrupted conflict. Too many nerve-shaking things had already happened that night for either of the young men not to drop their mutual squabble in the face of a common danger.

"Probably the Doctor," murmured Miss Cornelia uncertainly as the doorbell rang again. "He was to come back with some sleeping-powders."

Billy appeared for the key of the front door.

"If that's Doctor Wells," warned the detective, "admit him. If it's anybody else, call me."

Billy grinned acquiescently and departed. The detective moved nearer to Bailey.

"Have you got a gun on you?"

"No." Bailey bowed his head.

"Well, I'll just make sure of that." The detective's hands ran swiftly and expertly over Bailey's form, through his pockets, probing for concealed weapons. Then, slowly drawing a pair of handcuffs from his pocket, he prepared to put them on Bailey's wrists.

Chapter Fifteen
The Sign of the Bat

But Dale could bear it no longer. The sight of her lover, beaten, submissive, his head bowed, waiting obediently like a common criminal for the detective to lock his wrists in steel broke down her last defenses. She rushed into the center of the room, between Bailey and the detective, her eyes wild with terror, her words stumbling over each other in her eagerness to get them out.

"Oh, no! I can't stand it! I'll tell you everything!" she cried frenziedly. "He got to the foot of the stair-case —Richard Fleming, I mean," she was facing the detective now, "and he had the blue-print you've been talking about. I had told him Jack Bailey was here as the gardener and he said if I screamed he would tell that. I was desperate. I threatened him with the revolver but he took it from me. Then when I tore the blue-print from him-he was shot-from the stairs ——"

"By Bailey!" interjected Beresford angrily.

"I didn't even know he was in the house!" Bailey's answer was as instant as it was hot. Meanwhile, the Doctor had entered the room, hardly noticed, in the middle of Dale's confession, and now stood watching the scene intently from a post by the door.

"What did you do with the blue-print?" The detective's voice beat at Dale like a whip.

"I put it first in the neck of my dress —" she faltered. "Then, when I found you were watching me, I hid it somewhere else."

Her eyes fell on the Doctor. She saw his hand steal out toward the knob of the door. Was he going to run away on some pretext before she could finish her story? She gave a sigh of relief when Billy, re-entering with the key to the front door, blocked any such attempt at escape.

Mechanically she watched Billy cross to the table, lay the key upon it, and return to the hall without so much as a glance at the tense, suspicious circle of faces focused upon herself and her lover.

"I put it-somewhere else," she repeated, her eyes going back to the Doctor.

"Did you give it to Bailey?"

"No—I hid it-and then I told where it was-to the Doctor—" Dale swayed on her feet. All turned surprisedly toward the Doctor. Miss Cornelia rose from her chair.

The Doctor bore the battery of eyes unflinchingly. "That's rather inaccurate," he said, with a tight little smile. "You told me where you had placed it, but when I went to look for it, it was gone."

"Are you quite sure of that?" queried Miss Cornelia acidly.

"Absolutely," he said. He ignored the rest of the party, addressing himself directly to Anderson.

"She said she had hidden it inside one of the rolls that were on the tray on that table," he continued in tones of easy explanation, approaching the table as he did so, and tapping it with the box of sleeping-powders he had brought for Miss Cornelia.

"She was in such distress that I finally went to look for it. It wasn't there."

"Do you realize the significance of this paper?" Anderson boomed at once.

"Nothing, beyond the fact that Miss Ogden was afraid it linked her with the crime." The Doctor's voice was very clear and firm.

Anderson pondered an instant. Then —

"I'd like to have a few minutes with the Doctor alone," he said somberly.

The group about him dissolved at once. Miss Cornelia, her arm around her niece's waist, led the latter gently to the door. As the two lovers passed each other a glance flashed between them — a glance, pathetically brief, of longing and love. Dale's finger tips brushed Bailey's hand gently in passing.

"Beresford," commanded the detective, "take Bailey to the library and see that he stays there."

Beresford tapped his pocket with a significant gesture and motioned Bailey to the door. Then they, too, left the room. The door closed. The Doctor and the detective were alone.

The detective spoke at once-and surprisingly.

"Doctor, I'll have that blue-print!" he said sternly, his eyes the color of steel.

The Doctor gave him a wary little glance.

"But I've just made the statement that I didn't find the blue-print," he affirmed flatly.

"I heard you!" Anderson's voice was very dry. "Now this situation is between you and me, Doctor Wells." His forefinger sought the Doctor's chest. "It has nothing to do with that poor fool of a cashier. He hasn't got either those securities or the money from them and you know it. It's in this house and you know that, too!"

"In this house?" repeated the Doctor as if stalling for time.

"In this house! Tonight, when you claimed to be making a professional call, you were in this house-and I think you were on that staircase when Richard Fleming was killed!"

"No, Anderson, I'll swear I was not!" The Doctor might be acting, but if he was, it was incomparable acting. The terror in his voice seemed too real to be feigned.

But Anderson was remorseless.

"I'll tell you this," he continued. "Miss Van Gorder very cleverly got a thumbprint of yours tonight. Does that mean anything to you?"

His eyes bored into the Doctor-the eyes of a poker player bluffing on a hidden card. But the Doctor did not flinch.

"Nothing," he said firmly. "I have not been upstairs in this house in three months."

The accent of truth in his voice seemed so unmistakable that even Anderson's shrewd brain was puzzled by it. But he persisted in his attempt to wring a confession from this latest suspect.

"Before Courtleigh Fleming died-did he tell you anything about a Hidden Room in this house?" he queried cannily.

The Doctor's confident air of honesty lessened, a furtive look appeared in his eyes.

"No," he insisted, but not as convincingly as he had made his previous denial.

The detective hammered at the point again.

"You haven't been trying to frighten these women out of here with anonymous letters so you could get in?"

"No. Certainly not." But again the Doctor's air had that odd mixture of truth and falsehood in it.

The detective paused for an instant.

"Let me see your key ring!" he ordered. The Doctor passed it over silently. The detective glanced at the keys-then, suddenly, his revolver glittered in his other hand.

The Doctor watched him anxiously. A puff of wind rattled the panes of the French windows. The storm, quieted for a while, was gathering its strength for a fresh unleashing of its dogs of thunder.

The detective stepped to the terrace door, opened it, and then quietly proceeded to try the Doctor's keys in the lock. Thus located he was out of visual range, and Wells took advantage of it at once. He moved swiftly toward the fireplace, extracting the missing piece of blue-print from an inside pocket as he did so. The secret the blue-print guarded was already graven on his mind in indelible characters-now he would destroy all evidence that it had ever been in his possession and bluff through the rest of the situation as best he might.

He threw the paper toward the flames with a nervous gesture of relief. But for once his cunning failed-the throw was too hurried to be sure and the light scrap of paper wavered and settled to the floor just outside the fireplace. The Doctor swore noiselessly and stooped to pick it up and make sure of its destruction. But he was not quick enough. Through the window the detective had seen the incident, and the next moment the Doctor heard his voice bark behind him. He turned, and stared at the leveled muzzle of Anderson's revolver.

"Hands up and stand back!" he commanded.

As he did so Anderson picked up the paper and a sardonic smile crossed his face as his eyes took in the significance of the print. He laid his revolver down on the table where he could snatch it up again at a moment's notice.

"Behind a fireplace, eh?" he muttered. "What fireplace? In what room?"

"I won't tell you!" The Doctor's voice was sullen. He inched, gingerly, cautiously, toward the other side of the table.

"All right —I'll find it, you know." The detective's eyes turned swiftly back to the blue-print. Experience should have taught him never to underrate an adversary, even of the Doctor's caliber, but long familiarity with danger can make the shrewdest careless. For a moment, as he bent over the paper again, he was off guard.

The Doctor seized the moment with a savage promptitude and sprang. There followed a silent, furious struggle between the two. Under normal circumstances Anderson would have been the stronger and quicker, but the Doctor fought with an added strength of despair and his initial leap had pinioned the detective's arms behind him. Now the detective shook one hand free and snatched at the revolver-in vain-for the Doctor, with a groan of desperation, struck at his hand as its fingers were about to close on the smooth butt and the revolver skidded from the table to the floor. With a sudden terrible movement he pinioned both the detective's arms behind him again and reached for the telephone. Its heavy base descended on the back of the detective's head with stunning force. The next moment the battle was ended and the Doctor, panting with exhaustion, held the limp form of an unconscious man in his arms.

He lowered the detective to the floor and straightened up again, listening tensely. So brief and intense had been the struggle that even now he could hardly believe in its reality. It seemed impossible, too, that the struggle had not been heard. Then he realized dully, as a louder roll of thunder smote on his ears, that the elements themselves had played into his hand. The storm, with its wind and fury, had returned just in time to save him and drown out all sounds of conflict from the rest of the house with its giant clamor.

He bent swiftly over Anderson, listening to his heart. Good-the man still breathed; he had enough on his conscience without adding the murder of a detective to the black weight. Now he pocketed the revolver and the blue-print —gagged Anderson rapidly with a knotted handkerchief and proceeded to wrap his own muffler around the detective's head as an additional silencer. Anderson gave a faint sigh.

The Doctor thought rapidly. Soon or late the detective would return to consciousness-with his hands free he could easily tear out the gag. He looked wildly about the room for a rope, a curtain-ah, he had it-the detective's own handcuffs! He snapped the cuffs on Anderson's wrists, then realized that, in his hurry, he had bound the detective's hands in front of him instead of behind him. Well-it would do for the moment-he did not need much time to carry out his plans. He dragged the limp body, its head lolling, into the billiard room where he deposited it on the floor in the corner farthest from the door.

So far, so good-now to lock the door of the billiard room. Fortunately, the key was there on the inside of the door. He quickly transferred it, locked the billiard room door from the outside, and pocketed the key. For a second he stood by the center table in the living-room, recovering his breath and trying to straighten his rumpled clothing. Then he crossed cautiously into the alcove and started to pad up the alcove stairs, his face white and strained with excitement and hope.

And it was then that there happened one of the most dramatic events of the night. One which was to remain, for the next hour or so, as bewildering as the murder and which, had it come a few moments sooner or a few moments later, would have entirely changed the course of events.

It was preceded by a desperate hammering on the door of the terrace. It halted the Doctor on his way upstairs, drew Beresford on a run into the living-room, and even reached the bedrooms of the women up above.

"My God! What's that?" Beresford panted.

The Doctor indicated the door. It was too late now. Already he could hear Miss Cornelia's voice above; it was only a question of a short time until Anderson in the billiard room revived and would try to make his plight known. And in the brief moment of that resume of his position the knocking came again. But feebler, as though the suppliant outside had exhausted his strength.

As Beresford drew his revolver and moved to the door, Miss Cornelia came in, followed by Lizzie.

"It's the Bat," Lizzie announced mournfully. "Good-by, Miss Neily. Good-by, everybody. I saw his hand, all covered with blood. He's had a good night for sure!"

But they ignored her. And Beresford flung open the door.

Just what they had expected, what figure of horror or of fear they waited for, no one can say. But there was no horror and no fear; only unutterable amazement as an unknown man, in torn and muddied garments, with a streak of dried blood seaming his forehead like a scar, fell through the open doorway into Beresford's arms.

"Good God!" muttered Beresford, dropping his revolver to catch the strange burden. For a moment the Unknown lay in his arms like a corpse. Then he straightened dizzily, staggered into the room, took a few steps toward the table, and fell prostrate upon his face-at the end of his strength.

"Doctor!" gasped Miss Cornelia dazedly and the Doctor, whatever guilt lay on his conscience, responded at once to the call of his profession.

He bent over the Unknown Man-the physician once more-and made a brief examination.

"He's fainted!" he said, rising. "Struck on the head, too."

"But who is he?" faltered Miss Cornelia.

"I never saw him before," said the Doctor. It was obvious that he spoke the truth. "Does anyone recognize him?"

All crowded about the Unknown, trying to read the riddle of his identity. Miss Cornelia rapidly revised her first impressions of the stranger. When he had first fallen through the doorway into Beresford's arms she had not known what to think. Now, in the brighter light of the living-room she saw that the still face, beneath its mask of dirt and dried blood, was strong and fairly youthful; if the man were a criminal, he belonged, like the Bat, to the upper fringes of the world of crime. She noted mechanically that his hands and feet had been tied, ends of frayed rope still dangled from his wrists and ankles. And that terrible injury on his head! She shuddered and closed her eyes.

"Does anyone recognize him?" repeated the Doctor but one by one the others shook their heads. Crook, casual tramp, or honest laborer unexpectedly caught in the sinister toils of the Cedarcrest affair-his identity seemed a mystery to one and all.

"Is he badly hurt?" asked Miss Cornelia, shuddering again.

"It's hard to say," answered the Doctor. "I think not." The Unknown stirred feebly-made an effort to sit up. Beresford and the Doctor caught him under the arms and helped him to his feet. He stood there swaying, a blank expression on his face.

"A chair!" said the Doctor quickly. "Ah —" He helped the strange figure to sit down and bent over him again.

"You're all right now, my friend," he said in his best tones of professional cheeriness. "Dizzy a bit, aren't you?"

The Unknown rubbed his wrists where his bonds had cut them. He made an effort to speak. "Water!" he said in a low voice.

The Doctor gestured to Billy. "Get some water-or whisky-if there is any-that'd be better."

"There's a flask of whisky in my room, Billy," added Miss Cornelia helpfully.

"Now, my man," continued the Doctor to the Unknown. "You're in the hands of friends. Brace up and tell us what happened!"

Beresford had been looking about for the detective, puzzled not to find him, as usual, in charge of affairs. Now, "Where's Anderson? This is a police matter!" he said, making a movement as if to go in search of him.

The Doctor stopped him quickly.

"He was here a minute ago-he'll be back presently," he said, praying to whatever gods he served that Anderson, bound and gagged in the billiard room, had not yet returned to consciousness.

Unobserved by all except Miss Cornelia, the mention of the detective's name had caused a strange reaction in the Unknown. His eyes had opened-he had started-the haze in his mind had seemed to clear away for a moment. Then, for some reason, his shoulders had slumped again and the look of apathy come back to his face. But, stunned or not, it now seemed possible that he was not quite as dazed as he appeared.

The Doctor gave the slumped shoulders a little shake.

"Rouse yourself, man!" he said. "What has happened to you?"

"I'm dazed!" said the Unknown thickly and slowly. "I can't remember." He passed a hand weakly over his forehead.

"What a night!" sighed Miss Cornelia, sinking into a chair. "Richard Fleming murdered in this house-and now-this!"

The Unknown shot her a stealthy glance from beneath lowered eyelids. But when she looked at him, his face was blank again.

"Why doesn't somebody ask his name?" queried Dale, and, "Where the devil is that detective?" muttered Beresford, almost in the same instant.

Neither question was answered, and Beresford, increasingly uneasy at the continued absence of Anderson, turned toward the hall.

The Doctor took Dale's suggestion.

"What's your name?"

Silence from the Unknown-and that blank stare of stupefaction.

"Look at his papers." It was Miss Cornelia's voice. The Doctor and Bailey searched the torn trouser pockets, the pockets of the muddied shirt, while the Unknown submitted passively, not seeming to care what happened to him. But search him as they would-it was in vain.

"Not a paper on him," said Jack Bailey at last, straightening up.

A crash of breaking glass from the head of the alcove stairs put a period to his sentence. All turned toward the stairs-or all except the Unknown, who, for a moment, half-rose in his chair, his eyes gleaming, his face alert, the mask of bewildered apathy gone from his face.

As they watched, a rigid little figure of horror backed slowly down the alcove stairs and into the room-Billy, the Japanese, his Oriental placidity disturbed at last, incomprehensible terror written in every line of his face.

"Billy!"

"Billy-what is it?"

The diminutive butler made a pitiful attempt at his usual grin.

"It-nothing," he gasped. The Unknown relapsed in his chair-again the dazed stranger from nowhere.

Beresford took the Japanese by the shoulders.

"Now see here!" he said sharply. "You've seen something! What was it!"

Billy trembled like a leaf.

"Ghost! Ghost!" he muttered frantically, his face working.

"He's concealing something. Look at him!" Miss Cornelia stared at her servant.

"No, no!" insisted Billy in an ague of fright. "No, no!"

But Miss Cornelia was sure of it.

"Brooks, close that door!" she said, pointing at the terrace door in the alcove which still stood ajar after the entrance of the Unknown.

Bailey moved to obey. But just as he reached the alcove the terrace door slammed shut in his face. At the same moment every light in Cedarcrest blinked and went out again.

Bailey fumbled for the doorknob in the sudden darkness.

"The door's locked!" he said incredulously. "The key's gone too. Where's your revolver, Beresford?"

"I dropped it in the alcove when I caught that man," called Beresford, cursing himself for his carelessness.

The illuminated dial of Bailey's wrist watch flickered in the darkness as he searched for the revolver-as round, glowing spot of phosphorescence.

Lizzie screamed. "The eye! The gleaming eye I saw on the stairs!" she shrieked, pointing at it frenziedly.

"Quick-there's a candle on the table-light it somebody. Never mind the revolver, I have one!" called Miss Cornelia.

"Righto!" called Beresford cheerily in reply. He found the candle, lit it—

The party blinked at each other for a moment, still unable quite to co-ordinate their thoughts. Bailey rattled the knob of the door into the hall.

"This door's locked, too!" he said with increasing puzzlement. A gasp went over the group. They were locked in the room while some devilment was going on in the rest of the house. That they knew. But what it might be, what form it might take, they had not the remotest idea. They were too distracted to notice the injured man, now alert in his chair, or the Doctor's odd attitude of listening, above the rattle and banging of the storm.

But it was not until Miss Cornelia took the candle and proceeded toward the hall door to examine it that the full horror of the situation burst upon them.

Neatly fastened to the white panel of the door, chest high and hardly more than just dead, was the body of a bat.

Of what happened thereafter no one afterward remembered the details. To be shut in there at the mercy of one who knew no mercy was intolerable. It was left for Miss Cornelia to remember her own revolver, lying unnoticed on the table since the crime earlier in the evening, and to suggest its use in shattering the lock. Just what they had expected when the door was finally opened they did not know. But the house was quiet and in order; no new horror faced them in the hall; their candle revealed no bloody figure, their ears heard no unearthly sound.

Slowly they began to breathe normally once more. After that they began to search the house. Since no room was apparently immune from danger, the men made no protest when the women insisted on accompanying them. And as time went on and chamber after chamber was discovered empty and undisturbed, gradually the courage of the party began to rise. Lizzie, still whimpering, stuck closely to Miss Cornelia's heels, but that spirited lady began to make small side excursions of her own.

Of the men, only Bailey, Beresford, and the Doctor could really be said to search at all. Billy had remained below, impassive of face but rolling of eye; the Unknown, after an attempt to depart with them, had sunk back weakly into his chair again, and the detective, Anderson, was still unaccountably missing.

While no one could be said to be grieving over this, still the belief that somehow, somewhere, he had met the Bat and suffered at his hands was strong in all of them except the Doctor. As each door was opened they expected to find him, probably foully murdered; as each door was closed again they breathed with relief.

And as time went on and the silence and peace remained unbroken, the conviction grew on them that the Bat had in this manner achieved his object and departed; had done his work, signed it after his usual fashion, and gone.

And thus were matters when Miss Cornelia, happening on the attic staircase with Lizzie at her heels, decided to look about her up there. And went up.

Chapter Sixteen
The Hidden Room

A few moments later Jack Bailey, seeing a thin glow of candlelight from the attic above and hearing Lizzie's protesting voice, made his way up there. He found them in the trunk room, a dusty, dingy apartment lined with high closets along the walls-the floor littered with an incongruous assortment of attic objects-two battered trunks, a clothes hamper, an old sewing machine, a broken-backed kitchen chair, two dilapidated suitcases and a shabby satchel that might once have been a woman's dressing case-in one corner a grimy fireplace in which, obviously, no fire had been lighted for years.

But he also found Miss Cornelia holding her candle to the floor and staring at something there.

"Candle grease!" she said sharply, staring at a line of white spots by the window. She stooped and touched the spots with an exploratory finger.

"Fresh candle grease! Now who do you suppose did that? Do you remember how Mr. Gillette, in Sherlock Holmes, when he —"

Her voice trailed off. She stooped and followed the trail of the candle grease away from the window, ingeniously trying to copy the shrewd, piercing gaze of Mr. Gillette as she remembered him in his most famous role.

"It leads straight to the fireplace!" she murmured in tones of Sherlockian gravity. Bailey repressed an involuntary smile. But her next words gave him genuine food for thought.

She stared at the mantel of the fireplace accusingly. "It's been going through my mind for the last few minutes that no chimney flue runs up this side of the house!" she said.

Bailey stared. "Then why the fireplace?"

"That's what I'm going to find out!" said the spinster grimly. She started to rap the mantel, testing it for secret springs.

"Jack! Jack!" It was Dale's voice, low and cautious, coming from the landing of the stairs.

Bailey stepped to the door of the trunk room.

"Come in," he called in reply. "And shut the door behind you."

Dale entered, turning the key in the lock behind her.

"Where are the others?"

"They're still searching the house. There's no sign of anybody."

"They haven't found-Mr. Anderson?"

Dale shook her head. "Not yet."

She turned toward her aunt. Miss Cornelia had begun to enjoy herself once more.

Rapping on the mantelpiece, poking and pressing various corners and sections of the mantel itself, she remembered all the detective stories she had ever read and thought, with a sniff of scorn, that she could better them. There were always sliding panels and hidden drawers in detective stories and the detective discovered them by rapping just as she was doing, and listening for a hollow sound in answer. She rapped on the wall above the mantel-exactly-there was the hollow echo she wanted.

"Hollow as Lizzie's head!" she said triumphantly. The fireplace was obviously not what it seemed, there must be a space behind it unaccounted for in the building plans. Now what was the next step detectives always took? Oh, yes-they looked for panels; panels that moved. And when one shoved them away there was a button or something. She pushed and pressed and finally something did move. It was the mantelpiece itself, false grate and all, which began to swing out into the room, revealing behind a dark, hollow cubbyhole, some six feet by six-the Hidden Room at last!

"Oh, Jack, be careful!" breathed Dale as her lover took Miss Cornelia's candle and moved toward the dark hiding-place. But her eyes had already caught the outlines of a tall iron safe in the gloom and in spite of her fears, her lips formed a wordless cry of victory.

But Jack Bailey said nothing at all. One glance had shown him that the safe was empty.

The tragic collapse of all their hopes was almost more than they could bear. Coming on top of the nerve-racking events of the night, it left them dazed and directionless. It was, of course, Miss Cornelia who recovered first.

"Even without the money," she said; "the mere presence of this safe here, hidden away, tells the story. The fact that someone else knew and got here first cannot alter that."

But she could not cheer them. It was Lizzie who created a diversion. Lizzie who had bolted into the hall at the first motion of the mantelpiece outward and who now, with equal precipitation, came bolting back. She rushed into the room, slamming the door behind her, and collapsed into a heap of moaning terror at her mistress's feet. At first she was completely inarticulate, but after a time she muttered that she had seen "him" and then fell to groaning again.

The same thought was in all their minds, that in some corner of the upper floor she had come across the body of Anderson. But when Miss Cornelia finally quieted her and asked this, she shook her head.

"It was the Bat I saw," was her astounding statement. "He dropped through the skylight out there and ran along the hall. I saw him I tell you. He went right by me!"

"Nonsense," said Miss Cornelia briskly. "How can you say such a thing?"

But Bailey pushed forward and took Lizzie by the shoulder.

"What did he look like?"

"He hadn't any face. He was all black where his face ought to be."

"Do you mean he wore a mask?"

"Maybe. I don't know."

She collapsed again but when Bailey, followed by Miss Cornelia, made a move toward the door she broke into frantic wailing.

"Don't go out there!" she shrieked. "He's there I tell you. I'm not crazy. If you open that door, he'll shoot."

But the door was already open and no shot came. With the departure of Bailey and Miss Cornelia, and the resulting darkness due to their taking the candle, Lizzie and Dale were left alone. The girl was faint with disappointment and strain; she sat huddled on a trunk, saying nothing, and after a moment or so Lizzie roused to her condition.

"Not feeling sick, are you?" she asked.

"I feel a little queer."

"Who wouldn't in the dark here with that monster loose somewhere near by?" But she stirred herself and got up. "I'd better get the smelling salts," she said heavily. "God knows I hate to move, but if there's one place safer in this house than another, I've yet to find it."

She went out, leaving Dale alone. The trunk room was dark, save that now and then as the candle appeared and reappeared the doorway was faintly outlined. On this outline she kept her eyes fixed, by way of comfort, and thus passed the next few moments. She felt weak and dizzy and entirely despairing.

Then-the outline was not so clear. She had heard nothing but there was something in the doorway. It stood there, formless, diabolical, and then she saw what was happening. It was closing the door. Afterward she was mercifully not to remember what came next; the figure was perhaps intent on what was going on outside, or her own movements may have been as silent as its own. That she got into the mantel-room and even partially closed it behind her is certain, and that her description of what followed is fairly accurate is borne out by the facts as known.

The Bat was working rapidly. She heard his quick, nervous movements; apparently he had come back for something and secured it, for now he moved again toward the door. But he was too late; they were returning that way. She heard him mutter something and quickly turn the key in the lock. Then he seemed to run toward the window, and for some reason to recoil from it.

The next instant she realized that he was coming toward the mantel-room, that he intended to hide in it. There was no doubt in her mind as to his identity. It was the Bat, and in a moment more he would be shut in there with her.

She tried to scream and could not, and the next instant, when the Bat leaped into concealment beside her, she was in a dead faint on the floor.

Bailey meanwhile had crawled out on the roof and was carefully searching it. But other things were happening also. A disinterested observer could have seen very soon why the Bat had abandoned the window as a means of egress.

Almost before the mantel had swung to behind the archcriminal, the top of a tall pruning ladder had appeared at the window and by its quivering showed that someone was climbing up, rung by rung. Unsuspiciously enough he came on, pausing at the top to flash a light into the room, and then cautiously swinging a leg over the sill. It was the Doctor. He gave a low whistle but there was no reply, save that, had he seen it, the mantel swung out an inch or two. Perhaps he was never so near death as at that moment but that instant of irresolution on his part saved him, for by coming into the room he had taken himself out of range.

Even then he was very close to destruction, for after a brief pause and a second rather puzzled survey of the room, he started toward the mantel itself. Only the rattle of the doorknob stopped him, and a call from outside.

"Dale!" called Bailey's voice from the corridor. "Dale!"

"Dale! Dale! The door's locked!" cried Miss Cornelia.

The Doctor hesitated. The call came again. "Dale! Dale!" and Bailey pounded on the door as if he meant to break it down.

The Doctor made up his mind.

"Wait a moment!" he called. He stepped to the door and unlocked it. Bailey hurled himself into the room, followed by Miss Cornelia with her candle. Lizzie stood in the doorway, timidly, ready to leap for safety at a moment's notice.

"Why did you lock that door?" said Bailey angrily, threatening the Doctor.

"But I didn't," said the latter, truthfully enough. Bailey made a movement of irritation. Then a glance about the room informed him of the amazing, the incredible fact. Dale was not there! She had disappeared!

"You-you," he stammered at the Doctor. "Where's Miss Ogden? What have you done with her?"

The Doctor was equally baffled.

"Done with her?" he said indignantly. "I don't know what you're talking about, I haven't seen her!"

"Then you didn't lock that door?" Bailey menaced him.

The Doctor's denial was firm.

"Absolutely not. I was coming through the window when I heard your voice at the door!"

Bailey's eyes leaped to the window-yes —a ladder was there-the Doctor might be speaking the truth after all. But if so, how and why had Dale disappeared?

The Doctor's admission of his manner of entrance did not make Lizzie any the happier.

"In at the window-just like a bat!" she muttered in shaking tones. She would not have stayed in the doorway if she had not been afraid to move anywhere else.

"I saw lights up here from outside," continued the Doctor easily. "And I thought — —"

Miss Cornelia interrupted him. She had set down her candle and laid the revolver on the top of the clothes hamper and now stood gazing at the mantel-fireplace.

"The mantel's —closed!" she said.

The Doctor stared. So the secret of the Hidden Room was a secret no longer. He saw ruin gaping before him —a bottomless abyss. "Damnation!" he cursed impotently under his breath.

Bailey turned on him savagely.

"Did you shut that mantel?"

"No!"

"I'll see whether you shut it or not!" Bailey leaped toward the fireplace. "Dale! Dale!" he called desperately, leaning against the mantel. His fingers groped for the knob that worked the mechanism of the hidden entrance.

The Doctor picked up the single lighted candle from the hamper, as if to throw more light on Bailey's task. Bailey's fingers found the knob. He turned it. The mantel began to swing out into the room.

As it did so the Doctor deliberately snuffed out the light of the candle he held, leaving the room in abrupt and obliterating darkness.

Chapter Seventeen
Anderson Makes an Arrest

"Doctor, why did you put out that candle?" Miss Cornelia's voice cut the blackness like a knife.

"I didn't —I — —"

"You did —I saw you do it."

The brief exchange of accusation and denial took but an instant of time, as the mantel swung wide open. The next instant there was a rush of feet across the floor, from the fireplace-the shock of a collision between two bodies-the sound of a heavy fall.

"What was that?" queried Bailey dazedly, with a feeling as if some great winged creature had brushed at him and passed.

Lizzie answered from the doorway.

"Oh, oh!" she groaned in stricken accents. "Somebody knocked me down and tramped on me!"

"Matches, quick!" commanded Miss Cornelia. "Where's the candle?"

The Doctor was still trying to explain his curious action of a moment before.

"Awfully sorry, I assure you-it dropped out of the holder-ah, here it is!"

He held it up triumphantly. Bailey struck a match and lighted it. The wavering little flame showed Lizzie prostrate but vocal, in the doorway-and Dale lying on the floor of the Hidden Room, her eyes shut, and her face as drained of color as the face of a marble statue. For one horrible instant Bailey thought she must be dead.

He rushed to her wildly and picked her up in his arms. No-still breathing-thank God! He carried her tenderly to the only chair in the room.

"Doctor!"

The Doctor, once more the physician, knelt at her side and felt for her pulse. And Lizzie, picking herself up from where the collision with some violent body had thrown her, retrieved the smelling salts from the floor. It was onto this picture, the candlelight shining on strained faces, the dramatic figure of Dale, now semi-conscious, the desperate rage of Bailey, that a new actor appeared on the scene.

Anderson, the detective, stood in the doorway, holding a candle-as grim and menacing a figure as a man just arisen from the dead.

"That's right!" said Lizzie, unappalled for once. "Come in when everything's over!"

The Doctor glanced up and met the detective's eyes, cold and menacing.

"You took my revolver from me downstairs," he said. "I'll trouble you for it."

The Doctor got heavily to his feet. The others, their suspicions confirmed at last, looked at him with startled eyes. The detective seemed to enjoy the universal confusion his words had brought.

192

Slowly, with sullen reluctance, the Doctor yielded up the stolen weapon. The detective examined it casually and replaced it in his hip pocket.

"I've something to settle with you pretty soon," he said through clenched teeth, addressing the Doctor. "And I'll settle it properly. Now–what's this?"

He indicated Dale–her face still and waxen–her breath coming so faintly she seemed hardly to breathe at all as Miss Cornelia and Bailey tried to revive her.

"She's coming to —" said Miss Cornelia triumphantly, as a first faint flush of color reappeared in the girl's cheeks. "We found her shut in there, Mr. Anderson," the spinster added, pointing toward the gaping entrance of the Hidden Room.

A gleam crossed the detective's face. He went up to examine the secret chamber. As he did so, Doctor Wells, who had been inching surreptitiously toward the door, sought the opportunity of slipping out unobserved.

But Anderson was not to be caught napping again. "Wells!" he barked. The Doctor stopped and turned.

"Where were you when she was locked in this room?"

The Doctor's eyes sought the floor-the walls–wildly–for any possible loophole of escape.

"I didn't shut her in if that's what you mean!" he said defiantly. "There was someone shut in there with her!" He gestured at the Hidden Room. "Ask these people here."

Miss Cornelia caught him up at once.

"The fact remains, Doctor," she said, her voice cold with anger, "that we left her here alone. When we came back you were here. The corridor door was locked, and she was in that room–unconscious!"

She moved forward to throw the light of her candle on the Hidden Room as the detective passed into it, gave it a swift professional glance, and stepped out again. But she had not finished her story by any means.

"As we opened that door," she continued to the detective, tapping the false mantel, "the Doctor deliberately extinguished our only candle!"

"Do you know who was in that room?" queried the detective fiercely, wheeling on the Doctor.

But the latter had evidently made up his mind to cling stubbornly to a policy of complete denial.

"No," he said sullenly. "I didn't put out the candle. It fell. And I didn't lock that door into the hall. I found it locked!"

A sigh of relief from Bailey now centered everyone's attention on himself and Dale. At last the girl was recovering from the shock of her terrible experience and regaining consciousness. Her eyelids fluttered, closed again, opened once more. She tried to sit up, weakly, clinging to Bailey's shoulder. The color returned to her cheeks, the stupor left her eyes.

She gave the Hidden Room a hunted little glance and then shuddered violently.

"Please close that awful door," she said in a tremulous voice. "I don't want to see it again."

The detective went silently to close the iron doors. "What happened to you? Can't you remember?" faltered Bailey, on his knees at her side.

The shadow of an old terror lay on the girl's face, "I was in here alone in the dark," she began slowly —"Then, as I looked at the doorway there, I saw there was somebody there. He came in and closed the door. I didn't know what to do, so I slipped in-there, and after a while I knew he was coming in too, for he couldn't get out. Then I must have fainted."

"There was nothing about the figure that you recognized?"

"No. Nothing."

"But we know it was the Bat," put in Miss Cornelia. The detective laughed sardonically. The old duel of opposing theories between the two seemed about to recommence.

"Still harping on the Bat!" he said, with a little sneer, Miss Cornelia stuck to her guns.

"I have every reason to believe that the Bat is in this house," she said.

The detective gave another jarring, mirthless laugh. "And that he took the Union Bank money out of the safe, I suppose?" he jeered. "No, Miss Van Gorder."

He wheeled on the Doctor now.

"Ask the Doctor who took the Union Bank money out of that safe!" he thundered. "Ask the Doctor who attacked me downstairs in the living-room, knocked me senseless, and locked me in the billiard room!"

There was an astounded silence. The detective added a parting shot to his indictment of the Doctor.

"The next time you put handcuffs on a man be sure to take the key out of his vest pocket," he said, biting off the words.

Rage and consternation mingled on the Doctor's countenance-on the faces of the others astonishment was followed by a growing certainty. Only Miss Cornelia clung stubbornly to her original theory.

"Perhaps I'm an obstinate old woman," she said in tones which obviously showed that if so she was rather proud of it, "but the Doctor and all the rest of us were locked in the living-room not ten minutes ago!"

"By the Bat, I suppose!" mocked Anderson.

"By the Bat!" insisted Miss Cornelia inflexibly. "Who else would have fastened a dead bat to the door downstairs? Who else would have the bravado to do that? Or what you call the imagination?"

In spite of himself Anderson seemed to be impressed.

"The Bat, eh?" he muttered, then, changing his tone, "You knew about this hidden room, Wells?" he shot at the Doctor.

"Yes." The Doctor bowed his head.

"And you knew the money was in the room?"

"Well, I was wrong, wasn't I?" parried the Doctor. "You can look for yourself. That safe is empty."

The detective brushed his evasive answer aside.

"You were up in this room earlier tonight," he said in tones of apparent certainty.

"No, I couldn't get up!" the Doctor still insisted, with strange violence for a man who had already admitted such damning knowledge.

The detective's face was a study in disbelief.

"You know where that money is, Wells, and I'm going to find it!"

This last taunt seemed to goad the Doctor beyond endurance.

"Good God!" he shouted recklessly. "Do you suppose if I knew where it is, I'd be here? I've had plenty of chances to get away! No, you can't pin anything on me, Anderson! It isn't criminal to have known that room is here."

He paused, trembling with anger and, curiously enough, with an anger that seemed at least half sincere.

"Oh, don't be so damned virtuous!" said the detective brutally. "Maybe you haven't been upstairs but-unless I miss my guess, you know who was!"

The Doctor's face changed a little.

"What about Richard Fleming?" persisted the detective scornfully.

The Doctor drew himself up.

"I never killed him!" he said so impressively that even Bailey's faith in his guilt was shaken. "I don't even own a revolver!"

The detective alone maintained his attitude unchanged.

"You come with me, Wells," he ordered, with a jerk of his thumb toward the door. "This time I'll do the locking up."

The Doctor, head bowed, prepared to obey. The detective took up a candle to light their path. Then he turned to the others for a moment.

"Better get the young lady to bed," he said with a gruff kindliness of manner. "I think that I can promise you a quiet night from now on."

"I'm glad you think so, Mr. Anderson!" Miss Cornelia insisted on the last word. The detective ignored the satiric twist of her speech, motioned the Doctor out ahead of him, and followed. The faint glow of his candle flickered a moment and vanished toward the stairs.

It was Bailey who broke the silence.

"I can believe a good bit about Wells," he said, "but not that he stood on that staircase and killed Dick Fleming."

Miss Cornelia roused from deep thought.

"Of course not," she said briskly. "Go down and fix Miss Dale's bed, Lizzie. And then bring up some wine."

"Down there, where the Bat is?" Lizzie demanded.

"The Bat has gone."

"Don't you believe it. He's just got his hand in!"

But at last Lizzie went, and, closing the door behind her, Miss Cornelia proceeded more or less to think, out loud.

"Suppose," she said, "that the Bat, or whoever it was shut in there with you, killed Richard Fleming. Say that he is the one Lizzie saw coming in by the terrace door. Then he knew where the money was for he went directly up the stairs. But that is two hours ago or more. Why didn't he get the money, if it was here, and get away?"

"He may have had trouble with the combination."

"Perhaps. Anyhow, he was on the small staircase when Dick Fleming started up, and of course he shot him. That's clear enough. Then he finally got the safe open, after locking us in below, and my coming up interrupted him. How on earth did he get out on the roof?"

Bailey glanced out the window.

"It would be possible from here. Possible, but not easy."

"But, if he could do that," she persisted, "he could have got away, too. There are trellises and porches. Instead of that he came back here to this room." She stared at the window. "Could a man have done that with one hand?"

"Never in the world."

Saying nothing, but deeply thoughtful, Miss Cornelia made a fresh progress around the room.

"I know very little about bank-currency," she said finally. "Could such a sum as was looted from the Union Bank be carried away in a man's pocket?"

Bailey considered the question.

"Even in bills of large denomination it would make a pretty sizeable bundle," he said.

But that Miss Cornelia's deductions were correct, whatever they were, was in question when Lizzie returned with the elderberry wine. Apparently Miss Cornelia was to be like the man who repaired the clock: she still had certain things left over.

For Lizzie announced that the Unknown was ranging the second floor hall. From the time they had escaped from the living-room this man had not been seen or thought of, but that he was a part of the mystery there could be no doubt. It flashed over Miss Cornelia that, although he could not possibly have locked them in, in the darkness that followed he could easily have fastened the bat to the door. For the first time it occurred to her that the archcriminal might not be working alone, and that the entrance of the Unknown might have been a carefully devised ruse to draw them all together and hold them there.

Nor was Beresford's arrival with the statement that the Unknown was moving through the house below particularly comforting.

"He may be dazed, or he may not," he said. "Personally, this is not a time to trust anybody."

Beresford knew nothing of what had just occurred, and now seeing Bailey he favored him with an ugly glance.

"In the absence of Anderson, Bailey," he added, "I don't propose to trust you too far. I'm making it my business from now on to see that you don't try to get away. Get that?"

But Bailey heard him without particular resentment.

"All right," he said. "But I'll tell you this. Anderson is here and has arrested the Doctor. Keep your eye on me, if you think it's your duty, but don't talk to me as if I were a criminal. You don't know that yet."

"The Doctor!" Beresford gasped.

But Miss Cornelia's keen ears had heard a sound outside and her eyes were focused on the door.

"That doorknob is moving," she said in a hushed voice.

Beresford moved to the door and jerked it violently open.

The butler, Billy, almost pitched into the room.

Chapter Eighteen
The Bat Still Flies

He stepped back in the doorway, looked out, then turned to them again.

"I come in, please?" he said pathetically, his hands quivering. "I not like to stay in dark."

Miss Cornelia took pity on him.

"Come in, Billy, of course. What is it? Anything the matter?"

Billy glanced about nervously.

"Man with sore head."

"What about him?"

"Act very strange." Again Billy's slim hands trembled.

Beresford broke in. "The man who fell into the room downstairs?"

Billy nodded.

"Yes. On second floor, walking around."

Beresford smiled, a bit smugly.

"I told you!" he said to Miss Cornelia. "I didn't think he was as dazed as he pretended to be."

Miss Cornelia, too, had been pondering the problem of the Unknown. She reached a swift decision. If he were what he pretended to be —a dazed wanderer, he could do them no harm. If he were not —a little strategy properly employed might unravel the whole mystery.

"Bring him up here, Billy," she said, turning to the butler.

Billy started to obey. But the darkness of the corridor seemed to appall him anew the moment he took a step toward it.

"You give candle, please?" he asked with a pleading expression. "Don't like dark."

Miss Cornelia handed him one of the two precious candles. Then his present terror reminded her of that one other occasion when she had seen him lose completely his stoic Oriental calm.

"Billy," she queried, "what did you see when you came running down the stairs before we were locked in, down below?"

The candle shook like a reed in Billy's grasp.

"Nothing!" he gasped with obvious untruth, though it did not seem so much as if he wished to conceal what he had seen as that he was trying to convince himself he had seen nothing.

"Nothing!" said Lizzie scornfully. "It was some nothing that would make him drop a bottle of whisky!"

But Billy only backed toward the door, smiling apologetically.

"Thought I saw ghost," he said, and went out and down the stairs, the candlelight flickering, growing fainter, and finally disappearing. Silence and eerie darkness enveloped them all as they waited. And suddenly out of the blackness came a sound.

Something was flapping and thumping around the room.

"That's damned odd." muttered Beresford uneasily. "There is something moving around the room."

"It's up near the ceiling!" cried Bailey as the sound began again.

Lizzie began a slow wail of doom and disaster.

"Oh —h —h —h — —"

"Good God!" cried Beresford abruptly. "It hit me in the face!" He slapped his hands together in a vain attempt to capture the flying intruder.

Lizzie rose.

"I'm going!" she announced. "I don't know where, but I'm going!"

She took a wild step in the direction of the door. Then the flapping noise was all about her, her nose was bumped by an invisible object and she gave a horrified shriek.

"It's in my hair!" she screamed madly. "It's in my hair!"

The next instant Bailey gave a triumphant cry.

"I've got it! It's a bat!"

Lizzie sank to her knees, still moaning, and Bailey carried the cause of the trouble over to the window and threw it out.

But the result of the absurd incident was a further destruction of their morale. Even Beresford, so far calm with the quiet of the virtuous onlooker, was now pallid in the light of the matches they successively lighted. And onto this strained situation came at last Billy and the Unknown.

The Unknown still wore his air of dazed bewilderment, true or feigned, but at least he was now able to walk without support. They stared at him, at his tattered, muddy garments, at the threads of rope still clinging to his ankles-and wondered. He returned their stares vacantly.

"Come in," began Miss Cornelia. "Sit down." He obeyed both commands docilely enough.

"Are you better now?"

"Somewhat." His words still came very slowly.

"Billy-you can go."

"I stay, please!" said Billy wistfully, making no movement to leave. His gesture toward the darkness of the corridor spoke louder than words.

Bailey watched him, suspicion dawning in his eyes. He could not account for the butler's inexplicable terror of being left alone.

"Anderson intimated that the Doctor had an accomplice in this house," he said, crossing to Billy and taking him by the arm. "Why isn't this the man?" Billy cringed away. "Please, no," he begged pitifully.

Bailey turned him around so that he faced the Hidden Room.

"Did you know that room was there?" he questioned, his doubts still unquieted.

Billy shook his head.

"No."

"He couldn't have locked us in," said Miss Cornelia. "He was with us."

Bailey demurred, not to her remark itself, but to its implication of Billy's entire innocence.

"He may know who did it. Do you?"

Billy still shook his head.

Bailey remained unconvinced.

"Who did you see at the head of the small staircase?" he queried imperatively. "Now we're through with nonsense; I want the truth!"

Billy shivered.

"See face-that's all," he brought out at last.

"Whose face?"

Again it was evident that Billy knew or thought he knew more than he was willing to tell.

"Don't know," he said with obvious untruth, looking down at the floor.

"Never mind, Billy," cut in Miss Cornelia. To her mind questioning Billy was wasting time. She looked at the Unknown.

"Solve the mystery of this man and we may get at the facts," she said in accents of conviction.

As Bailey turned toward her questioningly, Billy attempted to steal silently out of the door, apparently preferring any fears that might lurk in the darkness of the corridor to a further grilling on the subject of whom or what he had seen on the alcove stairs. But Bailey caught the movement out of the tail of his eye.

"You stay here," he commanded. Billy stood frozen. Beresford raised the candle so that it cast its light full in the Unknown's face.

"This chap claims to have lost his memory," he said dubiously. "I suppose a blow on the head might do that, I don't know."

"I wish somebody would knock me on the head! I'd like to forget a few things!" moaned Lizzie, but the interruption went unregarded.

"Don't you even know your name?" queried Miss Cornelia of the Unknown.

The Unknown shook his head with a slow, laborious gesture.

"Not-yet."

"Or where you came from?"

Once more the battered head made its movement of negation.

"Do you remember how you got in this house?" The Unknown made an effort.

"Yes —I —remember-that-all-right" he said, apparently undergoing an enormous strain in order to make himself speak at all. He put his hand to his head.

"My-head-aches-to-beat-the-band," he continued slowly.

Miss Cornelia was at a loss. If this were acting, it was at least fine acting.

"How did you happen to come to this house?" she persisted, her voice unconsciously tuning itself to the slow, laborious speech of the Unknown.

"Saw-the-lights."

Bailey broke in with a question.

"Where were you when you saw the lights?"

The Unknown wet his lips with his tongue, painfully.

"I —broke-out-of-the-garage," he said at length. This was unexpected. A general movement of interest ran over the group.

"How did you get there?" Beresford took his turn as questioner.

The Unknown shook his head, so slowly and deliberately that Miss Cornelia's fingers itched to shake him in spite of his injuries.

"I —don't —know."

"Have you been robbed?" queried Bailey with keen suspicion.

The Unknown mumbled something unintelligible. Then he seemed to get command of his tongue again.

"Everything gone-out of-my pockets," he said.

"Including your watch?" pursued Bailey, remembering the watch that Beresford had found in the grounds.

The Unknown would neither affirm nor deny.

"If —I —had —a —watch-it's gone," he said with maddening deliberation. "All my-papers-are gone."

Miss Cornelia pounced upon this last statement like a cat upon a mouse.

"How do you know you had papers?" she asked sharply.

For the first time the faintest flicker of a smile seemed to appear for a moment on the Unknown's features. Then it vanished as abruptly as it had come.

"Most men-carry papers-don't they?" he asked, staring blindly in front of him. "I'm dazed-but-my mind's —all-right. If you-ask me —I —think —I'm —d-damned funny!"

He gave the ghost of a chuckle. Bailey and Beresford exchanged glances.

"Did you ring the house phone?" insisted Miss Cornelia.

The Unknown nodded.

"Yes."

Miss Cornelia and Bailey gave each other a look of wonderment.

"I —leaned against-the button-in the garage —" he went on. "Then —I think-maybe I —fainted. That's —not clear."

His eyelids drooped. He seemed about to faint again.

Dale rose, and came over to him, with a sympathetic movement of her hand.

"You don't remember how you were hurt?" she asked gently.

The Unknown stared ahead of him, his eyes filming, as if he were trying to puzzle it out.

"No," he said at last. "The first thing I remember—I was in the garage-tied." He moved his lips. "I was-gagged-too-that's—what's the matter-with my tongue-now-Then—I got myself-free-and-got out-of a window—"

Miss Cornelia made a movement to question him further. Beresford stopped her with his hand uplifted.

"Just a moment, Miss Van Gorder. Anderson ought to know of this."

He started for the door without perceiving the flash of keen intelligence and alertness that had lit the Unknown's countenance for an instant, as once before, at the mention of the detective's name. But just as he reached the door the detective entered.

He halted for a moment, staring at the strange figure of the Unknown.

"A new element in our mystery, Mr. Anderson," said Miss Cornelia, remembering that the detective might not have heard of the mysterious stranger before-as he had been locked in the billiard room when the latter had made his queer entrance.

The detective and the Unknown gazed at each other for a moment-the Unknown with his old expression of vacant stupidity.

"Quite dazed, poor fellow," Miss Cornelia went on. Beresford added other words of explanation.

"He doesn't remember what happened to him. Curious, isn't it?"

The detective still seemed puzzled.

"How did he get into the house?"

"He came through the terrace door some time ago," answered Miss Cornelia. "Just before we were locked in."

Her answer seemed to solve the problem to Anderson's satisfaction.

"Doesn't remember anything, eh?" he said dryly. He crossed over to the mysterious stranger and put his hand under the Unknown's chin, jerking his head up roughly.

"Look up here!" he commanded.

The Unknown stared at him for an instant with blank, vacuous eyes. Then his head dropped back upon his breast again.

"Look up, you—" muttered the detective, jerking his head again. "This losing your memory stuff doesn't go down with me!" His eyes bored into the Unknown's.

"It doesn't—go down-very well-with me-either," said the Unknown weakly, making no movement of protest against Anderson's rough handling.

"Did you ever see me before?" demanded the latter. Beresford held the candle closer so that he might watch the Unknown's face for any involuntary movement of betrayal.

But the Unknown made no such movement. He gazed at Anderson, apparently with the greatest bewilderment, then his eyes cleared, he seemed to be about to remember who the detective was.

"You're-the-Doctor—I—saw-downstairs-aren't you?" he said innocently. The detective set his jaw. He started off on a new tack.

"Does this belong to you?" he said suddenly, plucking from his pocket the battered gold watch that Beresford had found and waving it before the Unknown's blank face.

The Unknown stared at it a moment, as a child might stare at a new toy, with no gleam of recognition. Then—

"Maybe," he admitted. "I—don't—know." His voice trailed off. He fell back against Bailey's arm.

Miss Cornelia gave a little shiver. The third degree in reality was less pleasant to watch than it had been to read about in the pages of her favorite detective stories.

"He's evidently been attacked," she said, turning to Anderson. "He claims to have recovered consciousness in the garage, where he was tied hand and foot!"

"He does, eh?" said the detective heavily. He glared at the Unknown. "If you'll give me five minutes alone with him, I'll get the truth out of him!" he promised.

A look of swift alarm swept over the Unknown's face at the words, unperceived by any except Miss Cornelia. The others started obediently to yield to the detective's behest and leave him alone with his prisoner. Miss Cornelia was the first to move toward the door. On her way, she turned.

"Do you believe that money is irrevocably gone?" she asked of Anderson.

The detective smiled.

"There's no such word as 'irrevocable' in my vocabulary," he answered. "But I believe it's out of the house, if that's what you mean."

Miss Cornelia still hesitated, on the verge of departure.

"Suppose I tell you that there are certain facts that you have overlooked?" she said slowly.

"Still on the trail!" muttered the detective sardonically. He did not even glance at her. He seemed only anxious that the other members of the group would get out of his way for once and leave him a clear field for his work.

"I was right about the Doctor, wasn't I?" she insisted.

"Just fifty per cent right," said Anderson crushingly. "And the Doctor didn't turn that trick alone. Now —" he went on with weary patience, "if you'll all go out and close that door —"

Miss Cornelia, defeated, took a candle from Bailey and stepped into the corridor. Her figure stiffened. She gave an audible gasp of dismayed surprise.

"Quick!" she cried, turning back to the others and gesturing toward the corridor. "A man just went through that skylight and out onto the roof!"

Chapter Nineteen
Murder on Murder

"Out on the roof!"

"Come on, Beresford!"

"Hustle-you men! He may be armed!"

"Righto-coming!"

And following Miss Cornelia's lead, Jack Bailey, Anderson, Beresford, and Billy dashed out into the corridor, leaving Dale and the frightened Lizzie alone with the Unknown.

"And I'd run if my legs would!" Lizzie despaired.

"Hush!" said Dale, her ears strained for sounds of conflict. Lizzie, creeping closer to her for comfort, stumbled over one of the Unknown's feet and promptly set up a new wail.

"How do we know this fellow right here isn't the Bat?" she asked in a blood-chilling whisper, nearly stabbing the unfortunate Unknown in the eye with her thumb as she pointed at him. The Unknown was either too dazed or too crafty to make any answer. His silence confirmed Lizzie's worst suspicions. She fairly hugged the floor and began to pray in a whisper.

Miss Cornelia re-entered cautiously with her candle, closing the door gently behind her as she came.

"What did you see?" gasped Dale.

Miss Cornelia smiled broadly.

"I didn't see anything," she admitted with the greatest calm. "I had to get that dratted detective out of the room before I assassinated him."

"Nobody went through the skylight?" said Dale incredulously.

"They have now," answered Miss Cornelia with obvious satisfaction. "The whole outfit of them."

She stole a glance at the veiled eyes of the Unknown. He was lying limply back in his chair, as if the excitement had been too much for him-and yet she could have sworn she had seen him leap to his feet, like a man in full possession of his faculties, when she had given her false cry of alarm.

"Then why did you —" began Dale dazedly, unable to fathom her aunt's reasons for her trick.

"Because," interrupted Miss Cornelia decidedly, "that money's in this room. If the man who took it out of the safe got away with it, why did he come back and hide there?"

Her forefinger jabbed at the hidden chamber wherein the masked intruder had terrified Dale with threats of instant death.

"He got it out of the safe-and that's as far as he did get with it," she persisted inexorably. "There's a *hat* behind that safe, a man's felt hat!"

So this was the discovery she had hinted of to Anderson before he rebuffed her proffer of assistance!

"Oh, I wish he'd take his hat and go home!" groaned Lizzie inattentive to all but her own fears.

Miss Cornelia did not even bother to rebuke her. She crossed behind the wicker clothes hamper and picked up something from the floor.

"A half-burned candle," she mused. "Another thing the detective overlooked."

She stepped back to the center of the room, looking knowingly from the candle to the Hidden Room and back again.

"Oh, my God-another one!" shrieked Lizzie as the dark shape of a man appeared suddenly outside the window, as if materialized from the air.

Miss Cornelia snatched up her revolver from the top of the hamper.

"Don't shoot-it's Jack!" came a warning cry from Dale as she recognized the figure of her lover.

Miss Cornelia laid her revolver down on the hamper again. The vacant eyes of the Unknown caught the movement.

Bailey swung in through the window, panting a little from his exertions.

"The man Lizzie saw drop from the skylight undoubtedly got to the roof from this window," he said. "It's quite easy."

"But not with one hand," said Miss Cornelia, with her gaze now directed at the row of tall closets around the walls of the room. "When that detective comes back I may have a surprise party for him," she muttered, with a gleam of hope in her eye.

Dale explained the situation to Jack.

"Aunt Cornelia thinks the money's still here."

Miss Cornelia snorted.

"I know it's here." She started to open the closets, one after the other, beginning at the left. Bailey saw what she was doing and began to help her.

Not so Lizzie. She sat on the floor in a heap, her eyes riveted on the Unknown, who in his turn was gazing at Miss Cornelia's revolver on the hamper with the intent stare of a baby or an idiot fascinated by a glittering piece of glass.

Dale noticed the curious tableau.

"Lizzie-what are you looking at?" she said with a nervous shake in her voice.

"What's he looking at?" asked Lizzie sepulchrally, pointing at the Unknown. Her pointed forefinger drew his eyes away from the revolver; he sank back into his former apathy, listless, drooping.

Miss Cornelia rattled the knob of a high closet by the other wall.

"This one is locked-and the key's gone," she announced. A new flicker of interest grew in the eyes of the Unknown. Lizzie glanced away from him, terrified.

"If there's anything locked up in that closet," she whimpered, "you'd better let it stay! There's enough running loose in this house as it is!"

Unfortunately for her, her whimper drew Miss Cornelia's attention upon her.

"Lizzie, did you ever take that key?" the latter queried sternly.

"No'm," said Lizzie, too scared to dissimulate if she had wished. She wagged her head violently a dozen times, like a china figure on a mantelpiece.

Miss Cornelia pondered.

"It may be locked from the inside; I'll soon find out." She took a wire hairpin from her hair and pushed it through the keyhole. But there was no key on the other side; the hairpin went through without obstruction. Repeated efforts to jerk the door open failed. And finally Miss Cornelia bethought herself of a key from the other closet doors.

Dale and Lizzie on one side-Bailey on the other-collected the keys of the other closets from their locks while Miss Cornelia stared at the one whose doors were closed as if she would force its secret from it with her eyes. The Unknown had been so quiet during the last few minutes, that, unconsciously, the others had ceased to pay much attention to him, except the casual attention one devotes to a piece of furniture. Even Lizzie's eyes were now fixed on the locked closet. And the Unknown himself was the first to notice this.

At once his expression altered to one of cunning-cautiously, with infinite patience, he began to inch his chair over toward the wicker clothes hamper. The noise of the others, moving about the room, drowned out what little he made in moving his chair.

At last he was within reach of the revolver. His hand shot out in one swift sinuous thrust-clutched the weapon-withdrew. He then concealed the revolver among his tattered garments as best he could and, cautiously as before, inched his chair back again to its original position. When the others noticed him again, the mask of lifelessness was back on his face and one could have sworn he had not changed his position by the breadth of an inch.

"There-that unlocked it!" cried Miss Cornelia triumphantly at last, as the key to one of the other closet doors slid smoothly into the lock and she heard the click that meant victory.

She was about to throw open the closet door. But Bailey motioned her back.

"I'd keep back a little," he cautioned. "You don't know what may be inside."

"Mercy sakes, who wants to know?" shivered Lizzie. Dale and Miss Cornelia, too, stepped aside involuntarily as Bailey took the candle and prepared, with a good deal of caution, to open the closet door.

The door swung open at last. He could look in. He did so-and stared appalled at what he saw, while goose flesh crawled on his spine and the hairs of his head stood up.

After a moment he closed the door of the closet and turned back, white-faced, to the others.

"What is it?" said Dale aghast. "What did you see?"

Bailey found himself unable to answer for a moment. Then he pulled himself together. He turned to Miss Van Gorder.

"Miss Cornelia, I think we have found the ghost the Jap butler saw," he said slowly. "How are your nerves?"

Miss Cornelia extended a hand that did not tremble.

"Give me the candle."

He did so. She went to the closet and opened the door.

Whatever faults Miss Cornelia may have had, lack of courage was not one of them-or the ability to withstand a stunning mental shock. Had it been otherwise she might well have crumpled to the floor, as if struck down by an invisible hammer, the moment the closet door swung open before her.

Huddled on the floor of the closet was the body of a man. So crudely had he been crammed into this hiding-place that he lay twisted and bent. And as if to add to the horror of the moment one arm, released from its confinement, now slipped and slid out into the floor of the room.

Miss Cornelia's voice sounded strange to her own ears when finally she spoke.

"But who is it?"

"It is-or was-Courtleigh Fleming," said Bailey dully.

"But how can it be? Mr. Fleming died two weeks ago. I— —"

"He died in this house sometime tonight. The body is still warm."

"But who killed him? The Bat?"

"Isn't it likely that the Doctor did it? The man who has been his accomplice all along? Who probably bought a cadaver out West and buried it with honors here not long ago?"

He spoke without bitterness. Whatever resentment he might have felt died in that awful presence.

"He got into the house early tonight," he said, "probably with the Doctor's connivance. That wrist watch there is probably the luminous eye Lizzie thought she saw."

But Miss Cornelia's face was still thoughtful, and he went on:

"Isn't it clear, Miss Van Gorder?" he queried, with a smile. "The Doctor and old Mr. Fleming formed a conspiracy-both needed money-lots of it. Fleming was to rob the bank and hide the money here. Wells's part was to issue a false death certificate in the West, and bury a substitute body, secured God knows how. It was easy; it kept the name of the president of the Union Bank free from suspicion-and it put the blame on me."

He paused, thinking it out.

"Only they slipped up in one place. Dick Fleming leased the house to you and they couldn't get it back."

"Then you are sure," said Miss Cornelia quickly, "that tonight Courtleigh Fleming broke in, with the Doctor's assistance-and that he killed Dick, his own nephew, from the staircase?"

"Aren't you?" asked Bailey surprised. The more he thought of it the less clearly could he visualize it any other way.

Miss Cornelia shook her head decidedly.

"No."

Bailey thought her merely obstinate-unwilling to give up, for pride's sake, her own pet theory of the activities of the Bat.

"Wells tried to get out of the house tonight with that blue-print. Why? Because he knew the moment we got it, we'd come up here-and Fleming was here."

"Perfectly true," nodded Miss Cornelia. "And then?"

"Old Fleming killed Dick and Wells killed Fleming," said Bailey succinctly. "You can't get away from it!"

But Miss Cornelia still shook her head. The explanation was too mechanical. It laid too little emphasis on the characters of those most concerned.

"No," she said. "No. The Doctor isn't a murderer. He's as puzzled as we are about some things. He and Courtleigh Fleming were working together-but remember this-Doctor Wells was locked in the living-room with us. He'd been trying to get up the stairs all evening and failed every time."

But Bailey was as convinced of the truth of his theory as she of hers.

"He was here ten minutes ago-locked in this room," he said with a glance at the ladder up which the doctor had ascended.

"I'll grant you that," said Miss Cornelia. "But — —" She thought back swiftly. "But at the same time an Unknown Masked Man was locked in that mantel-room with Dale. The Doctor put out the candle when you opened that Hidden Room. Why? Because he thought Courtleigh Fleming was hiding there!" Now the missing pieces of her puzzle were falling into their places with a vengeance. "But at this moment," she continued, "the Doctor believes that Fleming has made his escape! No-we haven't solved the mystery yet. There's another element-an unknown element," her eyes rested for a moment upon the Unknown, "and that element is-the Bat!"

She paused, impressively. The others stared at her-no longer able to deny the sinister plausibility of her theory. But this new tangling of the mystery, just when the black threads seemed raveled out at last, was almost too much for Dale.

"Oh, call the detective!" she stammered, on the verge of hysterical tears. "Let's get through with this thing! I can't bear any more!"

But Miss Cornelia did not even hear her. Her mind, strung now to concert pitch, had harked back to the point it had reached some time ago, and which all the recent distractions had momentarily obliterated.

Had the money been taken out of the house or had it not? In that mad rush for escape had the man hidden with Dale in the recess back of the mantel carried his booty with him, or left it behind? It was not in the Hidden Room, that was certain.

Yet she was so hopeless by that time that her first search was purely perfunctory.

During her progress about the room the Unknown's eyes followed her, but so still had he sat, so amazing had been the discovery of the body, that no one any longer observed him. Now and then his head drooped forward as if actual weakness was almost overpowering him, but his eyes were keen and observant, and he was no longer taking the trouble to act-if he had been acting.

It was when Bailey finally opened the lid of a clothes hamper that they stumbled on their first clue.

"Nothing here but some clothes and books," he said, glancing inside.

"Books?" said Miss Cornelia dubiously. "I left no books in that hamper."

Bailey picked up one of the cheap paper novels and read its title aloud, with a wry smile.

"'Little Rosebud's Lover, Or The Cruel Revenge,' by Laura Jean —"

"That's mine!" said Lizzie promptly. "Oh, Miss Neily, I tell you this house is haunted. I left that book in my satchel along with 'Wedded But No Wife' and now — —"

"Where's your satchel?" snapped Miss Cornelia, her eyes gleaming.

"Where's my satchel?" mumbled Lizzie, staring about as best she could. "I don't see it. If that wretch has stolen my satchel — —!"

"Where did you leave it?"

"Up here. Right in this room. It was a new satchel too. I'll have the law on him, that's what I'll do."

"Isn't that your satchel, Lizzie?" asked Miss Cornelia, indicating a battered bag in a dark corner of shadows above the window.

"Yes'm," she admitted. But she did not dare approach very close to the recovered bag. It might bite her!

"Put it there on the hamper," ordered Miss Cornelia.

"I'm scared to touch it!" moaned Lizzie. "It may have a bomb in it!"

She took up the bag between finger and thumb and, holding it with the care she would have bestowed upon a bottle of nitroglycerin, carried it over to the hamper and set it down. Then she backed away from it, ready to leap for the door at a moment's warning.

Miss Cornelia started for the satchel. Then she remembered. She turned to Bailey.

"You open it," she said graciously. "If the money's there-you're the one who ought to find it."

Bailey gave her a look of gratitude. Then, smiling at Dale encouragingly, he crossed over to the satchel, Dale at his heels. Miss Cornelia watched him fumble at the catch of the bag-even Lizzie drew closer. For a moment even the Unknown was forgotten.

Bailey gave a triumphant cry.

"The money's here!"

"Oh, thank God!" sobbed Dale.

It was an emotional moment. It seemed to have penetrated even through the haze enveloping the injured man in his chair. Slowly he got up, like a man who has been waiting for his moment, and now that it had come was in no hurry about it. With equal deliberation he drew the revolver and took a step forward. And at that instant a red glare appeared outside the open window and overhead could be heard the feet of the searchers, running.

"Fire!" screamed Lizzie, pointing to the window, even as Beresford's voice from the roof rang out in a shout. "The garage is burning!"

They turned toward the door to escape, but a strange and menacing figure blocked their way.

It was the Unknown-no longer the bewildered stranger who had stumbled in through the living-room door-but a man with every faculty of mind and body alert and the light of a deadly purpose in his eyes. He covered the group with Miss Cornelia's revolver.

"This door is locked and the key is in my pocket!" he said in a savage voice as the red light at the window grew yet more vivid and muffled cries and tramplings from overhead betokened universal confusion and alarm.

Chapter Twenty
"He Is-The Bat!"

Lizzie opened her mouth to scream. But for once she did not carry out her purpose.

"Not a sound out of you!" warned the Unknown brutally, almost jabbing the revolver into her ribs. He wheeled on Bailey.

"Close that satchel," he commanded, "and put it back where you found it!"

Bailey's fist closed. He took a step toward his captor.

"You —" he began in a furious voice. But the steely glint in the eyes of the Unknown was enough to give any man pause.

"Jack!" pleaded Dale. Bailey halted.

"Do what he tells you!" Miss Cornelia insisted, her voice shaking.

A brave man may be willing to fight with odds a hundred to one-but only a fool will rush on certain death. Reluctantly, dejectedly, Bailey obeyed-stuffed the money back in the satchel and replaced the latter in its corner of shadows near the window.

"It's the Bat-it's the Bat!" whispered Lizzie eerily, and, for once her gloomy prophecies seemed to be in a fair way of justification, for "Blow out that candle!" commanded the Unknown sternly, and, after a moment of hesitation on Miss Cornelia's part, the room was again plunged in darkness except for the red glow at the window.

This finished Lizzie for the evening. She spoke from a dry throat.

"I'm going to scream!" she sobbed hysterically. "I can't keep it back!"

But at last she had encountered someone who had no patience with her vagaries.

"Put that woman in the mantel-room and shut her up!" ordered the Unknown, the muzzle of his revolver emphasizing his words with a savage little movement.

Bailey took Lizzie under the arms and started to execute the order. But the sometime colleen from Kerry did not depart without one Parthian arrow.

"Don't shove," she said in tones of the greatest dignity as she stumbled into the Hidden Room. "I'm damn glad to go!"

The iron doors shut behind her. Bailey watched the Unknown intently. One moment of relaxed vigilance and — —

But though the Unknown was unlocking the door with his left hand the revolver in his right hand was as steady as a rock. He seemed to listen for a moment at the crack of the door.

"Not a sound if you value your lives!" he warned again, he shepherded them away from the direction of the window with his revolver.

"In a moment or two," he said in a hushed, taut voice, "a man will come into this room, either through the door or by that window-the man who started the fire to draw you out of this house."

Bailey threw aside all pride in his concern for Dale's safety.

"For God's sake, don't keep these women here!" he pleaded in low, tense tones.

The Unknown seemed to tower above him like a destroying angel.

"Keep them here where we can watch them!" he whispered with fierce impatience. "Don't you understand? There's a *killer* loose!"

And so for a moment they stood there, waiting for they knew not what. So swift had been the transition from joy to deadly terror, and now to suspense, that only Miss Cornelia's agile brain seemed able to respond. And at first it did even that very slowly.

"I begin to understand," she said in a low tone. "The man who struck you down and tied you in the garage-the man who killed Dick Fleming and stabbed that poor wretch in the closet-the man who locked us in downstairs and removed the money from that safe-the man who started that fire outside-is ——"

"Sssh!" warned the Unknown imperatively as a sound from the direction of the window seemed to reach his ears. He ran quickly back to the corridor door and locked it.

"Stand back out of that light! The ladder!"

Miss Cornelia and Dale shrank back against the mantel. Bailey took up a post beside the window, the Unknown flattening himself against the wall beside him. There was a breathless pause.

The top of the extension ladder began to tremble. A black bulk stood clearly outlined against the diminishing red glow-the Bat, masked and sinister, on his last foray!

There was no sound as the killer stepped into the room. He waited for a second that seemed a year-still no sound. Then he turned cautiously toward the place where he had left the satchel-the beam of his flashlight picked it out.

In an instant the Unknown and Bailey were upon him. There was a short, ferocious struggle in the darkness —a gasp of laboring lungs-the thud of fighting bodies clenched in a death grapple.

"Get his gun!" muttered the Unknown hoarsely to Bailey as he tore the Bat's lean hands away from his throat. "Got it?"

"Yes," gasped Bailey. He jabbed the muzzle against a straining back. The Bat ceased to struggle. Bailey stepped a little away.

"I've still got you covered!" he said fiercely. The Bat made no sound.

"Hold out your hands, Bat, while I put on the bracelets," commanded the Unknown in tones of terse triumph. He snapped the steel cuffs on the wrists of the murderous prowler. "Sometimes even the cleverest Bat comes through a window at night and is caught. Double murder-burglary-and arson! That's a good night's work even for you, Bat!"

He switched his flashlight on the Bat's masked face. As he did so the house lights came on; the electric light company had at last remembered its duties. All blinked for an instant in the sudden illumination.

"Take off that handkerchief!" barked the Unknown, motioning at the black silk handkerchief that still hid the face of the Bat from recognition. Bailey stripped it from the haggard, desperate features with a quick movement-and stood appalled.

A simultaneous gasp went up from Dale and Miss Cornelia.

It was Anderson, the detective! And he was-the Bat!

"It's Mr. Anderson!" stuttered Dale, aghast at the discovery.

The Unknown gloated over his captive.

"I'm Anderson," he said. "This man has been impersonating me. You're a good actor, Bat, for a fellow that's such a bad actor!" he taunted. "How did you get the dope on this case? Did you tap the wires to headquarters?"

The Bat allowed himself a little sardonic smile.

"I'll tell you that when I—" he began, then, suddenly, made his last bid for freedom. With one swift, desperate movement, in spite of his handcuffs, he jerked the real Anderson's revolver from him by the barrel, then wheeling with lightning rapidity on Bailey, brought the butt of Anderson's revolver down on his wrist. Bailey's revolver fell to the floor with a clatter. The Bat swung toward the door. Again the tables were turned!

"Hands up, everybody!" he ordered, menacing the group with the stolen pistol. "Hands up-you!" as Miss Cornelia kept her hands at her sides.

It was the greatest moment of Miss Cornelia's life. She smiled sweetly and came toward the Bat as if the pistol aimed at her heart were as innocuous as a toothbrush.

"Why?" she queried mildly. "I took the bullets out of that revolver two hours ago."

The Bat flung the revolver toward her with a curse. The real Anderson instantly snatched up the gun that Bailey had dropped and covered the Bat.

"Don't move!" he warned, "or I'll fill you full of lead!" He smiled out of the corner of his mouth at Miss Cornelia who was primly picking up the revolver that the Bat had flung at her-her own revolver.

"You see-you never know what a woman will do," he continued.

Miss Cornelia smiled. She broke open the revolver, five loaded shells fell from it to the floor. The Bat stared at her-then stared incredulously at the bullets.

"You see," she said, "I, too, have a little imagination!"

Chapter Twenty-One
Quite a Collection

An hour or so later in a living-room whose terrors had departed, Miss Cornelia, her niece, and Jack Bailey were gathered before a roaring fire. The local police had come and gone; the bodies of Courtleigh Fleming and his nephew had been removed to the mortuary; Beresford had returned to his home, though under summons as a material witness; the Bat, under heavy guard, had gone off under charge of the detective. As for Doctor Wells, he too was under arrest, and a broken man, though, considering the fact that Courtleigh Fleming had been throughout the prime mover in the conspiracy, he might escape with a comparatively light sentence. In a little while the newspapermen of all the great journals would be at the door-but for a moment the sorely tried group at Cedarcrest enjoyed a temporary respite and they made the best of it while they could.

The fire burned brightly and the lovers, hand in hand, sat before it. But Miss Cornelia, birdlike and brisk, sat upright on a chair near by and relived the greatest triumph of her life while she knitted with automatic precision.

"Knit two, purl two," she would say, and then would wander once more back to the subject in hand. Out behind the flower garden the ruins of the garage and her beloved car were still smoldering; a cool night wind came through the broken windowpane where not so long before the bloody hand of the injured detective had intruded itself. On the door to the hall, still fastened as the Bat had left it, was the pathetic little creature with which the Bat had signed a job-for once, before he had completed it.

But calmly and dispassionately Miss Cornelia worked out the crossword puzzle of the evening and announced her results.

"It is all clear," she said. "Of course the Doctor had the blue-print. And the Bat tried to get it from him. Then when the Doctor had stunned him and locked him in the billiard room, the Bat still had the key and unlocked his own handcuffs. After that he had only to get out of a window and shut us in here."

And again:

"He had probably trailed the real detective all the way from town and attacked him where Mr. Beresford found the watch."

Once, too, she harkened back to the anonymous letters —

"It must have been a blow to the Doctor and Courtleigh Fleming when they found me settled in the house!" She smiled grimly. "And when their letters failed to dislodge me."

But it was the Bat who held her interest; his daring assumption of the detective's identity, his searching of the house ostensibly for their safety but in reality for the treasure, and that one moment of irresolution when he did not shoot the Doctor at the top of the ladder. And thereafter lost his chance —

It somehow weakened her terrified admiration for him, but she had nothing but acclaim for the escape he had made from the Hidden Room itself.

"That took brains," she said. "Cold, hard brains. To dash out of that room and down the stairs, pull off his mask and pick up a candle, and then to come calmly back to the trunk room again and accuse the Doctor-that took real ability. But I dread to think what would have happened when he asked us all to go out and leave him alone with the real Anderson!"

It was after two o'clock when she finally sent the young people off to get some needed sleep but she herself was still bright-eyed and wide-awake.

When Lizzie came at last to coax and scold her into bed, she was sitting happily at the table surrounded by divers small articles which she was handling with an almost childlike zest. A clipping about the Bat from the evening newspaper; a piece of paper on which was a well-defined fingerprint; a revolver and a heap of five shells; a small very dead bat; the anonymous warnings, including the stone in which the last one had been wrapped; a battered and broken watch, somehow left behind; a dried and broken dinner roll; and the box of sedative powders brought by Doctor Wells.

Lizzie came over to the table and surveyed her grimly.

"You see, Lizzie, it's quite a collection. I'm going to take them and ——"

But Lizzie bent over the table and picked up the box of powders.

"No, ma'am," she said with extreme finality. "You are not. You are going to take these and go to bed."

And Miss Cornelia did.

Made in the USA
Middletown, DE
27 March 2023